MOUNTAIN LAMB

"Show me how to kiss, Joe Meek. I think I will like it."

He took her into his arms then, cursing himself inwardly because his hands were trembling so, and once more placed his mouth to hers.

After a moment he pulled back and said, "Mebbe I ain't so good at it either. I ain't never loved anyone before."

"Keep showing me," Mountain Lamb whispered and pulled his face back to hers.

They kissed and held each other for a long while, until finally she asked, "Will we sleep together this night, Joe Meek? I am very ignorant. I have never done it before. It is something else that you will have to show me. All young women must have someone who will be their teacher in making love."

Joe rose, once more utterly uncertain of himself. But Mountain Lamb rose also and took his hand, stared back at the dying campfire, and allowed herself to be led to Meek's robes.

Bantam Books by Bill Hotchkiss

MOUNTAIN LAMB
SPIRIT MOUNTAIN

MOUNTAIN LAMB

Bill Hotchkiss

BANTAM BOOKS
TORONTO · NEW YORK · LONDON · SYDNEY · AUCKLAND

MOUNTAIN LAMB
A Bantam Book / May 1985

ISBN 0-553-24586-4

Published simultaneously in the United States and Canada

Bantam Books are published by Bantam Books, Inc. Its trademark,
consisting of the words "Bantam Books" and the portrayal of a rooster,
is Registered in U.S. Patent and Trademark Office and in other
countries. Marca Registrada. Bantam Books, Inc., 666 Fifth Avenue,
New York, New York 10103.

PRINTED IN THE UNITED STATES OF AMERICA

O   0 9 8 7 6 5 4 3 2 1

For Richard Berger (1916–1983),
in memoriam.

> *In his late sixties,*
> *He died alone—*
> *Alone in a small, weathered house,*
> *His private retreat,*
> *A place piled high with books*
> *And stacks of newspapers—*
> *And boxes and folders*
> *Crammed with his manuscripts:*
> *Collections of poems,*
> *Five novels in progress,*
> *Plays, essays, letters sorted*
> *To sequence, short stories,*
> *Fragments, fragments.*
>
> *This was a writer,*
> *His life's work heaped about him,*
> *So many things and all incomplete.*

Soldier, scholar, teacher, poet, traveler abroad,
member of the *California Historical Society*,
member of the *Range of Light* poetry group,
raconteur, enthusiast . . . .

CHAPTER ONE

The Daughter of Mauvais Gauche

Drums and singing.

And all the young people began to make the movements of the scalp-dance. As the celebration proceeded, a young woman who had come among these people as a visitor and who was believed to be the daughter of a great war chief—she decided to dance also. At first she did not know what steps to take, but soon she figured it out.

After a while she became aware of a delicious odor, one that was strange to her. The girl laughed and decided to follow the smell.

She came to a shelter made of sage brush, and now the odor was stronger. She stepped inside—and found two handsome young warriors, Bear-Man and Snake-Man. The first of these was dressed all in black, while the second wore clothing colored like a rainbow. They sat facing each other and passed a pipe back and forth. The burning tobacco produced the strange and wonderful odor.

The girl wished to smoke the pipe also, but the two young men were afraid that the other warriors would become angry. Yet she persisted, and so the men nodded, pulled the lodge flap closed, and offered her the pipe.

She took it into her hands, blushed, and lowered her eyes.

Bear-Man and Snake-Man grinned at each other as the girl touched the bit of the pipe to her lips and sucked the smoke into her mouth.

And immediately she fell to the floor of the lodge, unconscious.

When she awoke, it was the next morning. The lodge had become much larger, as tall as a medicine lodge. The walls were hung with shields and weapons of every sort, and a fire was blazing in the fire pit.

And sitting on either side of her, as if studying her features, were Bear-Man and Snake-Man. But both of them had become old men.

* * *

Umentucken, Tukutsey Undenwatsy. Bighorn ram of the mountain, his child. Mountain Lamb. Gotia's daughter.

She had many suitors among the Shoshones, but she had remained aloof and given encouragement to none. Nor had her father thus far in any way pressured her into choosing a husband, for he had brought no warriors into their lodge with the intention of arranging a match for her. The girl's mother had died of a protracted illness of fevers and coughing two years earlier, and now, at seventeen, Mountain Lamb had assumed the tasks formerly managed by her mother, and thus in most matters had become like a sister to Bad Left Hand, an assistant to his two wives.

It was well understood throughout the Shoshone village that the bride-price for Umentucken, Tukutsey Undenwatsy would be extremely high. Not only was she the warrior chief's daughter and important to him in the running of his own lodge, but she had gained a great reputation as a maker of moccasins and clothing, highly skilled not only in the cutting and sewing of leather and cloth but in design work with quills and beads and such dentalium shells as were sometimes acquired through trade with the Nez Percé and Umatilla peoples farther to the west and from the wide-ranging Bannocks. The shells had been garnered by those peoples from yet other tribes who had gotten them from those who lived at the edges of the Great Water, a place where none of Mountain Lamb's people had ever been.

Beyond her skills and her status as the chief's daughter and her seemingly quiet and pleasant personality, Mountain Lamb was considered very beautiful—tall and long legged, her face thinner and more finely chiseled than was usual among her people, narrow waisted, her breasts so prominent that at times she wrapped a band of the Whiteman's cotton cloth about her chest as a means of avoiding unwanted male attentions. The strategy was of little utility, however, and often she felt the eyes of the men upon her. When she took baskets of clothing to the river to wash, the young warriors would follow at a distance and whoop and show off. Even the women watched her constantly, but whether with envy or with admiration she was never quite sure.

In her mind's eye there was a special one with whom she would one day share her own lodge, but no such special person existed among Gotia's Shoshones. And even the prospect of marrying a younger man seemed dim—for what young warrior would possess a sufficient degree of wealth to pay the price that Bad Left Hand would surely demand? Her fate, then, seemed to lie in sharing a bed with one of the older men, but all such men possessed wives already. Her father's close friend Elk-Striker, for instance, a wealthy man who had at times shown interest in her—he had two wives. That was not a matter of importance to Mountain Lamb, however, for she felt no desire to share the warrior's robes. It was not that sharing a husband was repellent to her, for most of the men who managed to gain wealth and reputation, as Elk-Striker had, eventually took on more than one woman, as their situations accorded.

But still Mountain Lamb had this vision. . . .

One option seemed to lie in pursuing the role of shaman, the healer and interpreter of dreams and revealer of prophecy—a position that Shoshone women might aspire to. As she was well aware, Bear Woman, among the Doogooriga Shoshones, was seen as a very powerful leader and was respected by all, including Bad Left Hand. But to follow such a path, Mountain Lamb would need to live and study with an already-established medicine woman, and within her own village there were none.

And so she wore a chastity belt of woven horsehair and wrapped cotton bandings over her breasts and ignored the attentions of the young men and tried to remain happy as a grown daughter still living in her father's lodge.

Mountain Lamb and Plum Bush sat beneath a large cottonwood, near enough to the river that they could hear the murmur of the water and, from the pool farther downstream, the shouts of children swimming. Yet they were far enough away that no careless boy could spatter their work with mud. The day was pleasantly warm, and the two young women had brought their sewing outside. Both were at work on ceremonial clothing for the three-year-old son of Plum Bush and Mauvais Gauche, a boy called Frog-Catcher. The latter sat in the grass a few feet from his mother and elder sister and played listlessly with a toy horse that his father had carved for him.

The boy was too thin, his eyes ringed by dark circles and seeming too large for his face, and he was unnaturally quiet for one of his age.

Mountain Lamb, glancing up from the intricate flower pattern that she was working with blue and white beads, decoration for a tiny moccasin, saw that Plum Bush's fingers had

stopped moving at her own work and that the young wife's gaze
was again fixed upon the child, her face tense and haunted-
looking. Mountain Lamb's own eyes stung with tears of sympathy.
She knew what it was to watch a beloved one grow weaker day by
day, to see such a one slipping away into the Other World and to
be helpless to stop the process, for that was how it had been with
her own mother. Mountain Lamb knew that it was not a good thing
to think of the dead, and yet, even now, after two years, from time
to time her mother's face would appear in her mind as clearly as it
had when she was still alive, sometimes laughing, as when she
had teased the girl away from her fear after a nightmare, or with a
sly wink, as when she had slipped her daughter a special tidbit
from something she was cooking, sometimes lined and gentle and
painfully thin, the face she had worn during her final illness.

"Don't worry so, Plum Bush," Mountain Lamb said, trying
to put a cheerful, teasing note into her voice. "Sometimes I think
Frog-Catcher must believe he's sick because you're always
worrying over him. In a few days he'll be fine, and then my father
will call off the Spirit Dance, and all this work we've done on his
special clothes will be for nothing."

The young mother looked up at Mountain Lamb and tried to
smile, the dimple in her left cheek appearing for a second, but her
eyes were moist, and she had to glance back down at the work in
her lap.

"Perhaps you're right. And yet both Badger and Raven's
Beak did everything they could think of, but you can see that he
hasn't gotten any better. When Badger sucked that ugly flying
thing out of the back of Frog-Catcher's neck, I was certain he
would be fine. But there must still be something else. . . ."

"Nonsense," Mountain Lamb said with more conviction
than she felt. "Badger and Raven's Beak are old men. They are
good at dreaming things and telling about where the animals are
when the men wish to hunt, but what do old men know about
children? I think half of what they do is trickery. I have seen them
hide things in their mouths during a healing ceremony."

"You mustn't say such things," Plum Bush cried, shocked.

"It's true," Mountain Lamb replied. "I believe what I see
with my own eyes. The Spirit Dance will be much better, for then
all the prayer-thoughts of the whole village will be working to help
Frog-Catcher, not just the prayers of two old men. If they are such
good healers, then how was it that Raven's Beak had those boils

on his backside for such a long time? He couldn't sit down for nearly a whole moon."

Plum Bush giggled despite her worry, remembering; and Mountain Lamb peered around for something further to distract her father's wife.

"Look," she said. "There's Elk-Striker at our lodge again. Maybe those two wives of his won't feed him."

Plum Bush glanced toward where the short, thick-chested man, his face and arms a map of scars from old battles, had just squatted down in the shade of the lodge with Bad Left Hand. The chief was in the process of filling his long-stemmed pipe.

Plum Bush smiled, broadly this time, and the dimple revealed itself clearly.

"Perhaps. That must be why he is seeking a new wife. Or maybe he wishes to have a new woman for some other reason."

The two men were talking now, and their gazes turned toward the two young women. Mountain Lamb looked away quickly, her face flushing.

"Elk-Striker comes to see my father, that is all," she snapped.

"Of course," Plum Bush teased. "He could certainly not be interested in the chief's daughter, who is so ugly that the chief will probably have to give away all his horses just to get some toothless old man to marry her."

Mountain Lamb picked up the moccasin again and worked furiously, threading the tiny beads and stitching them into place.

"It doesn't matter to me why he comes," she muttered. "I will not be an old warrior's third wife."

"Why not? Elk-Striker is a great warrior. He can give you many nice things, and you won't have much work to do with two other women in the same lodge."

There was a note of hurt in Plum Bush's voice, and Mountain Lamb looked up at her, realizing that she had spoken rudely without intending to. She seldom thought of Plum Bush as her father's wife, not in the usual sense. The girl was only a year or two her senior, and they had been friends from childhood, long before Plum Bush had become Mountain Lamb's stepmother.

"I'm sorry," the chief's daughter said now. "I didn't mean that it isn't a good thing to marry a powerful, older man. I know that you are devoted to my father, and you have brought him much happiness."

"Gotia did me a great honor in marrying me, Mountain

Lamb," the girl said quietly. "You must remember that I was an orphan. And he has been the kindest husband I could imagine. I would not want a young warrior, not someone like Buzztail, for instance. Those are the kind who beat their wives and spend all their time gambling and chasing other women. You like him, I know that, but you must forget all about him."

"Buzztail is a fool," Mountain Lamb agreed. "And you are a very good wife to my father. You have given him a son, and that is what he wanted most in the world. I cannot think of a better marriage. I don't know what's wrong with me, Plum. Perhaps I'm still a child. Perhaps I want something that doesn't exist. Do you remember how it was when we were little girls, how we used to talk about who it was that we would marry? It was always someone tall and beautiful as a god, someone young and swift, and this magical being would look into my eyes and the whole world would turn inside out—the way things happen in stories, where lovers die for each other, and then they go into the Spirit World in search of each other. That is foolish, isn't it, my friend?"

"We are not children anymore." Plum Bush shrugged. "This is the world we have to live in. I am content with what I have. I only beg the Spirit Helpers," she added, her voice catching slightly as her gaze turned again toward her son, "that I may keep what I have."

Mountain Lamb glanced down quickly, ashamed at the seeming frivolity of her desire in contrast to her friend's very real anxiety over her little one. Even so, she could not quite silence the tiny, rebellious voice inside that continued to insist that she would never lie down with a man until it was *the* man. She stitched at her beadwork in silence for a time.

Frog-Catcher rose and stumbled over to his mother, whimpering and reaching toward her plump breasts.

"I'm hungry, Mother. . . ."

Plum Bush threw back her short cape and offered the child a nipple, gently stroking the soft hair at the back of his head and humming a soothing song as he nursed. But he suckled for only a brief time before he pushed away peevishly and then lay down with his head in Plum Bush's lap, toying with a fringe on her clothing and whining. Plum Bush continued rocking and singing softly, but she looked up at Mountain Lamb, her eyes wide and helpless.

"He hardly eats at all anymore," she whispered.

"It will pass," Mountain Lamb insisted. "I think children do these things to frighten their parents."

Plum Bush seemed hardly to have heard her. Mountain Lamb rose, brushing at the dust and leaves on her skirt. She put her sewing things into the leather pouch she used for that purpose and then bent and scooped Frog-Catcher up into her arms.

"Come, little bear," she called cheerfully. "The sun has gone behind the trees, and it's getting cold. We'll let your mother sit out here and worry while we go in by the fire and play. Perhaps she will turn into an ice maiden, like the one in the story, and she will have big icicles hanging from her nose and ears. Do you think she would be pretty like that?"

The child looked at Plum Bush and giggled before he remembered that he was supposed to be unhappy. Then the face wrinkled up again.

"I'm still hungry, but I don't like to eat," he complained.

"Hah!" Mountain Lamb cried abruptly, pretending to let the child fall and then catching him again. "I nearly dropped you. You must be getting slippery."

Frog-Catcher shrieked and then laughed again.

"Perhaps your mother won't freeze. Perhaps she will grow fur like the bears have. Yes, I think she will look much nicer that way."

The little body shook with laughter now. The joke seemed to improve the more Frog-Catcher thought about it, and he alternately closed his eyes and then opened them to look at Plum Bush again, whereupon he would cry out, "Furry Mommy!" and break into more uncontrollable fits of giggles.

Mountain Lamb hugged the frail boy, feeling something seem to expand inside her at the normal-sounding, childish merriment. Plum Bush smiled and rose to follow them toward the lodge.

I wonder if I will ever have one of my own? Perhaps I should not be so choosy. . . .

Bad Left Hand had also moved inside the lodge, and Elk-Striker had come with him. The two men sat near the rear of the dwelling, leaning against backrests and talking. Frog-Catcher climbed into his father's lap and began tugging at his braided hair. Bad Left Hand smiled indulgently and began jouncing the boy with his leg, singing a nonsense song.

Plum Bush went back out to fetch water in company with Likes Birds, the elder of the two wives. Mountain Lamb built up the fire and began to prepare the evening meal. As she moved about the lodge, she was aware that Elk-Striker's gaze was always upon her, watching her body rather than her face. She became acutely uncomfortable, feeling the blood rise into her cheeks. She turned away and tried to make her movements small and unnoticeable, but she still seemed to feel his eyes, his male eyes, moving over her body as if they were a pair of hands.

Elk-Striker is not a bad man, she thought. *It would please any woman to know that he desired her. He's a famous warrior, and everyone respects him.*

But still she felt his stare as a violation, as if he were undressing her without her permission. She wished to strike this friend of her father's, or to blindfold him, or else just to go to her sleeping place and hide herself in her robes. Instead, she forced herself to continue working quietly at the fire, all the time feeling as if things were crawling upon her skin.

Why do not Plum Bush and Likes Birds return? It does not take this long to bring water. Did my father tell them to stay away?

"You are fortunate in your family, Mauvais Gauche," Elk-Striker said, raising his voice so that Mountain Lamb would hear. "Your son will be a great warrior, and your women are handsome and good workers. My wives are ugly, and they nag at me all the time."

Bad Left Hand disagreed, as was proper.

"And this girl of yours has become a great beauty. Someone will bring you many horses for that one."

"She is not so pretty as many of the other girls in the village," Bad Left Hand replied. "And she is a very bad cook. I am sorry that you will be subjected to whatever she is preparing now."

"At the Whiteman's Rendezvous last moon, I bought too many beads and steel needles. These things aren't much good, and I don't have any use for them. Perhaps your girl can use them," Elk-Striker said, still addressing Bad Left Hand and handing the chief a pouch.

"Umentucken, come here," the chief called.

Keeping her eyes downcast, Mountain Lamb moved around the fire to stand before her father.

"My friend Elk-Striker wishes to give you these trinkets," he said, holding out the pouch.

"I do not deserve such fine things, Father," the girl said,

addressing the floor. "It would be better if your friend gave them to his wives."

"Elk-Striker wishes to give them to you," the chief insisted. "I do not know why, but that is his wish. You had better take them before he comes to his senses."

"I could not accept such a generous present," Mountain Lamb insisted, an edge of anger coming into her voice despite the modesty of her words. "The great warrior's wives are very beautiful and much better seamstresses than I. They will know how to make something fine with these beads and needles."

Bad Left Hand sighed.

"She is also a very stupid girl, my friend. She does not have the sense to take something that is much nicer than she deserves."

Elk-Striker abruptly changed the subject, and Mountain Lamb slipped away, going back to her task of cutting meat into the iron kettle that had been her mother's treasure, traded from the Whites of the Hudson's Bay Company many years before. She looked cautiously toward the men, and saw that Elk-Striker's face was stiff, impassive, but his eyes were no longer upon her. And after a short while, he rose and left the lodge.

Mountain Lamb fed two more sticks into the fire and pushed the pot to the edge of the flames. She knelt by the pit and continued watching the stew, as if it were necessary that she not take her eyes off it even for an instant. Now that Elk-Striker was gone, she quailed inwardly at what was certain to come next, for although she knew she could always bring the chief around to her side, still the man in a full-blown rage was an awesome phenomenon—and not one that she was pleased to have provoked.

Bad Left Hand did not speak for some time; rather, he sat and smoked a full pipe of tobacco, Frog-Catcher having fallen asleep on his lap. Mountain Lamb glanced quickly up at him from behind the curtain of her hair. The chief was not looking at her but at some point across the lodge. Mountain Lamb picked up a wooden ladle and began stirring the pot, although the contents weren't even warm yet.

Plum Bush and Likes Birds entered the lodge, breathing hard. There was the sound of water sloshing about in the hide buckets they carried. The two women looked from Mountain Lamb, intent on her cold stewpot, to Bad Left Hand, the latter sitting with his sleeping son and staring grimly into space.

"Oho," Likes Birds whispered, catching her lip between her

teeth and, setting the water down hastily, beginning to back out of the lodge once more.

"Stay, wife," Bad Left Hand ordered. "My son has fallen asleep, and now I have no one to talk with. Both of you, sit down."

"Mountain Lamb is right there, my husband," Plum Bush said. "Why do you not talk to her? Why did Elk-Striker leave so soon? You told us to—"

"I do not know who this person is," Bad Left Hand said. "I had a daughter once, but she insulted my oldest and best friend so badly that he will probably never wish to speak to me again, and now I have only one child, a son."

"My father tells stories of grizzly bears when all he has seen is a mouse," Mountain Lamb retorted. "I did not wish to insult his friend. Elk-Striker wished to give me some blue beads, but I thought his wives should have them. That is all that happened."

"Now she calls her father a liar!"

"But, husband," Likes Birds protested, "if Umentucken had accepted the beads, that would have encouraged Elk-Striker to court her. Wouldn't that have been wrong if she does not wish to marry your friend?"

"That is true," Plum Bush said.

"Now my wives argue with me also! I must be a child or a foolish old man with no lodge and no teeth, so that even the women refuse to have respect!"

Frog-Catcher came awake with a start and looked up at his father, eyes wide and frightened, his lower lip starting to quiver. Bad Left Hand hugged the boy close but continued to glare at his daughter and two wives.

"Do not be frightened, little warrior," the chief murmured. "You are my only child now. In a moment I will throw your mother and Likes Birds and this other person out of our lodge. Later I will go to find myself a good wife who will take care of us, one who will have proper respect for her husband."

Frog-Catcher began to cry, and Plum Bush stepped forward and took the boy into her own arms.

"Shame on you!" Mountain Lamb protested, her temper starting to rise now. "Father, you have frightened your son for no reason. Would you have me marry a man I don't wish to marry in order to avoid hurting his feelings?"

"What is so wrong with Elk-Striker?" Bad Left Hand complained. "You should be married by now. Umentucken, you find something wrong with every man who shows any interest in you. Soon the people will begin to think there is something wrong with you."

"Nothing is wrong with Elk-Striker, Father. He is a fine warrior and a very wealthy man. I just do not wish to marry him."

"I know what you want," Bad Left Hand said. "You want what all foolish girls want. You want some dashing young man, someone who is good to look at, even if he is worthless inside. But young men like Buzztail and Caribou Hoof are still very poor. What kind of a lodge would you have? You would freeze to death or starve to death."

"And you, Father, you want someone who will give you a hundred ponies for me so that all the people in the village will say, 'Look, there is the chief. He was given a hundred ponies for his daughter.' "

"No one would give a hundred ponies for you, Umentucken, not even ten. I should throw you out of my lodge for the way you speak. Your talk is shameful. It is only because I am forgiving and weak that I do not. Now I suppose I will have to give Elk-Striker one of my best horses to soothe his feelings, maybe the big Appaloosa. And I suppose I will still have you on my hands when I am a hundred winters old."

The time for the Naroya approached, the Spirit Dance that Bad Left Hand was giving for his ailing son, and the women in the chief's lodge were kept busy preparing food for the entire village as well as the friends and relatives from other villages who would come to participate. The dance was a solemn ceremony, but for the people it was also an opportunity to socialize, to eat, and to see old friends again.

During this time, Bad Left Hand indeed presented Elk-Striker with a fine Appaloosa stallion that he had traded from the Nez Percés for a great price. But in return the warrior made his friend the present of a prized rifle, a nearly new Kentucky, and so the friendship suffered no serious breach. Neither was Elk-Striker entirely discouraged from his courtship of Mountain Lamb. He did not come to the lodge for several days after the girl had refused his gift, but before too long he was visiting with his previous frequency. He gave Bad Left Hand a beautiful bone hair ornament to give to Mountain Lamb, not repeating his previous error of doing so in her presence. And although Mountain Lamb refused to wear it, neither would the chief allow her to return the gift.

The Spirit Dance lasted the traditional five days, with both men and women participating. The men formed a circle, and the women slipped in between the men, taking the hands of those on either side. Many girls took this opportunity to encourage the young men they were interested in, but Mountain Lamb was careful to avoid coming close to Elk-Striker or anyone else who could conceivably be considered a suitor.

The dance continued all day the first day, with the dancers shuffling first to one side and then to the other around a pine tree that had been cut and brought into the center of the village for the occasion. The ceremony continued through the night, around a blazing fire once the darkness had set in, with dancers who were exhausted dropping out from time to time to eat or to sleep for a short while before they returned. The chanting and the rhythmic movements went on without ceasing for the entire five days, and at times Mountain Lamb felt as if there had never been a time without the voices of the people, the singing, the chanting. It became a waking dream.

Little Frog-Catcher, dressed in his ceremonial clothes, was brought into the circle for everyone to see so that the people might think about him while they danced. But he was not made to stay there. Plum Bush brought him back many times during the course of the ceremony, however.

At last, at sundown of the fifth day, the dancing ended with everyone waving blankets and shrieking and pounding their breasts to drive away the evil spirits that might be troubling the sick child.

Now the entire gathering fell upon the feast, the elk and venison and mountain sheep roasted whole in fire pits, the platters of chokeberries and service berries, the stews and roots and greens that the women had prepared.

Now was the time for visiting, and the socializing with friends from other villages might go on for weeks on end.

Elk-Striker made several attempts to gain Mountain Lamb's company, but she was generally successful in avoiding him without being overtly impolite—by means of staying close either to Plum Bush and Likes Birds or to her two young male friends, Buzztail and Caribou Hoof, a pair with whom she had played since childhood and who had now set a pact between them, to die together in battle, should the need for that ever emerge.

Each of the young warriors suggested that she might wish to accompany him on an inspection of the willow glades along the river, but Mountain Lamb only laughed and observed that one of the mares in the village herd was in heat and no doubt wished to be serviced.

However serious either of the young men may have been, Mountain Lamb was confident that she could handle the situation as long as the two of them were together. And for a time neither young man was willing to let the other out of his sight.

In Bad Left Hand's lodge there were so many relatives and friends that it had been necessary for the women to erect a temporary shelter of brush and grass to accommodate the overflow. Among the guests was a sister of Mountain Lamb's mother, a woman called Morning. She had married a man from the Doogooriga band and lived with his people in the country a few days' ride to the north, near the Tetons. When it became apparent to everyone that Frog Catcher's condition was not improving, but in fact was growing steadily worse, Morning suggested that the young boy and his mother come back to her village with her, there to be treated by the woman healer, Old Fish, and her young assistant, Bear Woman, shamans whose fame had spread among all the Shoshone bands. Bad Left Hand consulted with Badger and Raven's Beak, and convinced the two medicine men that it was a good idea to seek out these women.

Mountain Lamb requested that she be allowed to accompany Plum Bush on the trip north, arguing that the child's mother might need her assistance. When Bad Left Hand consented, more easily than she might have imagined, she was pleased—glad to have an opportunity to make the trip, for she was becoming increasingly restless and confused. Her little brother's health was a great worry to her, but she was also concerned about herself. She felt that she was drifting, and she could not see a clear future.

Elk-Striker had become a relentless, although quiet, suitor. As often as not, whenever she stepped outside the lodge now to fetch water or gather berries, she would encounter the scarred-faced warrior along her path, and then she would have to pretend not to understand his subtle endearments. She did not want him. She did not want any of the men, young or old, who watched her as she walked about the village. And yet she would have to marry, for there was no other future that she could see. Perhaps time away from Elk-Striker, from her father, from the whole closed world of the village, where privacy was impossible and her future

husband was a subject for increasing speculation—perhaps away
from all this she would be able to think more clearly.

They set out for the north in a few days' time, Plum Bush,
Frog-Catcher, and Mountain Lamb in company with Morning and
her two sons, both boys in the stage of transition from boyhood to
manhood, as well as a number of others from Gro-wot's village
who had come for the dance. Riding on a brilliant early morning,
the sun just showing above the eastern mountains, Umentucken
felt an exhilaration, a sense of freedom, as if she were expanding
in some way to fill her expanded horizons. She felt almost as if she
had come to the surface after a long time under water, as if she
were drawing a first breath into air-famished lungs.

On the morning of the second day, however, Elk-Striker
caught up with the expedition, explaining that he had offered Bad
Left Hand his services to provide an experienced warrior to escort
the party, which was mostly women and children. Mountain Lamb
felt her newfound sense of freedom wither inside, even though she
sat her horse and faced straight forward, pretending that she hadn't
even noticed Elk-Striker's arrival.

For his part, the warrior did not press his suit, although he
made a great show of giving Mountain Lamb the choicest portion
of the deer he had killed for the party.

They arrived at the village near the base of the Teton Range
on the fourth day, and Morning took the visitors immediately to
Old Fish's lodge and introduced them to the medicine women.

Mountain Lamb was surprised at the warm greeting that both
the ancient shaman and the young one gave to the newcomers, for
the two medicine men in her own village adopted a very distant
and formal manner with the people. But Old Fish embraced both
young women as they were introduced to her, smiling with her
toothless lips and putting her papery cheek next to theirs, then
touching the child gently with hands so thin and dry they seemed
almost translucent.

Bear Woman, small and softly rounded and with a face so
delicately featured as to seem almost unreal, immediately picked
up Frog-Catcher and flipped him over her shoulder, holding him
there as he giggled helplessly. Then she swung him down and
knelt in front of him.

"I know you," she said. "You are the great warrior Frog-
Catcher."

"I am not a great warrior yet," said the boy, but his face wrinkled into a pleased smile as he looked up at his mother.

"Ah, but you will be," Bear Woman continued. "I have dreamed of you. I dreamed that you were coming to see me, and I hoped it was true."

She rose then, her hand upon the boy's shoulder, and addressed the women.

"When I heard of what had happened to Bad Left Hand's son, I wished that I could come with the others to the Spirit Dance, but I did not wish to offer my help until I was asked. I know that you have Badger and Raven's Beak, who are known everywhere as great prophets, and I was afraid I would insult them."

Old Fish nodded and said, "We added our prayers to the prayers that we knew were being offered at the time the dance was going on. As Bear Woman has already told the young warrior, she dreamed of the child during that time. She was very distressed because she felt certain that she could help but wasn't sure that you would bring him to us."

"We've brought gifts for you—" Plum Bush began, but the old woman cut her off.

"We will talk of gifts when we see what happens," she said firmly. "But if you have brought a little tobacco, I would accept that. Most people don't think of bringing tobacco to a woman, even if she is a healer. It has been many days since I smoked my pipe."

Plum Bush turned to Mountain Lamb with a helpless look, for it had not occurred to her, either, that the shaman might wish to have tobacco.

A thought came to Mountain Lamb, and she smiled and nodded.

"Mauvais Gauche sent along some tobacco for me to take as a greeting to Gro-Wot, your chief, for Man Without Wives is an old friend of his. I do not think your chief would mind if he had a good blanket instead of some of his tobacco."

The ancient face wrinkled into a wide smile, and Mountain Lamb went out to fetch the tobacco from her packhorse. She found Elk-Striker waiting near the lodge entrance, and he fell in beside her as she walked toward the brush corral where the horses had been taken.

"Umentucken, Tukutsey Undenwatsy," he began, speaking with a note of pleading that aroused her sympathy for the man at the same time as she wished passionately that he would leave her alone, "I have waited to speak to you for this whole journey, and you have never given me the chance. You know that I have been courting you for a long time now, even though you pretend not to notice. Now I am going to speak to you outright, even though the other men would laugh at me if they knew this."

"Elk-Striker, this is not the right time," Mountain Lamb protested—but he continued, refusing to be interrupted.

"This is like a madness with me," he said. "I feel that I must have you. You know that I would treat you well. I would always honor you above my other wives, and you would never have to do any of the hard work. I will never hit you—I couldn't. Your father has given me his blessing to court you, but he says that you must make up your own mind. Daughter of Bad Left Hand, you are the most beautiful woman I have ever seen. If you will not be my wife, perhaps I will become like the young warriors, and the next time we go to war with the Blackfeet or the Utes, I will become a Foolish One and set out to get myself killed."

He had gripped her arm as he spoke and forced her to stand still. Mountain Lamb was aware that several people had noticed what was happening—the older warrior holding the girl and speaking urgently—and these had paused to watch, some of them beginning to smile knowingly. Mountain Lamb's embarrassment and the coercion, both physical and psychological, that she felt he was employing caused her temper to flare, and she spoke sharply.

"Then you truly would be foolish, Elk-Striker. What man wants a woman who does not want him? I have other things to do, and since you have the answer to your question, I hope you will now let me go."

Elk-Striker gripped her arm more tightly for a second, until he noticed that the nearby onlookers had begun to grin openly. The look of pleading on his face had vanished and been replaced by an expression of growing fury, and Mountain Lamb felt a momentary shudder of fear. But then he merely dropped her arm and strode away without another word.

Mountain Lamb was troubled as she continued her interrupted errand. Once again she had hurt and angered her father's best friend.

"But it was his own fault," she said under her breath, annoyed. "He didn't have to come along on this trip. He should have seen that I had already said *no* to him. He was foolish to expose himself to an open refusal."

Old Fish was pleased when Mountain Lamb finally returned to the lodge, bringing with her a generous twist of tobacco. The medicine woman immediately filled her long-stemmed pipe, going through the familiar ritual of offering the smoke to the four directions and the sky and the earth before she settled back with a look of infinite content and drew in a great breath of smoke.

Mountain Lamb tried not to stare, but her eyes kept returning to the gnomelike figure, her head surrounded by a dense cloud. She had never before seen a woman smoke a pipe.

Bear Woman smiled.

"Old Fish says that this is part of her medicine," the younger shaman explained. "I am sure that this is true, because Grandmother Fish never lies, but sometimes I almost think she enjoys it."

The ancient one did not bother to reply and in fact gave no sign that she had even heard the comment. She continued to sit like some carved idol, expelling volumes of smoke. Indeed, Old Fish seemed almost to be falling into a trance, so still was she, and the others grew silent also, watching her and waiting for her to speak. Even Frog-Catcher was absolutely quiet, and Mountain Lamb thought that this, more than anything else, spoke eloquently of the commanding presence of the woman.

Only when the tobacco had burned out and the old shaman had tapped the ashes into the firepit and replaced the pipe in its leather case did she speak.

"This will be Bear Woman's healing, because she is the one who has dreamed of the child. She feels most strongly that she can help. Besides, I am beginning to grow old, and my medicine may not be as strong as it used to be. I will only assist with whatever I may have learned over the years. Bear Woman will one day be a greater shaman than I am. Perhaps she already is, but she is still young."

"Grandmother," Bear Woman teased, "I never know whether you are complimenting me or apologizing for me."

"The years take away strength, but they add knowledge and discipline," Old Fish continued as if there had been no interruption. "Bear Woman is the most powerful spirit I have ever known, though, and this is her healing. Here is what I think. I think there is need to begin as quickly as possible, so I think that today we should all be purified, and tonight will be for dreaming about this matter. That way we can begin the healing tomorrow. What do you say to this, Bear Woman?"

"I think that my grandmother is very wise, and that we will do as she says. But first I would like to speak with the boy and his mother and find out as much as we can about what has been wrong."

The old woman nodded, and the younger shaman knelt and began questioning, the boy first. She held his hands and looked directly into his eyes as she spoke, and waited patiently for his answers. She asked direct questions about how he felt, touched him in various places, and asked whether there were any pains. There were other questions that Mountain Lamb could tell were leading to the discovery of any possible infractions of taboo, whether intentional or unintentional. Bear Woman then questioned both Plum Bush and Mountain Lamb, using the same technique of looking intently into their eyes and speaking in a quiet, compelling voice. Mountain Lamb found answers being drawn out of her memory, things she had forgotten were there.

Somehow the sound of the shaman's voice and the quality of her stare were such that Mountain Lamb could not pull her own gaze away, and the lodge and the other people seemed to vanish, and Mountain Lamb's field of vision narrowed to the bright, brown stare of the other woman's eyes.

When the magician at last nodded and thanked her, Mountain Lamb felt as if she were returning from some distant place. She was stunned by the power of the woman's personality.

When the wife and the daughter of Bad Left Hand left the lodge to begin the purification rite, Plum Bush whispered to Mountain Lamb, "Did you feel what I felt?"

"I think so," Mountain Lamb replied. "If anyone can help Frog-Catcher, it is these women."

"Yes, yes, you are right."

Plum Bush and Mountain Lamb walked down the path to the pool in the river where the women bathed, following Bear Woman's directions. The medicine women had stayed behind to prepare the sweat lodge and the medicine lodge for the ceremony, and Morning had agreed to watch Frog-Catcher while his mother bathed. Mountain Lamb was still thinking about Bear Woman, about the strange power of the shaman.

Even Raven's Beak and Badger do not have such power, she thought. *The only other time such a thing has happened to me is during a long dance, where the singing and the movement and the drums have gone on for a long time, and the world goes away. But*

Bear Woman did this thing only by speaking quietly. Perhaps what I really wish is to be like her. Perhaps that is why I have never wished to marry any of my suitors.

It was early afternoon, and the light filtered through the leaves of willow and cottonwood at the river's edge, dancing on the water when the two young women approached the bathing place. No one else was bathing, and the only sounds were the gurgle of the stream and the song of a cicada sizzling on and on in the warmth of the day. Mountain Lamb had bent to untie one moccasin when she heard a man's voice calling to them.

Elk-Striker emerged from the trees, calling, "Plum Bush, wait. The shaman wishes to speak to you."

Plum Bush turned, startled.

"What is it? Is Frog-Catcher . . . ?"

"She did not say that. She only sent me to find you. She forgot something she wanted to ask you, maybe."

Plum Bush glanced at Mountain Lamb and then ran up the path.

"Wait, I'll come with you!" called Mountain Lamb.

"The shaman said for you to go ahead and bathe," Elk-Striker said.

I don't like the look in his eyes. Something is wrong here. . . .

Plum Bush had already disappeared, and Elk-Striker kept watching Mountain Lamb, who began edging away from him. In a movement so quick that the girl didn't see it, one powerful hand clasped over her mouth. She struggled wildly, but the warrior was solidly muscled, and she could not resist as he pushed her away from the stream and into the cover of trees, out of sight of the path. Here he paused, then lashed her wrists together with a length of rawhide and stuffed soft leather into her mouth to muffle her cries before he dragged her farther away from the possibility of accidental discovery.

She heard his breath whistling in her ear, forming words.

"You will not have me, proud one? You think you will not have me? You are too fine for an old, scarred-up warrior? I have known you since you were born, Mountain Lamb. . . ."

He pushed her down onto the soft earth and pinned her with his body.

"You will have me now." He grunted. "And then no one else will want to pay a fine price for you, and you will have to be mine. If I still want you. We will see."

As he spoke, he pulled up her skirt, working it up her thighs without releasing his weight enough to allow her to get up.

The sun still glittered through the leaves, and somewhere a sage thrush burst briefly into song.

This is not happening. This is a dream, and I will wake up. . . .

Mountain Lamb seemed to have a great deal of time to think. Elk-Striker had her skirt up around her waist and was holding her pinned with one arm while he reached around to draw his knife from its sheath in order to cut through her horsehair chastity belt. Mountain Lamb twisted violently to one side and found that her wrists had slipped free of the hastily tied noose. Without thinking, she reached quickly for the skinning knife at her own side, grasped the handle of the blade, and thrust wildly.

The knife plunged into the rear of Elk-Striker's thigh, and the man cried out and reached back to the wound. He drew his hand away and found it covered with blood. He stared open-mouthed at the blood and then at Mountain Lamb, and for an instant he raised his own knife as if to thrust it into her heart.

Mountain Lamb closed her eyes and turned her head away, but the blade did not descend. Instead, the pressure on her body relaxed and then moved off entirely, and she heard a long, low groan. She opened her eyes and saw that Elk-Striker had drawn away and was sitting, knees up, with his face in his hands.

"What have I done to you?" Mountain Lamb cried out, suddenly concerned for him. "Are you dying?"

He looked up at her now, and she saw that his face was wet.

"No, I will not die from this," he said, brushing at the blood on the back of his leg. "But perhaps I will die of shame. I do not know what I was thinking. Perhaps I will go tell your father what I have done, and he will kill me. I do not wish to live any longer."

"You must not do that," Mountain Lamb said, alarmed. "You are a great warrior, and my father needs you. You are like a brother to him. I don't want you to die, Elk-Striker. It's just that I don't wish to marry you."

The warrior laughed, ruefully, bitterly.

"I do not wish to marry you any longer, either," he said.

His face changed, and he groaned again.

"I am so ashamed," he continued. "I have heard in stories how sometimes men go mad with desire for a woman. I never thought that would happen to me. I promise you that I will never bother you again, Bad Left Hand's daughter. I will go away now."

"What will you do? Elk-Striker, you must promise me that you won't harm yourself. I will never tell anyone what has happened. Our village needs you. My father needs you. This is something that never happened."

"But I know, we know," he said. "I will go away from the village. I am not sure. Perhaps after I have been alone in the mountains for a time, I will be able to bear to face our people again. I don't know."

With that the powerful warrior Elk-Striker rose and shambled away, his head down. And Mountain Lamb watched him, not moving until he was out of sight.

CHAPTER TWO

Mountain Luck

Autumn encampment, 1831.

Cache Valley, where Bear River, rounding the Wasatch Range, turns southward toward the Great Salt Lake. And sunrise through low-hanging mists, thin trails of fog over the valley, orange-red sunlight spraying out from behind a curtain of lodgepole pines in a frozen explosion of brilliance. But there were no beaver ponds along the river here, for this segment of the Bear had long since been trapped out by the Whitemen who, years earlier, had come to the region in search of furs, men who had adapted to the Indian way of life in the endless forests and mountains and basins and deserts that either proved their strength or killed them.

These Americanos learned from the Redmen and from the land alike, drew their substance from the huge, sprawling terrain, gorged themselves on the flesh of buffalo and antelope and deer when the game was plentiful, and sometimes starved when the terrific cold of winter froze both creek and river. Yet the land provided for those whose strength and cunning and bravery were sufficient, for those who learned sign and the peaks and drainages of the continent.

Such men became their own law and discovered freedom in wildness. And though the search for Brother Beaver might take the trappers south to the Sangre de Cristos or north to the Milk and Marias and Columbia, east to the Bighorns and the Bear Tooth Range and the Absarokas, or west even to Oregon and California country—nonetheless, summer drew them back to Rendezvous: Henry's Fork, Cache Valley, Green River itself, the Seedskeedee as the mountain men called it.

And sunrise, burning through ghostlike trees in a spangle of light. Already the men in the encampment would be awake, with smoke rising from the vents in their elk-hide lodges. Odors of meat sizzling and coffee brewing in large fire-blackened pots.

* * *

For nearly a week the beavers at Joe Meek's uppermost set had ignored the castoreum-daubed willow switch that bent out over the shallow water beyond the driven stake to which the trap was affixed with a chain. And now it was time to pull iron. Another night or two as cold as the last would leave all the high-country beaver ponds frozen over and the trapping at an end. The cold weather was coming in early, too early. And now it would be necessary to drop back to the lower elevations.

This day he had finished his line early. His luck had been good, and he had taken four plew—*the stick's floatin' right*. So he waited downwind and close by the water's edge—had been waiting for nearly an hour.

"Come on, Brother Beaver," Joe mused, "come on up top for a nibble or two."

He was nearly ready to rise and head back toward the camp on Bear River when a nose appeared above the surface—a large male, the creature paddling its way to the pile of cut aspens and willow twigs stacked in a mound atop the bulge of the lodge. Joe slowly, carefully raised his Hawken, tapped the priming pan to assure detonation, and set his triggers and fired. The shot rang true, nailing the beaver through its skull.

The hide would be a good one, unmarred—a danger when one hunted old Mr. Castor with a rifle.

Meek waded out through the cold water, hip-deep by the time he reached the dead beaver, its webbed feet clinging even in death to the rough mud-and-stick side of the mound. He grabbed the animal by its broad tail, calculated the weight, and returned to where his unsprung trap lay submerged beneath half a foot of water close by the shore. Joe pulled the stake loose, retrieved the trap, and set it against the curtain of brush beside the pond.

With deft motions he skinned the beaver. The pelt would make a large brown oval when pegged for curing, and eventually it would find its way, perhaps even to Europe, to the shop of a skilled felt-master who would convert it into a hat, perhaps a gentleman's stovepipe.

But the tail—that was a different matter. It would be roasted and eaten back at camp, would sizzle and drip lard over the open flames. A delicacy among the mountain men, at least in late autumn and early spring, when buffalo hump-rib was a bit hard to come by.

The tail went into Joe's saddlebag, along with four others,

and the green hide went under the strap across the pack mule's midsection.

Joe mounted his pony and started downcountry.

Three hours of light left, he thought. *Mebbe I'll be back with the boys before sundown tonight. If Milt ain't busy with book-keepin', mebbe I can interest the old booshway in a few hands of cards.*

Joe was nearing the mouth of the lateral canyon and had just entered beneath a dense stand of tall, spindly firs when he heard the sound—a moaning, wailing, frustrated sound.

He drew his pony to a halt and studied the trees. At a second wail, he turned his head and saw what he was looking for.

"Yearlin' black bear." He laughed. "Cub up a tree, an' he cain't get back down. Clumb up too high, by gawd!"

No sign of mama or brothers and sisters. Just a single, precariously perched young black bear, clinging awkwardly to a pair of branches perhaps seventy feet up.

"What ye doin' up thar?" Joe called to the animal, noting the startle-response to the sound of a human voice.

The bear tried to edge around, slipped, and fell some ten feet to a lower branch sworl, where it managed to cling with its teeth and forepaws, pulling itself by inches in toward the bole of the fir. Once the bear had reached that relative safety, it hugged tightly to the center wood and let out a piteous howl—a whine and a coughing growl all at once.

"I done ye a favor, bear!" Joe called out. "Sure ye can get down now."

But the cub whined even more loudly, motionless, almost like a great furry knot.

Meek laughed and stared at the animal—a sensation of amusement and curiosity at the same time. If left to his own devices, how long would the little bear remain in the tree? Muckaluck, Antoine Godin's Flathead friend, had once described finding the remains of a starved-to-death cub high up in a tree.

Damned good climbers, unless they lose their nerve, Joe thought idly. *Then they get so concerned about not fallin' that they just plain won't come down—not until hell freezes over, they won't.*

The bear was looking down over its shoulder at Joe now, and the young, black-bearded trapper began to feel, in one way or another, as though he were responsible for the creature's predica-ment.

"Your mama chase ye up thar?" he yelled out. "It's the way of the world, friend. Just when we're startin' to feel real comfortable, *whump*, she shoves us out. Didn't happen with me quite that way, leetle friend, but it might of. Come on now, gawddammit, ye can get down. Give 'er a try!"

But the cub had no apparent intention of letting go of its death grip on the fir bole.

"Aw shucks." Joe groaned. "If ye think I'm goin' to climb up there an' save your apples, ye got another thought comin'. . . ."

The bear whimpered even more loudly.

Meek dismounted, walked to the base of the fir, and gazed up.

"Bite me, ye son of a female damned hound, an' I'll have your hide sure. . . ."

The first limb strong enough to support Meek's two-hundred-and-some-odd-pound body was at least fifteen feet above Joe's head. He double wrapped his rawhide lariat about a chunk of deadwood and tossed the line up and over the limb. Then, with both ends of the lariat in hand, he moved to the opposite side of the tree, checked his weight against the limb above, grabbed hold, and set his moccasins against the trunk. Up he went, agile, hand over hand, until he reached the first of the live boughs. Then he tossed down the deadwood and proceeded to hoist himself, branch sworl by branch sworl, until he had nearly reached the stranded cub.

The bear whimpered, started to climb higher, and then thought better of it.

"Listen, damn your eyes. No point at all in the both of us fallin' an' bustin' our necks. Now hyar's what I'm goin' to do, bear. I'm goin' to loop my rope over your head an' arms. No way I'm about to try haulin' a half-growed bear out of a tree otherwise. Remember what I said, now. Ye bite me, and your goose is cooked. Ye hear me, friend?"

But the cub wasn't even looking at Joe. He was staring straight up the tree, as if gaining the resolve to climb higher still.

Joe Meek pulled himself up one more set of branches until he was alongside the clinging cub. He set himself, made buzzing noises at the bear, and slipped the lariat draw-loop over the animal's head.

So far so good.

Now it was necessary to pull back the cub's forepaws, each in turn, so as to get the rope around the thick belly.

The young bear stiffened when Joe touched him, but after a few moments of petting, he relaxed. Joe took hold of one paw, pulled it loose from the tree, and was astounded at the strength of the eighty-or-so-pound creature.

The rope slipped down over the furry arms, and Joe laughed.

"That wasn't so bad, now, was it? Nigger, ye got a hell of a grip on ye, for sure. Come on now, big guy, one more. . . ."

The rope was in place, but the bear was clinging to the tree with all his strength, growling and coughing now, and then whimpering once again.

"Got ye!" Joe exclaimed. "But let me take another wrap on ye. Since I've gone to this much trouble, no sense in lettin' ye slip loose on the way down. Let me get my gawddamned hand under thar, now!"

Success—the bear was double-wrapped about his middle.

"Now, then. How does this child get ye loose from the tree? Ye're stronger than Bridger an' Frenchy Le Blueux together, an' ye got lots bigger claws. Don't be bitin' me now, ye fuzzy varmint. Just let old Joe pull ye loose. Wagh! This is like makin' love to a Blackfoot with a bad dose of the lice. Let loose, ye oversized hawg!"

Knees against the bole and one arm around the bear, Meek lunged backward, pulled the bear free, and nearly pitched himself out into space. The bear fell, but Joe grabbed the rawhide rope in time and hung on.

The cub dangled ten feet below him, squirming and screaming and trying to grab hold of the tree once more. With one hand Joe managed to tie the rope about his own middle, and, with the cub dangling beneath him, he started back toward the forest floor. Halfway down the bear clutched and held, and it took Joe some minutes to convince the animal that the two of them should continue their descent—and he did so only by explaining that the cub would otherwise be required to make it to the ground on his own.

"Ye've clumb down trees before, I know ye have. All right, by gawd, I'll untie ye. Thar! Now go on ahead, ye cursed beastie."

The cub finally got the idea and began, cautiously, to lower himself along the trunk.

Meek was at the last strong limb when the bear reached the

ground and, without so much as a snorted thank-you, sped off
upslope with amazing speed.

Meek swung himself down from the lowest branch, landed,
sat with his feet splayed out and his back against the trunk, and
bellowed with laughter.

"Coon," he addressed himself, "that was one of the most
dumb-ass things ye've ever done. . . ."

One out of many, the voice inside his skull remarked.

Meek nodded, accepting the judgment.

Then he rose to his feet, whistled, and walked toward his
patiently waiting horse and mule.

An uneasy truce existed in the autumn encampment. The
American Fur brigade under Vanderburgh and Drips, themselves
not familiar in any detailed way with the lay of the land to the west
of the High Shinin', and with inexperienced men to boot, were
under orders to dog the footsteps of the Rocky Mountain Fur
boys—seasoned trappers following such party chiefs as Robert
Campbell, Tom Fitzpatrick, Kit Carson, Jim Bridger, and Milton
Sublette.

When the free trappers, Pierre Le Blueux and Baptiste La
Jeunesse, rode into the RMF camp on Bear River, they found the
American Fur brigade lodge up right alongside Bridger and Fitz
and Campbell and the others.

"Baptiste, *mon fils*," Le Blueux grunted, "Drips and
Vanderburgh, they cannot catch *le castor, peut-être*, but they can
track down the other trappers. They hunt the same streams, and
neither side takes in a good harvest of plew. *Enfant de garce!* It is
no way to do things, this."

La Jeunesse, a tall, wiry man in his mid-twenties, a bearded
veteran with a knife scar above his left eye, glanced at the older
man and shrugged.

"It is not our fight, Pierre," he said. "Perhaps we have not
done well to come here, however, *c'est vrai*. Perhaps we should
ride on and make our winter encampment with our friends the
Shoshones. We could find an old squaw for the bald one and a fat
young girl for me—that way we would have something to do
when the streams are frozen and we can no longer set our traps."

"*Bâtard!*" Le Blueux laughed. "*Non*—let us go visit with
these friends. That is why we have come. It may be we will even
find out if what we have heard about our *compañero* Beckwourth

is true—that he is living with the Absarokas. It would be good to see that one again, *non*? Next summer, *peut-être*."

The American Fur Company trappers were indeed watching and waiting and following out behind Bridger and Carson and Campbell and the rest of the RMF men, never precisely trespassing upon staked grounds, but always staying close and trapping adjacent streams—in effect, learning their trade from the more experienced Rocky Mountain Fur men. RMF had been unable to get rid of this gang of unwelcome apprentices, and occasionally an RMF man, enticed by better wages, shifted his alliance to American Fur—"Gone beaver," as Joe Meek put it.

Meek and Doc Newell and Milton Sublette were engaged in a game of cards in the latter's tepee when they heard a whoop from Jim Bridger, whom they all called Gabe.

Joe squinted at Milt, his booshway, and then at Newell.

"Maybeso Gabe's drunk—or else somethin's up." Meek shrugged, laying out his cards and rising. He pushed his way through the lodge flap and stepped outside, the others following.

"Be damned," he said. "It's Pete Le Blueux an' his sidekick, sure as snake oil."

"Joseph, my friend," Milton Sublette agreed, "I do believe ye're right. The old man of the mountains has chose to grace us ordinary mortals with his presence."

"Well, shoot!" Newell added. "Mebbe the *ancien renard* has got some new stories this time around. It's a sheer wonder, just listenin' to him."

The newcomers were given a warm greeting, with much back-pounding and laughing.

By nightfall, a stiff, chill wind was coming down off the Wasatch Range, a precursor to the times of fierce cold that lay ahead; and the old friends gathered in Milt's lodge. As the steady currents of air buffeted against the stretched elk hides of the tepee, the men indulged in a bit of arwerdenty, the rot-gut whiskey reserved for such occasions. The lodgefire blazed, and the men dined on huge portions of roasted buffalo flesh—good fat cow, slain the day previous by Jim Bridger and Kit Carson, the two still debating whose rifle ball had *done kilt* the animal.

All the old compañeros were assembled—Le Blueux and La Jeunesse, Milt Sublette, Joe Meek, Doc Newell, Tom Fitzpatrick, Robert Campbell, Jim Bridger, Kit Carson, and with them half a dozen first-year men, greenhorns, brought into the lodge for the precise purpose of filling out the audience.

As they feasted on buffalo meat, Le Blueux rehearsed the story of how Jed Smith, the former RMF booshway, had kept a dozen or more beaver kits in his lodge.

"Enfant de Dieu!" Le Blueux laughed, puffing at his pipe as he did so. "Those little ones, they were into everything! Very fine animals—I do not know why it is we trap them. *Mais oui,* Diah's favorite, the beaver wore a red collar—what did he call it?"

"Red Collar," Meek volunteered. "Old Jed, he weren't strong on imagination."

"Ah yes! Red Collar," Le Blueux agreed, running his fingers over the bald spot atop his head. *"Oui.* Red Collar wore a red collar and a chain, *la chaîne.* Then this pet got away, and *Monsieur Smith,* he assembled a hundred of us and promised the one who captured Red Collar—what was it? *Alors,* ten pounds of coffee and ten pounds of *sucre* and two pints of rum. Yet the red-collared one, he was *très adroit.* None of us could ever catch him, *infortuné.*"

"She was one damned fine beaver, I'll tell ye," Bridger said, drinking off his whiskey. "Mebbe we ought to just tame 'em all. Then we could shear 'em, just like sheeps. Jed, he'd 've found a way of doin' 'er, too."

"It's the truth," Meek declared. "Beavers are the most harmless things in the world. Catch ye a beaver an' touch it an' it'll just turn up its head. Seen that lots of times, we all have. An' a kitten'll cry just like a baby. I'd never kill none of 'em if they wasn't worth five dollars, I swear."

"Good as any pet in the world," Carson said, nodding.

"Oui, oui," Le Blueux chuckled, "but these new men that Milton's *frère* has sent up to the Shining Mountains, they do not wish to hear about the little beavers. Joe Meek, *mon ami,* tell us about the time you jumped upon Ephraim, the grizzly. That is one good tale, *c'est vrai.*"

"Aw hell," Meek shrugged, "that weren't nothin'. I've just got good medicine for bears is all."

"Tell the damned story," Fitzpatrick said with a growl. "I've only heard it thirty or forty times. It's just startin' to interest this here coon."

"Yes, *oui,"* Le Blueux explained to the first-year men, "this is a story you must listen to very closely—so you will know what to do when it is your time to wrestle with Ephraim. You will see now why Joe Meek is known as *Bear-Killer*, even though he is only a young man."

Meek chewed off a mouthful of roast buffalo, drank what whiskey remained in his tin cup, cleared his throat, and began.

"Well—Mark Head an' Mitchell an' me were out on the Rosebud," Meek said, gesturing with his hands, "an' we set our iron in the water an' shot us a fat cow, just like the one we been chewin' on here. We ate what we could, an' put the best of what was left into hide sacks an' used 'em for pillows—that way the varmints wouldn't get to the meat. She was cold that night, snow on the ground an' all, an' when dawn come, I dreamt that somethin' heavy was standin' on me. I woke up quick, an' it wasn't no dream, nuther. Damned grizzly tryin' to get the meat from out of my goddamned pillow."

One of the new men spat into the lodgefire and muttered something under his breath.

"Lord's truth," Meek insisted. "Well, I kept quiet—an' the b'ar took the meat off a little ways an' ate at 'er. That was when old Mark raised up, an' back come griz. Damned if he didn't walk on top of me again. We started shoutin' then, an' Ephraim got downright puzzled. Finally he took off down the hill. After that we grabbed hold of our Hawkens, by gawd, an' went after the brute. Since I was the one got walked on, Head an' Mitchell let me shoot him—an' by heavens one good ball put griz flat on his back. When I was certain he was gone under, by gawd, I got up on his belly an' jumped around on *him* for a while."

Everyone laughed, even those who had chosen not to believe a word of the tale.

"It's like I was sayin'," Meek concluded. "Anyone out here that's able to hang on to his ha'r very long has got to have some kind of *medicine*. Mebbe you new fellas don't believe in 'er yet, but you will—ain't that right, Pierre? An' me, I've got *bear medicine*. Born with it, I guess. . . ."

When morning came, Pierre Le Blueux made his way to the lodge shared by Bad Hand Fitzpatrick and Gabe Bridger. He scratched at the entry flap of the tepee, whistled a chord or two from an old Quebec song, and entered.

"Pete the Good," Bridger nodded, "what gets ye up so early? Way I remember 'er, ye always slept in until mid-morning."

"Le Blueux." Fitzpatrick grunted. "How's the stick floatin'?"

"The *ronce*, it has stickers," Le Blueux answered. "Baptiste *et moi*, we like the idea of camping with you this *hiver*, but Drips and Vanderburgh? They are the enemy, *n'est-ce pas?* So perhaps we will find another place—we will go to visit Woman's Dress and his Shoshones."

"Had a feelin' last night ye might decide on that." Bridger grinned, gesturing toward the steaming coffeepot. "When ye find 'im, tell 'im Blanket Chief says for 'im to behave hisself. Likely as not, the old fraud's dreamin' up a whole new version of the future for us coons."

"*Oui*, one little *tasse*." Le Blueux grinned. "The winter chill, it is here this morning. But now we have these packs of plew. Do the booshways wish to buy them? They are *très* difficult to carry around."

"Seems like a child would l'arn better English after twenty, thirty years in the mountains, don't it, Tom?" Bridger chuckled.

Fitzpatrick poured the coffee, handed the cup to Le Blueux.

"Cain't give ye full Saint Louis price, Pierre," Fitz said, "not this time of the year. She's a long spell until Rendezvous."

"*Je comprends*. It is well. By summer we will have too many furs to carry to market. Friend of me, Baptiste, he catches *un grand nombre*. Soon there are no *castors* left in the mountains— then we will all have to become farmers of the dirt, *c'est vrai*."

The deal was struck quickly, and Le Blueux and La Jeunesse took on additional winter supplies, as well as some foofuraw for whatever Indian women they might discover in the course of their travels; and the further credits were duly entered into the Rocky Mountain Fur Company's logs, to be paid the following summer.

"Next Rendezvous we're gettin' together at your place, Pete," Bridger said, laughing. "Or is it your old friend Papin's? Anyways, Pierre's Hole she be."

Le Blueux shook his head.

"Pierre Tevanitagon—it is his Hole. This graybeard is innocent, *par ciel*."

"Appreciate it if ye didn't pass the word on to our American Fur friends, though," Fitzpatrick added. "We're hopin' to give them boys the slip. If they know where it is we're headin' come July, they'll be bringin' supply wagons up, like as not. Bill Sublette's haulin' our goods up country, an' we don't need any more competition than we've got right now. Anyone but you,

Pierre, an' this coon'd keep his yap shut. But ye're one of us, even though ye're on your own trail right now."

Le Blueux nodded.

"Years back," he responded, "La Jeunesse the Elder *et Papin et moi,* we work for them—for Astor and Pilcher. But now, with McKenzie—wagh! American Fur is the enemy. *Mais,* how do you get away from *Monsieur Drips?*"

"Quick move an' a fast ride to the forks of the Snake," Bridger answered, shaking his head in disgust. "That's what we got planned, anyhow."

The thick-shouldered old French Canadian pounded his friends on the back in turn and then proceeded to Milton Sublette's lodge, where La Jeunesse, Doc Newell, Joe Meek, and Milt were finishing their breakfast. Pierre communicated the transaction to Sublette, presented him with a scrawled note from Fitzpatrick, and Milt sent Meek and Newell to the supply lodges to take in the plew and to load the pack animals.

"Ah, Joe," Le Blueux grinned, "you should become the trapper *libre*. Come wander the mountains with us. Rocky Mountain Fur is very good company, but you will not become wealthy man."

"We've found some good country north of here," La Jeunesse added, "*très copieux*. The beavers, they make their nests in the trees—there are so many, *c'est a dire!*"

Joe Meek cinched the saddlebags and looked up.

"Hell, Pierre," he said, "old Milt'd fall in a crick an' drown himself if me an' Doc wasn't around to pull him out."

Newell whistled and continued counting furs.

"Well," Le Blueux snorted, "you will make your move when the time comes, *assurément*. Milt is a good man, but you must look out for yourself, *aussi*."

Meek ran his fingers over his beard.

"Gentlemen," he said, "it ain't that this coon hasn't thought about 'er."

A near-tragedy occurred the day following the departure of Le Blueux and La Jeunesse. A Delaware Indian named Gray, a chief among his own people, was in the employ of RMF as hunter and trapper; and Gray had brought along both of his wives and his daughter as well, an attractive young woman named Bent Feather. The girl laughed and smiled often, and as a result she had attracted several would-be suitors, including Doc Newell. But the Delaware chief was determined that his daughter should wed a young man of their own tribe when he and his family returned to the east of the Rockies the following year.

In camp were also a dozen or so more-or-less friendly Bannock Indians, who had come in to trade and had decided to set up their lodges for the winter. Bridger had warned against allowing the Bannocks to stay; but since their intentions seemed peaceful enough, the Pun-naks were permitted to camp in the space between the RMF men and the American Fur brigade under Drips and Vanderburgh.

Joe Meek, Doc Newell, and Milt Sublette were all present and were speaking with Chief Gray outside his lodge when the trouble began. The Bannocks, in a group, came swaggering by and commenced to shower verbal attentions upon Bent Feather as the girl was dressing out furs.

"Appreciate it if you coons would just keep on walkin'," Newell suggested. "Bent Feather don't want to listen to ye."

The Bannock leader sized up the three Whitemen and the Delaware chief. Then he spat at Bent Feather.

"Pun-nak pig!" Newell shouted, and the free-for-all was on.

Newell and Chief Gray both lunged for the offending Bannock, who, in turn, whipped out his skinning knife.

"Goddamn all of you!" Milt yelled.

He fired his horse pistol into the air and attempted to step between the Bannock leader and Doc and Gray.

The Bannocks surged forward, and Milt went down, clutching at his leg and cursing wildly—blood pouring copiously from the gash in his leathers.

"Hang on!" Joe Meek shouted, dashing toward his fallen booshway, cracking heads together and knocking men aside like so many tenpins. He wrenched the blade from the Bannock's hand, thrust both Gray and Newell back, and roared like a grizzly.

"I did not mean to cut Milt," the Bannock managed as the group stood about, shifting from one foot to another, thoroughly awed by Meek's amazing display of strength and authority. They stared down at the wounded RMF captain.

"See what ye've done, ye heathen son of a bitch!" Meek said through clenched teeth. "I ought to scalp the pack of you."

"I only wished to kill the Delaware," the Bannock protested.

"Well, you done 'er. Get the hell out of here, now. An' stay away from Bent Feather—you boys hear me?"

"We must do something, Joe," Gray said, kneeling at Milt's side, "before this one bleeds to death."

"Newell!" Sublette managed. "Run an' get Fitz. Tell 'im to bring his pine pitch an' bear grease. Fellas, I'm leakin' pretty fast."

Covert preparations had already been made for the RMF move north to the forks of the Snake, but now it was necessary to adjust the procedure. Major blood vessels in Milt's leg had been severed, and it took some time to stanch the bleeding. Fitzpatrick applied boiling pine tar to cauterize and seal the wound, and Sublette bit through his lip in the attempt to avoid screaming out. When the butchering was finished, Milt gratefully received the bottle of Fitz's best brandy and sucked at it, shook his head from side to side, shut his eyes, and said, "Goddamm it, Tom, why didn't ye tell me she was goin' to *hurt* that much?"

"Be fit as a fiddle in no time at all," Fitzpatrick assured him.

But it was evident to all that Milton Sublette was in no condition to make the ride north. At the same time, he knew that he simply could not allow his own bad luck to disrupt the purposes of the partnership—too much was riding on the season's take to allow that to happen.

As his friends were carrying him back to his lodge, Milt thought matters through; and when they laid him out on his sleeping pallet, he told Meek to fetch Bridger, Campbell, and Carson.

"Where in hell's Doc Newell?" Milt demanded.

"Still with Gray and Bent Feather," Meek answered. "I'll be right back with the other booshways, Milt. Jesus Christ, I ain't never seen a coon bleed the way you did—not an' live through 'er."

"Go on—get the boys." Milt groaned as he took another pull on Fitz's brandy.

The captains arrived at Sublette's lodge, and Bridger insisted that Milt drink a full quart-and-a-half flask of water.

"That's what the Injuns do," he said.

"It was Injuns that got me into this fix," Sublette argued. But he accepted the flask and began to drink.

"From what Meek says," Kit Carson put in, shaking his head, "a man my size'd be dead if he lost as much blood as you done, Milt. You damn near went under, nigger."

"A scratch, it were," Sublette said.

But he was having trouble keeping his eyes open.

"Anyhow," Milt went on, "I say we stick to the original plan—an' tonight's as good a time as any. Vanderburgh an' Drips, they won't be expectin' anything—not with me gettin' laid up. I'll stay here with Joe. That okay with you, old compañero? You other coons head on out, an' when I can ride again, we'll trail on after ye. Main thing is, get shed of the American Fur niggers. If we don't manage that, we'll have us a terrific shortage of plew come Rendezvous time."

The captains discussed the matter at length. Milt dozed off, and for a moment Joe Meek was afraid his friend had actually gone under. He shook Milt and woke him up.

"Cain't ye let a child sleep, dammit, Joseph?" Sublette demanded.

"Joe's just worried about ye, is all," Bridger remarked. "Old Bear-Killer ought to have been a mother, it's the truth."

"Where's Doc Newell?" Sublette went on. "Probably out in the willows with Gray's daughter. Done forgot all about his booshway."

"I'm right here, Milt," Newell said. "You was sleepin' when I come in."

Sublette squinted in the direction of the voice, nodded.

"After all this," he grinned weakly, "I hope ye're able to convince little Bent Feather to lodge with ye. Maybe she's worth it. Get ye a race of half-breeds an' teach 'em all to trap beavers."

The men laughed, and Meek pounded Newell on the back.

"Anyhow," Milt continued, "my head's set on it. Me an' the Bear-Killer will stay right here until I'm fit again. He'll take care of me while I live, and bury me if I die. The rest of ye make tracks for Snake River."

The RMF men pulled out before midnight, intending a forced march through the remaining hours of darkness and well into the following day. Joe Meek and Milton Sublette were left behind, in company with the scattering of Utes and Bannocks and the American Fur brigade.

The Bannocks, in a rare display of repentance and concern, did the hunting for Milt and Joe for nearly a week before they, too, vanished into the forest.

And shortly thereafter, to Meek's surprise, Drips and Vanderburgh pulled out.

The weeks drifted by slowly, and yet Sublette's wound

refused to heal. Milt could get about with a walking stick to aid him, but he was unable to sit his horse.

At the end of a full month, he said to Meek, "Joseph, my friend, I just cain't let this thing whip me. A crippled-up trapper ain't no good to nobody. What a goddamned piece of luck this has turned out to be. Close to the end of the year, an' I haven't been able to pull my own weight. You've been able to take some plew in between sessions of holdin' my hand, but most of the time ye've spent nursin' me. I'll make it up to ye, Joe, I swear I will."

Meek put more wood onto the fire, sat down on his own sleeping pallet, and looked across at Sublette.

"Milt," he said, "this coon figgers a friend has got to be good for summat. You'd do the same for me—now that's true, ain't it?"

Their eyes met, and a long and uncomfortable moment of silence followed.

"Of course," Milt answered finally. "But, Joe, you wouldn't be enough of a dumb-ass fool to step in between a bunch of hotheads, even if one of 'em was your own man. Well, maybe you would, too. Come to think of it, that's just what ye did while I was doubled up an' hanging on to my leg so's it wouldn't fall off."

"It's like the Injuns say, Milt. The Old Coyote Man's got a bum sense of humor—an' this is his country we're kickin' around in. Guess we have to play by his rules, at that."

Sublette reached out suddenly, and the two friends shook hands. Then they hugged and pounded each other on the back.

"Ye're a damned fine man, Joe Meek—more like a brother to me than a paid trapper. An' I won't forget, I promise ye."

"Shoot," Meek said, pulling away from the embrace. "Here we are, two grown men, carryin' on like a couple of squaws. I say it's time for a good snort of the arwerdenty an' then build up the fire an' get some shut-eye. She's a cold one tonight, Sublette."

Milt laughed.

"Look in my possibles sack," he suggested.

In the morning the tributary stream leading down to Bear River was frozen solid, and a chill wind was pouring in from the north. Winter had set firmly in, and the time for trapping was over until the spring meltout began some months hence. Days inched onward, and snow fell, covering the floor of Cache Valley to a depth of more than a foot. In the mountains the snowfall was much heavier, blocking the passes.

When a full six weeks had passed since Milt's knife wound, the booshway struggled out to his pony and up onto the animal's back. He gritted his teeth and began to pace the horse back and forth among the Ute lodges. Sublette was in obvious pain, but Meek made no attempt to stop him.

He's gutting it out, Joe thought. *A man learns to live with pain, or he don't survive—that's all there is to it. Milt's as tough as nails—if he thinks he can do 'er, why, it's certain he can.*

It was near sundown when Sublette came hobbling back into the lodge. He rolled onto his pallet, grimaced, and reached for the jug of arwerdenty. After a long swig he grinned at Meek.

"Tomorrow we head north, Joseph my lad," he said. "The damned leg's still half-numb, an' the rest of it's hurtin' like hell right now. But I can use 'er. Figger we ought to go find our compañeros. Ye up to it?"

"Just waitin' for you to ast me." Meek grinned.

Six weeks, and all that time Joe tending to Milt, nursing him, keeping the booshway's mind occupied by telling stories, boyhood in Virginia, coon-hunting ventures, the catching of a monstrous catfish that slipped away and back into the pool on Gervais Creek, never to take bait again. The lure of what lay beyond Cumberland Gap, putting dead animals into the old teacher's desk at school, and finally the episode of hitting the bald-headed grammarian over the head with the man's own alphabet board. Hunting for wild turkeys and playing with the sons of his father's Negro slaves. The preacher man coming to dinner every week. His own brothers Stephen and Hiram heading off somewhere West. Preachers, schoolteachers, stepmothers, civilization itself—just too much for a big boy with shiny black hair and a gleam in his eye to put up with. Head West, out to Saint Louis, life in the Vide Pôche district where he heard tales of places like the Grand Tetons and Seedskeedee and of men like Colter and Glass—and, dammit, Milt's own brother, Bill Sublette, wouldn't hire him on until Meek had stood toe-to-toe with him and stared him in the eye. But all of it, all of it was simply grist for the mill, words strung together to keep Milt's mind occupied, words to fill up the empty spaces between meals. Even as he talked on and on, Joe Meek knew that his own life story differed only in details and in circumstances from yarns any of the mountain men might have told, and that included Milt himself. But Meek talked on, almost desperately at times, in the attempt to force life back into Sublette—day after day in repetitive cycle as the suppurating wound refused to heal.

And by the end of it, Milton Sublette the booshway and Joe Meek the salaried trapper had become fast friends—an absolute bond had formed between them, one that neither found it necessary to remark upon, and yet one that both openly acknowledged as a simple fact of their existences.

With Milt more or less able to travel, given Joe's help, the two men set out to rejoin Bridger, Carson, and the rest of the RMF company. But more bad luck befell them on Blackfoot River, where they blundered through a heavy snowstorm and directly into a Shoshone encampment. A first response was one of happy anticipation—for the Shoshones were generally friendly toward the White trappers, "our Whites," as old O-mo-gua called the RMF men. Bear-Killer and Milt could envision hospitality, a warm lodge, the possible offer of Indian women for the night, and venison stew—perhaps even a feast of dog meat.

But Milt pulled his pony to a halt.

"I got a suspicion Old Coyote Man's playin' another one of his little jokes on us, Joseph," Milt said. "You know what bunch I think this is?"

The Indians stood about, solemnly observing the Long Knives through a curtain of falling snowflakes.

"Sure it ain't Mauvais Gauche's village?" Meek answered, his voice trailing off.

Bad Left Hand, Gotia, the unpredictable renegade Shoshone chief. Some years earlier he had nearly wiped out a brigade led by Etienne Provost—had invited the trappers to smoke the pipe of peace but at the same time had insisted that the presence of any metal would infringe the power of the medicine spirits, and Provost, against his better judgment, had actually fallen for the ploy—had ordered his men to stack their rifles away, pistols and knives as well. And then, at a word from Mauvais Gauche, the Shoshones had pulled out hidden knives and had jumped the trappers. Only with uncanny luck had any of Provost's men been able to escape with their topknots intact. . . .

"Yep," Milt answered, "I do believe it is. Be nice if Le Blueux was with us right now. That damned Frenchy can always figure some way out of a scrape."

"Any ideas, Milt?"

"Just keep amblin' along, I guess," Sublette answered,

waving to the sullen-looking Indians. "If they start comin' for us, spur your pony an' make for the damned medicine lodge. Old Le Blueux told me once that it works sometimes. Anyhow, we ain't got too much choice."

At that moment the Shoshone warriors began to approach the two Whitemen from either hand, and Joe and Milt dug their heels into the sides of their horses and went galloping toward the center of the village.

"Is that it?" Meek called out.

"Hope to God it is!" Milt shouted.

"Our luck, an' it'll be Gotia's gawddamned war lodge!" Meek yelled back.

The Shoshone warriors, yelling and whooping, had given chase.

Joe and Milt drew their ponies to a sudden halt in front of the decorated lodge, and Joe leaped down, grabbed hold of his booshway, slung him over one shoulder, and plunged ahead into the big tepee.

On either side of the lodgefire sat an old man. One was smoking a pipe, and the other was chanting. An otter-skin shield hung on a peg to one side, and various deerhide pouches were suspended here and there.

Smoke from the fire rose straight up and vanished out of the vent in the apex of the lodge.

CHAPTER THREE

In the Hands of
Mauvais Gauche

Once the world was peaceful, and no one went to war—but that was before the Long Knives crossed over the mountains where summer never comes—that was before the Shoshone People first acquired the Elk-dogs, or horses.

After that the world changed, and there was much fighting. The Shoshones drove toward the buffalo ranges east of the Shining Mountains and were pushed back again. Yet the People became friends with the Crows, just as they hated the Blackfeet.

West of the mountains, the buffalo themselves became few; and often food was very scarce. And that is why the Nation was dispersed into numerous small villages.

The Shoshones understood the great strength that comes of visions, and the shamans grew very powerful. Women as well as men might pursue the magic of dreams and prophecy, and a woman's vision was regarded as highly as a man's.

Sometimes the young bathed in icy waters, sometimes they tormented their flesh with thorns, sometimes they went to high places and fasted and chanted so that the Guardian Spirits might come to them.

A powerful vision meant that the shaman was blessed, and often in mid-winter a feast was held, lasting many days, and men and women would fall down unconscious, then revive and sing songs given to them in dreams.

Whiteman's horses, Whiteman's rifles, and Whiteman's disease—smallpox that left many, many dead, and those who lived were covered with running sores and scabs, and years later the terrible scars remained.

Once the world had been peaceful, but that was before the Whitemen came.

Mauvais Gauche summoned his daughter from the tepee and indicated that she was to follow him.

"You are interested in the medicine lodge," he said. "Now

47

we shall see what is inside. Perhaps the Evil Twins have come to pay us a visit."

Mountain Lamb walked two paces behind the chief as they crossed through the village.

"Something has happened, hasn't it?" the girl asked, at the same time brushing snowflakes from her hair. "I heard the warriors yelling just now."

"Long Knives, a pair of them," Bad Left Hand answered. "I think I will turn them over to the women for torture—you women are much better at that than the men. It's because you understand pain better. You must learn, daughter."

"Where are these men?"

"They have taken refuge with the shamans. I don't know why they were foolish enough to ride into our village, and I don't know why they ran into the medicine lodge. Whitemen are very stupid, and perhaps that explains it. These men wished to die, so now I will have to give them what they want. Are you listening to my words, Umentucken?"

"Yes, Father."

"Walk closer to my side, then. You are a grown woman and the chief's daughter besides. Do not trail behind me like a little one."

A crowd of warriors stood about the entryway to the magic lodge, parting to allow their chief and his daughter to go inside.

Badger and Raven's Beak, the two medicine men, had not moved since the unexpected guests had arrived. One smoked his pipe and stared at the Whitemen, and the other continued to chant, his voice a low, cadenced murmur. And sitting to one side, their pistols drawn, were the two trappers.

"I am Mauvais Gauche," the chief said after a moment, glaring haughtily first at the larger of the two men and then at the other. "You are trappers, or have you come to burn my village and kill our women and children? I remember you," he continued, gesturing to Milt, "from the Rendezvous at Bear Lake three years ago. Yes, three winters have passed since then. You were with Le Blueux and the Crow who was a trapper then but who has now returned to his own people. You are Bill Sub-lette's brother. That is what I think."

Milt lowered his pistol but kept it at the ready.

"Yes," he answered. "I'm Milton Sublette, a captain for Rocky Mountain Fur. We have always been friends with the Shoshones, Bad Left Hand."

"Who is this friend of yours, Sub-lette?"

"This here's old Joe Meek," Milt said.

"The man who is called Bear-Killer? I have heard of him—is that who you are, Joe Meek?"

Joe gave the hand gesture for *yes*, but he was looking past the scowling chief to the young woman who stood just behind him.

My gawd, what a fine-looking gal! This child's never seen an Injun female that could touch 'er—an' she's lookin' at me, too—I'm gettin' red in the face, gawddammit! Even if I was dreamin', I couldn't think up one like her, beautiful, beautiful, she damn well shines, this coon don't want to die now, not yet. . . .

"Do you not know how to speak English, Meek?" Bad Left Hand demanded.

"I hear ye, Mauvais Gauche," Joe answered.

That his wife? Old Injun bucks, they take young squaws so they'll have someone to take care of 'em when they cain't do it themselves anymore. . . .

"Sub-lette," the chief continued, "why have you entered the medicine lodge? If you wish to be friendly, why did you not come to me? Did you suppose my shamans would protect you?"

"The chief and his Long Knife friends disturb my song," one of the medicine men said in the tongue of the Shoshones—a language Sublette and Meek knew well enough, having done a good deal of both trading and trapping with one Snake band or another.

"I am sorry, Raven's Beak," Mauvais Gauche said. "I was told these Whitemen had entered the lodge, so I came to find out why."

"Take them away, then," Raven Beak answered.

"No—I will have to leave them here for a little while. If they go outside, the warriors will kill them. I must decide what to do with them. Should we burn them alive, do you think? Perhaps that would make the buffalo more plentiful in our lands once again. Or someone would have a bad dream so you would have something to explain to the People."

"It is up to you and your council," the second shaman remarked, a man who appeared to be nearly a century old. The hand that held the pipe was missing a thumb and one finger.

"I am still allowed to make decisions?" the chief asked, his face without expression. "Thank you, Badger. It is good to know that I still have some power in this village."

With that Mauvais Gauche turned and strode from the lodge,

the girl following him. But just at the entryway she turned back, stared first at Meek and then at Sublette, stepped sideways, and vanished.

Joe stood up, took two paces toward the shaman with the deformed hand, and asked, "Badger, is it? Who was the gal with the chief, old man?"

Badger put the pipe slowly back into its pouch before answering in Shoshone.

"She is the one who will devise your torture, Whiteman," he said. "Does that answer please you?"

Raven's Beak had begun to chant once again.

To the infinite displeasure of Gotia, his daughter had begun to plead for the lives of the two White trappers. In truth, the chief had intended nothing further than to allow the Long Knives to cool their heels in the medicine lodge for a time and to contemplate their fate before he gave them their liberty. Trade with the RMF Company was too important to hazard on behalf of the whims of a few riled-up young warriors. But now that Mountain Lamb was carrying on so, he had half-resolved, indeed, to burn the Whitemen alive. The latter course of action would be to the liking of the young men, in any case, for with the winter storms having moved in, it was no longer possible to do any trapping—and further horse-stealing ventures against the Utes to the south would have to be postponed until the advent of spring. Time for the mid-winter feast was nearly upon them, and death by fire would provide a fitting spectacle. There was little for his people to do during the cold times—other than to make whatever hunting ventures they could, for meat was always in short supply during the winter moons. Pemmican and camas cakes and smoked salmon, most of that acquired in trade from the Nez Percés, made dull fare after a month or so.

"The one with black hair is only a young man," Mountain Lamb protested. "He is not an enemy of our people. And the other is Sub-lette's brother—that is what you said. I have heard you brag that Sub-lette is your friend. Have you forgotten that now, Father? He is the one you trade with in order to get rifles and powder and shot and cloth and needles and vermilion. Why would you wish to kill your friend's brother?"

"Because they are Whitemen and cannot be trusted," Bad Left Hand replied. "No Long Knives are to be trusted. These men have violated the medicine lodge—if they were our friends, they would not have done such a thing."

"Is it not true than even an enemy may enter the magic lodge and receive protection and hospitality? When I was a child, an old Blackfoot did that, and you fed him and gave him his freedom."

"Still your tongue, Umentucken. Why must you always attempt to argue with me? You are not my wife. Daughters should not argue with their fathers. Be quiet now."

"Do not kill them, Father! It would only mean more fighting with Bridger and the other trappers. We would gain nothing, and we would have to find other Whitemen to trade with. It would be very foolish to kill these two men!"

"Mountain Lamb," the chief said, clipping his words. "You cause me to grow angry. I will have my wives pull off your fine clothing and whip you."

"They would not dare to do such a thing, and neither would you. Such a thing is not permitted among our people."

Bad Left Hand glared at his daughter.

"I think you wish to lie down with the black-haired one, the man called Meek," he answered. "Is that why you want me to spare their lives?"

"No," Mountain Lamb said quietly. "No—that is not what I wish. Why would my own father say that? But you must allow them to leave the village and travel on to wherever they were going. It was a mistake that caused them to come here—they must have been lost in the snowstorm."

Bad Left Hand started to turn away, but Mountain Lamb grabbed hold of his sleeve.

"Daughter," he growled, "take your hand away from me. You are not my wife, no matter what you think. Only a wife is allowed to speak in this fashion to her man."

"Then agree that you will let them go."

The chief, now boiling with anger, was quiet for a long interval before answering.

"I will do this thing," he said at last. "I will give the two Whitemen to you, if that is what you wish. And yet I do not think you will want them."

"My father has given his word," Mountain Lamb said. "He cannot take it back now. Tell me the rest."

"If you accept the gift of their lives," the chief replied, "you must leave the village with them and never return again for so long as I am alive. After that, I will be in the Spirit World and will no longer care if a disobedient daughter returns to her village. Yet after so long no one would wish to have you around, anyway. The men will no longer look at you with desire in their eyes, Umentucken. You will be old and worn out by then, for the Whitemen will give you children to care for and then abandon you. Is this the thing you would wish for, Mountain Lamb?"

The girl let out a little gasp and turned away—then swung back around to face her father.

"I accept the gift of the two Whitemen," she said. "I will leave the village with them, no matter what they do to me. At least I will be free, then. I will be able to choose my own mate, not either of the two trappers, but someone I myself desire. I will not have that freedom if I remain here. You would trade me to some old friend of yours in exchange for spotted horses and a new rifle."

"If that is what my daughter wishes," Bad Left Hand replied—but he still did not believe the girl actually meant what she said.

He turned abruptly from her and strode into his lodge.

As evening approached, Mountain Lamb showed no signs of having changed her mind; and Bad Left Hand began to feel genuine regret for having spoken as he had to his high-spirited daughter—one who was, he concluded, altogether too much like her father for her own good. He observed the girl making preparations for an extended journey, and so, unable to retreat from the position he had taken and feeling bound by his own words, he went out to where a great fire was blazing in the main fire pit of the village and undertook to harangue the warriors—hoping to convince them that wisdom lay in allowing the two Long Knives to leave of their own accord.

Most of the warriors and quite a number of the women, however, were steadfastly opposed to the idea. At the very least, the Whitemen should be obliged to fight for their lives in some sort of contest.

Only Badger, the ancient shaman, thought otherwise.

"My vision tells me," he said, "that we must let these trappers go. If we kill them, bad luck will come upon our people."

Raven's Beak, on the other hand, spoke in favor of burning the two alive.

Everyone was talking at once, and Bad Left Hand saw that

his words would be of little further avail in resolving the dispute. He shook his head, considered how much better things would be if the People were actually obliged to do what their chief told them, and returned to his lodge. He instructed Mountain Lamb to take the Whitemen's animals and get them across the river as well as she could.

Once outside and so out of sight of his wives, the chief embraced his daughter for a long moment, touched his fingers to her hair, and said, "You are just like your mother was. But perhaps it is time for you to go off on your own now, Mountain Lamb. Sometimes young men must do that, and perhaps the same is true of young women. But truly, I would not give you in marriage to anyone if you yourself did not wish it. Nor did I mean what I said about not coming back until after I am dead. I did not mean that part at all."

Then he turned and walked quickly toward the long, snow-covered meadows where the main herd of horses was kept. Snowflakes blew into his face, and for a moment he could not be certain tears were not running down his cheeks.

No guards were posted about the horses this night; everyone was in the village, beating drums and chánting and arguing about the fate of the two trappers. Bad Left Hand carefully walked completely around the horses, nodded, fired his pistol, reloaded as rapidly as possible in the near-darkness, and fired once more.

The ponies began to move away toward the west.

The shots, Bad Left Hand knew well enough, would be but faintly audible in the village. They would be heard, nevertheless, and the warriors would come running. Some would be certain that a band of Crows had sneaked in and stolen the ponies.

Skirting about the edge of the village, Bad Left Hand proceeded to the medicine lodge, which now, in deference to the new excitement with the horses, would have been left virtually unattended. Indeed, he found no one outside—and within were only Badger and the two trappers.

"I am not here," Bad Left Hand said to the old medicine man upon entering. "You have only dreamed this thing. You must tell the others that when you awoke, the Whitemen were gone. Right now the ponies have stampeded, and everyone is out chasing them."

"I understand the chief," Badger whispered. "You are not going to kill these men, then?"

Mauvais Gauche did not answer. Instead he addressed Milt and Joe.

"Follow me if you wish to live. I cannot control my warriors, but you have found a friend."

The three men waded across the shallow, icy river to where the horses were waiting. Waiting also was Mountain Lamb, astride her own pony and with a pack animal behind her.

Milt and Joe were astounded.

"She's goin' to lead us out of here?" Milt asked.

"Yes," Bad Left Hand replied. "And after that she will stay with you or go her own way, I do not know which it will be. Sublette, your brother is a man of honor. He is a brave man, and I trust him. Now I must trust you also, for my daughter, Mountain Lamb, rides with you. But if I should hear that harm has come to her, I will rouse all the Shoshone villages and ride after you; and when I find you, I will kill you myself. You know who I am, and you know I do not speak idly. There will be blood on the grass, and Umentucken, Tukutsey Undenwatsy will not dissuade me a second time. Meek and Sub-lette, do you understand my words?"

"Thank ye, Chief," Joe Meek blurted, and immediately wished he had not. But he made the hand sign for friendship, and hoped it was visible in the thin light of the chief's pine-pitch torch.

Bad Left Hand stared at the big trapper and shook his head.

"I think you must be the one," he said—and without any further words he turned and strode to the river's edge, waded into the water, extinguished the torch, and disappeared.

"I'll be gawddamned!" Meek said to Milt. "Gotia turned out to be a good old man. Cain't always believe what ye hear, I guess."

"Let's make tracks," Milt replied. "Hope the Injuns didn't pilfer the whiskey out of my saddlebag. That cold water has set this child's leg to aching something furious."

All night they rode northward through the darkness and the snowstorm that grew ever heavier with each passing hour. Even when grayness began to suffuse the snowy downfall, the girl continued to lead them—not speaking, not even looking back at them.

Joe and Milt spoke softly between themselves of the possible explanation for what had happened, but could come to no conclusions. They continued their ride, Milt in pain and from time to time pulling at his flask of arwerdenty. Behind them were the pack animals, and ahead was the tall, stunningly beautiful girl.

Whatever had happened, it was clear that they were in her hands—in her care. And for all they knew, Mauvais Gauche and perhaps a hundred of his warriors were not far away—were trailing them close and, now that morning had come, were observing them.

Finally Meek could take it no longer. He kneed his pony ahead and drew alongside the Shoshone girl.

"You speak English, ma'am?" he asked—and once again he was afraid he had said the wrong thing.

"Of course I do, Joe Meek," Mountain Lamb answered.

"This nigger don't understand. Why'd the chief—your daddy—let us off? An' where you takin' us, gal?"

"My father has spared your lives, and now I am leading you to safety. That is all. My father's warriors wished to kill you."

"In other words," Joe persisted, "old Mauvais Gauche *give* us to you, is that it?"

Mountain Lamb turned to him and studied his face.

"Yes," she said. "That is what happened. Joe Meek? You have very fine eyes, Joe Meek. They are brown, like a Shoshone's—not blue like some of the Long Knives'. Are your friend's eyes also brown?"

"Naw—they're gray, just like the sky is now. That long name your daddy called ye—what's it mean?"

"Oh," she said. "Mountain Lamb—the daughter of the bighorn sheep that lives on the mountain. *U-men-tuck-en, Tuk-ut-sey Un-den-wat-sy.*"

"Quite a handle." Meek grinned. "You sure are a *pretty* gal—ye don't mind my sayin' so, do ye?"

"I do not mind that," Mountain Lamb replied, looking away from Joe.

"An' Bad Left Hand ain't followin' us?"

"I do not believe anyone follows," she said.

"Well, damn then. Maybe we ought to stop an' have us somethin' to eat. Me an' Milt, we haven't had anything to chaw on since before we tumbled into that medicine lodge of yours."

"We can eat as we ride, Joe Meek. We must not stop until we are far from my father's village. Only then will we be safe. I have food in my saddlebags. Can you reach in for it."

Joe leaned over and managed to pull out two hardened balls of pemmican.

The closeness of the Indian girl, a sensation of delicate warmth, of strength and of softness at the same time, and the odor of her presence, like wildflowers and fear together. He wanted to reach out, to touch her, as if to prove to himself that she was indeed real and not part of an insane dream from which he would presently awaken. He could hardly breathe—had to force air back into his lungs.

Joe straightened up and raised the pemmican in one hand.

"Hey, Milt!" he shouted back. "We've done found us an angel! Pull on up an' chew on some Injun sausage!"

Gawd almighty. Joe Meek's in love. I don't know how it happened, an' it don't make no sense, but it's true, an' I know it as well as I've ever known anything in my damned life. Old Man Coyote's whims, maybeso. I thought I was whole an' strong an' by gawd a match for any man, White or Red. But now I realize I'm only half a man, an' I ain't never goin' to be complete until I've managed to make her love me too, until she's my own, my wife, Joe Meek's wife, by gawd. Umentucken, Tukutsey Undenwatsy— Mountain Lamb. But she'll need a civilized name too—Isabel, mebbe. Goin' to have to trap real beaver now—so's I can give 'er the finest wedding the mountains has ever seen. . . .

"Where we headin', gal?" Meek asked suddenly, breaking away from his reverie.

She smiled then.

"I don't know, Joe Meek. Where were you going before you came into my father's village?"

"North," he answered, "same as now. On our way to find Bridger an' Carson an' the boys. Milt, he took a bad wound in the leg, an' it ain't healed yet—so we had to stay behind when the others made tracks for the forks of the Snake. Other than that, this child didn't know where he was goin' until he met you. What I mean is—"

"Don't listen to him," Milt said as he drew alongside. "Cain't believe nothin' Joe Meek says—unless maybe it's somethin' about food. Give me some of that, Joseph."

Joe noted the quick glance Milt gave the Indian girl, nodded, and laughed.

"Mr. Sublette," he said quite solemnly, "I'd like you to meet Miss—Mountain Lamb."

"How do ye do, madam," Milt said, bowing forward in the saddle and grimacing from the pain he had momentarily forgotten.

"Wounded-leg," Mountain Lamb said, glancing sideways at Milt. "If you were Shoshone, that would be your name."

"Guess so," Milt agreed. "We owe you our lives, as I gather."

Mountain Lamb didn't respond.

"Fact is," Joe added, "we belong to her, Milt. It appears as how her daddy *give* us to 'er."

"At this moment," Milt grinned between mouthfuls of pemmican, "I cain't think of anyone I'd rather belong to. Joe, if I'm goin' to be Wounded-leg, Mountain Lamb here's got to have another name, too."

"Isabel," Joe insisted. "I done already picked one out."

"Isabel it is," Milt agreed.

Mountain Lamb looked thoughtful.

"What does that name mean?" she asked.

"Don't know," Joe replied. "Got a pretty sound to 'er, though. You like it?"

"All right, Joe Meek, I will have that name, then—even though it's not my real name."

Meek whistled and nodded.

But Joe was thinking of what old "Blackfoot" Smith had said to Kit Carson the previous summer:

"Valgame Dios! Your shanty is a poor make-out compared to this hyar Injun lodge. Leaky and cold and open to the weather, and whar's the fire when you come in at night half-froze for a hot kettle of soup? And your fingers too cold to strike a light. Why should you freeze all winter like a starvin' coyote? Your rifle shoots plumb-center; she makes 'em come; you kin throw plenty of fat cow, and you know whar to lay hands on a pack of beaver when you want it. It's time you womaned, Kit, and that's a fact. Maybe you're thinkin' of some sickly gal from the settlements, thin as a rail and pale as a ghost, pretty as a pitcher and so fofurraw she's good for nothin'. Maybeso you've sot your eyes on some wench to Taos or Santy Fee. Do you hear now? Leave the Spanish slut to her greasers and the pale-face gal to them as knows no better. Put out and trap a squaw, and the sooner the better. What a mountain man wants is an Injun woman. . . ."

The snow had ceased to fall, but the sky remained a uniform slate gray.

And the group of three rode onward, heading north,

Mountain Lamb in the lead and Joe Meek and Milton Sublette trailing a few yards to the rear.

Earlier, during the confrontation with her father and during the time when their fate was being placed in her hands and even through the long night hours of riding, Mountain Lamb's mind had remained both clear and purposive. She had not had time to question *what* she was doing, and so the matter of *why* had not been dealt with either.

And now, although she had the leisure to think through the entire sequence of events, she could find no reasonable answer as to what her motives had been.

Now I am exiled from my village. I cannot go back. Have I done this thing merely to get away from Elk-Striker? Not just him, but from being pushed, pushed silently toward a marriage with someone? Marriage simply because my father believes it is time? So now I am leading these two Whitemen somewhere, I don't even know where. For all I know, they will decide to kill me and scalp me. . . .

There was no explaining what she had done. Perhaps only someone like Bear Woman of the Doogoorigas would understand.

And the small, powerful woman came into her thoughts again, as she had so many times since the healing of Frog-Catcher, and once again Mountain Lamb began to rehearse the events in Gro-wot's village.

She thought of the knife that she had used to defend herself against Elk-Striker when the great warrior had begun to act like a man possessed by demons or evil dwarfs, the Nunum Bi. Or perhaps it was even the spirits of the Red-Haired Cannibals that had taken hold of him, she did not know. But she knew that she had lashed out at him with her knife, had fought back like a trapped animal, and that the wound she had given him had somehow led to where she was now, riding somewhere with two strange Whitemen.

Bear Woman.

I could be like her, Mountain Lamb thought. *But could I ever be powerful enough? I have had no dream vision, Coyote Man has not appeared to me to tell me that I should be a medicine woman. It is only that she . . . has power. I would like to have such power.*

Elk-Striker had come to his senses. The dribbling of his own blood from a wound given him by a young woman, the daughter of his chief and his closest friend, had caused him to apologize and to ride away, to find solace in the mountains. And she had returned, terribly shaken, to Bear Woman's lodge.

Yes, she remembered it all.

The two shamans themselves had built the fire outside the women's sweat lodge and had heated the stones to roll inside. Mountain Lamb's aunt, Morning, was instructed to take Frog-Catcher down to the river to bathe him, as it would have been improper to bring the boy into the women's lodge. When the stones were hot, the four women entered the lodge and sat naked in the near-darkness as the heat grew to the point where Mountain Lamb felt that she could bear it no longer—for in her village, only the men took sweat baths. At that point Morning rolled in more stones from outside, and Bear Woman pushed them to the center near the other stones, and they sweated even more. During the entire time, Old Fish kept up a faint, repetitive chant in a voice so low that Mountain Lamb couldn't understand the words. The rest of them sat in silence, perspiration running between breasts and shoulder blades, trickling off the ends of noses.

After what seemed a very long while, Old Fish signaled that it was time to go, and they rose and wrapped their robes loosely about them and ran to the women's bathing area along the river and plunged into the cold water, Mountain Lamb gasping at the shock. Then they returned to the dwelling lodge, where they dressed in clothing that had been smoked over sweetgrass. Frog-Catcher as well was ritually purified by being held in the sweetgrass smoke briefly, and then Old Fish explained to them that they must not speak again until the morning came. They must concentrate their thoughts on Frog-Catcher and what might be wrong with him, so that the Spirit Helpers would come.

Two Whitemen are riding behind me. They are my two Whitemen because my father has given them to me. But out here, so far from my village, what does that matter? They act friendly, but why should I trust them? Perhaps they will rape me and kill me. No, they will not do that—but why am I certain? Joe Meek and Milton Sub-lette.

Bear Woman had a three-year-old son, a child who Mountain Lamb had heard was half White. He was brought to the lodge by the aunt who kept him during the day. After an initial period of shyness, Frog-Catcher and Bear Woman's son, Little Red Bull, seemed to become great friends. Age-mates, and yet Bear Woman's child was so much larger, stronger. . . .

The son of a Whiteman, one whom she had loved and who had left her to raise the child alone.

Isabel. Joe Meek thinks my name should be Isabel.

The women and the two children slept in the medicine lodge that night, and in the morning Bear Woman said she had had a dream.

"Dragonfly came to me," she said, "and Thistle, and some of my other Helpers, and they all said the same thing. They don't always agree, and then I have to decide which one is telling the truth. But this time they all told me that Frog-Catcher has weak blood. They didn't say anything about anyone breaking any taboo or anyone putting a bad spell on the chief's son. The best thing for weak blood is fresh liver. We will find a hunter to get us a fresh liver—it doesn't matter whether it's deer or antelope—and then we will begin the healing ceremony."

"This is good." Old Fish nodded. "When someone's sick, it's always partly in his spirit and partly in his body. The liver will be good for Frog-Catcher's blood, and we will pray and sing and think about this boy, and the Helpers will come and do good for his spirit. Maybe he woke up too early from a dream, and his soul didn't get all the way back to him. We will all go search for his spirit."

"All of us?" Mountain Lamb asked. "I thought only shamans could do that."

"That is what some shamans say," Bear Woman replied, smiling mysteriously.

Old Fish smoked another pipeful of tobacco, and then she and Bear Woman sat down near Frog-Catcher, each taking one of his hands. They asked Plum Bush and Mountain Lamb to take their hands also. The older shaman began chanting, the younger one joining in on the first repetition of the song, Mountain Lamb and Plum Bush adding their voices when they had heard the chant enough times to remember the words.

The singing continued until the children became restless. The little ones were fed, although the women continued their fast. The shaman's son, Little Red Bull, attempted to engage Frog-Catcher in play, but the latter child seemed tired and cranky and began crying when his new friend pulled a colored pebble away from him. Then, at Bear Woman's direction, Mountain Lamb carried the sturdy, blue-eyed little boy to his aunt's lodge.

By the time she returned, Frog-Catcher had fallen asleep. And the ceremony continued.

Joe Meek's eyes are brown, like mine, like those of my people. And yet Bear Woman's child is also one of my people. The one with the black hair. He is only a young man. He is not an enemy of our people. And the other is Sub-lette's brother—that is what you said. Have you forgotten that now, Father?

Morning's two sons had been sent out to hunt, and then, toward afternoon, proud and beaming, they returned with a handsome buck. Bear Woman praised the boys extravagantly and removed the still-warm liver herself. She quickly pounded the rich meat into a paste and somehow, through the magic of her personality, persuaded Frog-Catcher to eat it.

Evening approached, and when Frog-Catcher was again soundly asleep, Bear Woman announced, "Now we will all go out to find this child's spirit."

Old Fish nodded and lit another ceremonial pipeful of tobacco, this time insisting that each of them make the offering to the sacred directions and take at least one puff. Mountain Lamb had to gag back a choking cough as she breathed in the acrid smoke. The four sat in silence as the old woman finished the pipe, and then Bear Woman spoke.

"We will look into the fire, for sometimes the embers hold pictures, and these can be helpful."

Old Fish softly hummed a chant in her whispery, cracked voice, and for what seemed a very long time there was no other sound in the lodge except the soft purring of the fire. Mountain Lamb stared into the glowing heart of the flames and gradually lost consciousness of the rest of the world. It was peaceful here, with the red embers and the soft, whispery chanting.

When Bear Woman began to speak again, her voice seemed to grow out of that peace.

"Now we are going on a journey," the voice said. "We are going uphill and downhill, we are crossing rivers. We are each going alone, but we are all looking for Frog-Catcher's shadow."

Mountain Lamb found herself in a high mountain meadow that blazed with summer flowers. Across the meadow, near a small stream, a raven was calling to her.

"Go up over that ridge," the bird said. "I think you'll find someone there."

She climbed the ridge and found herself, suddenly, face to face with the young medicine woman, who seemed to shine with light from within. Bear Woman smiled in recognition and hushed

Mountain Lamb with a gesture, pointing uphill to where a grizzly sat on his haunches, eating a salmon.

"I wish you'd leave me in peace," the bear said. "Go back home. The one you're looking for is where he should be."

The scene vanished, and Mountain Lamb was once again in the medicine lodge, staring into the fire. She looked up at Bear Woman and opened her mouth to speak, but just as in the vision, the medicine woman, smiling, gestured her to silence.

"Everything will be all right now," the young shaman said to Plum Bush. "Your son's shadow is where it belongs."

I will go with these two Whitemen only a little farther. They will find their friends after that, and they will never think of me again. Did I really believe that these two Whitemen could belong to me? I have spent my entire life dreaming, and now I have been dreaming again. I am foolish, proud, vain—just as my father has always said. And yet, if a man can look upon a woman and desire her, why cannot a woman look upon a man and desire him? I see myself making love with the brown-eyed one, Joe Meek. Is that not why I confronted my father and forced him to send me away from the village? Oh . . . oh, I have fallen into one of my dreams. Now where can I go?

Bear Woman will give me shelter, a place to stay. Perhaps she and Old Fish will let me assist them—perhaps they will even teach me their magic. . . .

The praying and chanting continued for three more days, and at the end of that time it seemed to Mountain Lamb that Frog-Catcher was getting better. For herself, she remained profoundly moved by the experience that, somehow, the shaman had caused her to have. Bear Woman wouldn't talk with her about it, but Mountain Lamb was sure that the healer knew exactly what had happened. More and more she was attracted by the idea that this, perhaps, was the life she wished to lead. At last she spoke with Bear Woman of the matter, some days after the conclusion of the healing ceremony.

"I have never wished to marry any of the men who courted me," she confided. "I was beginning to think that there was something wrong with me, but now I wonder if I have never loved a man because this is the life I was meant to lead."

The shaman stared into her eyes for a long while, as was her habit, before speaking.

"I do not know, Umentucken, Tukutsey Undenwatsy. I have loved a man, although he could not stay with me. Old Fish also married and raised children when she was young. These two paths do not exclude each other, but it could be that you are right. I am not old enough or wise enough to take a student, but perhaps Old Fish would be willing to have another assistant. I will speak with my grandmother of this matter, and we will dream upon it—if this is what you are sure you wish."

Mountain Lamb's own dreams that night were strange, confused, a welter of places she had never been and people she seemed to know but whom she was also sure she had never met. In the morning she could not recall enough to make sense of the visions.

Bear Woman, however, would not speak to her at all until she had consulted with Old Fish. The young shaman was troubled. When she did speak, she would not tell Mountain Lamb nearly as much as the girl wanted to hear.

"This is all I can tell you," Bear Woman said. "Your destiny is very different from anything you ever imagined. You are not ready to become a shaman because there is a man you love that you haven't met yet. You knew this already, Mountain Lamb."

"How could I have known that?" the girl asked, confused. But even as she spoke the words, it occurred to her that what the medicine woman said was true.

I do not understand. How could any of this have happened? But it has happened, and I am frightened because I have no idea as to where it will lead. Mauvais Gauche says that women should not be allowed to choose their men, for they would always choose badly. I have chosen badly, I am sure of it. Bear Woman chose badly also, and her man left her to raise his son. Am I willing to have that happen to me? I think about him, and it is hard for me to breathe. I do not even know him—I am foolish, I am foolish. But he is mine, even though he has no way of knowing it, and I am going to be his.

CHAPTER FOUR

Two Men and One Woman

Tricorn, bicorn, stovepipe, Paris beau, Quaker hat, lady's jockey helmet: beaver-felt hats. A hundred thousand pelts were needed each year for the gentry of Europe and America.

The process involved shaving the soft underfur from the skin, then twanging the string of a great bow, its vibration causing hairs to hook together. Then the matted pile had to be flattened and covered with damp linen and formed into a hood. Thickening and shrinking were brought about through the use of boiling water and acid. Then the material was beaten. The felt was molded over a wooden form, then dried and ironed—the nap raised with a wire paddle.

Castor canadensis.

The beaver's life cycle begins under ice in mid-winter—the sexual urges of creatures monogamous and true to their mates. When meltout comes, the pregnant female will drive away her two-year-olds, these exiled from both lodge and pond. And just before giving birth in May, she will chase out not only her mate but also the kits from last year's birthing. These exiles take up temporary residence wherever they can—abandoned lodges or holes in the bank.

Four to six little new ones, the young well developed at birth and able to swim within a single day. After that, the melancholy husband and the kits are allowed to return, the female mystery of parturition accomplished.

Spring and summer bring a new diet—all have had enough of willow bark. Now they devour fresh grass, fern and skunk cabbage, succulent bulbs, rushes and lilies, duckweed, columbine, Indian paintbrush and thistleroot. In particular beavers are said to savor mushrooms and the flesh of the crimson snowflower.

They stretch out on their lodge roofs and groom their coats, dabbing pungent castoreum from the glands just under the tails. But the slightest unexpected movement or noise can send them scuttling into the water, for they must be ever on the lookout for *coyotes, wolves, bobcats, wolverines, bears, and Whitemen with chains slung over their shoulders.*

During the trek northward, Mountain Lamb assumed the care of Milt—almost as a mother would tend to a sick child. The wound had flared up, and Sublette was thrown into periods of intense fever, his eyes glazed over and his incessant verbal outpourings often half-incoherent and at times utterly so.

Joe Meek awoke one morning to a world of dazzling light—sunlight glistering from snowbanks, the sky intensely blue, and snow falling in great bunches from the boughs of pine and cedar.

Mountain Lamb, a cloak pulled about her shoulders, had sat up with Milt throughout the cold night and had fallen asleep finally in a sitting position next to the booshway's robes.

Joe built a little fire and put coffee water on to boil. The bag of coffee beans was lank now, nearly empty. They'd tried stretching the precious stuff by adding dried juniper berries, but the resulting brew was extremely bitter—and the experiment had been discontinued.

Milt awoke, was feeling much better, and vented a string of ear-rattling curses against the entire Bannock Nation.

"Come on now, Milton, ye've got to keep a watch on your tongue. Got a lady present, as you'll recall."

"You got coffee over there, Joe, or are ye just cookin' water for the fun of it?"

They drank their coffee and ate cold breakfast and, with Milt feeling somewhat better, rode on down Blackfoot River toward the Snake.

Once on the floor of the basin, the snow was only a few inches deep and provided no hindrance to travel. The little caravan was able to make better time now, and by nightfall they had covered perhaps forty miles, as Meek guessed it. The sun flared deep crimson-blue to the west, and the three made camp beneath a thicket of winter-bare cottonwoods near the river. Mountain Lamb built a fire, and Joe tethered the horses in a protected area where wind had blown the snow away from numerous thick bunches of winter-yellowed grass. Then, his Hawken under his arm, he set off up a tributary creek toward a heavy stand of scrub cedar in hope of discovering game—for they had been without fresh meat for several days, and the supply of pemmican and jerky had diminished to little more than nothing.

Look at that, he thought.

Deer, half a dozen of the animals, clustered together in a ring, already bedded down for the night, faintly visible in the silver sheen of the half-moon. Meek settled carefully to one knee, tapped the firing pan, and drew aim.

With the explosion of the rifle, deer began to leap every which way, one passing within arm's length of where Joe knelt, vainly attempting to load for another shot. Then they were gone, the sounds of snapping brush dwindling in his ear.

"Comfortable like they was," he chuckled, "it's a damned shame to have disturbed 'em."

At the center of the small clearing lay a dead doe, its neck broken by the impact of the .55 slug. Meek shook his head, slit the throat, and, working rapidly in the thin light, gutted the creature, tossing the steaming viscera off into the brush, his deft hands having first extracted the gall and spleen, the skinning knife working almost with a will of its own. Then he cut out the liver, took a large bite, and savored the taste—hot, slippery, wild.

Joe hefted the animal over his shoulders, stooped to retrieve the old hex-barreled Hawken, and retraced his steps back to the camp area.

"Forget about the grease-balls," he said, laughing as he entered the ring of firelight. "Coons, we got venison for dinner this night. She ain't buffler nor antelope, mebbe, but she'll do."

"Bravo, Joseph!" Milt said. "We heard the shot an' was hopin' ye hadn't been target practicin'."

Mountain Lamb went to work on the deer, and soon generous portions of the hindquarter were cut away and spitted over the flames.

"Didn't find no coffee beans out there, did ye?" Milt asked.

"Not a one," Joe answered, poking at the fire.

When the meat was half-cooked, they began to eat, chewing and wiping at their mouths and grinning at one another. And Sublette, once his belly was full, limped to his robes, lay down, and wrapped them about himself.

"Not ever goin' to get used to bein' an invalid," he said. "No strength at all. Last hour or so before we made camp, an' I was about ready to fall off my pony. Didn't figger we could make it to the forks in one day, but old Joe seemed set on doin' 'er—so I just hung on. Now this nigger's goin' to sleep a spell. Wake me up when spring's arrived."

Within moments Sublette was snoring irregularly, his buffalo robe drawn up over his head.

Mountain Lamb had gone back to work butchering out the deer, and Joe sat by the fire, his chin in his hands, watching her.

So gawddamned beautiful it almost hurts to look at 'er.

"You are very close friends," she said suddenly.

"Oh—yep, that we are. Milt. He ought to of healed by now, Isabel. Somethin' wrong inside that leg—like maybe the knife point busted off against the bone. I don't know what it is. Some arteries severed, an' the blood ain't gettin' where it's supposed to. But he's a tough little bastard—he'll pull through. Just that it's takin' so damned long. Been close to two months now since she happened."

Mountain Lamb wrapped the meat inside the deer's hide and drew the makeshift bag together and tied it with strips of green rawhide.

"Joe Meek, you should hang this up in the tree, perhaps. The white bears are still asleep, but the black ones sometimes wake up and wander about."

"Guess we won't use it for a pillow, anyhow?" Meek grinned.

"I do not understand."

"Well, it's a long story—mostly about how dumb coons can be. A couple of seasons back, me an' Mark Head an' Mitchell were over on the Rosebud. . . ."

Joe began to tell his bear story, and Mountain Lamb came to the fireside and sat next to him as he talked. Even with the good fire burning, the night was becoming quite cold. The Shoshone girl pressed herself against him, and Joe had to force himself to stay where he was. There was a charge in her touch, in the warm pressure of her body next to his own.

When he'd finished the tale, Mountain Lamb laughed softly and squeezed his arm.

"You are a strong man, Joe Meek," she said. "You are also a good man. Sub-lette is fortunate to have such a friend. I think he would have gone to the Spirit World if you hadn't kept him from growing very dark inside. You would not let him give up, I believe."

"Milt's tough," Joe answered. "An' they ain't none better, not for my money."

"Put your arm about me," Mountain Lamb whispered. "It will not be so cold that way."

Is it possible? She wants some lovin'? Why do I feel so

ungawdly awkward around 'er? It ain't like I never been with a female woman before.

He slipped his arm around her waist and gently drew her even more tightly against his side.

But this ain't no ordinary female woman. I'm ass over teakettle in love with 'er, an' she knows it, too. Sure she does. Maybe she's just teasin' me an' is goin' to start laughin' at me in a moment or two. Why can't I say what I'm feelin'? An' Milt, he's fallin' for her too—I can tell it. Sick as he is, I can see him watchin' her as we traipse along. This whole thing's gettin' too complicated for me.

"Joe Meek," she asked, her voice subdued, "have you lain with many women? Probably with Whitewomen. With Indian women also?"

"Few times," Joe managed.

Mountain Lamb laughed suddenly.

"My people used to believe that there were no Whitewomen, only Whitemen. That is what my father told me. It was because for many years we had never seen any—only the men who came to trap. No Shoshone had ever been to any of the White villages then. He said that some supposed the Whitemen grew up out of the earth, like cornflowers in the springtime."

"Some of the boys has got wives back in the settlements," Joe explained. "An' all of us has got mamas, just like Injun folk."

"I know that. You don't have to tell me that," Mountain Lamb said, her voice piqued with mild indignation.

"Of course not," Joe said, nodding. "Of course not. Tell me, Umentucken, why'd you save our lives? You never explained that."

She laughed again.

"Oh," she said. "It was because—you have a good face. I told my father that you were too young to die. I—"

Joe turned on sudden impulse and put his lips to hers.

The girl stiffened, remained motionless, neither responding nor rejecting his kiss.

When he drew his head back from hers, she asked, "Is that what the Whites do? The other women in the village told me, but I did not understand. I don't know how to do it."

Joe stared at her, not at all certain he knew how to interpret what she had just said. Had he misread all the signs? Had he assumed something to be so merely because he wished it to be?

The perfect face, half-shadowed in firelight, the long braids of her hair both drawn around over one shoulder, the thin nose, high cheekbones, the brown eyes so dark that for the moment they appeared almost totally black, black with little orange waverings of reflected firelight in them—like a creature in a dream, a being magically transported to this moment, this place from out of the realm of phantomlike beings, from out of the place that her people called the Spirit World. . . .

"Joe Meek," Mountain Lamb said, her voice touched with a strange sadness, "why do you stare at me that way? I did not mean to displease you, but I have never lain—been—with a Whiteman before. I have never made love to any man. I did not know what to do when you placed your mouth upon mine—this thing, *kissing,* is something you will have to explain. Do not be angry with me, Joe Meek."

Cold fire swept over Meek. His face grew flushed, and when he attempted to speak, no words would come for an instant. He cleared his throat, reached over to touch her hand with his own.

"Angry? Lord, Isabel—Mountain Lamb—this child ain't angry. That's not it at all. I figgered you was angry with me. Dammit, gal, what am I tryin' to say? Tongue's all tied in knots. It's that I gawddamn love ye—can't explain it no further than that. Just happened, is all. An' this child knew it the first time he laid eyes on ye, when you followed your daddy into the medicine lodge. I—"

She put her fingers to his lips.

"Show me how to kiss, Joe Meek. I think I will like it."

He took her into his arms then, cursing himself inwardly because his hands were trembling so, and once more placed his mouth to hers.

After a moment he pulled back and said, "Mebbe I ain't so good at it either. I ain't never loved anyone before."

"Keep showing me," Mountain Lamb whispered and pulled his face back to hers.

They kissed and held each other for a long while, until finally she asked, "Will we sleep together this night, Joe Meek? I am very ignorant. I have never done it before. It is something else that you will have to show me. All young women must have someone who will be their teacher in making love."

Joe rose, feeling suddenly huge and clumsy, awkward, once more utterly uncertain of himself. But Mountain Lamb rose also and took his hand, stared back at the dying campfire, and allowed herself to be led to Meek's robes. Then they stood together in the shadows, and Meek shifted uneasily from one foot to the other.

"Give me your knife," she said.

"Knife? What—?"

"I must cut off my chastity belt. It is I who must do that, for I am the one who chose to wear it. After that, I will be free to be a woman."

Hesitantly Joe handed her the blade, half-supposing she would plunge it either into her own breast or into his. But instead she accepted it, staring into his eyes as she did so, and walked a few paces away, disappearing behind the bole of the largest of the cottonwoods. In a moment she returned, would not look up at him now, and moved slowly toward the fire, stood over it, and placed the garment of woven horsehair upon the still-flickering little tongues of flame.

When Mountain Lamb returned to where Meek was standing, she said simply, "This night I am yours. Please be gentle with me. Then I will do whatever you tell me to."

Sublette awakened momentarily, turned slightly, and saw his two companions standing together. He saw Meek draw back the robes; he saw Mountain Lamb slowly lie down. Then he turned his head the other way, aware suddenly of a new and different sort of pain.

Was it anger he felt toward his friend Joe?

No, he could not accept that interpretation of what he felt. The two of them sleeping together—it was natural enough. It was not a betrayal.

He closed his eyes, breathed deeply and evenly.

God bless the two of ye, he thought and willed himself back toward sleep.

When the journey was resumed the following day, something was different—and all three felt it, although they did not speak of it. But Milt laughed a bit more often than usual, and Joe went out of his way to defer to his friend in various small ways. For her part, Mountain Lamb was no longer riding on ahead—choosing, rather, to trail behind the two trappers.

It was late afternoon when Milt, leaning toward Joe and grimacing slightly, said, "You two made love last night, I take it?"

Meek had been expecting the question; but now that it had been asked, he wasn't certain how to respond.

Finally he said, "Well, dammit anyhow, Milt, this child's in love with her, an' I guess . . ."

"I knew it would happen," Sublette answered. "Joseph, I owe you my life—an' no real way of repayin' that. So what I'm sayin' comes hard to me— Is Mountain Lamb close enough to hear what we're sayin'?"

Meek glanced back, shook his head.

"Okay. Old compañero, I guess I love 'er too. She saved both our hides, an' she's tended me like a sister—or an angel. No—no—I understand what ye're thinkin', Joe. I ain't vexed with ye—no way I could be, not after what we've been through together. Here I am, half a man, less than that mebbe. I ain't even jealous. Well, mebbe a little bit. But ye're the one she's chose, an' I accept that. I love both of ye, an' I don't ever want anything to get in the way of that. But we've always been honest with each other, you an' me, an' I didn't figger this was any time to change that around. Joseph, I'll treat you two to the finest weddin' the mountains has ever seen, if it comes to that."

"Milt—gawdammit, this Virginia nigger don't know what to say. I loved her right off—an' I had a strong suspicion ye did too. When ye're a well man again . . ."

"We'll stay close friends," Sublette interjected, "the three of us."

"Mountain Lamb ain't chose me," Meek said. "Not yet, anyhow. She just chose me last night, is all. You're the booshway, Milt. Wouldn't be right for me to stand in your way if—"

"Ye're talkin' buffler droppings, Joseph, an' ye know it, too. Ye figger mebbe she's got a sister back there in old Gotia's village?"

As they drew to the crest of a low rise, Meek pulled his pony to a halt and raised his hand.

"Thar she is, Milt. Forks of the Snake, an' them's RMF lodges—only they's too many of 'em."

Sublette held his hand above his eyes and gazed toward the encampment as Mountain Lamb rode alongside the two White-men, glancing from one to the other.

"Have we found your friend Bridger and the other trappers?" she asked.

"That we have," Milt answered. "Only the stick's not floatin' so good."

"Looks like Drips an' Vanderburgh managed to track the boys down," Joe Meek said, spitting disgustedly into the snow.

"Camped half a mile upriver," Sublette added. "Ye almost have to admire their persistence."

Meek fired his rifle into the air, reloaded quickly, and fired once more.

And the three turned their ponies toward the RMF lodges. After a few yards, however, Mountain Lamb drew her horse once more to a halt.

"Perhaps I should ride no further," she said softly. "I have taken you to where your friends are. Now I would probably only be in your way. It is time for me to turn south once more."

Milt and Joe glanced at each other and then at Umentucken.

"You head back, then I'm headin' with ye—unless ye damned well tell me nay," Meek blurted.

"An' the booshway ain't letting his compañero ride off into the wilderness with no heathen Injun female," Sublette added.

"We want ye to come with us, Mountain Lamb," Joe said. "Me an' Milt both wants that."

"Both of you want me?" Mountain Lamb asked, looking first at Meek and then at Sublette.

"We'll set us up a lodge, a nice one," Joe added. "Isabel, I love ye—an' ye know that. Well, Milt loves ye too. That's what we was just talkin' about. Come with us, an ye're free to choose however ye want. Me or Milt, either one—or someone else, for that matter. Or we'll take ye back to your daddy's village when the moon of new grass rises, if that's what ye want when the time comes. After all that's happened, I figger the three of us is—well, *bound* together somehow. Am I talkin' out of turn, Milt?"

"My brother speaks for me also," Sublette agreed, nodding for effect. "Come with us, Umentucken."

The girl puzzled upon the matter for only a moment before answering.

"My father gave me two Whitemen as a present. But now that they have returned to their own people, I can no longer own them. Yet, if they wish me to remain with them, then it is well. We will live in the same lodge, then. This is a strange thing to me, but it seems right. Yes, I will go with you both. I will be the woman for both of you, if that is what you wish of me."

The lodge was built, a dwelling more elaborate than those of the other trappers—even of those who had womaned with squaws. And as the spring meltout began, an extremely successful trapping campaign took place. Not even the presence of the American Fur brigade proved particularly troublesome, for the various tributaries that found their way down to the Snake River were rich with beaver. The setting of iron into water now became an obsession for all the mountain men and for their various Indian allies as well. By the time of summer Rendezvous, the caches of plew would be very large indeed.

Joe Meek and Doc Newell, the latter still paying court to Bent Feather, though without significant progress in convincing Chief Gray of the wisdom of such a marriage, spent much of their time away from the central encampment, often being out on their lines for several days at a time.

Always, with Joe's departure, Mountain Lamb would become visibly nervous—and always she was utterly delighted when he returned to the little village. And in his absence, she tended to Milt and experimented with various spring herbage in a vain attempt to bring the booshway back to full health. But the horrible leg wound continued to erupt and drain from time to time. Despite the pain, Milt managed to hobble about fairly well. He had become quite adept in the use of his heavy walking stick and forced himself to make the best of a bad situation.

A No-ga-ie Shoshone medicine man was brought in at Bridger's insistence; but though he was paid the price of two fine spotted Nez Percé ponies, and though a sweat lodge was constructed to whose steam and heat Milt was subjected, in alternation with the freezing cold baths in the river, and though various powders and ointments were applied, the leg resolutely refused to mend.

"Wagh!" Milt growled at Joe one evening as the two of them and Mountain Lamb ate their evening meal. "This child's beginning to think he needs a new name—somethin' like *Stinkingleg*, mebbe. How much longer is it goin' to take, Joe? Way I am, I'm about as much good as tits on a boar hog. If it had been me the Injuns was chasin' instead of old Colter or Beckwourth, the race'd have lasted about two steps—an' they'd of had me."

"*Walks-with-a-stick*, maybe," Mountain Lamb suggested. "You complain too much, Sub-lette. Everything has been done that can be done. Now you must dream that your leg has healed. That is what I think. If one's dreams are strong enough, they can cause a thing to happen."

Sublette shook his head and bit off a chunk of roasted elk flesh.

"Any case, Milt," Joe added, "one leg or two, ye're the

only coon in this outfit as really understands about business dealin's. In the family blood, I guess. Now brother Bill, he's one of us—or used to be. An' he's our man—no offense, now. But when he brings supplies up country, he's intendin' to make a profit for himself, no two ways about that. Gabe an' Fitz an' Kit an' Campbell, they're your partners, but they're trappers, just like me. Ain't that Bill would cheat anyone—I don't mean that. But, Milt, RMF needs ye to kind of oversee what's goin' on with sellin' the plew an' buyin' the goods."

Milt laughed.

"Brother Bill," he agreed, "he's mountain man turned business man, that's for sure. But, Joseph, even when we were boys, Billy used to outwit me more often than not. I hear what you're sayin', though. Well, dammit, leg or not, I guess I'm not ready to give up the mountains yet."

The days drifted on, and the spring hunt remained highly successful. Despite the presence of American Fur, luck was holding out for the RMF men. Even though they were venturing ever farther north into Blackfoot territory, across the divide to the upper reaches of the Red Rock, the Madison, and the Ruby, Bug's Boys, for whatever reasons, had seen fit to leave the trappers alone. There were one or two scrapes, and for a brief interval in May, smokes were seen over the mountains to the north of the Snake Basin—and yet nothing came of it.

One party of three disappeared, but Bridger and Carson were convinced, or nearly so, that the men had simply deserted and had cast their lot with the Hudson's Bay trappers who worked the area to the west, along the Salmon River, in lands jointly occupied by Great Britain and the United States.

With various bands of Shoshone allies encamped along the upper reaches of the Snake, the American trappers were feeling not only right at home but even securely so.

Mountain Lamb had become a great favorite in the encampment and had, indeed, acquired numerous admirers—including several No-ga-ie braves. But when all was said and done, no one was particularly obvious in paying courtship to the beautiful woman who lodged with Milt and the Bear-Killer. If nothing else, the imposing form of the unpredictable Joe Meek was sufficient to prevent it.

When an American Fur man was bold enough to set some of his traps along the same drainage that Meek had been working, Joe lay in wait for the man, and a couple of rifle shots were actually exchanged. Newell attempted to calm Joe down, but Joe was having no part of it. He hunted the American Fur trapper on foot, hog-tied him, and then brought him back to the Snake River encampment secured to the back of a pack animal—rode up to the log shanty that Drips and Vanderburgh had put up, and dumped the man, still bound hand and foot, onto the ground.

That night Meek got roaring drunk and, with Newell and Mark Head and half a dozen other RMF men behind him, paraded in among the American Fur lodges and challenged one and all to a fistfight—shouting threats and insults alternately.

But there were no takers that night.

And a week later Meek rode in with a pair of grizzly hides tied up in great bundles. Joe said nothing, but the story got out that Meek had shot one and knifed the other to death. And some believed the tale and some did not.

The bearskin robes were given to Mountain Lamb, who dressed them out properly and cured them, using them thereafter to sleep between.

It was a matter of some debate as to whether Umentucken, Tukutsey Undenwatsy was Meek's woman or Sublette's. A few were of the opinion that Milt, half-crippled as he was, would be hard put to make love to a woman if he had to. And yet Mountain Lamb was, after all, in the booshway's lodge. And so was Joe Meek. It was a situation that most of the mountain men were either unable to understand or preferred not to think about.

Just the way things be.

Yet, within Sublette's lodge, all remained harmonious. Joe was often gone, and Mountain Lamb continued to care for Milt— the latter now visibly improved. At times he and the Shoshone girl would ride off together for an afternoon, and Sublette had now laid aside his walking stick, using it but rarely.

When Meek came in from trapping, Milt would leave the two alone and spend much of his time with the Blanket Chief, Jim Bridger, the name bestowed upon him several years earlier by the Crow Indians—*Casapy,* the man in charge of blankets.

Some nights the music of a mouth-organ and singing could be heard from within the lamp-lit hide lodge.

It was a situation the mountain men simply couldn't *figger.*

Now, for the past two weeks, Mountain Lamb had taken to wearing a loose-fitting dress rather than her former costume of tight-waisted deerskins. And Bridger, Carson, and Fitzpatrick winked at one another and grinned. But there were questions in their eyes.

Joe brought in a young buffalo cow, fat and prime; and Mountain Lamb prepared a feast of tongue and hump-rib, along with garnishings of ripe service berries and strawberries and wild parsnips and camas-cake bread. When the meal was finished, the three of them sitting about the open-pit fire she had built outside the lodge, she looked from one of her men to the other and said, "I have something to tell you, Joe Meek and Sub-lette."

"Well, out with 'er, gal," Meek said, laughing.

"Perhaps you do not wish to know," she protested.

"Of course we wish to know. What is it, Isabel?" Sublette demanded.

The firelight was in her hair, was gleaming from her dark eyes, was glinting from her even white teeth.

Joe nodded and grinned. No question—she was the most beautiful woman in the mountains. And whatever the arrangement among the three of them, he loved her with a fierceness and a passion that had changed his entire nature—in ways that not even he himself fully understood. He glanced at Milt, saw the deep love in the booshway's eyes as well, and then looked back at Mountain Lamb.

Umentucken placed one hand upon her belly—the gesture of new life within.

"When the leaves of the quaking aspen turn gold," she said, a faint smile playing about the edges of her mouth, "we will have a little new one."

From across the river a chorus of coyote song went up, and at that moment a horned owl swooped by, low to the ground, a silver-gray blur of feathers, visible for no more than an instant and then gone.

CHAPTER FIVE

Blood on the Grass

Pierre's Hole lies to the west of mountains that seem to rise from the center of the earth, the peaks a grand whim of Old Man Coyote, their cloud-hung summits some seven thousand feet above the basin floor and nearly fourteen thousand feet above sea level—the Big Tit Range, the Tetons. And down from this granite wall the Teton River drains westward and then north and then west again to confluence with Henry's Fork of the Snake, the waters flowing from glaciers and summer-long snows.

John Colter, who had been to the far Pacific with Lewis and Clark, was the first Whiteman to find his way to the mountains of the god. Then Astor's party, and later some French Canadian trappers, Pierre Tevanitagon among them: and they saw the big mountains from the westward basin and called them Le Trois Tetons, the three breasts.

The basin itself, nearly ringed by mountains, thirty miles long and fifteen wide—the bottomland open and level, treeless except where willows and cottonwoods and aspens crowd together in parallel, sinuous bandings along streams that feed down from the Tetons to the gathering river below. And here the grass is thick and good and capable of sustaining whole herds of ponies.

Look: hawks, herons, ospreys and eagles, whistler swans and trumpeter swans, vultures and kites.

Ungulates: the grazing people—moose, elk, and mule deer, blacktails, pronghorns, small bands of buffalo.

And the hunters: buffalo wolves and timber wolves, coyotes, mountain lions, grizzlies and black bears, wolverines and badgers.

Flowers: balsam root, camas, rydbergia, paintbrush, columbine, Parry primrose.

Many of the lateral creeks are dammed, and the still waters are punctuated by the stick-and-mud lodges of Brother Beaver.

And higher up, where the fir and spruce forest gives way to sheer, glistening sheaves of granite, there are the bighorns and the *shaggy mountain goats, the creatures browsing on low brush where the snow recedes.*

Despite their best efforts to get shed of Drips and Vanderburgh, and despite their once again following the strategem of making covert preparations and then leaving in the middle of the night, the hundred or so RMF men found their rivals from American Fur already encamped at Pierre's Hole when they arrived. RMF had crossed the mountains to the headwaters of the Snake and had moved downstream to the big bend, then northwestward back toward the forks. Once beyond the Elkhorn Peaks, they traversed a low pass and came down into Pierre's Hole—discovering American Fur's ninety men already set up, having taken the best grass and the best sites for themselves.

A simple matter, really. With advance information, Drips and Vanderburgh had not been surprised when RMF moved out under cover of darkness. Then, a day or two later, they set out on a leisurely jaunt up the Teton River to the Hole

Sublette, Bridger, Carson, and the others were furious at having been so totally outsmarted.

Free trappers and numerous Indians were coming in for the summer Rendezvous—Flatheads, Nez Percés, Shoshones, and Utes. By the last week in June even Le Blueux and La Jeunesse had arrived, their pack animals heavily laden with plew. Lodges were erected helter-skelter, and the area along the south branch of the Teton was actually getting crowded—a little makeshift city of nearly three hundred White trappers and close to a thousand Indians.

All that was missing was the supply of trade goods. Word had it that both Bill Sublette for RMF and Fontenelle for American Fur were coming up country with supply trains, overland from Saint Louis. Some talk, even, that old Etienne Provost, now working for American Fur, would be bringing in a quantity of goods from Astor's post at Fort Union.

If Fontenelle arrived first, then American Fur would get the majority of the trade, and RMF would be in bad straits indeed. The partners decided on a dual course of action. First, someone had to find out what the hell happened to Bill Sublette and the supply train—and to this end Tom Fitzpatrick saddled his fastest pony and, with a spare animal trailing behind, made tracks eastward through Blackfoot country to discover the whereabouts of the RMF supply train. Second, the partners resolved to meet with Drips and Vanderburgh—to make the astounding proposal that they share the mountains, divide the territory so as to provide for a maximum harvest of beaver for both groups.

Drips and Vanderburgh listened with interest as Bridger and Milt spoke of the advantages that would accrue to both groups of trappers. The two American Fur captains nodded frequently and asked a few questions and smoked their cigars. But when it was all over, Vanderburgh said, "Gents, what ye say sounds good. But to tell the truth, me an' Drips here has got our orders from the company. Even if she worked out like ye say it would, I reckon old Astor'd have our hides when the word got back to him. An' McKenzie, he'd have us shot an' hung an' scalped to boot. Sorry, gents, but we just cain't do 'er. Besides, rumor has it that Billy Sublette's gone under—the Blackfeet got 'im. One way or the other, if Fontenelle or Provost gets here first, I figger we'll have the mountain trade pretty much to ourselves. You boys know how to put iron to water, though, no two ways about 'er. We'll have jobs for all that wants 'em. That the way you see 'er, Mr. Drips?"

"My very thoughts." Drips nodded, pinching off the burnt end of his cigar and tucking the unused tobacco into his pocket.

First week in July 1832, and as yet neither supply train had arrived. The time for Mountain Saturnalia had come, but there was no whiskey to be had.

And neither had Tom Fitzpatrick returned.

Le Blueux, La Jeunesse, Meek, and Newell were idling their time away at a no-stakes session of hand game when a young Shoshone woman interrupted their sport with a message for Pierre. He spoke with the squaw for a few moments, coughed, and nodded.

When the Shoshone woman had departed, Le Blueux turned to his companions.

"Enfant de garce! This gray-haired old man, he wishes to go for a little ride, *monter à cheval.* Joe Meek, you come with me, *oui?"*

"Pierre, he is strange sometimes." La Jeunesse shrugged toward Newell. "Doc, we keep on playing, *peut-être?"*

Le Blueux and Meek readied their ponies quickly and within a few minutes had ridden away from the encampment.

"What's this all about, Pete the Good?" Joe asked.

"Monsieur Sublette and his wagon train, they are not far away. I thought we should lead them in *tout droit."*

Pierre's information had indeed been correct, and the two men intercepted Bill Sublette just a few miles to the north, at the forks of the Teton. Fontenelle, as it turned out, was far behind. Sublette, within sight of the American Fur caravan at times during the march up country, had taken a risky shortcut, and the gamble had paid off. RMF had won the race to Rendezvous! With Sublette were sixty new men and a generous supply of goods, including many kegs of straight alcohol that would be watered down and laced with everything from tobacco and licorice to pepper and perhaps even dried buffalo dung, thus producing the arwerdenty or whiskey of the mountains, the method of stretching and enriching having been devised by General Ashley at the first Rendezvous back in 1825, over on Henry's Fork of the Seedskeedee.

Bill Sublette's party, with Le Blueux and Meek prancing their ponies in ahead and firing off their rifles, arrived at the encampment in Pierre's Hole just after noon on the eighth of July. And by mid-afternoon of July eighth, mountain men and Indians alike were staggering about drunkenly, fistfighting, playing the hand game, wrestling, shouting, shooting at targets and at one another, cursing, and laughing. And RMF was taking in furs at an astounding rate. With sixty thousand dollars' worth of pelts of their own and the goods to trade for the plew of Indian and free trapper alike, the fortunes of RMF were soaring.

But when the caravan had entered the encampment, and the partners had come out to welcome Bill Sublette and his men in, Bill's first question was: "Whar's Broken Hand? He get it stuck in a tight squaw an' cain't work loose?"

Milt and Bridger and Carson and Campbell glanced uneasily at one another.

"Hopin' he was with you, Brother Bill," Milt said.

"What's happened, then?"

Jim Bridger shrugged.

"Gone under, mebbe. He went out lookin' for ye, Billy. That was near two weeks back."

"Like as not, American Fur set the Redskins on 'im," Kit Carson said, his voice trailing off.

"*Pieds Noirs,*" Bill Sublette said. "We run into 'em a few nights back—that God-cursed Atsina bunch. Mountain luck, that's all. Well, Broken Hand'll come back in if he's able. Ain't no one any tougher than Fitz. Let's get this show on the road—unpacked and open for business, that is. Then I wants to see that squaw of yours, Milt. Joe Meek here says she's a sight for sore eyes."

And the Rendezvous was on.

Bill Sublette saw to it that all the RMF men were properly outfitted for the coming season—and in the process took in some hundred and sixty-eight packs of beaverskins, as well as various quantities of muskrat and otter and rough fur.

Drips and Vanderburgh, with no supplies to sell, hung on to their own meager takings of plew and waited for Fontenelle—since they had no option to do otherwise.

By nightfall, great fires were blazing everywhere, and the drunken shouts of mountain men and Indians echoed across the basin. The men bragged and lied enormously for the benefit of the new men, the *mangeurs de lard,* that had come up country with Bill Sublette. More fistfights, and one of these encounters turned ugly and within moments each of the combatants had drawn his knife. The others drew about in a circle and watched, shouting encouragement, as the two proceeded to lunge at each other drunkenly; and before it was over, the trappers lay together in each other's arms, both dead.

A Ute brave sold his wife to three trappers in order to be able to buy more whiskey, and soon others followed suit. A few of the Indian women rebelled and went into business on their own—thus getting rid of the middlemen and thereby assuring that their sexual prowess would result in new supplies of beads and scarlet and yellow cloth, vermilion, and needles, hand-mirrors, and the like.

By midnight many had passed out—were lying here and there about the encampment. Occasionally someone stumbled over one of the sleepers, and the result was incoherent growling and cursing.

A red-haired Frenchman lay passed out in this manner. Stumbling over him and then kicking him with no response, a Spaniard, a Frenchman, and a Flathead poured their whiskey onto the man's hair and lit him afire. Within moments the man's head was enveloped in flames. A great commotion went up as the unfortunate wretch struggled to his feet, only to be hurled down again by other men who managed to burn their own hands in their efforts to put out the blaze.

By morning the victim of the prank was still alive, miraculously enough, thanks to the care of some Indian women who had smeared his charred scalp with bear grease and made him a skull cap of soiled linen.

And the encampment itself was strangely quiet—with only a

few souls moving about—most of the men still sleeping off the *grand* first day of Rendezvous.

Mountain Lamb had just finished bathing and dressing Milt's still-and-seemingly-perpetually-draining leg wound when Joe Meek entered hurriedly into the lodge the three of them shared. Milt struggled to his feet and drew on his breeches, and Mountain Lamb looked up and smiled—a question in her eyes. For a moment Joe forgot what he was about—his stare fixating on the figure of the six-months-pregnant woman whom he idolized.

"Just puttin' me back together, Joseph," Sublette blurted. "What is it, man? Ye looked like ye'd seen a ghost or summat."

"Is something wrong, Joe Meek?" Mountain Lamb asked.

"For a fact," Meek sputtered. "Milt, it's best ye come on over to Gabe's lodge and take a look-see for yourself."

"Goddammit, Joe, what's up?"

But Sublette was cinching his pistol belt about his middle and limping after Meek, out through the lodge flap.

It was Broken-Hand Fitzpatrick—only it looked more like a dead man who'd somehow managed to haul himself back out of the grave. Antoine Godin, an Iroquois hunter, and Muckaluck, his Flathead compañero, had brought Fitz in—a white-haired skeleton who could hardly hang tight to the cantle of his saddle, exhausted, starving, and weaponless.

"Tom!" Milt groaned. "What's happened to your ha'r? Great God, man!"

"Atsinas," Jim Bridger said. "Them spongin' Big Bellies. Tom's had a bit of a scrape with 'em, as it turns out."

"I got shed of 'em," Bill Sublette added, "but old Tom wasn't so lucky."

Fitzpatrick nodded weakly to Milt and Joe and continued to eat, washing his food down with what appeared to be a jug of Bill Sublette's private stock.

"Best we let him go on eatin'," Kit Carson grinned, "so long as he don't bust his belly open. Weren't there some poet did that once? Mebbe I never went to no school like some of you coons, but this child ain't stupid, no sir."

"Kit's right," Bridger agreed. "Chaw slow, Tom. Don't want ye bloatin' up like no damn cow."

"Somebody please-damn tell us what happened, by gawd!" Meek demanded. "Tom here was old Broken Hand when he left us, an' now he's White Hair. The Big Bellies got 'im?"

"Broken Hand, he got chased is all," Antoine Godin said, spearing himself a chunk of roasted elk and twisting his knife back and forth to shake the grease droplets from the meat. "Tom can correct me if I've got any of it wrong."

"Go ahead," Fitzpatrick mumbled, shaking his beard and wiping at his mouth.

"Think we'd best double up on the guards," Bill Sublette said and left the lodge.

"Muckaluck and I found him near the headwaters of the Madison," Godin began, "and it's only Whiteman's luck that he's still alive. Couldn't eat anything, ain't that right, Muckaluck? So we boiled him up a pot of broth and made him drink it. After that he started coming around. Seems like Tom wandered straight into the Big Belly village, and after that Bug's Boys set to chasing him. After that Tom's horse gave out, and he had to keep going on foot. Light and Darkness fought over him, but the Great Manitou must have seen what was happening and helped him. That's what I think, anyway. So Broken Hand kept running and hiding. The Gros Ventres already had his horse, but they wished to have his scalp also."

"Then Fitzpatrick says he hid in a hole," Muckaluck added.

"Yes. And he covered himself up with sticks and leaves and had to stay in the hole for more than a day. The Big Bellies were getting close, beating the brush and whooping. That's what Tom told us, ain't that so, Muckaluck? And the second night he crawled out and stumbled right back into the enemy's camp."

"Worst goddamn luck I've ever had," Fitzpatrick added between mouthfuls of roast.

"Then he went back to his hole, and the next day the Big Bellies looked for him some more. Even after they gave up looking, they stayed close and rode Tom's horse around."

"Then night came back, and he got away," Muckaluck said.

"Lost my Hawken, knife, the whole shootin' match," Fitzpatrick said.

"He crossed the river," Godin continued, "and after that he headed toward Rendezvous. Many times the *Gros Ventres* were close to him, and he had to hide again. And nothing to eat except berries and bark. When we found him, he thought we were Big Bellies also—ain't that right, Muckaluck?"

"Well, shee-it!" Fitzpatrick snorted, wiping at his beard. "What in hell would you coons of thought, for Christ's sake? I tell ye lads, I thought of preparing myself for death, an' I done committed my soul to the Almighty, an' that's the truth. After I done that, me boys, I don't recall nothin' until Godin here an' Muckaluck run onto me. These mountains ain't no place for a good Irish lad to be dyin', but that's what I figgered I'd come up with. She's bragh to be back with ye niggers, I'll tell ye."

Joe Meek broke into a fit of laughing, and the others stared at him in puzzlement.

"Coons," Meek declared, "at least now we got us a *genuine* Santy Claus to give us presents when the snows is deep this winter. Little scrape like that, Fitz, it ain't no reason to go washin' out your ha'r in chlorine water, not by a long sight."

"Someone stick a knife into 'im," Fitzpatrick said with a growl, and took a long pull from the jug of Billy Sublette's good whiskey.

Fontenelle had found his way to Rendezvous with a full supply of goods and a new company of American Fur greenhorns—but the Astor and McKenzie trader had little to do but to grubstake the company's men and to take in return the relatively few pelts that Drips and Vanderburgh's boys had accumulated. The prices on trade goods were lowered in an attempt to stir up business—but the only item that really went well was the whiskey, since Sublette's supply had been greatly diminished.

Attempts were made repeatedly to hire the RMF men away from their compañeros, but with scant success. For the moment, American Fur was in a bind; and yet, as Bridger and Fitz and the Sublettes and the others knew, the Giant of the River could afford to take temporary losses. And in the year ahead the competition would grow much more severe. The American Fur trappers were no longer as green as they had been. Indeed, they had gone a long way toward their goal of learning the lay of the land and the secrets of *beaver medicine*.

In addition, Nathaniel Wyeth had arrived in the mountains, having come up country with Bill Sublette and having brought twenty-four men with him—men totally inexperienced in the ways of the mountains and little more than novices at trapping. Wyeth's own brother had rebelled and, with seven of the original twenty-four, had turned back. But it didn't take the RMF captains long to realize that Wyeth was in the mountains and in the fur trade to stay, come hell or high water or Blackfeet. These men, too, would learn the lay of the land and the art of the trade.

All in all, the future of RMF looked anything but bright—despite the great success of Rendezvous.

But now the Rendezvous was drawing to its close, and Milton Sublette, determined not to allow his bad leg to get the better of him, had laid plans to explore the upper reaches of the Humboldt River in search of new beaver streams. And after some discussion with the other booshways, Milt decided to invite Wyeth and his men to accompany the little RMF party.

Le Blueux and La Jeunesse, on the other hand, suggested once again that Meek and Newell should go with them, as free trappers, into the dangerous lands to the north of the Snake, controlled by the Blackfeet but rich in fur.

"Mon ami," Pierre crooned, "the Mountain Lamb, it is you that she loves. *Vous et* Milt, you are close friends, yes? But what will happen when the new little one comes into the world? *Moi,* I think the child is yours, *non?"*

"Figure that's so, Pete," Meek agreed. "But it ain't like you think, not at all. Gawd knows, me an' Milt, we're in this thing together, thick an' thin. An' Isabel, she's . . . Well, dammit, man, she's safer with both me an' Milt with her. To tell the truth, I ain't got a pot of my own to piss in. An' Milt, he's one of the booshways. The three of us together, we'll make out."

"But when the young one comes," La Jeunesse asked, "then what happens? *A vrai dire,* I see trouble ahead. She will come with you, if you ask her to. *Je crois,* I believe it. I have seen her watch the two of you. A woman looks differently upon the man she loves."

"Coons," Meek explained, "ye just don't understand how it is with me an' old Milt. I love the man, an' damned if he don't love Joe Meek too. It's a strange sort of a thing we got goin', I admit 'er. Look, now. Mountain Lamb's done slept with Milt, same as she has with me. Could be it's his kid. But his or mine, that just ain't how it goes. It's our kid, no matter what color his eyes an' hair be."

Le Blueux scratched at his balding head.

"You know it will be a boy, then?" he mused. "How do you know such a thing, Monsieur Meek?"

"Don't make no difference which kind it be," Joe insisted. "I know you coons is tryin' to do me a favor—tryin' to help me out. An' I appreciate it, Pierre, damned if I don't. But Old Man Coyote sets these things up, an' us niggers has got to work our way through 'em."

Le Blueux laughed, pulled out his pipe, and set to packing the bowl.

"Baptiste, *mon fils*," he said. "The Bear-Killer, he has not been in *les montagnes* as long as you, and yet he knows which god to worship. He will be all right, this one, *c'est vrai*."

Milt saw to it that his little expeditionary force was well supplied—weapons, provisions, pack animals, and traps. The country that lay ahead of them was new. Milt figured to head southwest, keeping to higher ground above the Snake River Basin until he reached Salmon Falls Creek and then to work his way upstream into the ragged, mountainous terrain where the Mary's or Humboldt River was apparently sourced and then eastward, most likely, toward the Columbia Plateau, and then probably north toward the Wallowas and the Salmon River Mountains.

Perhaps his venture would take him through nothing but barren deserts, as some believed. But rivers didn't rise in deserts, or so he reasoned, and the streams that fed down to form the Humboldt were most likely fed by mountain snows high up. And the creeks that came down to form the river would have beaver along them.

In any case, with American Fur now west of the divide and grubstaked to stay awhile, the prospects of opening new territory were extemely appealing—if it was possible to do so.

Milt and Jean Baptiste Gervais would take along just fifteen men, including themselves and Joe Meek and Doc Newell, the latter morose because of the apparent failure of his suit for the hand of Chief Gray's daughter, Bent Feather. Mountain Lamb would accompany them too, of course, and would be the only woman on the expedition. And, this being the case, Joe and Milt between them decided to let it be known that Umentucken, Tukutsey Undenwatsy was, in fact, the wife of Milton Sublette.

Something about this arrangement nettled Joe at first—and he objected to the idea when Milt made the suggestion. But after a brief discussion, with Mountain Lamb listening silently, he came to see the logic of the plan. A single woman in the company of numerous mountain men was simply asking for trouble—unless she happened to be the wife of the booshway himself.

Joe and Milt were in the process of double-checking their supplies when the intense little New Englander, Nathaniel Wyeth, walked up. The man was grinning from ear to ear.

"Mr. Sublette," Wyeth began, "with your permission, sir,

I've invited Sinclair and his free trappers to accompany us. You've no objection, have you?"

Milt glanced at Joe, cinched a pack rope tight, and turned to Wyeth.

"Goddammit, Natty—why not just invite Drips and Vanderburgh to join us while ye're at it? The more coons we take with us, the less plew for any of us."

Wyeth braced himself and pulled back his shoulders.

"Mr. Sublette—you admit we may encounter hostile Indians? Well, you've got fifteen men. I have seventeen, including myself. Mr. Sinclair commands another fifteen. It seems to me, sir, that these reinforcements could well be to our advantage, if troubles arise."

Milt stared fixedly at Wyeth, saw that the man had no intention of backing down, and finally nodded.

"Elias Sinclair, eh? Natty, he's a Hudson's Bay man that's struck out on his own. Two years back he was workin' for American Fur. If ye an' yer Down-Easters are figuring on those boys backin' ye in a fight, ye probably believe that God walked on water. Besides, all those boys are on their own—Sinclair don't tell 'em what to do. But what the hell—they'll all have struck out for the woods long before we get to Mary's country. Okay, Nathaniel old coon. Get yer boots polished, an' let's head westward. The more the merrier, I say."

Wyeth's eyes had been blazing, but now he grinned again, bowed slightly from the waist, and walked briskly off.

"Strange he didn't invite along the Meskin army whiles he was at 'er," Joe Meek drawled.

"He just ain't thought about it yet, Joseph," Milt answered, pounding his friend on the back as he did so.

Milt's troupe had covered no more than six miles from the general encampment when trouble began.

Mountain Lamb saw them first and pulled at the fringe on Joe's sleeve.

"Indians," she said, pointing—"not Shoshones. Two groups. Those are Blackfeet, I think."

Milt already had his spyglass out.

"It's not bufflers," he said.

Wyeth came riding up, summarily grabbed the brass spyglass, and surveyed the situation.

"I told you," he said, his voice quavering. "I see a

hundred—no, more than that. Many more than that. Two hundred at least. Sublette, we have to retreat."

Meek studied the situation.

"The Big Bellies," he said. "Milt, they've got their women an' children with 'em, an' they're headin' straight back for the Rendezvous. I don't figger it."

Milt shook his head.

"That lead coon's carryin' a Union Jack—would you look at 'er!"

Elias Sinclair had now drawn up beside the others.

"Might be Absarokees," he suggested.

"Big Bellies," Meek insisted. "The Grovans, cousins to the Arapahos, in league with the Blackfeet. Friends, we got us *some* trouble."

"One way or another," Milt agreed, "it's Bug's Boys, the goddamned Blackfeet. Isabel, pull back behind us. Dammit, girl, do what I say!"

The chief of the Big Bellies was riding forward, tobacco pipe displayed across his forearm.

"You believe this, Milt?" Joe asked.

"Not for a minute."

"Maybeso he's not lookin' for a fight—not with the females an' the little ones along. But this nigger's willin' to bet these are the same boys that run Fitz damned near to death."

Wyeth said nothing, and Sinclair was shaking his head, his buffalo rifle primed and ready.

Antoine Godin and Muckaluck drew up alongside the others, and Godin was clicking his teeth together in a methodical two-beat rhythm.

"I have sent two of the Flatheads back to the Rendezvous for help," he said. "We will need help, I think."

"I do not trust these Indians," Muckaluck added.

"The chief wants to palaver," Meek said.

"Yes," Godin said quickly. "I will go talk with this Atsina. Is your rifle charged, Muckaluck?"

The Flathead tapped the pan of his weapon.

Godin didn't wait for word from Sublette—and he and his Flathead friend rode ahead.

"That's old Baihoh out there, the Atsina war chief—" Meek started to say.

But as Baihoh extended his right hand toward the big Iroquois, Godin yanked the man from his horse, and Muckaluck fired from almost point-blank. Gray-white smoke went up as the shot echoed across the basin, and the Gros Ventres yelled in anger and outrage. Now they began to fire.

Godin, despite the gunfire, leaped from his pony, scalped the fallen chief, the act taking no more than a few moments, shouted a war whoop, leaped back onto his horse, and he and Muckaluck galloped toward the astounded trappers.

The Gros Ventre women and children scurried for cover, and the Battle of Pierre's Hole was begun.

The two riders burst into the Rendezvous encampment, their horses badly lathered, shouting, "*Pieds Noirs*! Git yer guns an' ride—or old Milt an' the boys'll be done gone under an' out of beaver!"

Indeed, the battle was going thick and heavy, with smoke-flowers blooming all around Sublette and Meek and the others, from behind clumps of creosote and deer brush, dwarf cedars, junipers, thickets of willow and young aspen. Arrows drifting through the air as well, like little snakes that seemed to curve as they glided.

The Atsinas were armed quite well, perhaps as many as half of the warriors possessing rifles, and most of these new-issue Mackinaw guns, acquired from Kenneth McKenzie's American Fur post at Fort Union, at the confluence of the Yellowstone and the Missouri.

"Why in hell did Baihoh have his women an' children with him?" Joe Meek demanded. "Gawddammit, Godin, now ye've got us all in a fix—ye iggerant gawddamned Redskin Iroquois bastard!"

Antoine Godin fired, reloaded, and laughed.

"Stupid White-Eyes!" he answered. "These cousins of the Blackfeet were defeated by the Crows just two weeks ago—that is why so many are afoot. Longhair and the Crows took all their horses."

"But why'd ye shoot Baihoh? We might of got 'em to just pass on by. . . ."

"You do not understand Blackfeet, Joe Meek. They are never to be trusted. They would have taken our scalps and ponies. They would have had their fun with Umentucken. They would have mounted her until she was dead, even though she is with child. This Baihoh," he continued, holding up the bloody scalp and shaking it in the air, "he was the one who killed my father over at Godin's Creek. Did you not know that?"

"See your point, coon," Meek said, squeezing off a round from his Hawken.

By this time the Gros Ventres had taken cover beyond a small swamp that had been caused by beavers damming the stream, and gunfire and arrows were pouring in on the trappers. Milt had sounded a short retreat to a stand of aspen a few feet above the swamp, but the cover was insufficient, and already several men had been wounded.

Meek could see the Atsina women and children moving away on foot—no doubt to bring back the warriors from Baihoh's main encampment, wherever that was.

The standoff continued for a time, with neither side willing to make a concerted charge.

Then Bridger and Bill Sublette and Carson and Fitzpatrick and the others came riding in, and Milt's men let up a loud cheer.

"Milt! You stay with Mountain Lamb an' Wyeth's green-horns—keep those coons out of 'er. Come on, Bear-Killer, let's take it to these Red devils! I done made my will, an' I figger you have too."

Fifty or more experienced mountain men now advanced upon the Big Bellies' position across the swamp. Elias Sinclair, eager for the battle, was running ahead, roaring at the top of his lungs as rifle fire and arrows whistled about him.

Then, as if instantly frozen in mid-stride, the leader of the free trappers halted, did a crazy little step sideways, and slowly sat down.

When Robert Campbell reached him, Sinclair said, "Coon, take me to my brother if ye can."

With Meek's help, Campbell carried Sinclair away from the swamp.

Then Campbell and Meek hurried back, rejoining Bill Sublette and Jim Bridger where they had taken cover, close by the Indians' hastily constructed brush fort.

More men had poured in from Rendezvous by this time, and the trappers had the Atsinas completely surrounded. Even Wyeth had joined in, was leading a group of Nez Percés—though his Down-Easters had preferred to remain behind, with Milt and Mountain Lamb.

Bill Sublette moved out into the open to take a shot and was spun about by a ball from one of McKenzie's Mackinaw guns.

Again Meek and Campbell raced forward, picked up the wounded leader, and risked their own lives carrying him back across the swamp to safety.

The Atsinas were not firing so often by this time—were apparently running short on powder. But the gunfire from both sides continued, and the hours drifted onward. Further groups of men had been coming in from the Rendezvous encampment, and the mountain men and their Indian allies came to outnumber the Big Bellies by several hundred. The ring was drawn tight, and no escape seemed possible. And yet, from their favored position, the Big Bellies were nonetheless able to hold their own.

Some of the trappers rolled logs before them and were able to get into position to fire directly into the Indian stronghold. Another man, one of many who had been drinking heavily as the battle progressed, charged directly toward the Atsinas and took an arrow through the throat. He staggered about, trying to break off the shaft, screaming wordlessly, and was riddled with rifle fire.

Bill Sublette, his shoulder bound up, was back into the fray. Le Blueux and La Jeunesse stayed close to him—presuming, reasonably enough, that their former booshway was bound to get into more trouble if not watched out for.

"Dammit, Pete," Sublette complained, "we cain't just let these murderin' Red devils get away with 'er. Sinclair's gone under, an' half a dozen others as well. But what the hell do we do?"

"Enfant de garce, mon ami," Le Blueux said, lighting his pipe, "we do what they would do."

"Speak English, dammit! What's that?"

"Incendie," Le Blueux replied, "fire."

Word of the plan spread, but the Flatheads objected.

"The *Pieds Noirs* are rich," Muckaluck argued. "They have many presents with them. If we set fire to their cover, all will be destroyed."

"My friend's right," Antoine Godin agreed.

Then rumor spread that the main body of Atsinas had attacked the Rendezvous encampment, and Campbell and Fitzpatrick led most of the trappers back to the big camp. But nothing had been touched—no sign of any further Big Bellies.

By dawn the trappers were back at the battlesite, determined to put the Atsinas under. But when they opened fire on the Indians' position—nothing. The Big Bellies had escaped under cover of darkness. What remained were the bodies of nine warriors and two dozen dead horses. No scarlet blankets, no packs of plew, nothing.

And Le Blueux was slumped over the recumbent form of Baptiste La Jeunesse, who had taken an arrow in the back during the night. Le Blueux had cut out the shaft and, with Mountain Lamb's assistance, had applied such herbal medications as were available. Then, just as Meek and Fitzpatrick had returned from the Atsina stronghold, Baptiste La Jeunesse had shaken his head, closed his eyes, and gone under.

Carson, Meek, Newell, and a dozen of the Flatheads set off in pursuit of the Atsinas and returned a few hours later with an account of having come upon a dead warrior lying beneath a great pine. His woman had remained beside him.

"Come kill me!" she had called out to the trappers and their Indian allies. "The sun has gone out of my skies, and I wish to join my man in the Spirit World."

Meek drew back on his pony and yelled for the others to spare the Atsina woman; but the Flatheads were not to be convinced and immediately shot her dead.

Le Blueux had dug a grave, a hole six feet deep, in civilized fashion. He had borrowed Wyeth's Bible and had read a passage or two over his dead friend, tears all the while streaming down his weatherbeaten face. Then he filled in the grave and bound together a small cross to implant at the head of the mounded black earth.

Joe Meek stood next to the old French Canadian and was unable to think of any words that might comfort his friend.

"Baptiste, he was Catholic," Pierre Le Blueux said, wiping at his eyes. "He was not like the rest of us, Joe. I promised his father I would care for him, *enfant de Dieu!* I have taken two sons in the mountains, and now one is dead and the other may also be dead. Joe, it is time for this old man to go home, back to Quebec. I have been too long in *les montagnes,* too long I have been the wild man. But first I must visit the Absarokas to see if Jimmy Beckwourth is still alive, as we have heard. So many are dead now, *beaucoup—trop.* These *hommes* now, Jed Smith, Cahuna Smith, Pinckney Sublette, Godin the Elder, Alex Alexander, La Jeunesse the Elder, *trop, trop.* For you, Joe Meek, the world is still right, it still shines sometimes, *très resplendissant. Mais non,* not for this old Frenchman. It is time for me now to leave. . . ."

CHAPTER SIX

Dan'l in the Lions' Den

Grizzly.
Ursus horribilis.
Ephraim.
White Bear.
It was the grizzly who claimed that he, and not Old Man Coyote, had created the world. It is true that the creature has a ferocious disposition, but it receives its name from its silver-gray-to-brown coat. A full-grown male weighs a thousand pounds and sometimes a good bit more than that.

For the mountain men, those who had the ha'r of the b'ar in 'em, were accorded due respect—men who had tangled with grizzlies. Hugh Glass killed one bear, but the old sow tore him so horribly that Fitzgerald and young Bridger left him for dead and weaponless beside a pit they had dug for his grave—and Hugh crawled and hobbled and floated back to Fort Kiowa, eating rattlesnake, bugs, maggots, grass, and bark. Jed Smith drove off a griz, but it mauled him and chewed him and tossed him about and left him half-dead. Jim Clyman sewed together the great gash in his behind and stitched his torn ear together.

Face down the Blackfoot Nation, but don't front a grizzly— that bear could kill Gawd in a one-to-one contest. Ephraim is king of beasts in North America, and the impact from one blow of the huge clawed hand is often sufficient to break a buffalo's neck. It is brutally strong and despite its size is able to run as fast as a good horse. The grizzly is so heavy that it cannot climb a tree. It openly takes what it wants, and neither Indian nor Long Knife is wise to question its judgment.

White Bear, he eats anything—considers any living thing, plant or animal, his proper diet. In spring, just after hibernation, old griz is vegetarian. But before summer is over, the creature will have feasted on reptiles, amphibians, fish, birds, eggs, gophers, ground squirrels, grubs, insects, even badgers. It takes the prey of wolf and mountain lion and will kill old bull buffalo, moose, elk, and deer.

*Fortunately, Ursus horribilis does not seem to favor human
flesh.*

They had run into a few small bands of Shuckers, the ragged
cousins of the Shoshones, a people without horses or rifles. These
Indians, called Diggers by many, led a minimal existence
throughout the desert lands and in general posed no threat to the
Whites—inasmuch as only rarely would any of them come close
enough to put himself within bow-and-arrow striking distance.

But as Joe set and tended his traps along the Salmon Falls,
one of these Shuckers followed him, ghostlike, for three days.
Meek decided to ignore the man as best he could, building up a
big fire at night and sleeping away from it, his hand on his pistol
and his ear attuned to the slightest unexpected noises. As long as
the Shucker did no more than follow, Joe thought it best to ignore
the problem. But he felt almost as though he were being hunted,
and he didn't like it.

Late in the afternoon of the third day, Meek found the
Shucker with one of his traps, attempting to extricate the dead
beaver clamped between its steel jaws. Joe hoped that the
Shoshone lingo as spoken by Mountain Lamb and her people
would work. He demanded the return of trap and beaver as well.
But the Shucker responded first by brandishing a club and then
half-crouching and starting forward.

Meek pulled out his horse pistol and fired. The lead ball took
the Indian through the forehead, bursting out through the rear of
the skull.

When Joe related the matter, Nathaniel Wyeth became
furious.

"That Red heathen was harmless, Mr. Meek. I call what
you've done nothing less than murder. Why in God's name did you
do it?"

Joe glanced over at Milt and then spat upon the ground.

"To keep him from stealin' my traps is why."

"Take a man's life for that?" Wyeth sputtered.

Joe shook his head and walked away.

But by the next morning Nathaniel Wyeth and his men had
decided to strike out on their own, perhaps into Flathead and Nez
Percé country to the north of the Snake. The free trappers who had
remained with the party after Sinclair's death were of the opinion
that Wyeth's plan sounded better than Milt's, and so they
concluded to string along with the stiff-backed New Englander.

All in all, the parting was amicable enough, and the trappers shouted *Hurrah for the mountains!* and agreed that they'd be pleased to see each other again come Rendezvous time at Horse Creek, near the upper end of the Seedskeedee.

Milt, Joe, Mountain Lamb, and the band of RMF· trappers proceeded south along Salmon Falls, through a landscape of barren ridges and peaks at either side of the stream and finally to its headwaters beneath a high, pointed mountain that Milt dubbed The Matterhorn. They circled to the east and north of the mountain and came down to a small stream that flowed northward—not the Humboldt, they concluded. And so they continued, south now, through a low pass, until they came to a creek that seemed to be flowing in the right direction.

"Here's where your Buenaventura starts," Milt said as they paused to water the animals. "This is the one we all used to figure went clean to the Pacific, out through California."

"Don't look like much here," Meek suggested.

"Don't never amount to much, apparently," Milt said. "Four hundred miles long, an' she end up in a sinkhole out in the desert."

More Shucker Injuns now.

Half-starved and often utterly naked, the Indians flitted about through the shadows, keeping wary distance from the trappers. But curious—and more than a little attracted by the fire-stick weapons the trappers carried, weapons able to bring down game from a distance. An Indian who was able to obtain such a weapon would be able to feed his people on the meat of antelope and deer. And the iron traps—these would allow a much more systematic catching of wary beavers. Such a man would be delivered from a steady diet of mice, rabbits, and insects.

The Shuckers, Milt and Joe concluded, were after all not as harmless as they seemed. There was good reason to believe their arrowtips were poisoned, dipped in rattlesnake venom most likely.

Two days down the Humboldt drainage, a pair of Shuckers surprised Joe as he was setting traps. He fired once and, not taking time to reload his piece, set out running. The pair of short, brown men kept on his trail for nearly a mile, gaining ground all the time.

"They'd of stuck me full of poison arrows," Joe laughed, "if I hadn't of run into Godin an' Muckaluck. Those boys saved my beaver, no two ways about 'er."

Mountain Lamb burst into a fit of laughter, but Joe only scowled.

"What's so gawd-awful funny, Isabel?"

"These Indians are only half your size, Joe Meek. It is just funny to think of, that's all."

"Leetle bastards sure can *run*," Joe concluded, shaking his head.

The season had turned, with heavy frosts at night now, and Milt's party wandered from drainage to drainage throughout the barren lands that lay between the headwaters of the Humboldt and the Owyhee. Game had become so scarce as to be virtually nonexistent. No beaver, either, or anything else that might have provided purpose to their endless wanderings. Most of the streams had gone dry, and the men were forced to cut bark from cottonwoods and aspens to feed their horses—since there was never a sufficiency of grass along the arid ravine bottoms. Even when someone did manage to take an occasional beaver, it was discovered that sickness came from eating the flesh.

"Damn beavers, what there is of 'em is starvin' too," Joe lamented. "They been eatin' them wild parsnips—that's what makes us sick, I figger."

They were finally reduced to eating ants and grubs, just like the Shuckers. And they moved north toward the Snake River, hoping vainly each day that it would be possible to take some game. A few of the men even crisped the soles of their spare moccasins and ate those. At one point Milt ordered the men to bleed the pack mules for both drink and nourishment. An old mule, drained a bit too dry, staggered off and fell into a crevass, breaking its neck—but at the same time providing desperately needed meat.

Mountain Lamb, well into the ninth month of her pregnancy, became distant and noncommunicative. Joe and Milt, preoccupied with the very real problem of survival, chose to leave Isabel to her thoughts.

Why indeed, she often wondered, had she rashly left her own people to come adventuring with these two crazy Long Knives? She had dreamed of having a man of her own, but that was hardly the same as starving to death in a trackless wasteland with two Whitemen, one wounded and constantly ailing, the other forever deferring to his friend, sharing the two men, looking after them and being looked after in turn, and pregnant with a child whose birth, she realized, would most likely alter forever her relationship with both of the men.

Sometimes she listened to their whispered talk when they presumed her to be asleep. And she analyzed these exchanged bits of communication—seeking in them some hint as to what her own future might be.

Yes, she had indeed slept with each of the men—had been made love to by Joe Meek and had, in effect, made love to Sublette, the latter sometimes having gasped in pain when he attempted to mount her.

But then, once her pregnancy had begun to show in a noticeable way, all the lovemaking had ceased. No doubt they had presumed she had become delicate—fragile. And she had not questioned the matter. In any case, even among her own people, most women preferred not to take their men into themselves while they were with child.

And after a time, before the Rendezvous even, she herself had ceased to desire—whom?

Joe Meek.

It had never been desire that she felt toward Milt—only gratitude, care, a need to care for him, the leader who was obliged to live with constant pain.

All along it had been the big man, the Bear-Killer, who had occupied her thoughts in a way that drove all reason from her. His face, his disarming, intense brown eyes, his obsidian-black hair, and his strong, resolute, and yet good-natured face. In truth, that winter day in the medicine lodge it was Joe Meek that she had seen—Joe Meek and another Whiteman. It had been for his life that she had pleaded with Bad Left Hand, and it had been for him that she had impulsively left her own people.

That first time they had made love—how wonderful it had been, frightening also, the first time for her, the terrible euphoria of allowing a man to have his way with her and at the same time the need in her own blood for it. It was as if she had been suddenly a wholly different person, not Umentucken, Tukutsey Undenwatsy, but a woman instead of a child, a woman who had no need for any name whatsoever. And it was not even Joe Meek who had lain with her, who had pressed her legs apart and had gently, slowly entered into her body—it was a man who, like herself, had no name and had no need for a name.

Mountain Lamb placed one hand to her swollen belly and felt the child within her move slightly, a small, nudging kick. And at the same time she tried to recall exactly what it was that she had felt when the nameless man that Joe Meek had transformed himself into beneath the good warmth of the buffalo robes had begun to push his maleness into her.

It was his knife I used to cut away the woven belt of my maidenhood. . . .

Strange feelings, a fullness within her groin, sensations that were neither exactly pleasure nor pain but both at once—the flesh of her body stretching, tearing, the white fire of pain that burned toward pleasure at the same instant. And then, when he was fully within her and she was clinging to him desperately and the words *yes* and *no* were both exploding inside her brain, he began to work his body, a slow rhythm at first, and she was drawn into the circle of the great strength of those male arms, his bearded face against her own, and part of her wished desperately to be able to pull away and part of her wished even more desperately to be able to draw all of him, all of him inside of her body.

The quickening rhythm, the pain subsiding, her own excitement rising to heights she could never have guessed. And then, with every nerve in her being on the verge of explosion so that she feared she might actually die, he groaned, shuddered with clean, brutal strength, and engulfed her, his power vanishing, the male muscles relaxing, covering her totally so that she could no longer even breathe. But breathing did not seem important.

She bled afterward. She reached down and felt the blood with her fingertips, traced a design on her belly, and then, even without willing the action, reached for and held the sticky, softening penis of this man who had presided at her passage from girlhood to womanhood.

Another soft kicking sensation within her abdomen, and Mountain Lamb smiled.

The tired motion of the horse beneath her, Joe Meek and Sublette riding before her, the other trappers trailing behind. No talking from any of them, only grim silence as the seemingly endless trek continued. Blue autumn sky above, and a pair of vultures circling off to the north. A chill wind, but perspiration on her forehead. A locking of muscles across her belly, deep within her belly, and Mountain Lamb bit at her lip and closed her eyes.

The first spasm had come that morning, shortly after the day's ride had begun.

My child wishes to come out into the world now.

Perhaps it was but another false alarm.

Mountain Lamb waited, said nothing, half-consciously began to whisper a song—a patience-song she had learned from her mother. She had not reached the end when the pain hit her once again.

She cried out this time, and was immediately embarrassed for having done so.

I am afraid. . . . I do not know how to do this thing. . . . I have seen it happen, I was allowed to watch once when a child came . . . but I did not know then, I did not know how it felt, I could only suppose. . . . How will I know what to do? No women to assist me . . .

"Joe Meek!" she called out. "Joe—Sub-lette—I will have to turn aside now. I will be all right."

"Umentucken," Meek said, turning about in the saddle and drawing his pony to a halt at the same instant. "What is it, girl?"

Milt sensed immediately what was up—had been expecting it all morning. He waved Godin and the others ahead.

"Boys," he yelled, "keep headin' for the low pass. There's water beyond, I'll stake my good leg on 'er. Me an' Joe an' Mountain Lamb'll catch up to ye after a spell."

"Soon we have a new little one?" Muckaluck asked, laughing loudly. "All this past week your woman's breasts have grown larger, Milt. I keep track of these things."

The trappers gathered about, all of them grinning and nodding.

"We do not go on," Antoine Godin insisted. "We will kill more mules if we have to. We will eat crickets, just as the Shuckers do. But we are all the father of this child—and we wish to know whether it is a boy or only a girl."

"Gawddamned heathens!" Joe Meek spat out. "Do what Milt tells ye."

"We will pull Bear-Killer down and I will sit on him," Muckaluck said, laughing.

The men had already begun to dismount.

"Get some linen out of the saddlebags," Milt commanded, feeling the need to say something.

"We'll go with ye," Meek said in a half-whisper.

"No," Mountain Lamb answered. "I must do this thing myself. Men must not be present, Joe Meek. That is our way. I will go over into that clump of junipers. I will be all right. You stay here, both of you."

Mountain Lamb dismounted carefully and without further words began to walk away from the company of trappers. They, in turn, now glanced uneasily at one another and followed the slowly moving form of the tall Shoshone girl. When Mountain Lamb had vanished from sight, Godin pounded Milt on the back.

Within an hour Mountain Lamb had returned. In her arms was a wrinkle-faced little creature whose eyes were squinted shut and whose small head was covered with a light sheen of jet-black hair.

The men whooped and shouted and pressed forward for a look at the small wonder.

"What sort of varmint is it?" Godin demanded.

A strange, dazed sort of smile played about Mountain Lamb's mouth.

"He is a man child," she answered, glancing at Joe Meek.

"By the great, howlin' gawd!" Meek laughed.

"A boy!" Sublette mused. "What we gonna name the little feller?"

"Among my father's people, a shaman is called in to give the newborn its first name," Mountain Lamb said, glancing again at Meek and then at Sublette. "Perhaps we should wait before the naming. . . ."

"Muckaluck once wished to be a medicine man," Godin laughed suddenly, "ain't that right? You got any ideas, great shaman of the Flatheads?"

Muckaluck stood a bit straighter and gazed at the child—having instantly seized upon his friend's idea and having decided that he, indeed, was responsible for the naming of Mountain Lamb's newborn child.

"Last night I dreamed of a fish in the river," he said. "I dreamed of a salmon in the Snake River. The Snake is the river of the Shoshone People, and Umentucken is a Shoshone. I think the child's name should be *Salmon.*"

"He ain't a very big salmon, though," Meek said, grinning. "How about *Little Salmon?*"

"Sounds like a proper name to me, Milt agreed. "What do you think, Isabel?"

"I must try to nurse the child now," she said. "I am very tired and wish to lie down for a little while. Yes, I like that name. He will be Little Salmon."

The canyon beyond the low pass was dry except for one slight ooze beneath some basalt boulders. With some digging and scooping, the men were able to create a small catch basin from which it was possible to drink. The horses and mules stamped about in agitation but the water gathered too slowly to provide for the animals—and so Sublette's company moved on down the barren drainage, northward.

Hungry camp that night, and the remaining water in the one cask that they had managed to fill from the ooze was reserved for Mountain Lamb.

The group moved out with the first light, and by noon the canyon opened before them. The broad basin of the Snake River lay ahead, and as they rounded the last bend of the ravine, the men let out a whoop.

Snake River! Look at that big green son of a bitch!

The river, glinting in sunlight and lined by golden-leafed cottonwoods and willows, was still several miles ahead, at the foot of a broad alluvial fan. But the mules sensed water and began to run, kicking up their heels and making for the river. The packhorses followed, and the riding ponies champed at their bits.

Within the hour the trappers had reached the Snake, where they found their pack animals lying down, bloated with too much drinking, but nonetheless contentedly dozing in the sunlight, happily squashing the contents of the saddlebags with the weight of their bodies.

Trappers leaped into the cold water and rose to the surface, roaring and whooping.

"All right, Muckaluck, you Flathead savage, how do we get us some of them salmon you dreamed about? Got to be some kind of fish in the water, anyhow," Meek said, laughing.

"My people use nets—at the falls, when the salmon come upstream."

"We *know* that," Milt said. "Don't happen to have a net in your possible sack, do ye?"

"I have this," Godin said, holding up a two-inch-long brass pin. "This will work as a hook. Who has some line? Find me some crickets or worms, someone! Always the Indian has to look out for the Whiteman so that he will not starve to death in the midst of plenty."

Muckaluck began turning stones by the water's edge and quickly discovered a gray-white grub.

Godin fixed a flat pebble to a length of twine, tying it in place, attached the now-bent pin, and stuck the grub onto its point. He tossed the line into the river, and within moments the string went taut. Godin played the fish back and within a short interval had a foot-long salmon flopping about on the black stones of the river's edge.

"A little salmon it be!" Joe Meek cried out. "Boys, check through your gear—we needs some more pins, that's what. Anything ye can turn into a hook. Maybeso we'll eat tonight after all!"

Soon half a dozen lines had been fashioned, and the fishing began in earnest, and by sundown the trappers had managed to catch a large woven basket full nearly to the brim with trout and salmon. Fires were built along the river's edge, the men in high spirits and heedless of danger, and strings of fish were hooked through the gills and roasted.

The *starvin' times* were over.

The following day Meek and Muckaluck went out on foot and, their luck now having marvelously changed for the better, were able to bring down a pair of pronghorns and an old buck elk—an animal that, in better times, would have been spared on account of the probable toughness of his flesh.

Winter was coming on, and Milt's company had taken precious few beaver and had failed in the attempt to discover profitable new trapping areas. But enthusiasm nonetheless ran high.

"Bad times makes middlin' times look like good times when they come, coons," Joe Meek proclaimed. "Now what we gotta do is find us some beavers before the cricks all get friz."

The small party of RMF trappers rejoined their fellows at Big Lost River, a stream that inexplicably vanished into the till of cinderlike rocks at the foot of the mountains to the north of the Snake River.

And two miles upstream, Drips and Vanderburgh were encamped, having continued their dogged pursuit of their RMF competitors. Nathaniel Wyeth, having lost several of his men and having been deserted, as predicted, by the free trappers, had also come in to make winter encampment.

Bridger, Carson, Fitzpatrick, Campbell, Fraeb, and Gervais all made individual formal calls to Milt's lodge—for the specific purpose of paying their respects to Mountain Lamb and Little Salmon. For a mountain man to have children by one or another of his Indian wives, of course, was hardly an unusual thing. But Umentucken, Tukutsey Undenwatsy was unusual, as all agreed, in ways that went far beyond her almost unreal beauty of face and figure. And now, slim-waisted once again a month and more after the birth of Little Salmon, she was, the trappers agreed among themselves, even more strikingly beautiful than before—if that was possible. And the child, as Gabe Bridger proudly proclaimed, was his own godchild—and, clapping both Milt and Joe on the back so hard that each of the compañeros feared their backbones might have been permanently damaged, the Blanket Chief vowed he would look out for Little Salmon throughout his lifetime.

"Let's see." Meek grinned. "Old Jim here was born in eighteen and four. Little Salmon, he come along in late thirty-two. So that makes Gabe close to thirty years older, don't it? Now then, if Little Salmon lives to be seventy or so, Gabe'll have to make a century in order to keep his word."

"Damn right," Bridger growled, "an' I'll do 'er, too. Ye don't see me gettin' bald yet, like old Le Blueux, do ye? Hell no, ye don't. Milt, ye got to teach this Bear-Killin' kid of yours to learn some respect for 'is elders. An' that's what I am, Meek, your goddamn *elder*. Don't ye forget it, nuther."

"He'll be an ancient twenty-nine come spring," Meek bellowed, "an' already he acts like fifty. Livin' in the mountains don't make ye younger, Gabe, it makes ye older. So I figger mebbe ye'll have to live to be a hundred an' fifty just to take care of Little Salmon until he grows up."

"He's livin' in the mountains too, ain't he?" Bridger demanded in a way that put an end to all further discussion of the matter.

Tom Fitzpatrick never played the part of Santy Claus that year—and, indeed, the Whiteman's season of celebration was hardly observed at all in the winter encampment on Big Lost River. A terrible cold, alternating with periods of snowfall, had settled in over the Snake River Basin, and the temperature dropped at times to forty and fifty below zero. The lesser streams were solidly frozen, and game was desperately scarce. The old-timers, men like Bridger and Fitzpatrick, talked of the terrific winter of '27–28—a time of cold, those worthies opined, even more fierce than the present. That winter, also, had been spent near the Snake—the winter of the great battle with As-as-to's Siksika Blackfeet. Le Blueux had been there and La Jeunesse and Jim Beckwourth as well—and that crazy Red Beard Miller. It was Miller who'd crossed the river and used gunpowder to set the fire that had put Bug's Boys to rout. Then the endless snows and the breaking cold had come upon them.

"Five years," Bridger remarked, "an' our goddamn world's done changed on us. Lots of coons has gone under. Fitz, ye remember how we found old Jarvey—froze solid out in the woods?"

Fitz ran his fingers through his white hair and sipped at his cup of coffee.

'We stuck 'im in a snowbank, an' our Flathead friends done ate im," Fitzpatrick recalled.

"We'll all end up eatin' each other before this one's over," Bridger complained, "if we don't bring in some meat, that is. Meek, why don't ye go roust out a grizzly or two? Ye say ye've got bear medicine. Hell, man, there's lots of white bears holed up back in the lava rocks. Ain' nothin' wrong with bear meat, is they?"

Meek scratched at his mustache and then rubbed the tip of his nose.

"By the great blue gawd," he said, laughing. "Why didn't I think of that? Promise ye, Gabe, it'll be hump-rib of white bear tomorrow night. Got my word on 'er."

"He's serious?" Bridger asked, glancing at Fitzpatrick.

"Coons," Meek said, "Montain Lamb's got a sayin' for it. *Saunt-den-tickup, hintz. Saunt-den-duke.* Meat's meat, an' it's good meat, my friend."

First thing in the morning Joe rousted out Doc Newell and Antoine Godin.

"Goin' huntin', boys," he said, grinning.

"Nothin' to hunt," Newell responded. "Bufflers is all east of the mountains. Even the deers are hibernatin'."

"So are the b'ars," Joe explained. "You coons with me or not?"

They worked their way up Birch Creek, moving across the snow on foot and leading three pack animals. The temperature held steady below freezing point, and the sky was immense and cloudlessly blue.

By noon they had come across grizzly tracks, big ones.

"This bear, he is not sleeping," Godin remarked.

"Shore he is," Meek assured the Iroquois. "He just come out to relieve himself, is all. Not worried about him, are ye? Muckaluck always says ye're crazy for bears, just like me."

"Any coon what's crazy for b'ars is just plain crazy. That's what I'm thinking," Doc Newell growled. "Mebbe we can find a bighorn or two up on the rim north of here."

"You niggers got no stomach for bears?" Meek scolded. "Hell, I'll fetch this feller down by myself, then."

They followed the tracks, working their way up through a jumble of snow-covered basalt—were finally forced to tether their pack animals—and continued until they came in sight of what appeared to be a cave entrance.

Godin stopped and shook his head.

"Muckaluck likes to lie," he muttered.

"Hooray!" Meek laughed, suddenly doing a little jig. "Thar's meat, coons!"

At the entrance to the cave, Godin and Newell lost heart; and after some brief discussion, Meek concluded that he would go in alone. His companions nodded their agreement, but when Joe moved into the darkness, a pine-pitch torch in hand, his companions, Hawkens loaded and primed, were right behind him.

"Ain't no bears in here, Joe," Newell said. "Hell, we're just wastin' our time is all. Let's go find some bighorns."

"Gawd knows there be bears," Meek answered. "Lads, I can smell 'em."

Bears.

Three of them.

Grizzlies, curled up together, like so many camp dogs—a great sleeping mass of fur and muscle and bone and claws and teeth.

"Holy Jesus!" Newell gasped.

"We each shoot one, then?" Godin asked, starting to take aim.

But Joe Meek, excited as he was by their find, was warming also to the evident fear his companions were experiencing. He too was a little edgy—down to the soles of his feet, in fact. But the opportunity was simply too good to waste.

"Coons," he said, "ye got no sportin' blood a-tall. Pump galena into the brutes while they're sleepin'? No sir, that ain't the way."

"What, then?" Newell asked, edging backward.

"You two stand over where ye've got room to shoot without killin' each other. Me, I'm goin' to wake up his bearship and coax him out into the light."

"Goddammit, Meek . . . ," Newell started to protest.

But Joe had pulled out his wiping stick and was already advancing on the sleeping grizzlies.

Godin and Newell moved quickly to the cave's entrance and waited to see what would happen.

Joe lashed the biggest bear across its snout, then again. The grizzly came up roaring, and Joe headed for the cave's entrance, the bear in groggy pursuit.

Godin and Newell fired at the same instant, and the grizzly toppled forward, all four legs out, and slid a way down the snowy embankment.

"No more brains that your basic pissant," Newell mumbled as he immediately set to reloading his weapon.

"That's one!" Meek laughed and made his way back into the darkness of the cave, rifle and pine-pitch torch in his left hand and his wiping stick in his right.

Again a bear rushed out, this time only a couple of strides behind the whooping Joe Meek. Godin fired, and the bear fell, wounded, and was lashing his heavy claws at a boulder when Newell's shot to the throat finished him.

"Now once again!" Meek shouted and reentered the cave—but he came stumbling out backward and dived to one side as the third grizzly, already quite awake and fully roused, appeared.

Godin got off a shot, but Newell was still reloading.

Meek, sprawled in the snow, fired up at Ephraim from nearly point-blank range. The creature, stunned by the impact of the .55 ball, toppled over backward, thrashed about for a moment, and then lay still.

Meek stepped up upon the grizzly's huge chest and shouted, "Boys, we're Daniels in the lions' den, make no mistake about 'er! Dan'l war humbug—he couldn't shine in this crowd, by gawd! Ain't no one would believe that story nohow, unless she were winter an' the lions was suckin' their paws! Don't no one tell me no more about old Dan'l! Coon, we're as good Daniels as ever cotched beaver. Hooray for us!"

Godin and Newell looked at each other and shook their heads.

"Gone mad in the bush," Newell said. "Crazy as a rattler with its tail shot off . . ."

"I think it is time to send this one back to the settlements until he is well again," Antoine Godin concluded.

But he had already set to work skinning out the biggest of the grizzlies.

CHAPTER SEVEN

Free Trapper

The stream was called Ogden's River, Mary's River, and finally the Humboldt River. It flows four hundred miles from the high Rubies and the barren mountains to the north across and through seemingly endless wastelands to the Humboldt Sink, bad water, end of the river. And this is Nevada—the snowy place, as the name says.

But it's high country, sage-covered if anything grows at all, and traversed by numerous mountain ranges on a north–south axis, a vast, beautiful land if one is but able to value it for what it is—desert and oasis, mountains that melt in morning sunlight and seem translucent, violet to purple.

The winds blow, and tumbleweeds scatter and bounce about wildly, dust devils twist up the big basins, and cloudbursts fall from dark cumulus high up and sometimes never touch the floor of the desert, the rain evaporating as it falls. But sometimes avalanches of water come pouring down from ravines and spread out on their alluvial fans and sink into the sandy earth, whence myriad wildflowers that await the rains burst and bloom quickly and then vanish.

Piñon pines clot the ridges, and higher up, clustered about the greatest peaks, there are forests of fir and spruce, snowfields, vast domes of limestone and granite, bristlecone pines, the oldest of all living things.

Pronghorned antelope, mountain lions, jackrabbits everywhere, cranes and egrets and herons that live and nest in the marshes where rivers disappear. Big lakes here and there, remnants of a vast inland sea whose waters rolled during the ages of ice.

Heat and cold.

Sometimes no water for a hundred miles. Ask Jed Smith and Robert Evans and Silas Gobel—they crossed the big land on foot, from California across Nevada and back to summer Rendezvous at Bear Lake.

Along the western rim of Nevada rises the granite mass of the

*Sierra Nevada, jagged peak after peak, north to south. And
beyond these mountains that limit the desert are the dense forests
of the long ridges and the foothills and the oak-studded expanses
of the Great Central Valley of California—tall grass, deep black
soil, hot summers, a place where snow almost never falls.*

When the weather broke, shortly after the first of January in
1833, the RMF booshways decided to move camp. In addition to
the scarcity of game, rumor had it that there had been a smallpox
outbreak among the *Pi-at-sui-ab-be* Shoshones, a group that had
set up its winter village far down the Snake, below the big falls.
Even if the rumor was correct, the afflicted group was more than a
hundred miles away; but with a number of Shoshones living
among the Whites, the possibility of winter travel and hence of
infection provided a compelling reason for the move.

Where to?

"Through Blackfoot country, naturally," Jim Bridger opined.
"Ye know Drips an' Vanderburgh is goin' to follow us, so this
time we don't sneak out after dark an' ride like fools for two, three
days. No sir. We let the whole shee-bang come right along with us,
Wyeth an' his coons too. Bug's Boys ain't goin' to attack that
many of us, an' especially not with the American Fur bunch along
for the ride. McKenzie an' Chouteau been makin' friends with the
Blackfeet, tradin' with 'em an' all. Way I see it, we got built-in
protection."

"*Écraser toute opposition,*" Milt said, nodding. "Ain't that
what Chouteau's supposed to have said? Run us coons out of the
Shinin' Mountains. Well, Drips an' Vanderburgh want to do that,
they'll have to give us some free passage first."

"Wagh!" Fitzpatrick agreed.

"Up to Flathead Lake, mebbe?" Kit Carson asked. "We got
our Flatheads with us, Muckaluck an' the boys. Should get a fair
welcome, so long as them coons ain't starvin' too. Should work
out fine, me hearties. Old Muckaluck's always sayin', *Much
game, many animal people to eat.* Guess it's time we found out
about 'er."

"We been lookin' for new streams to work," Henry Fraeb
agreed. "Good place for the spring hunt, seems like. . . ."

Moving day was soon at hand, and the three contingents of
trappers, perceiving their common interest and the wisdom of
Bridger's plan as well, headed northward, up the Beaverhead to
the Salmon and then across Lewis and Clark's old Lost Trail Pass,

over the divide, and down to the drainage of the Bitterroot River, a stream that ran basically northward through a good valley to its confluence with the Flathead River, which, in turn, came down from Flathead Lake.

Half a dozen times during the three-hundred-mile trek they encountered small groups of Blackfoot hunters, but each time the pattern was one of mutual avoidance.

Once onto the Flathead River, the bitter cold returned, and yet the caravan was obliged to ride on, now within thirty or forty miles of their destination and anticipating a good welcome. Godin and Muckaluck and a group of the Flathead trappers had ridden on ahead to prepare the village for the new arrivals and had returned with news that all was well.

"Much game," Muckaluck reported. "All of my people are fat and happy. They welcome the trappers, and they wish to trade."

But now the mountain men trudged onward through wind and driving snow, an intense storm that had come spilling down from over the Mission Range, Arctic air from out of central Canada.

The long ride had taken its toll on Milt's reserves. His bad leg had flared up again, and he was running a fever.

"At least I'm the only one that ain't friz," he said, and laughed weakly.

Mountain Lamb grew fearful for Little Salmon. One of the infant's eyes persisted in gumming together, and the baby boy was coughing and sneezing and shivering.

"I must have another robe!" Mountain Lamb said.

"Saddlebags is all frozen tight," Milt answered. "Pull him in tight to ye an' lean forward more, Isabel. This damned wind cain't keep blowin' forever."

"Gawd!" Meek roared. "Take this, Umentucken!"

He pulled off his grizzly-fur capote, the one Mountain Lamb had made especially for him, and handed it to her. She protested, and Joe insisted—and so, knowing it was useless to argue with Joe Meek, she immediately bundled the child within the heavy garment.

Meek never wore a shirt even beneath the heavy grizzly skin, and now he was naked from the waist up. He shouted and laughed at the freezing wind against his chest and waved his arms about in the driving snow.

By the time they reached the first of the Flathead villages, just after nightfall, Joe was nearly frozen to death—hardly able to keep his saddle. Muckaluck ushered Mountain Lamb and her child, Milt, and Joe into an uncle's lodge, explaining the necessity in staccato bursts of his own language. The four were made welcome and a kettle of thick soup was offered to them and thankfully accepted.

Through the long night, wind buffeted the hide lodge and caused the lodgefire to flare and funk and flare again. Assisted by the uncle's two wives, Mountain Lamb ministered to Little Salmon, to Milt, and to Joe.

She would sleep, she decided, when her family was clearly out of danger.

The storm passed, and the three brigades of mountain men set up their own village about equidistant between two of the Flathead encampments. Game was indeed plentiful in this land, including buffalo, and Meek and the others were able to bring in a good supply of fresh meat—an almost unspeakable delicacy after the starvin' times that lay behind them.

One night, with Mountain Lamb presiding, Meek and Muckaluck staged an eat-out. Before it was finished, with both men belching and groaning in their sleep, each had consumed close to ten pounds of buffalo, as Milt reckoned the matter. But as to which man had been the winner, Sublette was not about to say.

A week later Joe and some others found a small group of Blackfeet on a peninsula in Flathead Lake.

"Tan my britches!" Joe laughed. "Them's Bug's Boys, just sittin' there an' waitin' to go to the Spirit World."

Meek and Godin and the others opened fire, and the Blackfeet, inexplicably without weapons, were forced to dive into the icy waters of the lake and swim for their lives.

The trappers jumped up and down and yipped their delight.

But at that moment a much larger delegation of *Pieds Noirs* appeared, and Joe and the others immediately saw the wisdom of running to save their scalps. The Blackfeet, howling in rage, gave chase, and the race was on.

With luck and good running, they made it to the trappers' encampment, and the Blackfeet held back—though they were still shouting and eager for battle.

The Mexican free trapper Loretto had a Blackfoot squaw. He came forward and told Fitzpatrick and Bridger not to worry—that he would be able to intervene. No one had been killed as yet, and battle could be averted.

"Señor Gabe, these *hombres*, they will not wish to fight. We will give them some presents, *sí? Amigos—muy buenos.*"

Bridger and Fitzpatrick gave signal for truce, and they met with the Blackfoot chieftain halfway between the two forces. At this point Loretto's squaw happened to recognize her brother among the warriors and called out to him. The brother started down toward his sister, and Bridger picked up his rifle. The Blackfoot chieftain, a man fully as large and strong as Gabe, managed to wrestle the weapon away from him, and instantly gunsmoke went up on both sides. The battle was begun.

The *Pieds Noirs* took Loretto's wife with them to the hillside, and Loretto went into a panic. He turned, ran to his lodge, scooped up their infant child, and rode directly in among the startled Blackfeet—amid much shouting and yelling. Loretto's squaw pleaded for his life, and her brother intervened with the party chief, who thought the matter over and ordered Loretto returned to his White friends. But the wife and her child would remain with the Blackfeet.

Then the shooting began once more.

The battle was a standoff, and eventually the Blackfeet withdrew, taking Loretto's wife and child with them. Beyond that, the trappers had lost three men, all from the RMF brigade, and six horses. Jim Bridger, whose luck was running poorly that day, had taken two arrows in the back. Tom Fitzpatrick used his skinning knife to cut out one of the arrowheads, but the other remained embedded.

When the butchery had proceeded as far as Fitz could take it, Bridger sat up, groaned, shook his head, and demanded some whiskey. He drank copiously and said, "Aw, hell, boys, this coon'll be all right. Ye know meat don't spile in the mountains."

In his empty lodge, Loretto was also drinking heavily—and tears were running down his cheeks.

And the day following, Milt took a high fever and became delirious. Joe and Mountain Lamb sat up with him throughout the long night, both fearful that their friend would die. Joe tried to remain cheerful, allaying Mountain Lamb's fears. But then he too broke down and finally strode out into the darkness and roared at God at the top of his lungs.

At length, the smell of morning coffee brought Milt back to his senses.

"Damn me," he said. "I don't know where I been, but I had

some of the damnedest dreams. Isabel, could ye pour a sick man a shot of that coffee if she's ready?"

The winter wore on, and the Blackfeet stole a number of the trappers' horses, including Jim Bridger's big white stallion, an animal named Grohean, Gabe's favorite. Bridger, Kit Carson, Joe Meek, Mark Head, and some others gave pursuit and were able to overtake the Indians.

The *Pieds Noirs*, not particularly interested in fighting if a fight could be avoided, decided to parley. After some considerable talking, during which the Blackfeet correctly determined that they had the trappers outnumbered, they agreed to part with five of the least-valuable horses, but not the others. As to Grohean, the Blackfoot party chief insisted, he had been a Blackfoot pony all along—stolen by the thieving Crows two years earlier.

"Well, coons," Meek shrugged, "it's take what they give us an' go home with our tails atwixt our legs—or fight. This nigger says fight."

Bridger was furious and agreed immediately.

"Not sure she's worth it, James," Kit Carson said, "but hell, I'm with ye. Let's have at 'er."

A battle ensued, arrows whistling through the trees and galena thumping through the air. So much powdersmoke was rising, Joe reflected, that from a distance the woods seemed to be afire.

Kit Carson and Mark Head led a charge and succeeded in running two Blackfoot warriors into a pocket among some trees. Meek stumbled up the hill behind Carson, glanced over, and saw an Indian about to fire on the unsuspecting Mark Head. Kit saw it too and fired immediately, the ball from his Hawken striking the Blackfoot in the side of his head and causing his skull to explode with the impact.

Another Indian emerged from behind a boulder and leveled his piece at Kit—who had not yet had time to reload. Kit leaped and danced about like an Indian in the attempt to spoil the Blackfoot's aim, but to little avail. The McKenzie fusee exploded, and little Kit Carson was spun about, the lead having grazed his neck, passing completely through his shoulder.

Meek fired from nearly point-blank, and his shot ripped through the Indian's stomach, throwing him backward onto the snow, his legs twisted together and his arms straight out in a bloody cruciform.

Head came running back down the hill, and he and Joe carried Kit back to cover.

The battle was over, and the Blackfeet had vanished, Grohean with them.

"Guess we can buy us some new ponies from the Nez Percés," Bridger said. "I'm sure gonna miss old Grohean, though. Loved that damned horse. Ye think Kit's goin' to make it, Joe?"

Carson was still alive, half-conscious.

Through a night of terrible cold the trappers nursed the little firebrand who, at just over five feet, was in many ways taller than any of them—and they knew it. At times Kit came to his senses, and at other times he drifted off—even stopped breathing.

"Come on, ye leetle fool, live, dammit!" Bridger crooned. "Ye always insisted ye could whup me if ye had to—well, whup this, by golly! Ye can do 'er, Kit."

The cold became so intense that blood flowing from Carson's wound actually froze.

Bridger wiped away the blood and started crying and cursing alternately.

Meek watched, shook his head, and thought of his own friendship with Milt—a friendship that was just as deep as that of Bridger and Carson but that was, owing to the fact that they both loved the same woman and were living with her together, beginning to show signs of stress.

Maybeso I ought to just move on an' leave 'em together. But gawddammit, how can I do that? I love that gal so much I cain't even think what it'd be like livin' without 'er.

"Best ye get some shuteye, Gabe," Joe said. "We'll stay up with 'im. Christopher ain't goin' beaver tonight, I'll guarantee 'er."

Bridger looked up, shook his head.

An' Milt. He's more my brother than Steve or any of 'em. How much longer's he got in the mountains? That leg's goin' to have to come off, that's what I think. Wal, if he can do 'er one-legged, he will. Damned if he ain't tougher than the lot of us. . . .

It was still dark when Carson stirred and then, his mouth wide with pain, sat up.

"Winged me, by God," he said, trying to laugh. "Gabe, between us, we're plumb full of holes."

* * *

The long spring hunt had been a good one for Drips and Vanderburgh's bunch and for Wyeth's too, as well as for the RMF brigade. Many of the Flatheads had also taken to trapping and had their own packs of plew. Milt traded for the furs until the supply goods had run dangerously low. Vanderburgh, with goods left over from the previous Rendezvous, did an even better business. And yet many of the Flatheads refused to sell at all, preferring instead to accompany the trappers to the Horse Creek Rendezvous, where the arwerdenty would be abundantly available.

Old Man Coyote dropped a last few inches of snow over the mountains during the first week in May, but it melted quickly and the days, quite long at this time of the year, were turning hot. Everything was blooming wildly, and the horses gloried in the new grass. The rivers were singing, high with meltoff from the mountains, and the trapping season was over. Pelts taken during the preceding two weeks were of distinctly inferior quality, even those from the high country where the snows still lay heavy in places.

Meek pulled his traps, the last man to do so, and rubbed them up with tallow—to be put away now until the autumn hunt began. He'd worked with extreme diligence all through the spring, and he had a handsome collection of plew to show for his efforts. The company got its share, of course, but nonetheless Joe was feeling just a mite pleased with himself. Various possibilities would now be open to him—matters that he'd think about and decide on when the time was right.

Black Harris rode in. The old-timer had been down country and had just returned to the mountains, bringing some interesting if not particularly welcome information with him.

In the first place, riverboats were now working the Big Muddy on a regular basis clear up to the American Fur post at Fort Union, at the confluence of the Missouri and the Yellowstone. Further, these specially designed craft, suited to shallow-water navigation, had even been up the Yellowstone as far as Fort Cass, at the mouth of the Bighorn.

And McKenzie, as spokesman for American Fur, had made something of a fuss about the matter of bringing liquor in for the Indian trade. Regulations had been there, of course, all along, and permits had been required for some time. But now the U.S. Cavalry would be in the business of enforcing the law.

"But Billy Sublette," Harris told them, "he's bringin' up more damned booze than ye can shake a stick at. Strange thing is, rumor has it he's done made hisself some kind of arrangement with McKenzie. Don't make no sense to this coon, but that's the scuttlebutt back in Saint Louis."

"Sublette's in with American Fur?" Bridger asked, his forehead wrinkled in astonishment. "No way that could be true, no sir."

"Yep," Milt said. "It could be true at that. Bill's my own damned brother, but he's always looked out for himself first, last, an' always. An' that's the truth."

The talk went on. Jed Smith had gone under—the rumor of the preceding year was true. Comanches had harvested him down on the Cimmaron River. And Hugh Glass and Edward Rose were dead, both of them put under by the Arikaras, not far from Fort Union. Jim Kipp had Glass's rifle, *Old Bullthrower*, up on the wall of his office at Fort Union. Pierre Le Blueux had indeed gone down country, but not back to Quebec, as most of the RMF men had supposed. Last heard of, Le Blueux was in New Orleans.

"Wearin' out the ladies of the evening, most likely," Harris suggested.

"He'll be back," Meek said. "I dreamed about the big Frenchy the other night."

"Figger he will," Harris agreed. "His old compañero Beckwourth—a mite before your time in the Shinin' Mountains, Joseph, my lad—but he's alive an' well. Better off than any of us coons, I should say. Wagh! Gabe, ye'll be glad to hear this. Not only were them rumors about Beckwourth bein' with the Crows true, but now the some-bitch is their head chief. I just missed 'im at Fort Cass. Sam Tulleck, he told me all about 'er. Rotten Belly, the old chief of the Mountain Crows, has gone under—an' damned if the council hasn't chose Beckwourth to be the new head honcho. It's true, I tell ye—no two ways about 'er."

Bridger burst out laughing. He and Beckwourth had been out tending traps the day Nigger Jim had gotten kidnapped by the Crows.

"With Beckwourth an' the Crows," Bridger chuckled, "an' Behele with the Pawnees, an' Garreaux with the Arikaras, we're fair on our way to havin' a *civilized* coon in charge of all the tribes. Now if we could just sneak one of the boys into As-as-to's place, we'd have the *Pieds Noirs* on our side, mebbe."

"Forget about Garreaux," Harris said, shaking his head. "He's bad, that one. No friend of ours. The Rees is as unpredictable as they ever was."

"All the same," Bridger insisted, "if push come to shove . . ."

"It were Garreaux an' his Injuns that put Glass an' Rose under. It's gospel, Jim."

"Come on, Mose," Milt put in, "haven't ye got any good news for us?"

"Expect I have." Harris laughed. "Milt, your brother's bringin' some guests up country with 'im. That's what I heard, now. A painter named Cat-lin, or some such, is comin' to Rendezvous to do our portraits, an' Dr. Benjamin Harrison—related to the goddamned old governor of Indiana—is comin' out here for 'is health! How about that one? Ain't all, nuther. There's this Scot nobleman, *Sir* William Stewart, filthy rich an' rarin' to spend it all. Billy Sublette's bringin' him along, too. An' probably some genuine Christian missionaries, an' more damn rotgut than's ever been known in the mountains. Right under the noses of the soldier boys. He'll get here with it, too, ye can bet on 'er."

Milt turned immediately to Tom Fitzpatrick.

"Ye feel up to a little travelin', White Hair?" he asked. "Go down country an' check on Billy?"

"Exactly what I had in mind."

Bridger, Fraeb, Campbell, Carson, and Gervais all nodded at once.

"First off," Bridger said, "if Billy don't get here before Fontenelle, we're in big trouble no matter how ye cut it. An' second off, if Billy Sublette's makin' deals with American Fur, us niggers is about to go out of business. This side of the mountains is all we got left, lads."

So it was all changing.

Joe Meek shook his head and went off hunting for a few days, mostly to be by himself and to sort things out. He rode as high into the mountains as the remaining snows would allow, bagged a pair of mountain goats, butchered them and filled his saddlebags with meat, set up camp next to a little lake, built a campfire, and stared into it.

Could be Little Salmon's Milt's kid after all. No way of tellin' yet, not from the looks of him. An' Umentucken—she ain't sayin' nothing. She steers a path between me an' Milt like she don't want to consider what's goin' to happen tomorrow nor the day after, nuther. An' me an' Milt, time was when we was just like brothers, for a fact. Now there's somethin' gettin' in the way of it.

*Umentucken, Tukutsey Undenwatsy, that's what. Gawd curse my
soul, if I wasn't so crazy in love with that gal, I'd just ride away
from the whole thing—strike out for Oregon country, mebbe, I
don't know.*

He put more wood onto the fire, lay back, and listened to a
wolf howling off across the ridges, the cries followed directly by
the yipping of coyotes.

*Coyotes runnin' with a wolf, or is it a wolf runnin' with
coyotes? Problems like that vex me. Which way is it?*

Meek cupped his hands and howled back at the animals,
howled several times.

Silence for a minute or more. And then the coyotes sent up a
terrific barking and yowling, their voices echoing back and forth
from mountainside to mountainside.

"Good eatin', brothers!" Joe yelled out—and listened as his
own voice bounced back and forth from rockslide to rockslide.

Now the animals chose to ignore him, and he laughed softly
to himself.

He stared at the reflection of the moon on the surface of the
little lake and thought about swimming out.

"Catch the moonlight if ye can, child," he said and nodded.
"Only ye can't, there's no way. By the time ye get there, she's
gone—slipped on ahead of ye."

*It don't do no good to love a woman what don't love ye back,
nuther. Mountain Lamb, she cares for this bear-killin' nigger, but
like a sister, just the way she cares for old Milt. An' damned good
to us she is, by gawd. At the first, she wanted me—she did for
sure. An' it were right, right for both of us. Guess that's when I
made my mistake—feelin' sorry for Milt, an' all. I done sent her in
to lie down with him because I loved him too. After that she were
different. An' then come Little Salmon, an' me an' Milt the pair of
us ended up with a friend instead of a lover.*

Something splashed out in the lake, and Joe wondered if it
was a big fish or an otter.

*Gawd, this coon's pure miserable. Don't know what he's
goin' to do. I could ast her to marry with me, an' she'd probably
do 'er. But then we'd have to go somewhere else. Most of the
coons figger Isabel's Milt's woman anyhow. Hell, he's the
booshway, ain't he? An' besides, he couldn't get along without her
to take care of him. That'd be the end of the mountains for Milt,
no question.*

Meek stood up suddenly, stripped off his bearskin capote and his moccasins and breeches, ran for the water's edge, dived in, and swam toward the undulating, silver reflection of the moon.

"Just like I thought," he bellowed, spitting out a mouthful of water, "it's slippin' away from me. . . ."

The Horse Creek Rendezvous began, and once again Bill Sublette won the race across the Rockies. He brought with him the various people whom Mose Harris had mentioned and a few more to boot. Joe Walker was there, heading up an exploratory expedition under Captain Benjamin Louis Eulalie de Bonneville, and the proposed destination, no less, was California itself.

"California, by gawd!" Meek said. "Maybeso this coon would like to trail along. . . ."

He sold his furs, took on supplies for the following year, and then to everyone's surprise insisted on clearing his accounts with RMF.

"No need to do that, Joe," Milt protested.

"Yes, there is too. I'm goin' to be a by gawd free trapper, Milt. She's time I struck out on my own. That's what you done years ago, an' that's why ye're the booshway an' a rich man by mountain standards. Wal, Joe Meek's got it in 'im, too."

Having settled accounts, Joe proceeded to the lodge he and Milt and Mountain Lamb and Little Salmon shared.

"Gal," he said, "now you listen to me, hear? Ye know I love ye more than even my own black soul, an' I'd do anything ye told me to, no matter what. But look here, I'm goin' to strike out on my own, an' Gawd knows where I'll end up. The spotted pony ye like—he's outside the tepee. An' the saddlebags is loaded with presents for ye an' Milt."

"Joe Meek," she protested, "I do not understand what you're saying. Why . . ."

"Has to be, is all."

"Are you leaving, Joe Meek? I will come with you, then. Wherever you wish to go, Little Salmon and I will go with you."

"Ain't in the cards, gal. Just ain't. I done thought the whole thing through."

"Joe, I will go with you no matter what you say. I will follow along behind you until you tell me to come live with you. I do not wish to live without you."

"Isabel . . ."

"Joe, I am going where you go."

"Dammit, gal, ye don't want to see the Bear-Killer bawlin'

like some fool woman, do ye? Now listen. I thought it through. Ye're goin' to marry Milt, proper like, that's what. That's what I want ye to do.''

"You want me to do that?" Mountain Lamb asked, her voice quavering.

"Damn right. That's what ye got to do. I love ye so much . . . I'm goin' crazy . . . I don't know what I want."

"Marry Sub-lette?"

"Yes, an' no arguments, nuther. An' if he won't do 'er, I'm goin' to kill 'im on the spot. I mean that, Isabel. An' then I'm goin' to put a round of galena into my own skull."

He turned and ran from the lodge, oblivious to her cries of anguish.

By nightfall Meek was blind drunk. He and Godin, after drinking together for several hours, got into a fistfight and punched each other bloody and senseless and then fell into each other's arms and passed out.

Three days later he was still drunk—sick drunk, either passed out or drinking again so that he would pass out. When a rabid wolf came wandering into the Rendezvous, attacking several men and squaws and causing the deaths of two, Joe Meek was unconscious, lying in his own vomit in the open field where Jim Bridger shot the animal. Jim looked down, figured the wolf had bitten Meek, then turned him over and saw that, beyond the bruises left by Godin's fists, the man was unharmed.

"Coon," Bridger said, "let me get ye back to Milt. Mountain Lamb'll bring ye around."

"Leave me be, Gabe," Meek managed, his voice a series of stutters and slurs. "Don't want to see nuther of 'em—never again. Don't like 'em. Don't want to be around 'em. Tell Milt to marry 'er or I'm goin' to slit 'is gawddamned throat. Leave me be, Bridge, or I'll put ye under, too. . . ."

When he awoke again, his vision blurred and his head pounding, his brother Stephen was leaning over him.

"Stevie, is that ye?" he managed. "Where am I? We back in Virginia, an' I done dreamed all this? My head hurts, Gawd it hurts. I'm sick, Steve, I'm sick. I've been havin' the damnedest dreams. . . ."

Stephen Meek dragged Joe to his feet and assisted him to a lodge, forced him to drink a full pot of coffee, and left him to sleep some more.

When he finally came out of it, Meek staggered about and demanded something to eat.

"Brother Joseph," Steve chided, "I gather you've decided to live, then. Just happen to have a kettle half-full of venison stew. . . ."

He ladled out a bowlful for Joe and handed it to him. Joe ate, willed himself to stop gagging, and finished the portion—handed Stephen the empty bowl and indicated that he wished some more.

"Hungry, is he?" Stephen grinned.

"Damned right. You heard whether that damned Milt Sublette's married Isabel yet? That's what I want to know. Hurry up with that boiled deer meat."

"The one they call Mountain Lamb?" Stephen asked. "Well, he did. Big, fancy weddin', with lots of presents. Word has it that you're the one she wanted, Joe. If you're looking for a squaw, I don't know where you're likely to find a better. That's the most beautiful woman I ever saw, Joseph, White or Colored or Injun. The boys are all sayin' that you've lost your goddamn mind, Joe. I don't understand a damned bit of it."

Meek attacked the second bowlful of venison stew and didn't look up until he was finished.

"I don't understand 'er, nuther," he said. "Stevie, what in hell ye doin' out here?"

When Joe Walker had guided Bonneville's troupe to the eastern edge of the broad salt desert that lay beyond the big lake variously known as Weber's Lake, Bridger's Pond, and Great Salt Lake, he called for a night-long forced march. Mid-morning found them amid a seemingly endless white plain glittering under the fierce August sun. A little stream shimmered its way along through the beds of rock salt, and the horses and mules had to be forced away from it—the water being bitterly saline. There was no shade whatsoever, and the temperature had risen to well over a hundred degrees.

"This is a fine place you've brought us to, Mr. Walker," Benjamin Bonneville said, sleepily drinking tepid water from his flask. "I see no way the men are going to be able to get any rest— a man would bake to death within an hour."

"Guess us coons ought to keep goin', then." Joe Walker grinned. "This nigger didn't figger on sleepin' for a spell yet anyhow."

Bonneville removed his worn officer's cap and rubbed disconsolately at the top of his bald head.

"The greatest mistake of my life was when I decided to take you under my wing. You've been leading me into hell-holes like this ever since—and I keep being naive enough to follow."

"She'll all come out lookin' good," Walker growled. "Wagh! With ye an' Zenas writin' everything down for the sake of hist'ry, them Easterners'll figger we was out for a leetle Sunday jaunt."

"Coons," Joe Meek yelled out from behind, "let's keep movin'! The horses is half-blind, an' the mules is balky. What we stopped for, Cap'n?"

Bonneville cursed under his breath, shot a final ugly glance at Walker, and gave the gesture to move forward.

They rode on into the night, reached the low rim of mountains, and made camp beside a small, oozing swamp beneath a treeless rim—the water little more than slime, but at least potable. And neither the men nor the horses and mules, at this point, were particular.

The night was cold, and Joe and his companions sat huddled about their sagebrush campfire and chewed on dried buffalo meat—meat they had taken in a good buffalo hunt over on the Seedskeedee before moving westward.

"Nothin' to drink, but at least we ain't goin' to starve for a while," Joe mused.

With no more than the idea of trailing along, Meek had approached Captain Bonneville—thinking the trip to California would be "a damned feather in a man's cap." But Bonneville, once he realized he was talking to Bear-Killer Meek, had hired him on—and Stephen and Muckaluck and half a dozen of his Flathead kinsmen as well.

Was Bonneville just looking for new trapping grounds, or was he actually in the employ of the United States government? Rumor had it that the boys in Washington City were laying plans to extend the nation's boundaries into Texas and California as well as the Oregon country. Well, that didn't make any difference to Joe Meek.

Bonneville's party now numbered forty-three men, some of them mere greenhorns, *mangeurs de lard,* and some of them, like himself and Joe Walker, experienced mountain men.

One way or another, they'd make it through to California. What would happen after that Meek neither knew nor much cared.

He had resolutely put one lifetime behind him, had left the woman he loved even if he couldn't drive her out of his thoughts, and he was determined to make a success of whatever happened.

Zenas Leonard came stumbling over to Joe's campfire, sat down, and began to ask questions. Was it true that Joe was familiar with the Mary's River? Would there be good grass along it? Were the Shuckers as harmless as he'd been told?

"Depends on what you've been told," Muckaluck said, laughing.

"As long as ye don't drink no green mule-blood," Meek added, "ye'll be all right, lad. Ye see, the Shuckers, they dip their arrowheads in rattlesnake pizen. But it don't affect ye none so long as ye ain't been drinkin' mule's blood. The red kind's okay, but leave the green stuff alone."

"Joe Meek," Leonard grinned, "you're more stuffed with buffalo dung than any man I've ever known."

"Not buffalo dung," Stephen Meek put in. "Just plain *badness*. He's been that way ever since we were kids together. It is true you're writin' a book, Zenas?"

"A journal, anyway," the young man admitted. "Maybe it'll be something for my grandchildren to read one day. Who knows— I might even manage to get it published eventually. People back East are extremely curious about what's out here."

"Tell ye what I think," Meek drawled. "The mountains'll get to ye, just like they do to most of us coons. Me, I don't figger I'll ever walk east of the Mississippi again. Another year, an' most like you'll feel the same way, Zenas. Get some sleep, my friend. It's still a far stretch to the Mary's, an' we'll be lucky to find any water that's better than what we've got hyar."

After a lengthy discussion with Joe Walker, Captain Bonneville and his two military aides turned back the way they had come, Bonneville having concluded that wisdom lay in returning to his fort on the Seedskeedee and thence on north to Snake River country. The Mexican government in California, already suspicious of the presence of any Yankees whatsoever, would be even more difficult to deal with if the expedition gave sign of somehow having been sponsored by the United States government— something Bonneville's own presence would surely indicate. Besides, with the venture well under way and with Joe Walker and Joe Meek both in on it, there was little need for Benjamin Bonneville to waste further time wandering across alkali and salt flats. Let Walker and Meek tend to the deserts and mountains and possible problems with hostile Indians. That's what they were being paid for, after all.

The mountain men moved on, and two days later they found themselves on a creek that wound its way down to a confluence with a somewhat larger stream that began, apparently, in the ranges to the north. Grass was suddenly plentiful, and thousands of waterbirds waded about in shallow swamps, nesting about the small river's margin and screeching at the approach of the riders, their wings hurtling them upward in a muffled, clattering noise.

To the southwest rose the great wall of the Ruby Mountains, the peaks still touched with snowdrifts that looked as if they might last out the season.

But an increasingly large band of Shuckers was following them now, keeping their distance, moving silently and implacably behind the expedition.

"Damn Diggers!" Joe Walker huffed. "Wagh! They ain't got nuther rifles nor horses, boys, an' they wants ours. Hell, mebbe they don't even know what rifles be. An' that's the worst kind of Injun. She'll come to a showdown soon, by gawd. That's what I think."

Meek glanced back over his shoulder and nodded.

"Persistent niggers," he said.

CHAPTER EIGHT

The Stars Fall Over California

Sierra Nevada—Mount Joseph, as Jed Smith had called the entire range.

He and Gobel and Evans crossed the mountains in May of 1826 and found themselves in a blizzard. Horses and mules fell to their deaths, and Jed and his companions stumbled onward toward a hoped-for salvation in the Nevada deserts.

The mountain range runs southeast to northwest along the edge of California—the big snowy mountains. A tipped shelf of granite overlaid in places by basalts, fifty to eighty miles across and four hundred miles long and rising to extremes of more than fourteen thousand feet in elevation. A single block of the earth's crust, geologists say, tilted upward toward the east, its westward slopes overlaid with igneous rocks and metamorphic slates and deposits of tertiary marine gravels and sands that contained more gold than anyone had ever imagined. Gold in the sands, more gold down deep in the seams of quartz that thread the gray-black diorite. Silver deposits along the east face of the range.

The largest trees in the world grow in isolated groves in the high forests—Sequoia gigantea.

Green rivers tumble down from snowfields and the glacial remnants of the last Ice Age, snowmelt foaming through long, deep canyons, the waters gathering, working their way to the big valley and forming the San Joaquin and the Sacramento, these joining and issuing into the Pacific Ocean through a broad bay where cities would one day rise.

But the gold was as yet hidden, the rivers uncharted, the forests untracked except by the Maidus, the Miwoks, the Yanas, the Yokuts, the Washos, the Monos—peaceful people who lived in a world of plentiful game and who gathered acorns and leached them and made cake and flour from them.

The women commonly went bare-breasted, their long black hair unbound, their brown skin glistening under the sun. And one girl, frightened of Jed Smith's men, screamed and ran until her heart burst and she fell dead.

*All one mountain, as Jed Smith saw it—the last and greatest
barrier to the land of California.*

The Shuckers continued to follow, sometimes like curious
children, and sometimes making noises that sounded distinctly
bellicose. Occasionally Meek could understand what they were
saying, but often not—the language was Shoshonean or closely
related to it, as he gathered.

At times the party had difficulty in finding sufficient fuel
along the little desert river. Wood was scarce, and there were, of
course, no buffalo chips. If bison had ever inhabited this strange
land, they must have vanished long since, perhaps at the time
when the waters receded. For surely, as Zenas Leonard noted in
his journal, much of the desert country was undoubtedly an
ancient lakebed or the floor of an inland sea. Great Salt Lake, as
huge as it was, must have been no more than the pitiful remnant of
a body of water of far vaster proportions. And the land that lay
along the Mary's River was apparently at the very center of a
world in which the rains had simply ceased to fall—but for what
reason? What could possibly have accounted for a climatic change
of such scope? No conceivable answer seemed to account for it—
unless the lands had been covered by waters from Noah's Flood.
Or perhaps some other huge flood that old Noah had not known
about.

Leonard shook his head and whistled, removed his cap, and
dabbed a handkerchief at his face.

Walker and Meek came riding up, and Walker was humming
to himself:

> *Old Ben Bonneville's a fine old soul*
> *With a buckskin belly an' a rubber bunghole.* . . .

"Your little verse amuses you, I take it?" Zenas Leonard
asked.

"By gawd, didn't realize what I was singin'." Walker
laughed. "Listen, young feller, we got to do something about
these damned Diggers. I tell ye, they's gettin' ready to jump us."

"Do you agree, Mr. Meek?" Zenas asked.

Joe nodded.

"Me an' Milt had trouble with 'em up in the mountains last
year," he replied. "Thing is, Zenas, these boys live off of birds

an' beavers mostly. They've seen our traps, an' they want 'em—simple as that."

"Perhaps we should give them some traps, then," Leonard suggested.

"Then they'd want more," Walker said, spitting tobacco juice. "Stick's floatin' bad now, an' she'll get worse if we give in to the Red divvels. 'Spect we should teach 'em a lesson instead. . . ."

"It might work at that," Joe Meek agreed. "Maybe we need to show 'em what a good Hawken'll do. Blow a few herons or geese out of the water while the boys is watchin'. Mebbe they'll get the idea."

That afternoon the Indians set fire to the grass downriver from the White brigade. And in the evening a delegation came in and demanded to talk with the *chief*. Walker nodded, and he and Meek confronted the band of Shuckers.

"It's like I figgered," the Bear-Killer said, shrugging. "They want traps, an' they want us to give 'em some of our *firesticks* an' show 'em how they work. In exchange for that, they'll let us go. Figure they've got us surrounded by now, I guess. The chief here says he's got about two hundred Injuns all around us, if I'm gatherin' what he's tellin' me."

"Raggedy cousins of the Shoe-shines," Walker said, nodding. "I can make out most of what they're tellin' us. But, nope, this child ain't buyin' it."

Walker lifted his rifle and fired it into the air.

At the report, the Shuckers turned and ran for their lives. But it wasn't over yet. By the next day the Indians were back, having convinced themselves that the *firesticks* were capable only of making noise.

Walker ordered a display of power, and a group of the mountain men blazed away at some ducks on the river, killing a half-dozen of the birds and of course sending the others buzzing skyward.

The Indians fled again, but the next day they set more fires and killed a couple of pack animals by means of poisoned arrows. At last the Shuckers drew their full number, now considerably more than two hundred, directly in the way of the mountain men's progress.

Walker ordered that two or three of the Indians should be shot, hoping that this would finally solve the problem. But the men's tempers were short after the weeks of harassment. When

Joe Walker fired, all the rifles came up, and gunsmoke filled the afternoon air. Meek waved his arms about and called for a cease-fire, but to no avail. Within a few moments the trappers had slain nearly fifty of the Indians, and the remainder had fled, kicking up their heels as fast as they were able.

Meek was angry, and Zenas Leonard was sick at what he considered a wanton act of butchery.

"Guess I half-agree with ye," Meek told the young man, "but this thing's gettin' on the boys' nerves pretty bad. Still, mebbe they don't feel so good, nuther. Ain't nobody in much of a mood to take skulps."

The Mary's River died in a broad sink in the desert, and Walker passed beyond it and continued west toward the distant long white wall of mountains, the Sierra Nevada—what Jed Smith had once named Mount Joseph. Beyond those mountains, the men knew well enough, lay California—a place where the snow did not fall during the winter months.

Joe Walker was of the opinion that their best chances lay in moving south, keeping to the base of the range, and skirting the extremity. The year had now run into early October. With the aspens up high already a brilliant golden color, and clouds hanging above the mountains, snows could be expected during any attempted crossing. Smith's account of the range had circulated widely among the mountain men, and, even allowing for the usual amount of exaggeration, the risk of being caught in a blizzard in the high country was evident to all.

Joe Meek, however, was willing to give the Sierras a try; and after some consultation with Walker, it was decided that Joe and Stephen and Muckaluck and his Flatheads would attempt a crossing and, God willing, rejoin Walker and the others out in the Big Valley that was said to lie beyond the Sierra Nevada.

Meek's party proceeded toward the mountains, encountered a clear, fast-flowing river—one that must also have ended out in the desert somewhere—and worked their way up into a canyon that eventually opened out into a wide glacial basin at the foot of ramparts of snow-draped granite, below which nestled a beautiful blue-green lake.

Muckaluck gazed up at the snow-hung domes and at the black clouds overhead.

"We do not go this way," he said. "Soon it will snow some more, and we will lose our horses and mules. Perhaps we could get across, but the animals cannot. Maybe we should catch up with Joe Walker and the others."

"I figure he's right, Joseph, Steve Meek agreed. "This doesn't look like much of a possibility."

Meek shook his head and grunted.

"The Bear-Killer don't tuck his tail between his legs an' run for the lodge," he said. "Let's move down out of the basin to where that river forked—take the north branch. Sure as hell, there's a way *somewhere*."

The party backtracked, rode north through high forests and meadows, over a redstone rim, and down into a wide valley that was still green even this late in the season. Bands of antelope and deer gazed at them curiously, apparently not even frightened, and thus provided easy targets and a source of fresh meat. Midway up the valley, a huge honey-brown grizzly reared up on its hind legs, wagged its head back and forth in an apparent attempt to determine what these strange animals were, men on horseback, growled several times in warning, and then moved off nonchalantly as the men stared in admiration.

"Now that was a bear!" Stephen crowed. "Why didn't you shoot him, Joseph?"

"Even b'ar medicine's got its limits." Joe laughed. "That fella must be as old as the mountains themselves. What nigger'd want to shoot such a varmint? What's the matter with ye anyway, Stevie?"

From the valley's northern end, a small river drained away westward, its canyon turning down into the mountains themselves. Joe led his men on into the canyon, the going so precipitous in places that it was necessary to lead the horses, the river winding and tumbling, the mountain walls about them now two and three thousand feet above their heads.

By early sundown a heavy rain had begun to fall, and the men strung up haphazard shelters. An old punk log, brought down perhaps by high wind a year or two earlier, provided dry wood for the campfires, and Joe and the boys relaxed as well as they were able.

"I thought you said it did not rain in California," Muckaluck complained. "I have never seen so much rain in my life, Joe."

"Snow," Meek answered. "I said it don't snow."

"What was that on the mountains, then?" Muckaluck persisted.

"It don't snow down in the valley, you iggerant savage. As it is, you'll be complainin' the day they hang ye, even if the coons is usin' a new rope."

"My people do not hang anyone. Only the Whites do that. But one day we will all act together and drive the Long Knives out of our lands. Perhaps we will make an exception for you."

"Might be good if ye did," Meek answered. "What ye think about 'er, Steve? Leave the Red heathens to their mountains an' b'ars?"

"I think this river's going to wash us right down the canyon before morning if it don't stop raining. That's what I think."

"I wish we had not come," Muckaluck said suddenly. "I miss Antoine. He is my good friend, and I miss him."

"Likely." Meek grunted.

"Do you think we will ever find our way back, Joe? Bridger and Godin and all the others, they are our friends, even little Kit Carson."

The image of a tall Shoshone woman flared in Meek's brain, the sound of her voice. She was calling to him, calling him to come back to her. . . .

The rain continued throughout the night, and by morning the river had become a howling torrent of brown water, carrying fallen trees with it, even moving the boulders in its bed. Further progress down the canyon was clearly impossible, and so Meek led his little brigade upslope to the crest of the canyon wall. But at the increased elevation the rain became snow, a heavy, swirling, wet snow that draped the big firs and pines.

"Caught betwixt the Devil an' Old Man Gawd," Joe sang out. "Keep with 'er, lads! There's flatlands an' oak trees ahead, even though we cain't see 'em yet. Just gotta keep movin' is all."

The mountains around them were no longer ice-capped peaks—just huge, rolling giants of mountains, heavily forested and seemingly endless—the back-and-forth trenches of the rivers, thick brush, fir tangles, big pines with bark plates three times the size of a man's hand.

They'd worked their way down out of snow country now and were in mixed forest—various kinds of oaks, some huge and some small, pines interspersed with cedars and firs. Rain continued to fall, and any slope whatsoever quickly became a quagmire beneath the hooves of horse and mule.

When the rain became too intense for them to make headway, the men simply holed in. But everything was sopping wet—no wood for burning. They wrapped themselves in their saturated robes and tried to sleep.

Then the big storm was past, and the sky burned cloudless blue.

From a long, oak-studded ridgecrest they looked down on the wide expanse of the Sacramento Valley, could see the Coast Range far to the west, the higher elevations limned in white. And out in the valley, thrusting up like a miniature set of Tetons, a small mountain range entirely to itself, blue gray and gleaming in the brilliant autumn sunlight.

That night, now down into a land of green grass and tules and clumps of oaks, they became aware of shooting stars streaking the night—on a far more frequent basis than any of them could remember.

"Old Man Coyote is giving us a sign of something," Muckaluck insisted.

"Could be the end of the world's comin' on." Joe Meek laughed. "Mountain Lamb, she used to tell us about how old Badger, the medicine man of her people, had predicted a time when all the stars would fall from the sky."

A silence hung in the air after Joe had spoken. It had been a long while since he'd mentioned Mountain Lamb's name, something he'd made a point of not doing. And now, suddenly, he could feel the loss of her, a tangible sensation, a dull pain that he had previously not allowed himself to experience.

Finally Muckaluck spoke.

"Why did you let Umentucken, Tukutsey Undenwatsy marry Milt? I do not understand why you did that, Joe."

"Shoot, old friend. Guess I don't understand 'er any more than ye do."

They rejoined Joe Walker's band about a hundred miles south of the little range of mountains in the center of the valley, the sacred hills called Estawm Yan, as they learned—for they had met with various groups of Indian peoples along the way, villages that belonged to the Maidus, Indians who obviously were unfamiliar with starvin' times, people who were able to live on the bounty of the land about them—small elk and deer and jackrabbits and mush made from acorns. The Indians were shy and usually avoided Meek and his men, but some of the Maidus treated them with great hospitality and claimed to remember earlier bands of Whitemen who had come into their lands. One chief had an old flintlock Hawken, the weapon badly rusted and long since nonfunctional, which he used as a kind of staff. He wore a netted hat and a tule loin covering and was able to speak a ragged, half-forgotten form of English. The Maidu chief's name was Oleli-Koto, which, Joe was gradually able to deduce, meant Coyote-Hat or Hat-Coyote. And it was from Oleli-Koto that the trappers learned of the whereabouts of their erstwhile traveling companions.

Oleli-Koto asked a strange thing. He wished to know if the Whitemen (for he did not distinguish between the Meek brothers and Muckaluck and his Flathead companions) were causing the sky to fill with fire at night.

Joe gave some foofuraw as presents to Coyote-Hat's band and continued on down the valley, crossing high-flowing rivers with especial difficulty, hunting as they went, and rejoined Joe Walker and his men near a wide, shining river they supposed must be the San Joaquin.

Walker had taken his men far south along the high wall of the Sierras in search of an easy pass without danger of the possibility of becoming marooned among the granite wastes, but they had not found what they sought. Instead, the mountains grew higher and more precipitous. When a band of Indians, close by a large, brackish lake, told Walker of a path leading westward to the Great Valley, Joe turned his men westward. Two days of toil had taken them to the summit, but what lay beyond was a seemingly endless expanse of granite crags and spires, frozen lakes, and snow-clotted forests of dwarfed evergreens. Food supplies were exhausted, and severe cold and rough terrain took their toll upon the horses as the beasts grew stiff and balky—for they were also without feed. The men were on the point of rebellion, with considerable talk of turning back and returning to Rendezvous country for the winter hunt. Only Joe Walker's iron will prevented the proposed retreat from the mountains.

When two of the horses seemed on the point of death, the animals were slaughtered, and Walker's men enjoyed a feast of horseflesh.

"Under the circumstances," Walker grinned at Meek, "it were better'n hump-rib, I'll tell ye. Until then, we hadn't had nothin' in our meat bags for three, four days."

They worked their way slowly ahead through the frozen wilderness, killed some more horses, and came at length to the limits of the snow. From atop a high, barren rim, the men gazed down at a green valley into which they were unable to descend, a valley into which waterfalls of amazing heights cascaded over sheer granite faces. But there was no way down, and so they continued doggedly westward. When one of the men was able to shoot a deer, it was a matter for celebration, and Zenas Leonard made a journal entry that read, "This was the first game larger than a rabbit we had killed since the 4th of August when we killed the last buffalo near Great Salt Lake. . . ." By this time the going was fairly easy, and Walker's brigade passed through groves of trees of gigantic size and finally down into rolling hills and thick stands of acorn-bearing oaks, a land of plentiful game and friendly Yokuts Indians. On October 31, as Zenas Leonard noted in his journal, the party reached the floor of the Great Valley of California.

"At least us coons didn't get wet," Joe Walker said, laughing. "Nary a droplet of rain until after we moved north up the valley—and then it was just easy an' gentle like."

The men exchanged tales of their wanderings, and afterward Walker produced what he claimed to be the last of his rum. He and Leonard and the Meek brothers had a snort or two in the privacy of the little tent that Walker had strung up.

Again the night sky flamed with long streamers of blue and blue-green.

"An extensive meteor shower, apparently," Leonard said. "It's been going on for four days now, and each night is more spectacular than the one before."

"The Maidus—Injuns up north of here," Meek explained, "they's worried. Think mebbe the world's endin'. Muckaluck an' my Flatheads, they been mutterin' prayers to Old Man Coyote."

"What about you, Joe?" Walker asked, clapping the Bear-Killer on the back in a rare display of friendliness and warmth. "You worried too?"

Joe looked at his empty rum cup and shook his head.

"Hell," he responded, "I done ruint my world already. Don't make this child no difference if the earth-ball turns upside down now. Just the same, I don't reckon it will. They's plenty of stars left in the sky, for that matter. Fact is, I ain't noticed a one that's missing yet—for all the fireworks."

Joe Walker growled wordlessly and then wondered if possibly, just possibly, they'd be able to buy some more rum from the Californios at Monterey.

During the night, rumbling noises came up from within the earth, and for a few moments the ground itself shook. Horses reared and screamed and went plunging about through the celestially flame-lit darkness. Walker stumbled out of the tent, caught his balance against another heave of the earth, and bellowed, "Round in the horses, boys! It ain't nothin' but the waves slappin' against the shores of the gawddamned Pacific Ocean!"

By morning the laws of terrestrial order seemed once again to have asserted themselves, and the mountain men continued their trek westward, swimming their animals across the San Joaquin River and proceeding through a range of low, rolling hills.

Once across these, they ran into a detachment of Mexican soldiers under the command of Captain Luis Branciforte, who demanded that they identify themselves and explain their purposes. Without waiting for an answer, Branciforte went on with a short harangue asserting the sovereignty of Mexican California in behalf of Governor José Figueroa and castigating all American adventurers. He then ordered Walker and his men to depart from California, back the way they had come, as soon as it was expeditious for them to do so. Otherwise, he implied, the consequences could prove serious indeed.

"*Comprende, señores*?" Branciforte asked, bowing, saluting, and, with a flourish, snapping the heels of his riding boots together.

"Aw, hell!" Walker snorted. "We ain't invadin' ye, Cap'n. Jest out lookin' for beavers is all. Say, you boys got any tequila with ye?"

Branciforte, neatly uniformed and wearing both a military saber and a brace of pistols, stared at the disreputable-looking leader of the mountain men, began to laugh, and then said, "*Todo el mundo—seguir, por favor*. Follow along behind, if you please. For now I will be your *dueño*."

Both Walker and Meek had certain misgivings about being led along by Branciforte and his men, but forty veterans of the High Shinin', they assured themselves, were easily a match for any two hundred Mexican regulars—and the captain had, after all, only twenty-five soldiers with him. And so the parade continued, down to an inland body of water, the shores of which served as pasture to numerous longhorned cattle tended by tame Ohlone

Indians, men who were either owned or employed by the San Jose Mission.

In the shallow waters of the tidal mudflats a sperm whale was stranded, a matter of great wonder to Muckaluck and the Flatheads and to nearly all the Whites as well. Fifty or so Ohlones were gathered nearby, sitting about an open fire, waiting for the huge aquatic mammal to have done with its death throes so that they could begin with the business of slaughtering it.

"Now thar's a fish what *be* a fish," Meek said to Muckaluck. "Ain't it the damnedest thing ye've ever seen?"

They rode on past, following Branciforte and presuming they were being escorted to the mission. Meek noted that Joe Walker seemed strangely calm about the entire business and wondered, not for the first time, why Bonneville had sent them into Mexican California. Did it have something to do, as a number of the men had surmised, with the possibility of California eventually becoming United States territory?

Indeed, Luis Branciforte led the trappers to the *Lagoda,* an American ship of 292 tons, anchored at the upper end of the bay, and, taking Walker and Zenas Leonard with him, went aboard. Within a short while a series of dories came ashore, and the entire troupe of mountain men were invited aboard, where John Bradshaw, the vessel's captain, entertained the men, providing food and drink and information about the local geography. San Francisco, Captain Bradshaw said, lay forty miles to the north, and Monterey, the capital of the province of California, was beyond the low ridges to the west, sixty miles distant, on the margin of the Pacific Ocean.

At length the mountain men returned ashore, and Branciforte escorted them to the San Jose Mission, where they spent the night within the walls of the adobe stockade, being treated kindly by the padres and having their evening meal brought to them by smartly costumed Ohlone women, some of them quite attractive but none of them able to converse in English.

"What in the name of gawd's balls is goin' on, Zenas?" Meek demanded from the Keeper of the Journal. "We prisoners, or what?"

"No, no, of course not, Joe. Walker delivered a letter to Bradshaw, according to plan. Everything's quite under control. In the morning we're on our way to Monterey. The ocean, Joseph. That's the only natural boundary for the United States—so we might as well take a look at it."

"Whar the governor's at—Figueroa? You sure these coons ain't plannin' on putting us coons on trial or some such?"

"No chance of that," Walker said, sitting down next to Meek, a heaped plate of food in hand. "But we've got to follow procedure. An audience with his worship, old man Figueroa, has already been arranged. These Californios ain't like the rest of Mexico. Nope, California's almost like a damned separate country. They've already had a showdown or two with the Meskin gov'ment, an' Figueroa's their boy. He's bustin' up the big church ranchos, so to speak, kind of spreadin' power around. We'll get permission to stay the winter all right, cotch beavers wherever we can find 'em."

"It'll be a few years down the line, not so many," Zenas Leonard put in, drinking wine from a flask and offering it to Meek, "and then this will all be a part of the United States. That's what Captain Bonneville has said all along. What we've got here is a basic Spanish version of medieval Europe. The Indians are slaves, little more. They're not going to fight for their overlords, not by a long shot. And the overlords, in any case, have very little loyalty toward Mexico."

"Bunch of damned theory," Meek said, growling. "I thought we come hyar to hunt beavers."

"A couple of regiments of bluecoats could take over the country, in all likelihood," Zenas insisted.

"Hell, Zenas," Walker chuckled, "I figger me an' Joe here an' a hundred of our old mountain compañeros could do the job right now—if that's what Bonneville wanted. That bald-headed bastard could be king out hyar, if he had the nerve for it. Or Cap'n Bradshaw, for that matter. You see the cannons on the *Lagoda?* Even them would be enough to blast hell out of Monterey, that's what I'm thinkin'."

Meek took another pull at the wine flask and then handed it to Walker.

"You two are damned politicians, that's what I figger," he said, grinning. "Me, all I want to do is find a good woman an' a can of good old arwerdenty—them an' beavers. Politics is for coons what never grew up in their heads. An' right now I don't feel good about bein' cooped up inside these hyar walls, no sir."

Before them rolled the great western ocean, blue and gleaming, the waves coming into the white sands of the beach in long bands of foam—and pelicans and cormorants and herring gulls gliding and swooping above the water.

"She's pretty, all right," Joe Meek said, "but the air smells funny. Damn salt water, I guess."

Seals and sea lions at the foot of the rockheads to the south of the village of Monterey, and half a dozen small sailing craft at anchor. Farther out, the *Lagoda* rode the waves, Captain Bradshaw having brought his craft around to Monterey and arrived shortly after the Walker brigade had reached the settlement.

Somewhere at the far end of the village someone was playing a guitar and singing. The voice was dulcetly female.

"Don't suppose any of these señoritas is for hire, do ye, Joe?" Walker asked, grinning, his eyes glinting with sunlight.

"Could be," Meek answered. "Ain't none of us has had a woman in quite a spell. . . ."

"Except Zenas hyar," Walker said, winking. "I saw him makin' off with that leetle gal with the big tetons, headin' for the bush, they were."

Leonard flushed, shaking his head in denial.

"Wal, we'd all best get our fill of it tonight. B'ar-Killer, it's your job to keep the men in line. I mean that, now. Everything's gone smooth as hell, so far, an' we can't afford any trouble. Tomorrow we're headin' back toward the San Joaquin. But tonight's fandango time, so let's have a good one."

In the encampment to the east of Monterey, the mountain men combed their beards and put on whatever clothing they considered their best. Their spirits were high as they departed for an evening of festivities in the little Mexican city.

Once in the village, Meek danced with several of the young women, had a standoff with an enraged boyfriend, and then, when he realized the señorita in question had highly serious eyes for him, he decided that the better part of valor lay in returning to camp. The girl was quite attractive and obviously had mating on her mind, but something inside Joe had turned off.

Umentucken, dammit, ye're the one this child wants to be with. Why'd ye have to go an' marry Milt, anyhow? All right, I know I told you to do 'er. But ye never took my advice before, so why . . . ?

Zenas Leonard was there also, apparently in a downcast mood.

"Come on, then," Meek said, pounding Leonard on the

back, "let's play draw poker for matchsticks an' rifle balls. Give us somethin' to do."

When the first of the men, singing and laughing, began to traipse back into camp well past midnight, Meek and Leonard stood outside their tent and watched. For a time meteors streaked the sky, just as they had that night out in the Big Valley, but the display was short-lived.

"Wal now, that's somethin', I should say. Maybe the world's goin' to end after all."

"No, Joseph Meek," Leonard responded. "I should say it's just beginning. This is a rich land, and its future is clearly not Mexican. One day these valleys will be among the finest agricultural areas in the world. What part we play in this, who knows?"

Meek grunted, a sound that indicated neither agreement nor disagreement.

"I'm lonely, Joe," Zenas Leonard confided. "Francesca Olivero—and she's engaged to be married. She likes me, I can tell. But we're worlds apart. There's a river running between us that's so wide we can't bridge it."

"Swim your pony across, then." Meek chuckled.

"Things don't bother you, I guess. Somehow or another, you always seem able to laugh at yourself. But me, I . . ."

Meek stared at Zenas Leonard, nodded, shrugged, and whistled softly.

Ye don't know how much gawddamned pain's inside this skull of mine. I'm like a weasel-sucked egg, to tell the truth. Empty an' useless. Everything's gone wrong, an' I caused it. Can't live with it, an' I can't ride away from it nuther.

Half a continent eastward, Mountain Lamb had also watched the falling of the stars. The strange foreigner, Sir William Stewart, and his friend Dr. Harrison, the White shaman, had explained the cause of shooting stars several nights earlier—and certainly neither of those men seemed particularly worried about what was happening in the sky in a way that had never happened before within anyone's memory.

Blanket Chief Bridger and Washakie, the powerful leader of the Wind River Shoshones, had also been present and had listened with interest. Mountain Lamb had studied the faces of these two for clues as to whether she herself should give credence to what Stewart and Harrison were saying.

Bridger had seemed to grant assent, although somewhat halfheartedly; Gabe's friend Washakie, however, had clearly not believed what the strange Whitemen were saying. Mountain Lamb had no trouble reading that message—so clearly was it imprinted upon the Shoshone chief's face.

She wondered what Milt or Joe might have thought, had they been there to listen.

It was Dr. Harrison who had convinced Milton Sublette to return to the East in order to receive proper medical treatment for his bad leg that had still, after all that time, refused to heal.

Things had happened so rapidly at Rendezvous. Joe Meek had gone crazy and had left her, had gone with the bald-headed man to the Far Water. And Milt, in the aftermath of Joe Meek's sudden removal from their lodge, had convinced her that Joe would be back, all in a matter of time, and that in the meanwhile she must marry him. In this way, Milt had explained, she would be protected—for now he, too, would have to leave her. Harrison had said so—it was the only way for him to have a chance of saving his leg. Amputation was inevitable, the doctor had insisted, without the sort of medical care that he could receive in the settlements.

She was numbed by the whole thing, heartbroken that Joe Meek would leave her, heartbroken that Sub-lette was also to go away for perhaps as long as a year. At first she had resolved to return to her father's village—to take Little Salmon and ride alone until she discovered the whereabouts of Bad Left Hand. But Milt had assured her that he would return as soon as he was able to do so and that she would have the protection of Jim Bridger and the others if it was clear and unquestioned that she, Mountain Lamb, was wife to Milton Sublette and not simply an unattached Indian woman.

At length she came to see the wisdom of what Sub-lette told her, and she consented to whatever ritual he wished to enact. And so the marriage had come off, in grand style as it turned out, with the trappers in high spirits and with the giving of many presents. Indeed, the men provided her with so many things that the lodge was not sufficient to accommodate everything—to say nothing of the total of eight horses, three of them beautiful spotted Nez Percé ponies. In addition, Joe Meek himself had left her with many gifts.

By mountain standards and by the standards of her own people as well, Umentucken, Tukutsey Undenwatsy was now a wealthy woman. Should she then later decide to return to her father's people after all, she would not be obliged to marry anyone unless she wished to do so, if indeed anyone wanted her—for such was the common fate of Indian women who had taken White trappers for husbands and then were deserted by them, left with a child with no father, a child who would live its life with only conditional acceptance among the people of the village.

And after Milt had departed at the conclusion of the Rendezvous, accompanying his brother, Bill Sub-lette, eastward to the great villages of the Whites, Mountain Lamb found herself dreaming again and again either that Joe Meek had returned or that he had simply been playing one of his tricks on her—that he had known of Milt's departure all along and had come laughing and singing back to their lodge, bringing her yet more presents.

But the days and weeks and then months drifted by, and yet she was never awakened by the strangely melodic sound of Joe Meek's voice.

From the beginning, she had not truly believed that Sub-lette would ever return to her—even though Bridger and Godin and Carson had insisted that he would.

Then they had moved to the Wind River, to a winter encampment near the river's headwaters, near the big mountain the Whitemen called Pinnacle Buttes. Chief Washakie's people were nearby, people who spoke a language only slightly different from her own, a tribe closely related to her own people who lived to the north, near the Snake River.

Almost from the beginning, Mountain Lamb began to receive the attentions of various Shoshone braves—attentions that pleased her but that she did nothing to encourage. Even Washakie himself, after visiting her lodge in the company of Bridger and Carson, had proceeded to leave several handsome gifts, some knives and some scarlet and yellow cloth, as well as numerous portions of fresh meat. And he had hinted that with only three wives, his own lodge was far too large. Perhaps she should live with him?

Mountain Lamb gave the great chief to know that she was flattered that he should look kindly upon her, but that she was the wife of Bridger's friend Sub-lette and that he would surely return to her at the next Rendezvous. Washakie could accept this. In fact, he praised her for being faithful to her absent husband. Many women in her position would not be, he told her.

After that it was never necessary for her to go hunting on her own, for Bridger and Godin and the other Whites and Washakie's

men as well kept her amply supplied with fresh meat and with
various other foodstuffs as well. Everyone came to know her, and
all treated her cordially. Indian women came to her for advice and
often invited her to accompany them—to harvest camas root, wild
plums, berries, medicinal herbs, and the like. And for Bridger and
Godin and Carson she worked at scraping and curing beaver pelts
and in return received a certain number of furs with her own
insignia affixed.

Little Salmon was healthy and growing rapidly, a year old
now and already talking and walking. The child had an uncanny
capacity for getting into things and making messes—so that at
times Mountain Lamb almost regretted that the child had ever
learned how to walk in the first place. Except that even before,
while still crawling about, Little Salmon had discovered the joys
of tipping things over and strewing articles about the lodge.

The autumn had not been a particularly good one for Blanket
Chief Bridger and his RMF partners, however—and when a
dispatch had been sent East during the moon of yellow leaves,
separate messages actually, to Milt and to Bill Sublette as well—
the news was dreary.

"Won't help old Milt to heal up," Bridger had told her, "but
won't put 'im under, nuther."

And Godin had shown her how to write her name, *Isabel*,
and she had copied the odd marks at the bottom of the letter to her
husband.

"At least," Bridger grinned, "we can tell the old hard head
that Drips an' Vanderburgh ain't followin' us around no more.
An' Wyeth's boys, they's off on their own too. We're taking in a
pretty good bunch of plew, even if prices are droppin'. Mountain
Lamb, I tell ye, things is goin' to get better when Milt and Joe get
back. I miss them coons, damned if I don't. Just the way Godin's
pinin' for that worthless Muckaluck, I guess."

"Will they really come back, Jim Bridger?" Mountain Lamb
asked.

"Course they will, pretty face. Course they will. . . ."

What was in his eyes? Did Bridger mean what he was
saying? Or did he only hope that it was true?

Other things as well, she knew, had gone wrong. There had
been several encounters with Siksika Blackfeet in the mountains
to the north, and three trappers had been killed. Several others had
been missing for some time. Then White Hair Fitzpatrick had
gone to trade with the Cheyennes and the Crows and had gotten

involved in some kind of battle between the two tribes. As a result, the Crows had chased Fitz out of the Bighorn Basin and had stolen his furs and his horses as well. Bridger was of the opinion that Sir William Stewart's quick temper had brought on the theft. The Scot nobleman had foolishly drawn a pistol on the chief of the Mountain Crows, a man whose white name was Beckwourth, close friend to old Pierre Le Blueux. Whatever had happened, the plew had shown up at the American Fur Company post at Fort Cass, and one of Fitz's men, a bad-natured sort named Red Beard Miller, was missing and presumed dead.

"Old Red Beard," Bridger had said, "he's played both sides against the middle for years, from Ashley's time on. First with us, then with American Fur. Lived with the River Crows for a couple of years, in fact—did his part to bring them coons around to McKenzie's side. Wal, if he's gone under, it ain't no great loss, not as I figger it. Shore wisht we had them ponies back, though. Mebbe we'll have to go horse-thievin', just like the Injuns. . . ."

But now Umentucken was watching the stars fall, the sky blazing with strange lights, streaks of blue-white that continued to glow in the air long after they had ceased to be brilliant. She thought about the magic lights that hung in the northern sky during the winters, glowings that would sometimes appear night after night and at other times would come only once or twice all winter.

"Reflections from Old Coyote Man's lodge in the Spirit World," her father had told her when she was still a child.

When such lights appeared, the medicine men would build a fire in the great fire circle and sit up until very late, humming and chanting and studying the glowing patterns that sometimes seemed to be virtual curtains of fire in the sky.

Mountain Lamb wondered if Dr. Harrison and Sir William Stewart had explanations for those lights as well—or if anyone in the world truly knew why such things happened.

Old Coyote Man, is this something you are doing? Is this truly the signal that the world is ending and that a new world will emerge? The old stories tell us it has happened before, perhaps it has happened many times. But can my two men see this firefall also? They are far away from me now, Coyote Man. Are the same things above them as are above me now? Or is it only here that the heavens flare so? If they have also seen these things, Old Man Who Does Everything, then could you not tell them that Umentucken, Tukutsey Undenwatsy is very lonely? Could you not tell them that I wish them to return to me, that I would be a better woman to both of them, that we would once again be happy together in our lodge?

Fires blazed in the heavens. Great burstings of light, spreading, showering down, glowing so that the sky was filled with strange, inchoate images that resembled many things and yet nothing at all. Explosions and whistlings that seemed to come almost as indecipherable answers to her questionings.

If it is not possible for both of them to return, then perhaps one of them? Bring Joe Meek back to me, Old Man Who Does Everything. I do not ask for myself alone—Little Salmon must have his father to teach him those things that only the father can teach his son. Even if this is the time when everything in the world is changed, that is still true. I wish for my son to live and to grow strong and to be a man and to have children of his own. That is the way it has always been, that is the way it must be now also. I am even willing to go into the Spirit World and my dead body lie out in the forest to be torn by wolves and badgers if that will bring Joe Meek back to us. I love him, and yet I have never told him that Little Salmon is his son. I was wrong—is that why you have taken him from me? I love him. I wish to lie down with him once again.

The sky grew quiet now, and the stars that gleamed down were the same stars that Mountain Lamb had always remembered. That was the way the two Whitemen had said it would be—and yet how did they know? Perhaps they did not know—had only guessed—had only hoped that it would be so.

And along the east, beyond the long shoulder of the mountain, a faint grayness had begun.

False dawn, first dawn, she thought. *The morning will be here soon. And before long it will be the shortest day. After that the days will grow longer once more. The great storms will come, but eventually they will melt, and the new grass will come up from the earth.*

CHAPTER NINE

A Message From Gotia

Old Coyote Man was wandering around, but then he grew very tired. His claws were worn to nubs, and half the teeth in his mouth were broken.

"It is hateful to grow old," he said. "I do not like it at all. Where are my grandchildren? I used to be able to depend on them, but now they have gone away to raise families of their own."

A young bull buffalo approached Old Man, sat down, and listened to Coyote's complaints for a long while.

"Well," the buffalo said, "I can make you young again. You'll still be an old coyote on the inside, but I can give you the body of a fine, strong buffalo."

Old Coyote Man laughed and asked, "How can you do this thing?"

So they went to Bear Butte and ran around in circles until they both fell down into a ravine. When Old Coyote Man got up and stared at his reflection in the water, he realized that he had been turned into a buffalo calf.

"Thank you," Calf-Coyote said.

But the buffalo turned away from him.

"I have no time to amuse children," he said.

Calf-Coyote snorted and ran. He wallowed in mudholes, and he ate all the grass he wanted. It was good, he decided, not to have to hunt.

Seasons passed, and Calf-Coyote grew bigger and stronger all the time. He found a young buffalo woman and copulated with her. He was not even unhappy when she kicked him in the face.

Then one day he met an aged coyote out on the prairie.

"I can help you," Calf-Coyote said. "Come with me to Bear Butte."

When they got there, the two of them ran around in circles and finally fell down into the ravine together, raising a great cloud of dust in the process.

But when they opened their eyes and stared at their

reflections in the water, all they saw were two old, ragged, toothless coyotes.

The camp dogs cried out a frenzied warning, and Washakie's Wind River village of Shoshones and mountain men was immediately galvanized into action. Men stormed out of their lodges, rifles in hand, to see what the disturbance was all about.

Early-morning redness glinted from the great uplift of Pinnacle Buttes, the light reflecting and glittering from patches of snow between the spires.

Mountain Lamb rose immediately, drew the robes carefully back around Little Salmon, and moved quickly to the lodge entrance. Pulling the flap, she could see warriors hurrying about, seemingly in all directions. Jim Bridger and Washakie stood together across the way, the two leaders staring westward.

The dogs continued to bark for a few moments and then grew still.

Three riders were entering the village, two young warriors and an older man, the apparent leader. He was dressed in full regalia, his face and forearms carefully painted—a short, powerfully built man whose dress and bearing proclaimed him an accomplished warrior.

Washakie's men came up on either side of the trio, making a show of force but otherwise holding their distance.

The lead rider drew his big Appaloosa stallion to a halt and called out in a booming voice.

"I am Elk-Striker of the Goshute Shoshones! I bear a message from Bad Left Hand to his brother, Washakie. Has Old Coyote Man led me to the right village?"

A chill passed through Mountain Lamb as she recognized her one-time suitor, the warrior she had stabbed as a means of discouraging his unwanted attentions. Elk-Striker, her father's closest friend. . . .

What message could this be from Mauvais Gauche? Had Elk-Striker, in fact, come looking for her?

She watched as Washakie and Jim Bridger walked casually toward the three mounted Shoshones. She saw Washakie's men draw back in deference both to this bold intruder and to their own leader.

Elk-Striker made the hand sign for peace, and Washakie gestured the signal for welcome. Then Elk-Striker dismounted, and he and Washakie made their formal embraces.

What was the meaning of this surprising visit?

Mountain Lamb turned, reentered her lodge, and knelt at Little Salmon's side. The child was still sleeping quite peacefully, and Mountain Lamb ran her fingers gently over the bridge of the boy's nose.

She waited, none too patiently, in her lodge, nursing Little Salmon as she did so and taking keen pleasure in the sensation of the child's greedy mouth sucking at the nipples of her breasts. But sometimes the small teeth would clamp down too tightly, and Mountain Lamb would pull away and shift the child from one breast to the other.

Joe Meek liked to do that too. I was very puzzled the first time he did it, and I wondered if maybe his mother had weaned him too early. White women do not like to nurse their little ones—that is what I have heard. Then I began to like it also.

At length the child was sated and seemed content to sleep some more. Mountain Lamb gently placed him back on the sleeping pallet and pulled the robes around him. Even with the lodge fire rekindled, it was still cold. Soon it would warm up, and then the child would awaken once again.

Fifteen moons, she thought, *and how quickly he grows. Now that he knows how to talk, I will never have any peace again. But when he is older, it will be different then. Then I will have someone, even if Sub-lette and Joe Meek never come back. We will be all right, Little Salmon and I.*

But as she looked ahead to the years of the boy's growing up, the thought that the child would have no father was impossible to deal with.

Idly she toyed with the idea of taking another husband, perhaps even someone from her father's village. Perhaps even Elk-Striker himself—supposing, of course, that the old warrior still had eyes for her.

Was that possibly the reason he had come, a long ride, and in winter? Or was it something else, a warpath perhaps? The need for some new alliance between the northern and southern Shoshones?

"How could my father even know that I am living here?" she said aloud.

But the question answered itself. Washakie's people, after all, retained their contacts with their cousins to the north. And, in any case, if a thing happened at the summer Rendezvous, word of it was eventually spread throughout the mountains, from band to band and from tribe to tribe.

The daughter of Mauvais Gauche had been living with Bear-Killer and Milt Sub-lette. Bear-Killer went crazy and rode away with Joe Walker. Then Sub-lette married Umentucken, Tukutsey Undenwatsy and left her because he had a bad leg and thought that only the Whiteman's medicine could heal him. She is there in Washakie's village, living in a lodge by herself, and the only man she has is her young son.

Yes, Mauvais Gauche would know. And no doubt he had known all along what had happened to her and what she was doing. Yet he had made no attempt to get a message to her, until now—if indeed that's what Elk-Striker's business was about.

But neither had she, in fact, made any attempt to get in touch with her father. There had been hard words at the time of their parting.

You must leave the village with them and never return again for so long as I am alive. . . .

But when he had seen that she intended to leave with Meek and Sub-lette, then he had softened toward her—had embraced her.

I did not mean what I said . . . I did not mean that part at all. . . .

Why, then, had Elk-Striker come to Washakie's village? Having heard that her two Whitemen had left her, did he now intend to renew his suit? Would he offer presents and beg her to come live with him? Perhaps something had happened to his two wives, and now he hoped that she would be persuaded.

"This is foolishness," she said aloud. "No man in his right mind would ever wish to marry a woman who had stabbed him. He would always be afraid to go to sleep at night."

She rose from the cushion upon which she had been sitting, and had already taken a couple of steps toward the entryway when she heard the scratching on the leather flap.

She prepared food for Elk-Striker and his two young companions, men her own age and with whom she had grown up in Gotia's village: Caribou Hoof and Buzztail. Even before she had left her own people, these two young men had distinguished themselves as warriors, having stolen horses from the Blackfeet and having struck coup in a battle against the Pun-naks, the war-like tribe who spoke the language of the Shoshones but who were allied with the Blackfeet. Each, at one time or another, had suggested that she might wish to go to the willows with him, propositions made in such a fashion that she was required to do no more than to smile and shake her head. Each had grinned and had promised that he would ask again later, *after you have begun to bleed like a woman.*

"Yes," she had said. "After that happens."

She had already been in her sixteenth year at the time, but such had been the willful pretense, satisfactory both to her and to them.

Little Salmon stayed close by his mother as she prepared coffee and pemmican balls, as she warmed up a pot of venison stew from the previous evening's meal. Only when she served the food did he approach the three men and demand to know which one of them was his father.

The three laughed and glanced at one another and at Mountain Lamb.

"I will be your father—if Umentucken will have me as her husband," Buzztail said, chuckling.

For this remark he drew a hard stare from Elk-Striker.

"Then who are they, Mother?" Little Salmon asked.

"Quiet, child," Mountain Lamb said, a casual sternness in her voice. "Elk-Striker. When you entered the village, I heard you say you had a message from Mauvais Gauche—for Washakie. Am I permitted to know what this message is?"

"Everyone in Washakie's village heard him say it," Caribou Hoof said, chuckling. "Elk-Striker's voice is as loud as the thunder. I almost turned my pony about and rode for home."

"Sometimes when he shouts like that, the rain begins to fall," Buzztail agreed.

"Ignore the young ones, Umentucken," Elk-Striker said. "It is bad for an older man to have to make a long journey with two warriors who can only amuse themselves by talking all the time. Next time I ride with them, I will cut their tongues out first so that I do not have to listen to their babbling. Yes. Your father's message is for you as well as for Chief Washakie. And it is a serious message that he has sent. I am almost afraid to tell you."

"I wish to know. Tell me now."

"The chief is very sick. He has been sick for more than two moons, and he has grown very thin. You would recognize him, but he would seem much changed to you. Neither Badger nor Raven's Beak has been able to help him, and now he has decided that it must be time for him to go to the Spirit World. And that is why he has sent me to find you. Bad Left Hand wishes to see his daughter again before he dies."

"What is . . . wrong?" Mountain Lamb gasped, a terrible, cold, heavy weight seeming to settle over her shoulders. "Does he have the Whiteman's disease that killed my mother?"

"It does not seem to be like that," Elk-Striker answered. "It is strange. Sometimes I can tell that he is hungry, and yet he refuses to eat. His spirits are good, and he does not sleep any more than he ever did. But he continues to grow thin. I almost believe that it is all because he has decided to die."

"I do not understand."

"No one understands," Buzztail said. "Bad Left Hand is a great chief, but he is very strange. I even thought that when I was a young boy. But perhaps you can understand, since he is your father, Mountain Lamb."

"No," she repeated. "I do not know why he would wish to die. Those in his lodge . . . are they well, Elk-Striker?"

"Yes," the scarred, thick-muscled old warrior said, nodding. "Everyone is well. Plum Bush and the others are all in good health. And little Frog-Catcher is growing rapidly. He is even able to ride one of your father's ponies now, though sometimes he falls off. Bad Left Hand takes a great interest in him, and has made him a small bow and arrow."

"I do not think Bad Left Hand will die," Buzztail said. "Whatever he is doing, he still seems as strong as ever to me. He will not die until after his son has grown up. That is what I think."

"Elk-Striker?" Mountain Lamb asked, turning back to the older man.

"I hope my young friend is right. This will be the first time in his life, but perhaps it is so. Bad Left Hand has told me that he will die soon, and that is why he has sent me and these two noisy ones to find you. It was not because your Whitemen have left you, Mountain Lamb. You must not think that. It is true that we have heard what happened, but that is not the reason we have come. No, your father wishes so see his daughter again before he goes into the Spirit World."

"Then I will go to him," Mountain Lamb answered. "I love him very much. Do you know that, Elk-Striker? Only I think he wished me to be his son instead of his daughter. I am very glad to hear that Frog-Catcher is growing up strong and healthy. My father must be very pleased to see it happen. Then. . . ."

Her voice broke off, and she had to blink back the tears that had started to her eyes.

"What is it, Umentucken?" Caribou Hoof asked, starting to rise from where he was seated.

"No," she said. "I am all right. But this has come so suddenly. I . . . Then why would my father wish to die? It cannot be that. I think he must have the lung disease, just as my mother did. Let us leave today. My lodge will stay here, I will not take it down. It must be here when Joe . . ."

Elk-Striker squinted at her, looked puzzled.

"Never mind," she said. "I will need to pack only a few things. I will take my pony and one pack animal. You did not bring any packhorses with you?"

"No," Elk-Striker said. "I wished to find you as quickly as possible, for it is that time of year when heavy snows can come with no warning. Perhaps we should have brought extra horses with us, for then we could have switched from one medicine dog to another when the first horse grew tired. But that is not what we did."

"That is why he brought us along," Buzztail said. "So that we could do the hunting for him. He did not want to have to carry meat with him."

"These two do not even know which end of a rifle to shoot with." Elk-Striker sighed. "They would have starved to death if I had not been with them."

"Give me just a little time," Mountain Lamb said. "I will be ready to go in a short while. First I must speak to Washakie's wives and to my friend Bent Feather. Then I will be ready. Where is our village now—is it south of Snake River or north?"

"North," Elk-Striker replied. "Mauvais Gauche has made winter encampment at the foot of the mountains on Big Lost River."

By nightfall Mountain Lamb and her three Shoshone kinsmen had left Washakie's village behind, having crossed the low pass to the west of the Wind River drainage and having come down into the canyon of the Gros Ventre River. Sunset blazed over the high ranges, and pale fire burned on the snows of Doubletop Peak to the southwest, with lesser lights glinting from the crowns of Sheep Mountain in the distance and the Pyramid due west of their encampment on a level shelf covered with sparse timber and meadows some several hundred feet above the churning waters of the stream.

"Here we are safe," Elk-Striker said. "We will not be surprised by any band of renegade Utes. Those people have no sense of decency. That is what I think. It will be very cold tonight, and we will need to build a good fire."

"If there are any renegade Utes," Buzztail remarked, "they will see our fire up here on the mountainside and come to scalp all of us."

"You see how these young warriors are, Umentucken?" Elk-Striker asked. "They speak before they think. Does the foolish one believe he can see the river trail from where we are?"

"Of course not," Buzztail said quickly. "Already it is too dark to see the river."

"You could not see the river even if it were broad daylight," the old warrior said, laughing. "And that is why no one on the river trail will be able to see our fire, so long as we do not burn the entire forest. But I do not believe the Utes will be out looking for us in any case. Why should they? I think they are far away, at Bear Lake perhaps, and warm inside their lodges."

"I think Elk-Striker wishes his two slaves to gather the firewood," Caribou Hoof grumbled. "That is why he makes a big issue out of nothing. Next he will wish us to cook his meal for him too."

"I will do that," Mountain Lamb volunteered. "I think all three of you like to play these word contests. Come, let us hurry. We will wish to be on the trail early in the morning."

Soon the fire was burning nicely, with chunks of resin-filled wood popping and snapping and throwing off curls of dark black smoke. Mountain Lamb carefully spitted small chunks of venison and set some cakes of camas flour to steaming by the fire's margin.

Elk-Striker's eyes were upon her almost constantly, and Mountain Lamb's thoughts grew troubled. Would her father's old friend now renew his suit, the suit that had ended so disastrously two and a half years earlier? Sub-lette and Meek were both gone, and she had been left with a child. Such, as all knew, was often the way of relationships between the mountain men and their Indian wives—and so Elk-Striker would believe, naturally enough, that she had simply been deserted and left to fend for herself and her young son. Under normal circumstances, Elk-Striker would never be one to take in such a woman and with her the responsibility of raising a half-breed child. But he had cared for her once, and his friendship with Bad Left Hand all but dictated that he offer her a place in his lodge.

Mountain Lamb understood all this and appreciated it. But for the same reasons that she had rejected Elk-Striker in the first place she would have to reject him again. No, it would never be possible for her to return permanently to her father's village.

Am I being foolish, full of pride, stubborn? That is what my father often told me. And it is true—I do not believe that Sub-lette will ever return to me. He would if he could, for he loves me. But his brother and his family will never let him. I do not know why the leg refuses to heal, but nothing has helped. It is the way of things. I must accept what has happened, for there is nothing else that I can do. Bear Woman bore a child to the Whiteman called Red Bull, and he left her—he left her even without knowing that he had fathered a child. But she has managed to survive on her own—she has not been forced into taking a husband she does not wish. Her power with medicine is respected by all, and her son is accepted by his people. Perhaps I too could do such a thing.

She spread out a worn leather mat, piled the food upon it, and nodded to the three men.

But not in my father's village. Bridger and Washakie and Carson and the others—they are my people now. I am one of them, and that is where I wish to live. Little Salmon will grow up to be one of them.

Little Salmon was, at the moment, sitting on Buzztail's lap, and the warrior was cutting off small portions of meat for him—holding the child awkwardly, but at the same time rather evidently pleased with himself.

Elk-Striker tore off a chunk of meat, chewed, swallowed, and wiped at his mouth. Then he grinned.

"See?" He chuckled. "Buzztail is trying out fatherhood. Already he is thinking of the son he may one day have. . . ."

Buzztail looked embarrassed, but Mountain Lamb smiled.

Caribou Hoof burst out laughing, caught himself, and attempted to put on a more serious face.

Little Salmon stopped eating and looked about, puzzled, but nonetheless pleased that he was momentarily the center of attention.

The meal was finished quickly, and the Shoshones spread out away from the fire and pulled their robes about them. Mountain Lamb took the opportunity to nurse her son, not having wished to do so in front of the three men. Among her own people, the act of nursing a child was performed openly enough, but she had been with Sub-lette and Joe Meek long enough to have adopted many of their ways. And from the beginning it had been obvious to her that both of the mountain men were conspicuously ill at ease when she undertook to nurse the child, though they both pretended otherwise. So after a time Mountain Lamb had begun to give the boy suck when the two men were out of the lodge—unless the child's hunger cries dictated otherwise.

She had just finished and had lulled Little Salmon to sleep when she became aware that someone was crouched next to her. She felt for the horse pistol that Milt had given her and then turned slowly toward where she sensed the man's presence.

It was Elk-Striker.

"Are you awake?" he asked.

"Yes."

"Umentucken, this is difficult. But there is something I must tell you. You know that Bad Left Hand and I have been on many warpaths together, so now you must listen to my words. Are you completely awake, Mountain Lamb?"

She let go of the pistol and sat up slowly so as not to disturb the sleeping child.

"I am awake. What do you wish to say to me, Elk-Striker?"

"Once I loved you and wished you to be my wife," he said, speaking slowly, picking his words. "This is the third winter since that time, and much has happened. I still care for you, Umentucken. That is the truth, and I admit it. I did not think I would after so long, but as soon as I saw you, I began to feel just as I did before."

"I am sorry," Mountain Lamb replied. "I do not wish to make you unhappy."

"I know that. And you are the daughter of the one man that I myself love most in the world—and that is why I set out to find you so that you would go to him. He asked me to do this thing, and I was glad to do it."

"Thank you. I thank you for that, Elk-Striker. But . . ."

"No. Let me finish what I must say. You have lived with two of the Whitemen and have married one of them, but now they have both left you. I would do anything for Bad Left Hand and for you also, Mountain Lamb. But I must tell you this. I am a wealthy man. I have taken many coups, and I have a fine herd of horses. I am also very good at trapping, and I sell the furs to the English Whitemen."

"Elk-Striker is a great warrior. I know you care for me, and I never meant to kill you that time. I was young then, and I acted in a crazy way. But even now it is still . . ."

"Let me finish, Mountain Lamb. Even when you were a little child, you would never let anyone finish what he was saying. Do you remember that I held you in my lap when you were very small, just as Buzztail was holding your son tonight?"

"I do not remember. . . ."

"Well, it is true. But this is what I am trying to tell you. It is proper for a wealthy man to have several wives, if that is what he wishes. So it is with me. I have married three more times since you left our village. I have five wives now, and that is all my lodge will hold. Now I think that you must find a younger man."

Mountain Lamb began to laugh, softly at first and then more loudly, until Little Salmon stirred, his small hands clutching at her dress.

"Quiet, quiet, Umentucken. You will waken the others. I did not wish them to know I had come to talk with you."

"Five wives?" Mountain Lamb gasped, hardly able to contain herself. "Either you will live forever, or else they will exhaust you totally and you will die in your sleep. I am pleased for you, Elk-Striker. No, do not worry about me. For a woman, I am also very wealthy. You saw my lodge. And I think my husband will return to me. He said he would, and I believe that he will. Go get some sleep now. Five wives, Elk-Striker?"

The old warrior was chuckling and nodding.

Then he was gone, disappearing into the shadows. Mountain Lamb turned over once more, drew the buffalo robes up over her head, and pressed her lips to Little Salmon's forehead. The child murmured something indistinguishable, and then his breathing became regular once again, and he slept soundly. Mountain Lamb lay awake for a time longer, relieved at Elk-Striker's good fortune, if good fortune it was, and relieved as well that this one problem, at least, would not have to be dealt with.

As she drifted into sleep, she heard the words *Joe Meek.* It was her own voice.

The weather was deteriorating rapidly, and by the time the small caravan had reached the Snake River Plains, a light snow had begun to fall. As the hours passed, the snowfall intensified, and by nightfall of that day, the fifth since they had left Washakie's village, their horses were struggling forward through a windblown torrent of whiteness, already drifting to depths of three feet in places.

"We must find shelter," Elk-Striker insisted. "This storm only gets worse. By morning it will bury us alive."

"It is growing dark rapidly," Mountain Lamb said. "Soon we will not even be able to tell which direction we are traveling."

"We should turn south, back toward the river," Caribou Hoof declared. "There are willows and elders close by the water—the trees will give us some protection."

"No, the other way," Buzztail said. "I know this place. Just to the north there's a rimrock with caves in it, small ones, holes in the rock, but big enough for four big Goshutes and one very small one. Do you know the place I mean, Elk-Striker?"

"Yes!" the old warrior called out, his affirmation nearly lost in the keening of the wind-driven snow. "I killed a big white bear among those rocks many years ago. Buzztail is right. It is probably the first time in his life. On a good day it would be less than an hour's ride from here. But today it will take much, much longer. Even by darkness we will be able to find those rocks, so long as we don't get turned completely around. It is a long rim, and we cannot miss it. It will tell us when we get there."

They turned their ponies northward, at an angle to the blown snow now instead of directly into the force of it. But even as they plodded along, the horses having to struggle desperately at times, Mountain Lamb was aware that the temperature was rapidly dropping. She clung to the reins of her pony with one hand and clutched at the buffalo robe she had pulled about her shoulders with the other.

"I'm hungry, Mother," Little Salmon managed from within the protecting folds of the heavy robe, his voice barely audible.

"Soon," she answered. "We will be there soon. . . ."

This is not a good day to die, not good at all. I am not ready for this to happen. I cannot let it happen.

Then, after what seemed an interminable interval, the little band of Shoshones became aware that the terrain was rising, the snow-blanketed earth rocky and broken.

"This is the place!" Buzztail called out. "I will go on ahead and find a place of shelter."

"We will all go together," Elk-Striker said. "How would I ever find my way back to the village of Mauvais Gauche without you to guide me? If you go into the storm alone, you will certainly get lost and freeze to death. Then none of us will get home—

because we will have no leader. Have you thought of that, Buzztail?"

"Listen to what Elk-Striker says," Mountain Lamb insisted. "He is wiser than the rest of us put together. We must do as he says."

"I tell you I can find a good place," Buzztail persisted. But the tone of his voice indicated that he had accepted the older warrior's judgment.

They led their ponies upslope, fighting against the dark weight of snow, stumbling at times, the horses stumbling forward also. Buzztail took Little Salmon from his mother's arms, hoisted the child onto his shoulders, and moved forward.

Then the long shelf of high rocks rose before them, its presence felt more than seen, a darkness held within a greater darkness. The Shoshones moved along the base of the rim, searching for cave or crevass or overhanging stone—anything that might provide a degree of shelter from the cold wind and stinging wetness.

An hour or more they struggled along, not even attempting to speak to one another, pulling the recalcitrant ponies, their hands numb, their faces nearly without sensation.

Then they were out of it—the hard presence of the wind vanished. They pulled in against a smooth face of stone, the rock free of snow, and groped forward, inward, away from the keening blast of the storm.

Caribou Hoof managed to ignite a pitchy torch, and the sputtering flames revealed jagged walls of lava stone, a channel-like tube leading back under the rim, a protected area large enough to accommodate both humans and animals.

The ponies snorted, suddenly in better spirits, snuffled about in search of edible vegetation, found none, and began to stamp their hooves on the cindery floor of the hollow.

"First Old Coyote Man has given us the storm, and now he has given us this hole in the mountain," Umentucken said, smiling through lips that were still without feeling.

"Old Man is like Buzztail," Elk-Striker agreed. "He never pays any attention to what he is doing. We must all huddle together now and hope that the feeling comes back into our hands and feet. We cannot build a fire because there is nothing to burn. But we will be all right if we all get under the robes together."

"My stomach hurts, Mother," Little Salmon complained.

Mountain Lamb took her child and drew him to her.

"Do not cry, do not cry. I will nurse you now. Everything will be all right now, little one. Then we must sleep and wait for the morning."

It was nearly dawn when Mountain Lamb awoke from a dream, half-believing that she was back inside her own lodge, with Joe Meek and Milton Sub-lette both sleeping close to her. Then she heard the restless lip-flutterings of the horses, and she remembered who these men were whose bodies pressed close about her. She reached down involuntarily for Little Salmon, the child pressed tightly to her abdomen and sound asleep.

Something was changed.

She drew the robe away from her face and stared into the darkness—aware only then that the temperature had unaccountably risen, that the air inside the cave was in fact almost warm.

A white burst of illumination revealed the cave mouth and the interior walls as well, even the lank forms of the horses. Then, within a few moments, a long, heavy rattle of thunder came wheezing through the cave, a sound like some gigantic bear groaning heavily in its winter sleep.

"Old Man has seen the error of his ways," Elk-Striker whispered. "He has remembered you, Umentucken, Tukutsey Undenwatsy. You do not remember, but I remember. This same thing happened on the night of your birth. A Melting Wind has come to save us. Our Umatilla friends call it the Chinook."

"You are awake?" Mountain Lamb asked, startled at the old warrior's words. "Yes, I can feel it. The air feels like . . . springtime."

"We are all awake now," Buzztail complained. "I suppose our great leader will now wish to get up and do a rain dance. But I wish to sleep some more. My feet are still cold."

"What is happening?" Caribou Hoof demanded, sitting up suddenly and reaching for his rifle.

"A dream came to me is all," Elk-Striker said softly as he turned to one side beneath the pile of robes and prepared to sleep once more. "I have dreamed that the snow all melted, and only the two young men starved to death. That is all."

Mountain Lamb laughed, shaking her head in the darkness.

Again the white blush of lightning, and again the long roar of thunder.

"I am hungry," Buzztail said. "I think I will investigate what's in the saddlebags."

"Go out and find firewood while you're at it, then," Caribou Hoof suggested. "Build us a big fire, and perhaps Elk-Striker will make us a pot of good broth when the morning comes. Either that, or be silent and let me sleep."

Little Salmon pressed more tightly to Mountain Lamb's midsection but did not awaken.

And then the only noises were those of the restless shiftings about of the ponies and the sustained and continuous rumblings of thunder.

The Melting Wind brought with it a warm and insistent rainfall, and the snowcover seemed to disappear as if by magic. As Mountain Lamb stared down from the entrance to the lava cave, stared off across the seemingly endless near-flatness of the Snake River Plains, she could fancy that the blanket of whiteness was disappearing before her eyes.

Buzztail came up behind her and stood silently for a time before speaking.

"It is only three days of riding to the village now, if all goes well—and Old Man does not change his mind again. It is good to pay reverence to this god, for otherwise he makes bad things happen. Sometimes he does anyway."

"The snow will soon be gone," Mountain Lamb agreed, "but then all the creeks and little rivers will be flooding. And we must still cross the Teton and the branch the Whites call Henry's Fork. Then Camas Creek and Beaver Creek. I remember all of this. Is the village in the same place it was five years ago, the new-grass time when the Piegans attacked our village and my father and Elk-Striker and the other men drove them away?"

"Yes, that is the spot," Buzztail said. "The same place. Fifteen miles to the south of where Big Lost Creek disappears into the rocks. You remember well, Mountain Lamb."

"How could I forget such a thing? I had only left the coming-of-age lodge the night before, and I was still half-afraid that Nunum Bi, the evil dwarf, would grab hold of my hair. You and Caribou Hoof were still boys then—and all of you were playing kickball with the buckskin stuffed with rabbit hair. And that was when Old Badger the prophet suddenly began to shout that the Piegans were going to attack us."

"Caribou Hoof and I had already been on more than one horse-stealing venture," Buzztail declared, his pride up. "But that is when it happened. And right after that, two of the scouts came riding in with news that the Piegans were only an hour's ride away from the village. But when they reached us, we were ready for them."

"And you scored your first coup that day," Mountain Lamb said, nodding.

Buzztail, rather obviously pleased that Mountain Lamb should remember his victory, put his hand to his forehead and gazed off across the plains, as if searching for possible enemies.

"Where are the Foolish One and the Beautiful One?" came a deep voice from inside the cave. "Now the meal is ready, and not enough people to eat it all."

Buzztail and Mountain Lamb glanced at each other and smiled.

"I asked him once to show me which of his scars is the one you gave him, Umentucken. But he wouldn't. Did you really cut him with your knife?"

"I was foolish then," she answered. "But he tried to force me to marry him, and I did not wish to do that. He is different now also. He is a very good man, I think."

"Five wives." Buzztail grinned. "That is probably too many even for Elk-Striker. But maybe that is why he is so much easier to get along with now."

"I will eat everything myself, then!" came the voice from within the cave.

By noon the heavy snowfall of the preceding afternoon and night was nearly gone, with only large patches remaining here and there on areas of higher ground. The warm rain continued to fall, and the Shoshones made their way northward to the Teton River. This stream was indeed running much higher than normal, and yet the crossing was made without undue difficulty, despite the increased force of the current.

The following day the rainstorm abated, and great blue fractures appeared in the cloud cover, with bursts of pleasant sunshine coming through. The snow was entirely gone, and crickets and tree frogs were singing loudly as the group made camp that evening.

The following day they came to Beaver and Camas creeks, just at the confluence of those two streams, and proceeded on to Mud Lake.

With an early start the next morning, and with a sustained march throughout the day, it would be possible to reach the

Goshute village by nightfall or shortly afterward. Elk-Striker discussed the matter with his companions, and finally they all decided that it would be better to make one more camp—so as to be able to enter the village at mid-morning. An entry by night could well result in confusion and the possibility of their being mistaken for prowling enemies.

"Our people fear the darkness more than they need to," Elk-Striker said. "Perhaps we would be wise if we ceased to frighten the children with stories about the bad muguas, the evil spirits and the Nunum Bi dwarfs and the red-haired cannibals and all the rest of it. And yet we have always told these stories, and that is the way of things."

"Anyway," Caribou Hoof agreed, "it is best that we do not frighten the people and cause them to murder us before they realize who we are."

"That would not be a problem," Buzztail said, shrugging. "When we get a mile or two from the village, Elk-Striker could begin singing. His voice is so loud that everyone would know who was coming."

"Or else they would ambush us and throw rocks at us to keep him out of the village," Caribou Hoof suggested.

Elk-Striker turned toward Mountain Lamb and raised his palms in a gesture of futility.

"Why did I agree to let these two Foolish Ones come with me?" he asked.

At mid-morning of the second day, the party entered the village of Bad Left Hand. A swarm of children and dogs came running out to meet them, and Elk-Striker stood tall in his stirrups and waved to one and all.

Suddenly the entire village was aroused, the people laying aside whatever tasks they were involved with and coming quickly to welcome those who had returned.

The village was clearly not in mourning, Mountain Lamb noted with a terrific sense of relief, for she had half-supposed that her father might have died during the time it had taken Elk-Striker and his two young friends to find their way to Washakie's encampment and to return with her.

Mauvais Gauche was still alive, then.

Mountain Lamb took a deep breath, exhaled, and made polite nods to these people, once her own people, whom she had not seen for more than two winters.

Caribou Hoof let out a whoop, and immediately he and Buzztail urged their ponies forward and began to engage in a spontaneous display of trick riding, much to the delight of the onlookers and of the females of marriageable age in particular.

Elk-Striker, grinning from ear to ear, dismounted from his big Appaloosa and was quickly enveloped in a group of five women, two of them with young children close at their heels.

Now, for the first time since the beginning of the journey northward, Mountain Lamb felt completely alone—a stranger suddenly among people who had once been her own people. But then, perhaps it was so that she had never truly belonged to Gotia's band, had never been one with them. Some lack in her own make-up, something inside her that had precluded her from entering into the rhythm of tribal society. Like a young man who, unable to deal with the realities of the fierce male groups and uninterested in either warfare or the stealing of horses, chose to draw apart, to become an artist or a healer or even to adopt the dress of the women and so in effect to become one of them. Such men might even eventually gain positions commanding genuine respect, like O-mo-gua, Woman's Dress, who had become the leader of his own band and whose reputation as a prophet was renowned.

Had she not run away with Joe Meek and Milton Sub-lette, perhaps she would have taken on the costume of a young man and so have made the attempt to find acceptance among them. Certainly, from the very beginning, Mountain Lamb had known that whatever her life might eventually hold, she would never be able to follow the complex and yet simple and certain ways of tradition.

Now the people seemed almost to ignore her—and, indeed, perhaps they did not know how to react to her. What stories had been told at the time of her leaving? Would Bad Left Hand have claimed that he had accepted a bride-price from the Whitemen? Or would he have chosen to remain silent on the matter, allowing speculation to run wherever it might?

The rebellious daughter, she who rejected Elk-Striker and even tried to murder him, the one who remained in her father's lodge rather than taking a husband. . . .

She guided her pony toward the lodge of Bad Left Hand, the signal design on the stretched elk hides immediately recognizable.

"Will my father be here?" Little Salmon asked suddenly.

Mountain Lamb was startled by the child's words, but she merely shook her head and hugged the boy. Then the two of them dismounted and tethered both the riding horse and the pack animal. Mountain Lamb walked hesitantly to the lodge and forced herself to scratch on the entry flap.

A voice bade her enter, and, with Little Salmon close beside her, she slipped inside—there to be greeted warmly and embraced by Plum Bush and by Likes Birds, the elder of Bad Left Hand's two wives.

"Little Sister," Plum Bush rejoiced. "How good it is to see you in our lodge once more. Sit down now, for we must paint your cheeks with vermilion. That is the sign for peace, and you have forgotten to do it. You have been away too long, Umentucken, Tukutsey Undenwatsy."

"I will get the crimson powder," Likes Birds said. "Yes, just a moment now."

Mountain Lamb allowed herself to be guided to a couch, but poor Little Salmon was captured by the portly Likes Birds and lifted into the air and pressed tight to the woman's ample bosom. Mountain Lamb and Plum Bush both laughed at the boy's feeble attempts to retain some dignity, these unexpected from one so young. And laughter rang through the lodge, the time of restraint now fully broken, the tension created by the sudden meeting now vanished.

"Where is Frog-Catcher? He must be much larger by now," Mountain Lamb exclaimed. And then, her voice growing more subdued, "Where is my father?"

The two wives glanced at each other and then back at Mountain Lamb. Likes Birds released Little Salmon, and the boy scrambled back to stand next to his mother, pressing against her shoulder as she sat on the oval couch of deerhide stuffed with pine needles.

"Elk-Striker told me that Bad Left Hand was ill, and I . . ."

"What the man with the scarred face told you was true," Plum Bush answered. "But I do not think you need to worry any longer."

"Right after Elk-Striker and the two Foolish Ones left to find you," Likes Birds added, "our husband suddenly began to demand that food be prepared. He has been eating like a famished bear ever since."

"He does not speak of going to the Spirit World anymore," Plum Bush said. "Right now he is out riding with Frog-Catcher, his son. He is teaching the boy how to stalk rabbits, I think."

"Now," Likes Birds said, returning from the far side of the lodge, "we must paint the cheeks of this young mother so that she can approach her father in the proper way. Mauvais Gauche has missed you very much, Umentucken. I don't know why you did what you did, but now you are home. And Bad Left Hand will be very happy."

"I am home," Mountain Lamb said, "but I will not be able to stay for very long. My . . . husband . . . will return to Washakie's village in the time of the new grass, and I must be there to meet him."

Mountain Lamb left Little Salmon with her father's two wives and rode alone up into the hills beyond the encampment. After some searching, she spied a war horse and a pony, the animals tethered beneath a large cottonwood at the edge of a meadow. She continued on downslope to where the animals were standing, dismounted, and tethered her own horse.

At the far side of the meadow were two figures, one large and one small. Both were crouched, with bows drawn. Then the arrows leaped out, almost at once, and a jackrabbit leaped once and lay dead.

She walked slowly toward the hunters.

The boy saw her first and pointed. The man nodded.

Mountain Lamb stopped, waited. A lump had formed in her throat, and she was aware that her hands were trembling.

The man and the boy, in no apparent hurry, approached her.

"Umentucken," the man called out. "Is that you?"

"Yes, Father," she answered.

"So you finally decided to come visit me," Mauvais Gauche said. "Or did Elk-Striker tell you I was dying, and so you decided to come home to see me buried?"

Uncertain of the tone of her father's voice, Mountain Lamb stared down at her moccasins and waited.

"It's about time you got here," Mauvais Gauche continued. "What took you so long?"

"I am here now, Father," she said.

"I know I told you never to return so long as I was still alive," the chief muttered, "but you also know that I changed my mind about that."

Frog-Catcher, suddenly growing shy, hesitated and then fell in behind his father.

"Elk-Striker told me that you had decided to go to the Spirit

World," Mountain Lamb managed, the tears threatening to come even though she had told herself that she would never cry at the time of their meeting.

"Yes, well," Mauvais Gauche grumbled. "Well, I changed my mind about that, too. Women are not the only ones who have the right to change their minds."

Then they were standing close to each other, and he said, "You are as beautiful as ever, my child."

She threw herself into his arms then, at the same time fighting to hold back the sobs. He held her tightly, and she closed her eyes.

Then the chief held her back at arm's length, as if to look at her more closely. And Mountain Lamb wiped at her eyes.

"I wish to know one thing," Mauvais Gauche exclaimed. "Where is my grandson? Did you think I wished to see you only?"

"Did you bring my . . . nephew?" Frog-Catcher asked, his hands on his hips. "Did you bring him with you, Mountain Lamb?"

CHAPTER TEN

Return to the High Shinin'

For a long while it was held that Columbus had discovered America, the Beautiful Land; but then it was determined that Vikings, the Wichinga, wandering seafarers without homes, had crossed the Atlantic far earlier. Others pointed out that the Indian Peoples had found their way to America across a supposed Bering Land Bridge thousands of years earlier still.

However, Indian legend asserts that First Man and First Woman came into existence here on the land some call Turtle Island. Now a few archaeologists believe it may have been so—skulls, spear points, shards, bone-bending tools, fire pits. All of these point to human occupation far older than European Cro-Magnon remains. But scientists are like religious zealots and consequently have trouble dealing with new evidence.

In any case, at the time the Whitemen came, Mexico City was the largest metropolis in the world. And to the north, along the Rio Grande in present New Mexico, lived the Pueblo Peoples, peaceful folk who found war abhorrent. If one took a scalp, he had to blacken his face in shame. These were farming people, descendants of the Anasazis and the Cliff Dwellers. Numerous villages—the Acomas, the Zunis, and the Hopis, their dwellings high on the shimmering mesas.

A life of toil and ceremony and peace. The people were crafters of beautiful, multicolored pottery, and they wove textiles for their clothing and hunted rabbits and deer. Summers were spent farming, the winters spent weaving—cotton dresses, white kilts, black and red designs, diamond shapes, diagonals. And their baskets were woven so tightly that they could be used for cooking. Whirlwind, kachina, geometric patterns.

The Spanish came looking for cities of gold and found the Pueblos instead, people who had only a different sort of treasure.

"To the north still farther," the Pueblos said. "The Pawnees are the ones who have the gold."

And the Spanish set off once more.

*The elders smiled and nodded. With a little luck, the savage
Pawnees would kill and eat the Spaniards.*

*But instead the Pawnees stole Spanish horses, Magic Dogs,
Medicine Dogs. And after that everything changed.*

The long, warm rains of January and February finally abated,
and evidence of spring was everywhere in the valley of the San
Joaquin River. The winter months had been spent trapping and
hunting, the results surprisingly good. But now, with warm
weather setting in so much earlier than was ever the case in the
Rocky Mountains, the quality of fur began to deteriorate much
earlier.

Joe Walker called his brigade together and announced that the
men should pull in their traps in preparation for heading back
toward the High Shinin'.

A week later, with all gear stowed on the backs of the pack
animals, the mountain men moved out, following south along the
San Joaquin River and then up one of its tributary streams. To the
west of their route were marshlands and a broad, shallow lake
where countless waterfowl swarmed, ducks and geese almost
without number, and numerous egrets and cranes and herons as
well. The small elk of the valley roamed in herds of considerable
size, and occasionally a great golden grizzly allowed its presence
to be known. These bears, Meeks noted, seemed in some
intangible way more graceful of movement and handsomer than
their Rocky Mountain cousins. It crossed his mind to shoot one of
the monsters and take its hide back to Rendezvous country to
show Bridger and Carson, who were certain to be skeptical of his
descriptions, but somehow or another he found that he simply
wasn't interested in bear-killing. Now that they were actually
heading home, that alone was on his mind.

After two days of heavy rains, the sky cleared—and the great
mountain wall to the east loomed white and distant above them.
Then cold fogs settled in, fog thicker than any Meek had ever
experienced before, so that for several days the caravan was
unable to get under way until the sunlight had begun to penetrate
the thick overcast that seemed, in fact, to rise straight out of the
damp earth.

Mountain rims rose above them on three sides now, the Sierra
apparently curving westward and fusing with the coastal ranges.
The river they were following veered east, emerging from the
mountains under a big range of treeless hills, its hitherto slack

current plunging along and beginning to take on the appearance of a genuine high-country stream. Stephen Meek let out a spontaneous whoop, and the rest of the brigade began to do likewise, urging their ponies ahead.

They made their way up canyon and finally into high, sage-pocked land, encountering no wasteland of granite spires and snowdrifts. Walker, in particular, felt a genuine surge of personal satisfaction, knowing he had this time managed to round the southern extent of the worst part of the Sierra and had found a pass that would, in times to come, allow even for wagon travel.

At the summit he called a halt and yelled out, "Joe Walker's Pass, by thunder! I knew it was hyar all along!"

The weather remained fair, and the crossing was accomplished without difficulty, the party entering into the desert region beyond.

But here Meek and his friends parted company with Walker, electing to proceed into the Great Southwest, to New Mexico and the Hopi villages, thinking to make their spring hunt north of Taos, in the Sangre de Cristo Mountains. Walker, on the other hand, was intent upon heading directly back to Rendezvous country and on to the Snake River Basin, where Bonneville, he presumed, would be waiting for his return.

The men embraced, advised one another to stay on good terms with Old Man Coyote, and fired their Hawkens into the air. Meek pounded Zenas Leonard on the back, swore he'd have his revenge if the journal was eventually found to contain anything but the truth, and suggested that Zenas take a Flathead squaw when he reached Snake River country.

Recalling tales of Jed Smith's misadventures with the Mojave Indians on his ill-fated second expedition to California, Meek at first determined to avoid these people. Nine men, however well armed, stood little chance against as few as fifty truly malicious Indians, even if the Redmen lacked rifles. But as luck would have it, Joe managed to stumble directly into a Mojave village on the western bank of the Colorado River. What appeared at first to be a bad situation proved otherwise, however, and the Mojaves hailed them in and treated them with great hospitality, trading them extra horses and quantities of dried meat for some badly worn service pistols.

Heartened by their good fortune, Meek's small brigade crossed the red-brown waters of the Colorado and continued southward along that river to the mouth of the Bill Williams River and up that stream and so eastward into the drainage of the Little Colorado, where, to their utter astonishment, they encountered an RMF party led by Fraeb and Gervais.

Joe recognized Kit Carson from half a mile off, whooped and shouted at the startled Stephen Meek, Muckaluck, and the others, put his heels to his pony's sides, and raced down upon the RMF men, fired off his rifle so that his intentions would not be mistaken prior to his being recognized, came in yelling *Hoorah for the Mountains!,* leaped from his pony at full run, tackled the astonished Carson, and dragged him from his horse, the two of them sprawling onto the sandy ground, locked in mock combat.

"Ye ain't grown none!" Meek roared. "Still ain't but half the size of a pissant!"

"Fraeb!" Carson called out. "Pull this overgrown kid off me or by the blue Jesus I'll cut 'is heart out an' feed it to my mule!"

Meek flipped Carson around, rose to one knee, and lifted him onto his shoulders—while Kit, with catlike quickness, twisted from Joe's grasp and drew a headlock on the Bear-Killer.

"Uncle!" Meek yelled. "I give in, Kit. Never was one to pick on anybody bigger than me!"

Then the two were embracing as the others were clustering around them.

Stephen Meek and Muckaluck and the Flatheads nudged their ponies forward and within moments had joined the RMF brigade.

Steve shook his head and glanced at Muckaluck.

"Was he always this way?" Muckaluck asked.

"It's a classic case of growing down mentally while growing up physically," Stephen Meek explained.

Muckaluck scowled.

"Now you forget how to talk English?" he asked. "Wagh!"

The trappers ascended the mesa to visit the Hopi villages, to trade, and to relax.

Moqui. Hopituh. The Peaceful Ones.

The Indians made the trappers welcome indeed, but one of the shamans explained to Fraeb, Gervais, Carson, and Meek that Hopi women were not, perhaps, like the women of some of the other Indian Peoples with whom the trappers had been in contact. There would be no selling of the women's sexual favors, as among the Utes or the Pawnees. All Nations, the shaman explained, had their own traditions and their own rules of moral conduct. And guests were expected to observe these rules.

"The Hopi men take but one wife," he continued, "and each man is expected to be faithful to his mate. We are divided into clans, and all are expected to marry within their own clan. We do not have what the Whitemen call prostitutes. No, my friends, we are simple people. We are farmers at heart, and we work very hard. You are welcome among us and are honored guests for so long as you respect our ways."

For two days the RMF men managed to behave themselves, despite the curious glances and friendly smiles of some extremely attractive young women. Fraeb and Gervais had given strict orders that the old shaman's words were the law.

But beyond the pueblo were some irrigated fields in which produce was already growing quite abundantly, the result of considerable agricultural industry, warm climate, and sufficient water.

The pea vines in particular caught the attention of the trappers, and, not being men given to nicety, they proceeded to tramp through the neatly tended rows of green stuff and to pull off handfuls of peapods.

The Hopis came swarming out, indignant with protest.

The mountain men, most of them firmly convinced that the *Hopituh* hadn't shown them proper respect in any case and not about to put up with a pack of shouting Injun divvels, lifted their rifles and opened fire, sending a dozen or more Peaceful Ones to the Spirit World.

Kit Carson and Joe Meek came running out, shouting at the tops of their lungs, but the issue had already been settled—and the only solution lay in a hasty retreat back down off the mesa.

When they had put a number of miles between themselves and the enraged Hopis, Fraeb called a halt and threatened to horsewhip all who had been involved in the killings. But the trappers merely glared back and patted the stocks of their Hawkens and Kentuckies.

The issue was closed, and the RMF contingent moved on toward the northeast.

"Guess we don't belong to that crowd," Meek said to Kit Carson. "And yet the both of us just sat there on the fence an' watched 'er start up."

"Were a mistake to have gone there in the first place," Carson said. "But there ain't no way we could of knowed what was goin' to happen, Joe. By the Mornin' Star an' the Manitou, I swear I never expected it, this child didn't."

Meek shook his head.

"My faithful compañero, Muckaluck," Joe said, his voice trailing away, "he was one of the first niggers to fire. . . . "

Carson shrugged.

"Guess them boys is just too civilized for Whitefolks to be around," he said.

The party followed the Rio Grande north toward San Luis and the Bayou Salade, the South Park of the mountain men. But as they rode, Carson endeavored to persuade Meek to join him on a hunt into the lands of the Comanches.

"Never been down that way," Meek said. "You know that country, Christopher?"

"Not very good," Carson admitted. "But Billy Mitchell— he's up for 'er, an' he knows it like the back of his goddamn hand, he does for a fact. Hitched to a Comanche squaw once an' lived with 'em. Claims he was lookin' for gold, an' when he didn't find none, he lit out. Anyhow, he's willin' to guide us. Good beaver, Joe. You're a free trapper, an' me, I'm thinkin' to be one of the booshways. Coon's got to look out for hisself, or he ain't goin' to get looked out for at all."

"Stephen, he's wantin' to get back to Saint Louis," Joe said. "Had about enough of the High Shinin', as I figger it. An' Muckaluck's been pinin' for Antoine Godin ever since we set out for California. I don't know, Kit. Think mebbe we ought to keep ridin' north."

Bill Mitchell noted the two of them talking and urged his pony ahead, drew up alongside Meek and Carson.

"Got him talked into 'er?" he asked, gesturing to Carson.

"Just about," Kit answered. "Mainly because I got somethin' he'd like to know about, an' I'm not spillin' the beans unless he comes along."

"Kit, ye little runt," Joe bellowed. "Ye expect a grown man like me to fall for that sort of rot? Think I ain't got the ha'r o' the b'ar in me or what?"

"He's got it *on* 'im, anyhows," Mitchell said, laughing. "Only damn fool in the mountains that wears his grizzly, an' that's the truth."

"Don't even wear a shirt underneath," Carson agreed. "An'

that bearskin's probably got more lice than six wild varmints put together."

"No more than your greasy buckskins, ye worthless bastards. What's this you think I'd want to know about, Kit? Come on, old compañero, don't be holdin' out on me. Wagh!"

Carson winked at Mitchell.

"Like I said, Billy, I just about got 'im convinced."

Stephen Meek and Muckaluck and his Flatheads rode on north with Fraeb and Gervais, and Kit, Joe, and Billy Mitchell struck out for Comanche territory. For the first two days of their ride Joe pretended to have forgotten all about the *special* bit of information that Kit had promised to impart, but when they camped the second night, he could could contain his curiosity no longer.

He built a small fire under an overhang of rimrock, put on a pot of coffee, sat down, and glared at Carson.

"So what was ye goin' to tell me?" he demanded.

"Thought ye'd never ast," Carson replied. "Wait till the coffee's ready. Man needs a swig of java if he's goin' to tell a good story."

"Ye squinty-eyed little runt, ye're goin' to tell me now or I'll cut off your nuts an' feed 'em to the hawgs."

"Peevish, ain't he?" Carson winked at Mitchell.

"What I think it is, he probably ain't even interested," Mitchell said, laughing.

"By gawd, I'll stab ye!"

"Wouldn't never find out then, now ain't that true? Simmer down, old coon. Okay, hyar she is. Serious, now. I'm tellin' ye the truth."

Meek gritted his teeth.

"*What* truth, dammit?"

"Wal," Kit said, savoring the instant, "first off, your friend's done left the mountains."

Joe stared into Carson's glittering eyes.

"Milt?" he asked, a sudden, powerful wave of feeling surging through him. "When?"

"Just about the time ye took off with Cap'n Bonneville, as a matter of fact."

"An' he took Mountain Lamb with him?"

"Nope," Carson continued. "That ain't what he done. No sir. Doc Harrison that come up country with Billy Sublette told

Milt that he had to have citified medical help or he was goin' to lose that bad leg of his. An' that's why Milt married Umentucken—so's she'd be protected. Milt never figgered on you lighting out the way ye done. So anyhow, Gabe's lookin' out after 'er. Anyone so much as thinks about beddin' her, an' Bridger cuts 'is throat. Just like havin' the toughest big brother in the mountains, as I see 'er."

The coffee was ready, and Joe stood up, poured out a tin cup full for each of them.

"Milt'll be back," Joe said. "An' if not, by gawd, I'll see to it that kid of his gets raised an' mebbe even sent to school back East somewhere. I weren't much for school myself, but Little Salmon's probably goin' to turn out a lot smarter than me. Milt's damn smart, an' that's the truth. Otherwise brother Billy'd own the whole damn mountains by now."

"Don't know about that," Carson said. "But it don't make no difference. Little Salmon's *your* kid, Joe. Umentucken told Milt before they got hitched, an' Milt told Gabe, an' Gabe told me."

"I knew about 'er too," Mitchell put in. "I heard it from Black Harris. Guess mebbe Campbell told him."

"You boys is blowin' boiled buffler dung into my ear, ain't ye?" Joe said, spitting on the ground. "That ain't no way to treat a friend. . . ."

"Hell, Joseph, everybody that was left at Rendezvous after ye took off probably heard," Mitchell said. "Ain't never been no secrets among us thieves."

"Besides," Carson added, "we all suspected it from the beginning. Stove up the way Milt was an' in pain most of the time, he weren't in no shape to—"

"Well," Meek interrupted, "I love that gal, an' that's a flat fact. But she's Milt's wife an'. . . ."

"Milton, he don't figger to come back—not on two legs, anyhow. And, Joe, dammit, Milt told all of us that we were to see to it that you come back to 'er if we could ever find ye. I don't understand the whole thing, but I know this much. Milt was your friend, an' he cared about ye—just like I care about old Gabe, for instance—an' like ye do too. We got to trust each other because they ain't nobody else we can trust. I'm tellin' ye the truth, coon. You're the one that Umentucken loves the way a woman loves a man. Milt, he knew it too. An' that's why he told us to haul your young ass back to 'er."

Meek's head was spinning—too much information, too quickly. But then he began to laugh—pounded his legs and laughed until his eyes were watering so much that he could barely see the faces of his companions in the firelight.

"So ye dragged me off to where the Comanches are goin' to skulp all three of us . . .," he managed.

"Now, Joe," Mitchell crooned, "they ain't goin' to do that. Comanches is plumb peaceful folks. Gentler than old Jed Smith's pet beaver pups."

The third morning brought company—welcome company, as it turned out. Muckaluck had changed his mind and had persuaded three of the Delaware Indians from the RMF brigade to accompany him—Tom Hill, Jonas Blunt-Claws, and Mark Head, one of Meek's old trapping companions.

"Wal, coons, it appears our party's gettin' a mite bigger." Kit Carson grinned, obviously pleased. At this point he had with him what amounted to a respectable little company of trappers.

"I was afraid I'd get lost without Joe Meek to show me the way home," Muckaluck said. "And these three *White* Indians begged me to let them come with me."

"*White* my ass!" Mark Head growled. "Only good Injun's a civilized Injun. Truth is, me an' Jonas an' Tom figgered Joe could protect us from the b'ars, an' Kit an' Billy'd find the beavers for us. That's why we're out here, ain't it?"

"Suppose ye've rode all night an' now you niggers want to sack out," Mitchell said, growling. "Well, boys, ye're out of luck. We're just headin' on."

"*Whitemen* need sleep," Muckaluck said, stopping to whistle a bit. "Real Injuns don't."

"Then have a bite to eat," Meek put in. "We're ready to roll, so to speak."

"The ponies have wheels now?" Mark Head asked.

The band of seven moved on, crossing the mountains and drifting down onto the plains along the Purgatoire River, trapping as they went.

The take was good, and it was often possible to *cotch* the beavers with balls of galena rather than taking the time and effort to use traps.

But best of all, there had been no trouble with the Indians whatsoever, Comanches or otherwise. In fact, nearly a month went by without so much as a single glimpse of an Indian.

Aside from a few days of torrential thunderstorms, the weather had been most cooperative. One afternoon they'd been obliged to take cover beneath some cottonwoods when the sky poured down a shower of hailstones large enough to crack open a man's skull, or nearly so. And several times they were able to watch from a distance as tornadoes zigzagged their way across the plains, sucking up clouds of dust and breaking off trees as they went.

But now it was close on to the first of May, as nearly as the trappers could figure it, and the furs they were taking were of diminished quality.

It was time to head for the mountains beyond the Seeds-keedee—where, with luck, they'd still be able to take some prime pelts from the high meadows and the streams of rushing snowmelt.

They were crossing some bare prairies, the land undulating and treeless, when Kit called a halt.

"Somethin's up. I kin smell 'er," he said.

"Pawnees, mebbe?" Joe asked. "Hell, Christopher, them boys is all out huntin' bufflers—an' I expect the herds are all away to the east of here. That's why we ain't seen no sign."

"Don't know what kind they be, but I smell Injuns. Use your damned sniffer, Meek."

"He smells himself," Jonas Blunt-Claws suggested. "Whitemen don't bathe often enough."

"Ride on," Carson said softly. "But, gents, keep your eyes peeled. . . ."

On the low ridge ahead, completely motionless, an Indian scout. Then, realizing he had been spotted, the man scrambled over the crest and was instantly out of sight.

"Appears Christopher was right," Meek said.

"Comanche," Mitchell added. "An' there's probably five, six thousand of the coons on the other side of the rise. Any ideas, Kit?"

"Thought you said they was harmless," Meek said, growling.

"Mostly they are," Mitchell answered.

"Pull in the mules," Carson said. "I hear the Red divvels comin'."

The Comanche war party poured down from the ridge, lances waving, eagle-feather crests, the warriors' bodies nearly naked and gaudily painted, war whoops echoing.

"Looks like they was gettin' ready to pay the Pawnees a visit," Joe said, "an' they found us instead."

"What do we do?" Muckaluck cried out.

"Must be two hundred of 'em, this child figgers," Meek said, turning his pony about.

"Mule fort!" Carson yelled, leaped from his pony, and, knife in hand, slit the throat of one of the pack animals.

Joe and the other trappers did likewise, stabbing and shooting their livestock. Those not put down immediately took to their heels and pounded away over the plains, taking with them furs, gear, and all.

The Comanches charged directly at the trappers, who, in turn, began to fire from behind the cover of their slain mules and horses.

The Comanches, hurling spears, sent up a dreadful howl and parted to either side of where the trappers lay pinned down, and passed beyond them.

The trappers reloaded immediately and spun about, expecting a second wild charge.

No question: the fat was in the fire. Three of the Comanches lay dead beyond the mule fort.

"Hyar they come again!" Joe called out.

"Injuns fire first," Kit shouted. "Then the White niggers. Don't want our rifles all empty at once—she's the onliest chance we got!"

"We're dead players," Mitchell said, groaning.

"Hold your fire, Billy," Joe hissed.

Again the Comanches passed by, this time raining arrows, most of which lodged into the carcasses of the dead mules.

Meek took aim, squeezed off his round, and nodded as a Comanche warrior threw out his arms, spun from his pony, and pitched down into the cloud of dust from the horses' hooves.

"Keep your wipin' sticks hot," Carson sang out.

But the Comanches turned immediately about, certain that the trappers' guns were empty, and began a return charge. Now they sensed an easy victory—merely a matter of riding the trappers down and sticking them with lances.

But the charge split apart once again, the Indians' horses refusing to approach the heaped bodies of dead mules and ponies—they smelled the blood of their own kind.

One of the Comanches, staring back from astride his balky

war pony, called out: "Mit-chell! I recognize you now, Lean Bull! Your hair will hang from my lodge pole!"

"One of your cousins, I gather?" Meek asked, turning toward Mitchell.

"Nice friendly folk," Carson muttered, reloading as fast as he could.

Muckaluck tapped his priming pan to assure detonation, aimed, and squeezed off his shot. Mitchell's *cousin* grasped for his throat, the blood spraying outward, and fell beneath the churning hooves of his own horse.

"Injuns fire!" Carson commanded, and the three Delawares drew aim and shot.

One Comanche wounded, two more on the ground.

The horses were going crazy, lashing out with their hooves, milling about in fear and confusion, and the Comanche party leader shouted the retreat.

"Got time to breathe a bit before we go under anyhow," Meek said, laughing. "Boys, I ain't had so much fun since we hung Grandma. . . ."

Once again the Comanches charged, whooping and screaming. Now those who had either rifles or pistols were using them, and lead as well as arrows thumped into the carcasses of the mule fort. But, miraculously, none of the trappers was hit.

The Comanche medicine man, waving his gourd rattle as though it had the power to deflect Hawken lead, urged his horse forward and came slowly and directly toward the trappers.

"We *need* this one," Meek said, aiming his piece and firing.

The medicine man, his face a mask of amazement as he stared down at the hole that had suddenly appeared in his abdomen, made a brief attempt to hold his intestines in place and then soundlessly slipped to the earth.

The Comanches drew back to the base of the rise and began to talk things over.

"With Gawd's own luck," Meek said, loading again, "the niggers'll decide their medicine's no good for today. If they hold off until dark, maybeso we can slip away."

"Likely they forget to bring their mule medicine with 'em," Carson suggested.

A group of Comanche women had now appeared and were tending to the wounded. After a time a few of them approached the mule fort to drag off their dead.

Midday, and blinding sunlight. No shade, not so much as a

flask of water. Throats parched, and clouds of shiny black flies swarming about the dead animals, drawn by the crusting blood.

"I throw dung at you!" one of the women called out. "It will give you something to eat! I will piss on your scalps when our men have finally killed you!"

"Bad tongue," Mitchell said, "but she shore is a purty little thing, ain't she?"

The trappers grinned.

"Come here so I can fuck you!" Muckaluck shouted, waving his rifle in the air.

"White cowards!" the young woman shouted back. "Men who sleep with deer!"

Mark Head, thinking of the coup of killing an Indian woman in full sight of her men, raised his rifle.

"Don't do 'er, coon," Carson ordered. "We got us plenty of other targets out thar. Another time, another place, an' ye'd be thinkin' about playin' kissy-face with 'er. Anyhow, it's like Billy says. She's just too damned purty to kill. An' a damn brave squaw, too."

"Shoot!" Head mumbled. But he lowered his rifle.

Afternoon wore on, and the fighting diminished. Instead, the Comanche braves seemed more inclined to show off their horsemanship, displaying marvelous tricks, spinning their animals about, shooting from behind their horses' necks and from under their bellies, rushing toward the dead mules and letting arrows fly. The braves had braided hair rope into the manes of their ponies and, swinging from these, were able to shield themselves from possible return fire by the trappers.

"They *are* a wonder to behold," Joe Meek said.

The trappers did not even bother to fire back. Better, all things considered, to save their powder and play for time. If the Comanches wanted to spend the afternoon bragging and showing off, so much the better. The longer it went on, the better were the chances for an escape. And even the slimmest chance, Meek figured, was better than no chance at all.

If thar's any way whatsoever of gettin' back to Isabel, I mean to do 'er. I sure ain't ready to start pushin' up petunias, no sir. We're as good as dead men, but we still got a lee-tle chance. . . .

At last the sun blazed crimson over the far, white mountains, and somewhere not too far away the crickets had begun to sing.

Meek stood up, reached down to run his hand along the side of one of the dead mules, whistled softly to himself.

"So many arrows in 'em they look like great big porkypines," he said.

"Will the Comanches give us a chance to slip away?" Muckaluck demanded. "That is what the Flatheads would do. That way they can track us down later or let us go if something more interesting happens."

"Good question," Carson said. "Any case, they ain't no point in stayin' here."

The seven trappers shouldered what equipment they could—their robes, rifles, knives, and axes—and, leaving all else behind, crawled away from the mule fort and into the chill darkness of the prairie night.

"Let's head for the High Shinin'," Meek suggested. "Mebbe the Comanches'll go on after the Pawnees or whoever it was they was goin' to steal horses from. Mebbe we can find Frapp an' Jarvey up in Bayou Salade. . . ."

They worked their way up a shallow ravine and then began to run—a steady, ceaseless dog trot that, although they had had no water since early morning, they were somehow able to maintain until sunrise. Thirst tormented them, and by first light all of them were sucking air through mouths parched and swollen. Exhaustion, pain, a weariness so heavy that even Joe Meek had cause to wonder if his thumping heart might not just rear up and say *no more*. . . .

A smell of water, and they kept going, down off a crest to the shadowed forms of some young cottonwoods.

A rivulet, glinting in the half-light of dawn.

They drank—too much and too quickly, but they could not control themselves. Muckaluck got cramps and writhed about in the grass as the Delawares, their voices cracked and half-audible, pronounced the ultimate insult:

Stupid as a Whiteman.

Meek belched, coughed, and burst out laughing in spite of himself.

"Wagh!" he managed. "Christopher, we're busted as empty barrels. Powder's wet an' no fire. On foot, an' nary a pot to piss in. If a coon follows old Kit Carson, he might save his skin, but whar's his gawddamned mule?"

CHAPTER ELEVEN

Isabel

The drama, human and otherwise, continued apace.

Coyote pups followed their parents about and pounced upon lizards and even high-country toads—but these poison-skinned creatures they soon learned to leave alone, at mother's urging. Antlers of male deer in velvet, new fawns, the little ones spotted and long-legged and clumsy. Beavers devoured their favorite kinds of vegetation, and black bears snorted and growled and wallowed in mud holes.

Bonneville built a stockade the mountain men dubbed Fort Nonsense, a post that was never used. McKenzie, King of the Missouri, planted corn at the mouth of the Iowa River—to be used in the still he placed inside his river craft, The Yellowstone. And Milt Sublette, not trusting his brother, had made arrangements with Nathaniel Wyeth to bring in supplies for the next Rendezvous. There were rumors that Bill Sublette had been conniving with McKenzie and American Fur.

Robert Campbell supervised the building of a post to be called Fort William, after Billy Sublette, supposedly to compete with American Fur on the river.

And both Sublettes had been sick and near to death on the way downriver in '33.

Medicine Calf Beckwourth and Long Hair had turned their Crows into the scourge of the mountains and were at war with the Blackfeet, the Cheyennes, the Arapahos, the Assiniboines, and the Utes. War fever spread like grassfire.

Wyeth let General Clark in Saint Louis know about McKenzie's distillery, and American Fur disclaimed all knowledge of the matter. Senator Benton attempted to defend the company.

Astor had retired from the fur trade, and McKenzie, erstwhile King of the River, was sent to Europe—but before he went, he made a deal with Billy Sublette, the latter now backed by General Ashley's fortune.

Very complex.

Black Harris came overland with information about Fitz's

*debacle with the Crows, and Bill Sublette headed for '34
Rendezvous to foreclose on RMF debts.*

*In the mountains, the beavers were building new lodges of
sticks and mud, oblivious to the human turmoil their very
existence brought into being.*

"That damned Coyote Gawd has got a very peculiar sense of
humor," Joe Meek remarked. "Do you coons realize that we're
the *most* impoverished niggers in the Rocky Mountains?"

"Only one thing to do," Carson said.

Near the northern end of the San Luis Basin they found what
they were looking for and more than they could have hoped for—a
Ute village, broad meadows and numerous horses grazing, many
of the animals no doubt stolen from either the Cheyennes, with
whom the Utes were perpetually at war, or from the Pawnees, with
whom they usually pretended to be at peace. Perhaps a thousand
or more animals and, as the trappers quickly determined, guarded
by only half-a-dozen boys who were far more interested in riding
about and in doing mock battle than in keeping proper watch on
the herd.

But beyond the prospect of horses, something else of rather
significant interest: a number of Whites were living among the
Utes, an American Fur detachment as it turned out.

For three days Meek, Carson, and the others studied the
situation and at length discovered the area where, or so it seemed,
the company men had cached their furs.

"Coons," Meek grinned, "we got to figger out how to put all
this together. If we can pull it off, I expect we can make up for our
losses."

"*La récolte grande*, as Frenchy Le Blueux used to put 'er,"
Carson said, laughing. "What ye got in your bonnet, Joseph?"

"Wisht Pete was here." Mitchell sighed. "He had more
talent for this sort of thing than any nigger I ever met."

"Well, he ain't,," Joe said. "So we got to figger 'er out on
our own. Wonder if the old coon's ever goin' to come back to the
mountains. . . ."

"Already has, is what I hear," Mitchell said. "Supposed to
be over with Beckwourth an' them horse-thievin' Crows. Anyhow, he passed through Fort Union last fall—told Kipp that's
where he was headin'."

"You figger that's true, Kit?" Joe demanded.

"Damned if this child knows. How ye figger to get us some ponies an' some furs into the bargain?"

"Muckaluck an' Jonas an' Mark an' Tom can get the horses," Joe suggested. "Injuns is good at that sort of thing. For them, it ain't like stealin'."

"Of course it isn't," Muckaluck agreed.

"So about sundown, us White coons dig out some of the plew. Muckaluck, at midnight you boys bring in some animals. Need some ropes, too. Figger ye can do 'er?"

"Ponies picketed near the lodges," Jonas Blunt-Claws said. "They will be all ready to go."

"How do ye get past the camp dogs?" Carson asked. "Ye thought about that or not?"

"We are not like stupid Whitemen," Mark Head answered. "Leave the horses to us. You dig up the furs. We will be rich men yet."

It took Joe and Billy and Kit about an hour to break through into the hollowed-out fur cellar—and wouldn't have taken that long if they'd had proper tools to work with. But with hand axes and fingernails, nonetheless, they were able to manage.

But just as they finished removing a dozen bales of plew, they heard voices—the voices of Utes who had been apparently engaged earlier in drinking quantities of Kenneth McKenzie's rotgut whiskey, courtesy of their American Fur guests.

The mountain men froze, weapons in hands, and waited for whatever was about to happen. Luck was with them, and the intoxicated Utes staggered past in the darkness, hardly even aware that they were proceeding in a direction away from the village. Their arms were about one another, and they were singing and chanting and talking all at once.

As quickly as possible, Joe and Bill and Kit replaced the security logs and heaped some dirt and leaves over the evidence of their excavation.

It was just midnight, give or take a few minutes, when the Flathead and the three Delawares arrived with a string of twenty horses.

"We didn't even have to kill the boys they had left as guards," he said. "No, we hit them over their heads and gagged them and tied them up. The men will find them in the morning and let them go. With so many horses, the Utes will not even notice."

"What about these?" Carson asked. "War ponies—all ready to be rid."

"The Utes will notice," Mark Head admitted. "And they will raise a party and come after us."

"In that case, gents," Joe Meek suggested, "we'd best get loaded an' be on our way."

"How many furs?" Muckaluck wanted to know.

"Just a few, old nigger," Joe Meek said, chuckling. "Dozen packs is all."

"A dozen packs?" Jonas whispered, amazed.

"Should of took thirteen, but we didn't know how many ponies you coons would bring us." Carson laughed. "Come on, let's get 'em loaded. Goin' to have swayback horses as it is, I'll tell ye!"

"If we can pull this off," Joe said, "we're rich men—rich men, boys. Why, at five dollars American for each fur, that's— let's see . . ."

"Meek ain't too good with numbers," Mitchell added. "At five dollars times twelve hundred skins, that's . . ."

"Six thousand dollars," Tom Hill said.

"A thousand apiece," Muckaluck said.

"Naw, it ain't," Meek said, laughing. "But it's a good bit. Near eight hundred and fifty to the man."

"Might not be five-dollar skins," Carson continued. "Let's don't get our hopes up. Any case, it's still a long way to Green River country. What can be stole one way can be stole the other. Let's get a move on, niggers. . . ."

Ham's Fork of the Seedskeedee, and already, in the last week of June, the trappers and their Indian cohorts were coming in.

American Fur had pulled most of its operations east of the mountains, and there would be no supply train from Fontenelle this Rendezvous. Instead, the trappers were anticipating the arrival of Nathaniel Wyeth, who had entered into an agreement with Milton Sublette to supply the needs of RMF. And word had it that Milt himself would be with the little New Englander.

It was into this atmosphere of expected carnival time in the mountains that Carson's brigade rode, their animals exhausted but laden with furs.

"By god, ye done good, Kit!" Bridger crowed. "If ye weren't such an ugly leetle coon, I'd pick ye up an' kiss ye! An' old Bear-Killer an' Billy Mitchell! By the beard of Jesus's mother, we'd about given up on the lot of ye!"

The men embraced all around, and Antoine Godin broke

through the crowd, glared at Muckaluck, turned, and walked briskly away.

"Antoine!" the Flathead shouted. "I have brought you many presents!"

He ran after his friend, tackled him, and the two went sprawling in the dust, kicking and pummeling each other.

"Does a coon's heart good," Joe Meek roared, "just to watch 'em. . . ."

"Big Joe," Bridger said, "I figger they's someone who's been waitin' an unholy long time to see ye. The lodge is over next to mine," he added, pointing.

Meek took off running, caught himself, slowed to a casual walk, and began whistling as he went.

Mountain Lamb heard the notes, warned Little Salmon to stay inside, and came running out.

And then they were both running.

She leaped into his arms, and he whooped as he swung her about, lifted her over his head, and roared with laughter.

"Set me down again so I can kiss you, Joe Meek!" she implored. "You have been gone so long—I have—missed you very much, Joe Meek."

He set her feet back on the earth and then felt suddenly and terribly shy with her. But Umentucken was oblivious to his moment of reticence and threw herself into his arms once more, her mouth pursed and searching upward for his, her eyes closed, the sunlight gleaming from her drawn-back and braided black hair, little fingers of shadow about her cheekbones, a faintly discernible sheen of perspiration over her smooth forehead.

"Ye ain't changed," he managed.

Mountain Lamb kissed him again, pushed her head up under his chin, and began to laugh and cry at the same time.

"Of course I have not changed," she sobbed. "Why should I change, Joe Meek? It is so—good—to have you back. I have dreamed about you often—I have worried about you so much—I do not want you to go away with that bald-headed Captain Bonneville ever again. Will you promise me that, Joe Meek?"

Joe looked down at her, saw love in her eyes, hoped to *Gawd* that it was love he saw. And then he looked past her at someone else.

A child.

"Little Salmon?" he asked, amazed.

"He is your son, Joe Meek. I never told you that before—I should have told you. . . ."

"The boys told me," Joe said, reaching down and gathering in the child with one arm.

And the child, clearly trying not to, began nevertheless to cry—fear and wonder of this large, bearded individual who had seemed nearly to devour his mother and would now probably kill him and eat him for dinner.

They found themselves riding together far up the Big Sandy, toward the high peaks of the Wind River Range.

Joe had chosen to respect Milt's prior claim to the hand of Umentucken but had nonetheless put up his own lodge adjacent to hers and had undertaken to hunt for her and to take care of her—not that Mountain Lamb was in particular need of further protectors.

But evenings he spent in the lodge with the woman he loved and the child who, as he was now convinced, was his own. After so long a parting, it took a bit of time to get reacquainted. And Little Salmon, of course, had no memory of the big, bearded man who his mother explained to him was in fact his father. But the man and the little boy were soon playing together, with Joe carrying the child about on his shoulders. Meek used his hands to create shadow patterns of various animals against the stretched hide of the tepee and growled and told the child about strange places he had been to and about the White bears he had killed.

Little Salmon was awe-struck and yet immensely pleased with his huge new playmate, and, as Mountain Lamb noted, the Bear-Killer himself seemed as contented as at any time since she had first met him—that day, now two and a half years past, in the medicine lodge in her father's village.

And yet, despite her hints, Joe Meek returned to his own lodge each night to sleep.

"Milt's comin' up country with the supply train, Isabel. Don't matter none what either of us wants, we got to wait. We both owe old Milt too damned much to do anything behind his back. It's just what's *right* is all."

Turning away from him, she had said, "You used to wish to lie with me, Joe Meek."

"I still do, dammit, Isabel. But ye're *married* to Milt, an'. . . ."

"Milt told me to live with you when you came back," she had protested.

"We gotta have patience, Pretty Face," he had said, and had turned and left the lodge.

But the following day, when Meek had told her he was going hunting and had ridden off toward the Wind River Range to look for mountain goats and bighorns, Umentucken, Tukutsey Undenwatsy left Little Salmon with the wives of Washakie and, her pistol and the rifle Joe had given her in hand, mounted her own pony and began to follow.

On the second day, just as he was making camp beside the river, she dismounted and stepped forward into the circle of light from his campfire.

Meek spun about instantly, threw himself flat, and leveled his pistol at her.

"Have I come all this way for you to kill me?" she asked, the firelight glinting in her eyes and from her teeth as she smiled at him.

And that night they slept in each other's arms—touching, holding each other, but not entering into sexual concourse.

Now they were riding together, side by side, toward the high granite peaks whose upper slopes still lay deep beneath the snowdrifts of the preceding winter.

A great horned owl sat perched on a pine limb above their heads, watching sleepy-eyed as they passed but not taking flight. Deer were out and about in the grass of the high, lush meadows and also watched curiously and were in no great hurry to run from the man and the woman who rode together. And near the center of the meadow, where the waters of the stream were pooled and still behind dams the beavers had constructed, Joe and Mountain Lamb could see V-like bandings, their points moving ahead and finally disappearing near the humped mounds of sticks and mud that were the beavers' lodges.

An osprey screamed at them from a spruce beyond the meadow, the bird intent upon fishing and not wanting to be either disturbed or observed.

They drew their ponies to a halt and waited to see what the little fish-eagle would do.

After a time the cries ceased, and the osprey took to the air, fluttering mothlike above the shallow beaver pool. Then it dropped down a few feet and held there, hovering just a man's height above the surface.

Then it splashed into the water, its wings beating against the surface, screamed once again, and rose into the air, its talons empty, and spun up to perch once more in the spruce.

"Even leetle white eagle, he misses sometimes," Joe said, laughing.

"I don't think he wanted us to see that," Mountain Lamb said.

And from across the way the osprey began once more to shriek at them, the bird's voice now filled with terrible indignation.

By sundown they had reached a shallow tarn high atop a boulder-strewn ridge crest—groves of flamelike hemlocks near the water, paintbrush and columbines in bloom, and carpets of forget-me-nots among the stony flinders of the far rise—blue, yellow, white, and violet. The colors were still faintly visible in the rich, crimson-yellow of alpenglow.

Early that morning Mountain Lamb had used her rifle to bag a young buck, her quickness of response and the accuracy of her shot surprising Joe. But he had seen Mountain Lamb use a weapon before—knew she could handle the short-barreled Hawken nearly as well as any man.

Now she cut steaks, spit them, and placed them over the flames of the campfire Joe had built. He, in turn, got his small, battered coffeepot (one thing he'd been unwilling to leave behind on the night he and Carson and the others had left their mule fort), fetched water, and set the pot beside the flames while he crushed a small handful of coffee beans by placing them on a smooth-faced slab of granite and tapping them with the side of his hand ax.

Within a short time, the meat and the beverage were ready, and Joe and Mountain Lamb partook of their evening meal.

Afterward, Meek lay back and gazed off across to the dull purple shadows of the high peaks, their crowns still tipped with a faint, glowing light.

Along the water's edge the crickets were singing, and a bullfrog groaned—perhaps calling to one of his own kind to come join him. Even a big frog in an otherwise empty pond was only a little frog.

"He calls to a mate," Mountain Lamb said as the amphibian hummed and sighed. "If he calls well enough, a woman frog will hear him and come. That is how it is with the frog-people."

Joe wondered how it was with the human-people. But he only shook his head so that his beaver cap fell off.

"Things do *shine* tonight, don't they Isabel?"

"Yes," she answered, and rolled over upon him and placed one hand between his legs, squeezing softly.

Bear-Killer Meek.

Umentucken, Tukutsey Undenwatsy—bighorn ram of the mountain, his child.

What thoughts flamed in the skulls as the thing desired so long and so intensely by both began to happen? Whatever scruples the conscious minds may have had were now suddenly gone— conscious mind itself drugged by resurgent flamings in the blood, in the soft ache of groin and breast and mouth and the rhythm of breathing changed, all mind in abeyance and only the passionate need of body for body, of the male for the female and the female for the male. They bit at each other, clawed, touched gently, clung fiercely—and then, within what were only moments but that seemed like gasping eternities, the male hardness entered and the inward-drawing force of the female opened to receive. Two bodies one then, a new being, a new creature that knew nothing of time and was oblivious to time and yet contained all time within itself, a creature that had existed from the dim beginnings of life itself in its blind need to rejoin and retangle the minute and coded spindles of life that had been drawn apart long, long ago in a tidepool beneath alternations of lightning and blazing sunlight, all this in a dimness, and ancient, down the constantly altering track of billions of years. . . .

Then the male gasping, the muscles going slack, lungs sucking for air. And the female dreaming, she could go on forever she believed at that moment, and she clung to him, was utterly unwilling for him to withdraw from her.

Lying together then, not even fully unclothed in their haste, but each aware of the other's heartbeat, of the warmth and the smell of the other, each clinging to the other.

And as the great gray owl of the mountains drifted its cries across the high ridge where hemlocks and stunted junipers grew close to a shallow tarn of dark water and a single bullfrog moved quickly beneath a granite slab that overhung the pond's edge, weightlessly alive and sentient in its own liquid element and its eyes blinking slowly and reflecting not only the thousands of white points of light in the heavens but also the ebbing glow of a campfire across the water, a man and a woman, now without either names or identities of any sort, moved downward into their separate caves of sleep.

* * *

It was not Wyeth and Milt but Bill Sublette and Robert Campbell who arrived at the Rendezvous at Ham's Fork with a store of supplies and mountain whiskey.

"Wal dog my cats," Jim Bridger said, shaking Bill Sublette's hand with an enthusiasm that made the mountain-man-turned-trader half-flinch. "Thought ye'd left the High Shinin' for good. Whar's Milt an' Wyeth, Billy?"

"Tell ye the truth, Gabe, Wyeth's on his way up country with a supply train of his own—an' brother Milton's with 'im, though how he can ride, I don't know. He's lost thirty pounds an' looks like death warmed over. This'll be his last trip west—I can guarantee 'er."

"This nigger don't understand, Billy," Henry Fraeb said. "We made our arrangements with Nat Wyeth. . . ."

"Gents," Sublette answered, "times is bad. Saint Louis beaver prices is way down—I hate to tell ye that. Old Astor's retired, an' American Fur's in the hands of Chouteau an' his boys."

"Meanin' McKenzie's running the show?" Bridger asked.

Bill Sublette spat a stream of tobacco juice and shook his head.

"King of the River's lost his crown, I'm afraid. He's on his way to Europe for a leetle vacation. Big to-do about a distillery that Mack had in the hold of his riverboat. Could be Wyeth's the one that blew the whistle on 'im."

"We cain't buy your goods," Fraeb said. "We done got a deal with Wyeth. Milt an' the rest of us set 'er up. . . ."

"Boys," Sublette said slowly, "looks to me like ye don't have no choice in the matter. I'm here, an' I'm openin' up the trade. You don't buy from me, an' I'll be obliged to foreclose on the notes of credit I hold, an' that would be the end of RMF. As it is, I've made a leetle deal with American Fur—that's why Drips an' Vanderburgh ain't out here pesterin' ye no more. American Fur's got the other side of the mountains an' the *Pieds Noirs* trade, ye've got this side. Didn't figger ye was interested in dealin' with Bug's Boys anyhow. An' that's the way it's got to be."

Bridger, Fraeb, and Gervais looked at one another.

"Guess mebbe we ought to palaver with Fitz before we decide anything," Bridger said, forcing a grin. "How far back's Wyeth an' Milt?"

"Couldn't tell ye," Sublette answered. "I guess they'll be

along in a week or so, if the Injuns don't put 'em under. The tribes are all at each other's throats. Old Long Hair's got his Crows riled up, an' somehow that's got everybody riled up. Coons, my boys is gettin' the goods ready for trade. Come on, let's wet our whistles. When ye've thought 'er over, ye'll see that I've saved your Rocky Mountain asses. Got a genuine surgeon with me, Gabe—ye still got that arrowhead stuck in your back? If it's botherin' ye, we'll cut 'er out. That way ye'll have room for a new one. . . .''

Rendezvous was on, and the trappers quickly exchanged their furs for weapons and traps and supplies from Bill Sublette's hastily set-up lodges. The trade was brisk, even at the new price of a dollar a pound—two to three dollars for a skin. The RMF booshways held back a few of their skins in deference to Wyeth, and Carson's bridgade held back most of theirs. But Bill Sublette, through his superior skill in crossing the mountains and through his willingness to turn the financial screws a bit, had nearly all of the trade.

When Wyeth, in the company of Cerré and about forty others, arrived, there was little for him to do except curse in proper New England fashion at the RMF booshways.

"Whar's Milt, gawddammit!" Joe Meek interrupted. "I don't care about the rest of 'er. Whar's Milt?"

Nathaniel Wyeth bit at his upper lip and then rolled a cigarette and lit it. But his hands were shaking with partially suppressed rage.

"Joseph Meek," he said, "I've got a message for you. Milton had to turn back—about two weeks up from Council Bluffs, it was. He's a strong man, an iron will. But that leg of his abscessed and for a day or two I thought he was finished. He pulled himself back out of the pit, though, and I sent three of my greenhorns back to the settlements with him. Milton said to tell all of you that he'd see you before the snows fly, unless thay had to shorten his leg a mite. That's how he put it, gentlemen. The man's got a will like iron. But I believe Milton's days in the mountains are finished. I may be wrong, but that's what I think."

Joe glanced at the others and then stared at the ground.

"Joseph," Wyeth continued. "Milt said that if you had returned from California, I was to *order* you to take Mountain Lamb. Since you're just a bit bigger than I am, I don't feel in a position to do any ordering. But that's what Milton said. And he mumbled something about *lovin' the both of 'em, by the blue Jesus*. His own words, Joe."

"You're a good man, Nat Wyeth. Better'n any of the rest of us coons, likely," Joe said softly. "No matter what Bridger an' the boys has had to do to get Billy Sublette off their backsides, me an' Carson an' our bunch have got some skins for ye."

"We all have," White Hair Fitzpatrick added. "Couldn't hold back many, but we've got some. Enough to keep ye goin' for a time. An' them supplies ain't a complete loss, Wyeth. Maybeso ye can set up to trade all year. That's what I'd do, sure as buffler dung."

Bill Sublette and Robert Campbell wandered over to join the conversation.

"Wal, Nat," Billy Sublette said, laughing. "It were a good race ye run me across the Ammahabas. But I guess my mules was just a tad bit faster or summat. This year I won. Next year Old Man Coyote'll likely be on your side."

Wyeth was bristling with indignation, but he controlled his voice.

"Mr. Sublette," he said slowly, "indeed you won the race— even though I didn't know until I was clear to Fort Union that a race was on. And by that time you were more than a week ahead of me. Nonetheless, you were the winner. But, Mr. Sublette, I intend to plant a boulder in your garden, and I don't believe you'll be able to move it. So perhaps only time will tell who has actually won this race."

With that Wyeth turned on his heel and walked away.

Bill Sublette laughed.

"You boys figger he's gone Rocky Mountain loco, or what?"

"Never knew Wyeth to say anything he didn't mean," Joe Meek mumbled.

And the RMF partners fixed their attention upon Tom Fitzpatrick's face.

Wyeth did what trading he could and then moved his supply train north toward Snake River. The Rendezvous was over, and the RMF partners were left wondering how much longer they themselves would be able to survive in the mountains. The trade was in bad straits indeed, with prices down and with severe competition from both American Fur and from Bonneville's men and now from Wyeth's brigade as well.

Wyeth, Meek told the others, intended to cache his goods, set his men to trapping, and head east for the settlements.

"Get backin' for a permanent tradin' post," Joe said. "He figgers to do business with the Shoshones an' the Flatheads an' the Nez Percés an' mebbe even the *Pieds Noirs*. He says to tell you boys that if ye run short of supplies, to haul along some plew an' come visit 'im at Fort Hall on the Snake."

"Fort Hall, eh?" Bridger asked.

"Guess that's what he intends to call 'er," Meek said, shrugging.

"Who the hell's *Hall?*" Carson wanted to know.

"Likely one of Nat's rich Boston friends," Bridger said, his voice trailing off.

CHAPTER TWELVE

Bear Contest

These are the names of artists who, in the 1830s and after, attempted to portray and preserve something of a doomed world: George Catlin, Alfred Jacob Miller, Carl Bodmer, Jules Tavernier, Woodrow Crumbo, John Mix Stanley, Henry Farney, C.M. Russell, Frederic Remington, William Cary, Rudolph Kurz, Charles De Granville, O.C Seltzer, Albert Bierstadt. . . .

Several paintings come to mind.

Miller's rendering of Joe Walker and his Indian wife, the two of them riding into Rendezvous, Walker's horse stepping proudly forward, an insane look in its eyes, Walker wearing a short-brimmed sombrero with feathers, his Hawken across his knees, the Indian woman, her features indistinguishable, riding behind at a discreet distance.

Another Miller painting of a trapper taking an Indian bride. The long-haired trapper is wearing a blue coat, the barefoot girl a white dress of deerskin. An Indian war chief, in full headdress, a bear- or eagle-claw necklace looped across his chest, holds a lance, menacing, from the right side.

A Bodmer painting of the Missouri River under heavy skies, a cloud of vultures swarming, Whitemen coming ashore, well armed, to drive away two grizzlies from what appears to be a buffalo carcass.

One by Cary—a hundred or more Indians engaged in watching a riverboat on the Missouri, perhaps McKenzie's The Yellowstone, smoke trailing from the craft's stack. At the painting's center are Indian mud lodges—to the right the ramparts of a fort and trading post.

Catlin's depiction of a Mandan village, earth-and-timber lodges surrounded by a stockade. Numerous Indians, many of them on the roofs, a girl astride a white pony, a young man with a tame wolf, buffalo skulls on the dome of the medicine lodge and grotesque figures hoisted on poles above, three black and one white. In the distance, beyond the stockade, is the burial ground.

Another by Catlin: Indians hunting buffalo, one bull down,

*its eyes wild, another about to be slain. Buffalo disappearing over
low hills.*

Two more by Miller:

*Green River Rendezvous, Indian lodges in the distance
painted with pale yellow clay, and in the left foreground—is that
Washakie on a white stallion, Jim Bridger behind him and
wearing a suit of metal armor, the gift of Sir William Stewart,
ordered from Scotland and shipped to the American West?*

And one entitled Indian Encampment, *a mountain elder in
the right foreground, behind it a tall skin tepee, the entry flap held
open by a thin pole. Another lodge in the background. The sky is
brooding, as though rain would come soon. Campfire, left
foreground. A beautiful horse. Three old women in the background. Four braves in the foreground, but the face of only one is
visible. Foreground center, in a white deerskin dress, a stunningly
attractive young woman, small-breasted, her face animated as she
speaks, a skinning knife held in her left hand.*

*It is probably early morning. It is probably evening. It is
probably no time at all. It is probably a time that never existed
and which will always exist.*

When Bill Sublette once more made his way eastward, a
letter went with him—one addressed to Milt Sublette in Saint
Louis—or, for that matter, wherever Bill should happen to find his
brother. The missive's primary message had to do with the formal
disbanding of RMF. Henry Fraeb and Jean Gervais had pulled out,
and Robert Campbell was now in league with Bill Sublette,
working hand-in-glove with the American Fur Company. But Tom
Fitzpatrick and Jim Bridger had elected to stay on as partners—
and, in Milt's absence, they had included him in. It would
henceforth be Fitzpatrick, Bridger, and Sublette—unless Milt said
different.

Further, unable to do otherwise as long as Bill Sublette held
notes of indebtedness against them, the two partners had agreed to
purchase their next year's supplies from American Fur, via the
elder Sublette. An account was given of Wyeth's resolve to set up
a permanent trading post on the Snake River, and a cryptic note
was added about the *damn-fool* activities of Jason Lee, the
Christian missionary Wyeth had brought to Rendezvous *to help
the Injuns find God.*

Cerré was now in charge of Bonneville's trappers, and Joe
Gale, formerly one of Bridger's men, was heading up Wyeth's

contingent, having been lured away by higher wages. And the free trappers—Carson, Meek, Mitchell, Muckaluck, Godin, and the Flatheads—were keeping camp with the partners.

All in all, Milt, things ain't as good up here as they once was. . . .

Bridger's bunch moved north to the headwaters of the Seedskeedee and began the fall hunt. Joe Meek found himself working with greater diligence than ever before. Despite falling prices, now he had a specific goal—marriage to Umentucken come next summer's Rendezvous.

It was possible, Joe knew, that Milt might yet return to the mountains—and as long as that was true, he couldn't feel right about making his *womaning* a formal thing. Yet now, after all, Milt had sent specific word. And Joe and Isabel were indeed living together in the same lodge, as much man and wife as any trapper and his squaw in the Rocky Mountains. But summer would be the right time for the marriage. Joe wanted to do it right—*the biggest gawddamned mating in the whole history of the High Shinin'*. If the situation was, indeed, just a bit complicated, it didn't make any difference. Joe Meek and Mountain Lamb. He'd put on a show that was worthy of the woman he loved, a chief's daughter, after all, and the most beautiful woman in the mountains, to boot.

The various gifts and finery that he meant to present her with would cost money, however. And that required a plentiful harvest of plew. No two ways about it.

With Washakie's Wind River Shoshones encamped next to them, the trappers were generally immune to attacks by hostile Indians; but word had it that all the tribes were up, and there was trouble in the mountains.

Word came in that Joe Gale's group had been set upon by the Blackfeet, who had killed several men and had stolen some of the cached furs. Meek and Carson and their cohorts decided to pay Gale a visit, against Bridger's advice, and rode into Gale's camp to find a battle in progress.

The Blackfeet, of course, had returned to finish what they'd started.

Gale and a dozen of his men were pinned down and nearly out of gunpowder—just holding on and hoping. Joe and Kit and the Flatheads and the three Delawares came down on the band of Blackfeet from behind, rifles and pistols snapping to deadly effect. The *Pieds Noirs,* not at all certain that a hundred or more trappers might not be following close behind, took to their ponies and headed northward toward the Three Forks of the Missouri.

A week later, a number of Washakie's horses disappeared overnight, and the general feeling was that some marauding Crows, notorious for their thefts of livestock, had *borrowed* the animals.

Two days later, however, half a dozen Bannocks were caught in the act, and all were gunned down and scalped. Meek undertook to track back to their camp and found the trappers' stolen horses grazing peacefully in a high meadow near Green River Lakes.

Despite all the *doin's,* the fall hunt went on, and Joe was taking in a considerable number of furs. Not only was Mountain Lamb extremely diligent and even expert at the dressing of the plew, but occasionally she accompanied Joe on his haunts. Little Salmon, now two years of age, was old enough to be left for a few days at a time with Washakie's wives, or with Bent Feather, Chief Gray's daughter—the latter still being courted by the utterly determined Doc Newell and still being withheld from marriage by her father.

On one such venture Joe and Mountain Lamb, working their way up a drainage back in the Wind River Range, and within sight of Gannett Peak, discovered that several of their traps had been robbed.

"Bannocks again, I suspect," Joe remarked, and then cursed softly so that Mountain Lamb would not hear him.

"Are they still close by, do you think? Perhaps we should not go any farther. . . ."

A rifle ball ripped bark from the young pine against which Meek was leaning, and an instant later came the report of a rifle.

Joe spun about, pulled off a shot from his pistol, and yelled for Mountain Lamb to get to her pony.

Two more shots humming close by, and then they were riding, urging their horses downstream and then forcing the animals upslope toward the ridge crest.

Shouts from below.

"They're after us, gal, and they ain't friendly, nuther. Stick close behind me. . . ."

Over the ridge and down a shallow ravine, the ponies plunging onward, leaping fallen logs and scattering shards of stone from beneath their hooves.

"Cave on ahead!" Joe called out. "She's big enough for the

horses too. They want to take us, they goin' to have to pay a price!"

Mountain Lamb followed unquestioningly, and when Joe drew his pony to a halt and began leading the animal upslope toward a thick cluster of aspens, she did likewise.

Behind the trees and almost totally concealed was a cave entrance, the opening some ten feet tall and nearly as wide, a fracture between slabs of granite, with some jagged boulders before it.

Joe and Mountain Lamb cajoled and pushed their spooked ponies back into the darkness, hobbled the animals, and took position behind the protection of the boulders.

"Will they find us here?" Mountain Lamb asked.

"Afraid so, Pretty Face. If they can follow horse-sign, they will. We didn't exactly cover our trail. . . ."

Now they could hear the voices of their pursuers—close by, just on the other side of the aspens.

"It's the Bannocks, all right," Joe said. "An' it sounds like they want our ha'r—mine, anyways. They'll want somethin' else from you. Isabel, ye get as far back into the cave as ye can. Crouch low and stay hid in the darkness. An' don't make no noise, no matter what happens out here."

"I'm staying with you, Joe Meek. I will keep the rifles loaded for you."

Meek saw the wisdom of what she proposed and squeezed her arm.

"Okay, okay. We might as well go up in flames together, then. Let's see if we can give them boys a little tussle first, though. . . ."

For nearly an hour they listened as the Bannocks fussed about down below them and yet made no attempt to continue their pursuit.

"Aren't they going to attack us, Joe Meek?" Mountain Lamb asked. "I don't understand."

"They're stewin' about 'er, Pretty Face. We got position on 'em, an' they're tryin' to figger out how to get us without takin' no losses of their own. Truth is, the Bannocks is like mischievous kids. It ain't even that they got any grudge against us, I don't expect. Like coyotes huntin' lizards, even when they don't want to eat 'em."

"Or spiders?" Mountain Lamb asked. "Yes, I have seen coyotes doing that."

"Or mebbe they're waitin' for some of their friends to show up. More of 'em there is, the braver they get."

At that moment boulders began to crash down from above, hurtling past the cave's entrance and bounding downslope. Dust swirled up and drifted back into the darkness.

"What is happening?" Mountain Lamb cried out.

"Tryin' to shut us up in our own hole, likely. . . ."

Whoops and shouts from the aspen grove.

Meek slipped forward, wriggled his way along the base of the cliff face for a short distance, drew aim, and fired. One of the two Bannocks above the cave mouth cried out and then pitched forward, the body arcing through space and landing with a muffled thud on the granite lip directly over the cave. The legs hung over, spasmed, and were still.

Once back beside Mountain Lamb, Meek roared at the Indians.

"This here's the Bear-Killer, boys! I'm not lookin' for trouble, but I'll kill an' scalp the lot of ye if I have to! I ain't riled yet, but I'm goin' to be real soon. No way ye can get to me, but I'll pick ye off, one by one!"

Three shots in answer, two of them flattening themselves against the rock and the third humming back into the cave and sending the ponies into a frenzy of snorting and whinnying.

Silence for a moment.

"Give us your horses!" a voice came up in English. "Then we will let you go! I know who you are, Bear-Killer. You take the beavers from our streams. Now you must give us your horses in return!"

"Will they go away if we give them the animals?" Mountain Lamb whispered.

"Naw," Joe answered. "They're playin' for time while they figger out what to do, just like I am."

The dead Bannock on the lip above fell, landing on his shoulder in front of the boulders behind which Joe and Mountain Lamb were crouched, the form sprawling, the neck snapping backward under force of impact.

"Figger we'll have another visitor in about ten seconds," Meek said. "He's up above us. . . ."

A very live Bannock leaped down, whooped, and lunged forward into the cave, a pistol in both hands.

Joe and Mountain Lamb fired at the same instant, and the

Bannock, struck in mid-chest and through the throat, collapsed at their feet.

Screams of rage from below.

"I told ye—ye damned Red divvels! I'm gettin' riled now! I'm goin' to come out an' put the rest of ye under!"

Then a voice from the aspen grove.

"Bear-Killer! How many men are with you?"

"Half my brigade!" Joe shouted back. "Me an' eight others. Unless ye got about fifty coons with ye, we're goin' to skulp the lot of ye!"

"You lie, Bear-Killer Meek. You have only one other. Do you think we are fools?"

"Come on up an' have a look around, then," Meek answered. "Hell, we won't hurt ye none!"

The exchange of words was followed by nearly an hour of sporadic rifle fire, gradually diminishing. For his part, Meek shot only once in a while, hardly bothering to aim.

"Nothin' to shoot at—cain't see a one of 'em. But we got to keep up a show, Pretty Face. Otherwise they might come chargin' up the hill."

When the balls of galena had ceased to hum into the cave mouth, Joe cupped his hands to his mouth and shouted down toward the aspens.

"Ye want these two dead braves with their topknots still in place? Come on up an' get 'em then. I calls a truce!"

"Why should we trust you, Bear-Killer?"

"Why should I trust you boys? Ye're the ones tryin' to kill me an' my men."

"Do you give us your word, Meek?"

"Ye got it!"

An indistinguishable babble of voices from the aspen grove, and at length one brave, unarmed and hands held at shoulder height, began to walk cautiously up the slope.

"Got ye in my sights," Meek called out. "Keep comin'. I ain't goin' to shoot as long as ye don't try nothin'!"

The Bannock hesitated, cast a glance back toward his fellows, then continued his advance. When he reached the body of the warrior who had fallen from above, he lifted him in his arms, turned, and worked his way slowly back down the slope.

"We cannot get to the other one without entering the cave!" the voice sounded up to Joe and Mountain Lamb.

Joe thought about the problem for a moment, then lifted the

dead Bannock and strode out in full sight and placed the body against the face of the granite cliff.

"Ye trusted me. Now I'm trustin' you boys. Here he is. Come an' get 'im!"

"How many men are with you, Bear-Killer?"

Joe, moving quickly back into the protection of the cave, sang out, "I lied a bit! Only four of my boys is with me!"

"You are still lying," the Bannock chieftain returned. "I think you have only one man with you. No more than two shots ever came at once!"

"Just savin' powder is all!" Joe called back, grinning and chuckling to himself.

"Where are the other horses then?" the Bannock demanded.

"My Delawares got 'em hid, that's where. Boys, we're losin' our patience real fast!"

"You only have a squaw with you!" the Bannock returned.

"Come on up an' have a look, then!"

Silence.

"Godin, dammit, hurry up with that keg!" Joe commanded, not loud—but loud enough, he hoped, that his words would carry downslope.

"Have you gone crazy?" Mountain Lamb whispered. "No one is here but you and I, Joe Meek."

"Antoine, don't argue! Gimme the damned thing. . . ."

Continued silence from below. Then the Bannock party chief himself emerged from cover and, weaponless but deigning to raise his hands, came walking up the slope. When he reached his dead warrior, he grasped the body, stared into the dark opening in the cliff face for a long moment, and turned and started downslope. Once to the aspens, the party chief called out, "I did not know that the Iroquois was a woman's dress! We will go to bury our dead now, Joe Meek. But we will take the rest of your traps with us. Next summer maybe we will sell them to you!"

Within a few minutes Joe and Mountain Lamb observed the Bannock party moving off through the sparse forest—six riders and two bodies draped over the backs of two other ponies.

Joe stood up, took Mountain Lamb into his arms, and said, "Isabel, ye want to make love right now? All of a sudden I'm wantin' ye real bad. . . ."

"My husband has lost his mind," she protested, clinging to him with one arm and running her other hand down over his belly.

"Could be," Meek said, laughing. "But could be we've just

saved our hides. Anyhow, we ain't goin' nowhere until it's come darkness.''

"What if they return with others?" she asked.

"What if they's just around the bend, waitin' for us?" He grinned and then bit at her neck.

Heavy snows, and the winter encampment at the head of Seedskeedee drew in upon itself. The fall hunt had been a great success for Joe and Mountain Lamb, and Bridger and Carson and the others had done well also. Now the snows fell day after day, and the drifts were beginning to mount, a strong east wind, down from the high mountains, piling snow heavily against the exposed sides of the lodges.

But inside, the fires were burning, and life slowed to a comfortable lull. Joe and Mountain Lamb calculated the return their combined efforts would bring them and made love during the long nights after Little Salmon had fallen asleep. One time the child awoke when Joe and Mountain Lamb were engaged in each other's embrace, and he pulled at his father's hair and cried out, "Don't hurt Mother, Joe! Please don't kill her!"

The man and the woman groaned, drew apart, and comforted the child.

"Joe Meek was not hurting me," Mountain Lamb explained. "No, he was giving me pleasure. When a man gives a woman pleasure, that is how new little ones come into the world. After a time the new one is born."

The child was not fully convinced.

"Joe was holding you down and biting at you," he protested.

"It's all right, son," Joe assured him. "Umentucken's tellin' ye the truth. Let's all go to sleep now. . . ."

Little Salmon curled up beside Mountain Lamb and was soon once more asleep, and only then did the mother place her hand where it was said a wife should always place her hand.

Joe groaned as he felt his blood begin to rush once more.

"I will give my husband some pleasure now," Mountain Lamb whispered. "Then perhaps he will give birth to the next child. . . ."

"Isabel," Joe managed. "I don't think it's goin' to work, but I'm up for tryin' 'er."

"Yes," Mountain Lamb laughed softly, "I can tell that you are. That which rises has already risen, Joe Meek. Now I will

chew on it for a while. After that you will leave me alone and let
me sleep. . . ."

Food supplies were running low, and hunting had become
quite difficult; and when Jean Marteau reported a small herd of
buffalo mired in the snowbanks only a few miles from the
encampment, there was great rejoicing, and the hunters went out
immediately and were able to bring in considerable quantities of
fresh meat.

"Cold as she is," Bridger grunted, "ain't no problem with
smokin' the meat. Just hang 'er out an' freeze 'er is all."

"Oui!" Marteau laughed. "Now we have become like the
Esquimaux, n'est-ce pas?"

"Way this damned wind keeps blowin'," Bridger laughed,
"that's what we're goin' to end up with, all right. Igloos—ain't
that what they're supposed to call 'em?"

A break in the weather, and Joe, Kit Carson, and Marteau
went out in search of more buffalo—inasmuch as one of
Washakie's scouts had reported coming across sign of a hundred or
more animals in the foothills to the immediate west of the
encampment.

Luck was with the three hunters. They found the buffalo, a
couple dozen of them, chewing peacefully at matted grass where
winds had cleared most of a small prairie of snow.

Joe loaned Marteau his *buffler pony* and set off on foot
toward the big brown cattle, a Kain-tuck long rifle in hand. Kit
trudged along beside him, the two of them intending to set up shop
just downwind of the buffalo, while the Frenchman was supposed
to circle the little herd and create sufficient distraction when the
animals began to run so that the charging creatures would move
toward the rifles rather than away from them.

Joe and Kit took their positions on a slight rise of ground,
well within range, lay down, braced themselves, each selecting a
likely-looking cow, and fired.

The two buffalo went down, and instantly and quite uncharacteristically, the remainder of the group began to run,
heading straight toward Marteau.

The Frenchman had fired off both his rifle and his horse pistol
in the attempt to turn the buffalo when Joe's horse, rearing,
pitched the man heavily to the ground. The buffalo pounded past
him and vanished over the far rim, but Marteau did not move.

Kit ran for the pony, mounted it, took off after the buffalo, was able to catch up with the animals against some bluffs where the snow still lay deep, and was able to bring down another two of them.

When Joe followed with the pack animals, he found Kit busy with the butchering.

"Marteau all right?" Kit asked.

"Didn't check," Joe answered.

"Wal, Big Joe, goddammit. Ye got to use your head sometimes. Wouldn't it be a good idee to see if he's dead or not?"

Meek nodded but said, "What'll I do with 'im if he *is* dead?"

"Cain't ye pack 'im back to camp?"

"What good's a dead man? Mebbe we ought to bury him out here. Figger he'd like that better."

"Go check on 'im, ye bull-headed nigger. An' if he's gone under, then pack 'im back to camp."

"Pack, hell!" Joe responded. "I'd ruther pack a load of meat."

"Dumb-ass coon," Carson said, growling. "Go see if he's okay an' let me keep workin'."

Joe mounted his pony and headed back toward where they'd left the unfortunate Marteau.

The Frenchman was sitting on the ground, shaking his head and smoking a cigar stub.

"Jean!" Joe called out. "Ye ain't dead, then?"

"*Enfant de garce!*" Marteau yelled. "Of course I am not dead. Do dead men sit up and talk?"

"Ye've got a point thar," Meek answered.

Spring meltout began, and Bridger suggested that the trappers leave the protection of Washakie and his Shoshones and move north some two hundred miles to the big bend in the *Roche Jaune*, at the mouth of Boulder Creek. The land lay in an overlap zone between the Blackfeet and the Crows and as a result might reasonably be expected to be free of either Nation except for wandering groups, each on its way to prey upon the other. And even that complication seemed fairly slight until after the spring buffalo hunts—at which time the minds of the warriors would turn to the less immediate needs of exacting revenge upon their enemies for griefs real or imagined. And by that time the trappers would be on their way back to Rendezvous country.

In any case, the Crows seldom if ever attacked the Whites, Fitzpatrick's misfortune notwithstanding, and the Blackfeet were presumed less hostile since As-as-to and the others had perceived the advantages of dealing with the American Fur posts at Fort McKenzie and, to a lesser extent, at Fort Cass—where the Crows themselves did their business. And a force of more than a hundred mountain men was a power to be reckoned with. Bug's Boys were not ones to take on the Blanket Chief's trappers en masse. So long as the spring hunts were carried on by men in groups, most of the trouble could be avoided.

They struck across to the Hoback and then north along the Snake River into Jackson's Hole, encountering only a couple of small bands of Shoshones who had set up their villages at the base of the Teton Range.

O-mo-gua, or Woman's Dress, the widely revered medicine man who had been present at several of the Rendezvous and who knew Bridger well, advised the trappers that they would encounter little snow among the high forests around Yellowstone Lake.

"Any *prophecy* for us, my friend?" Bridger asked.

Woman's Dress stared toward the glittering spires of the Tetons, the Mountains of the Shoshones, and finally spoke in a low voice.

"Yes," he said. "I have dreamed often, Blanket Chief. And I have not always wished to see what I have been shown. A time of great sickness is coming for the Redmen, but I do not think my people will die. This will come within one winter or perhaps two, but it will come. I see villages of Siksikas, Piegans, Bloods— other villages along the Big River. Only a few old women remain alive. These times of sickness have come before, and now they will come again. I have dreamed this thing."

Bridger nodded. He knew well of the ravages of both smallpox and the lung disease upon the Indian Peoples. What he had not seen with his own eyes he had been told about when he had first come to the mountains back in '23. Hugh Glass had told them stories of what it had been like—the same Hugh Glass whom he and Fitzgerald had left for dead only to have the old man show up again at Fort Henry, blood in his eye and greatly of a mind to lift Bridger's scalp. But then, instead of coming at him, Glass had said, "Aw, hell, you're just a fool kid. This child forgives ye. . . ."

"What do you see in store for me an' my boys, O-mo-gua?" Bridger asked.

Woman's Dress nodded and gestured with his palms up.

"Soon you will work for those who followed you about in the

mountains," he said. "And after that a time will come when you will no longer wish to catch the beaver. But there will be very few beavers then to catch anyway. All things are changing, Blanket Chief. Only the mountains remain forever."

They made their way past the big lake and through the land of geysers—an area hardly unfamiliar to Joe Meek, who had once avoided death from freezing and starvation by staying close to a bubbling hot spring and discovering that deer and elk came close to graze where the snows were melted out by the warm water that spilled into small marshes throughout the area.

Mountain Lamb had often heard of the land of spouting waters, but this was the first time she had seen them. Many among the Shoshones believed the area to be possessed by devils who lived just beneath the surface of the ground.

Joe explained that *It probably ain't so,* and since he had made the pronouncement she accepted it, but she was still relieved when the party had passed beyond the valleys where the steam came up from the earth, hissing and gurgling and spitting.

On through the Yellowstone Canyon, taking care to detour wide around a Blackfoot encampment that Muckaluck, riding ahead as scout, had reported.

When they reached Boulder Creek, they found the Yellowstone itself still frozen in places—though the ice was cracked and broken and the going was rotten.

The lodges were erected, and a majority of the men went directly to trapping.

Meek, Muckaluck, Godin, Mitchell, and the three Delawares, however, took up Bridger on his offer of pay and traveled eastward, down the Yellowstone, in search of buffalo. Finding sign of the big animals near the mouth of Clark's Fork, the hunters turned their mules up that stream and continued on for a full day without success.

That night Billy Mitchell awoke the camp with his screaming. Everyone was up quickly, and Joe piled wood on the dwindled campfire.

"Goddamn dream, I guess," Mitchell stammered. "The biggest damn white bear ye ever seen come up to me an' insisted on shakin' my hand. Wal, I weren't willin' to do 'er, but the bastard made me anyhow. That's when I woke ye all up. Hell, I'm acting like a greenhorn kid or an old squaw."

Antoine Godin had lit his pipe.

"Be glad it wasn't a female white bear," he said.

"Why's that?" Mitchell demanded.

"She would not have wished you to shake her hand," Godin replied, his face utterly without expression.

The men roared with laughter.

"Ain't funny," Mitchell persisted. "What's a dream like that mean, anyhow?"

"I have b'ar medicine," Meek said, half-chuckling. "So I'm the best one to say. Ain't that right, boys?"

Sensing a tale coming on, the other trappers agreed.

"So tell me," Mitchell said, growling.

"Now old white bear," Meek explained, "he's a powerful devil, an' that's the truth. Ast Muckaluck if that ain't so."

Muckaluck, his face solemn, nodded.

"So the way this child sees 'er, Billy, ye'd best keep your eyeballs peeled tomorrow—or ye're goin' to end up shakin' hands with Bull-zee-bup hisself. An' that, old compañero, means ye're goin' under. Now let's all get some shut-eye. Mitchell, he won't have no more bad dreams now that I've explained it all."

The men laughed and jeered at Mitchell, who offered to slit Joe's throat and then returned to his robes. But whether he slept anymore than night, no one ever knew.

First light found them back on the trail of the elusive buffalo. Luck was with them, and they came upon a small herd of perhaps a hundred animals. The trappers formed a loose *surround*, after the fashion of the Indian hunters, and closed in, firing from several sides at once. By the time the buffalo had spooked and run, a dozen animals lay dead.

Immediately Meek and his men set about skinning and butchering the creatures, and by mid-afternoon they had their mules heavily packed and were ready to return to Bridger's camp.

But near the confluence of the Clark's Fork and the Yellowstone they came upon a group of nine Blackfeet, and the Indians, apparently believing themselves more than a match for the trappers, responded by firing off their fusees.

A ball of galena narrowly missed Joe, twisting his head about and tearing off his beaver hat.

Bullets sang through the air, and Mitchell was down—had fallen from his pony.

Powdersmoke rising, half-obscuring the Blackfeet—who, fortunately, as Joe observed, were afoot. Meek leaped from his mule, pulled Mitchell to his feet, and dragged him back toward relative safety.

"Don't explain no more of my damn dreams," Mitchell said, clutching at his bleeding arm. The ball had gone completely through his biceps, and he was losing considerable blood.

Joe pushed Mitchell up onto his pony once more, slapped the animal on its rump, and called for the other trappers to stand and fight.

But it was too late. The trappers, pack mules and all, were in full retreat. Meek cursed, leaped onto his own mule, and kicked its sides.

The creature only brayed and continued standing stock-still.

"Gawd save both of us, mule, ye better get movin'. Come on now, ye long-eared hawg!"

Bug's Boys were closing in, yipping and screaming, and still the mule, despite repeated thumpings to the ribs, refused to move an inch.

Joe was ready to leap down and run for his life when the mule finally smelled something, either fresh blood or the Blackfeet themselves, and thundered forward like a racing horse from Carolina.

"Good mule!" Joe yelled, looking over his shoulder at the pursuing Blackfeet now far behind him.

The mule ran as no mule before it had ever run, and within half a mile Joe drew alongside his fellow trappers.

"Run for your lives, niggers!"

"Thought you wanted to *stand an' fight,*" Antoine Godin called back. "What happened to your backbone, Bear-Killer?"

"Fight, hell," Meek retorted. "There be a thousand of the Red divvels!"

The mule plunged on ahead, and Joe was unable to control the frenzied animal. The Yellowstone lay directly before him now, and the mule was heading straight for it.

Mules cain't walk on ice, an' the gawddamn river's friz. What's this child goin' to do?

At the river's edge the mule stopped, its tongue lolling. The creature was completely run out.

Joe jumped down, pulled loose his pack of blankets, and began to lay them out, one after another, on the ice. Then, cursing and belaboring the animal with a section of cottonwood branch, he forced the mule ahead.

The mule, finally taking to the idea, began to cooperate, and just as man and animal reached the bank, the Blackfeet appeared across the ice and opened fire once again.

Meek threw back a single round from his Hawken, mounted the mule, prayed that the varmint had caught its breath, and made for the brushy woods beyond.

Once back at Bridger's camp, the other hunters laughed loudly and jeered at any defense Meek attempted to make of his *bravery*.

Joe took it all good-naturedly, for he could do little else.

Finally he said, "Aw, hell, boys. Live an' let live. But if she comes to one or the other, this nigger would ruther live."

Mountain Lamb, Joe discovered, was far more sympathetic to his account of what had happened. She was delighted with him for still being alive, and that night they made love three times.

But in the morning, Joe was still a bit nettled by the thought that anyone had actually questioned his courage. He sulked about, was short-tempered even with Mountain Lamb, and finally rode off into the woods alone to regroup his thoughts.

And that night, around the big fire, he engaged in a bragging contest with Howard Stanbury, a young lieutenant of the United States Cavalry. Stanbury had brought in a small detachment of soldiers during Meek's absence.

Stanbury was a big fellow, and very full of himself—certain he could whip any man in the mountains in a fair fight, White or Indian either. When, at length, tempers began to flare, the lieutenant found himself standing nose to nose with Bear-Killer Meek. And only at this point did he begin to have second thoughts about a fistfight.

Despite the remonstrations of both Jim Bridger and Kit Carson, the two concluded that they would shoot it out with rifles at thirty yards.

"So who's goin' to command yer soldier boys when Joe here puts ye under?" Carson asked the lieutenant.

Stanbury pulled off his military jacket and tossed it to the ground.

"You take over, little man," Stanbury snarled.

Carson pulled his knife and started forward, but Bridger restrained him.

Meek bellowed with laughter and slapped the stock of his Hawken.

"Come on, coon," he shouted. "I ain't skulped no army boys in six, seven months now. Be good to get back into practice. . . ."

At that moment a huge grizzly came lumbering into the camp, stopped, stood, and gazed dimly about.

"Have a contest on the b'ar, then," Carson shouted. "Countin' coup on a white b'ar is powerful. Ye got teeth for it, soldier boy?"

Joe let out a whoop and ran for the bear, drew out the rifle's wiping stick on the run, and proceeded to lash the astounded giant with the hickory shaft. Three times he struck, and the grizzly roared its rage and punched at Joe with a huge paw.

Meek leaped out of the way, set himself, and fired his Hawken.

The bear was dead on the ground before Stanbury could even set his triggers.

The officer strode forward, stared down at the slain monster, and turned to shake Joe's hand.

"Mr. Meek," he said, "that's the most astonishing thing I've ever seen. That bull-slinging contest of ours—you weren't bragging at all. Just telling the truth. You've made a believer out of me."

Joe shook the lieutenant's hand, squeezing just a bit harder than necessary, and grinned from ear to ear.

"Just that I've got powerful *b'ar medicine* is all. Come on—let's go see if Bridger's got any ee-legal whiskey in camp. Mebbe we could both do with a snort. Ye want the hide of that varmint? She's yours. . . ."

CHAPTER THIRTEEN

Marriage in the Rocky Mountains

High on the back of the continent he trudges across snowbanks, stops, suddenly aware of the creature before him—a mountain goat. The eyes are suspicious but not particularly afraid.

The goat paws at loose rocks, and pebbles fall, sifting downward, leaping out into space, almost drift with currents of air in their descent—three thousand feet down to the floor of a big glacial basin.

The goat is not concerned that his fleece is in terrible shape, hanging in yellow-white streamers with the spring shed.

The man is not armed, and the mountain goat chooses to ignore him, returns to browsing.

Elevation ten thousand feet: great chunks of granite, slabbed off, tumbled, ice-scoured domes, orange-gray, rich with feldspar. Whitebark pine below, blue spruce, clumps of gooseberry, sage-green lichens spattering the rocks.

The man moves downslope, comes to a little river flooding and ripe with snowmelt—it hurls itself down, a thundering torrent over the granite, white-gleaming in sunlight, a branch of Clark's Fork of the Yellowstone. The water bursts its whole energy into a hundred-foot trench, a swirl and explosion and foaming roar of white water.

Small spruces cling to granite by melting snowbanks. They drip, drip in the sun-glittering spray.

The stream gathers and surges onward, down the mountain, other falls, deep blue canyons, out into a valley far below.

This water, the man knows, will journey four thousand miles—to the Missouri—to the Mississippi—to the Gulf of Mexico. But here it pounds through boulders below him, and he lies back against a young pine. For this moment he is alone, as if there were no other human presence in the entire Absaroka Range.

He stares fixedly at the boiling white current, a constant writhing and thunder of mist-smoke.

What is it he sees? Something barely visible, half-formed in the upsurge of cold steam?

The face of Old Man Who Does Everything. . . .

After the soldiers had left, a large force of Blackfeet approached the trappers' encampment. Outnumbered perhaps four or even five to one, Bridger, Carson, Meek, and all the others were nevertheless ready to fight.

The mountain men began immediately to fortify their position, and for a time Mountain Lamb simply watched. Then she put Little Salmon into the care of Bent Feather and hurried to where Meek was digging and hurling rocks and earth up against a log abutment.

"What can I do?" she asked.

"Whar's the Whale?"

"With my friend. Here, I'll help dig. Are the Blackfeet certain to attack us, Joe Meek?"

"Think ye're gettin' to like firefights," Joe said, grinning. "Know who your daddy was, but I figger your mama must of been a mountain lion or summat. Yeah, we need to take this up about another half-foot or so."

"You did not answer me, Joe."

"Don't know for sure what they got in mind," he replied. "The Blackfeet ain't actin' natural. Right now a bunch of 'em's out on the island poundin' drums. But I guess they've decided to hold off until tomorrow, anyhow. They don't want to fight us coons until their medicine's *powerful*."

Kit and Gabe came up from behind and began laughing.

"What do ye honchos figger is so funny?" Meek demanded. "Them boys ain't out there playin' us no serenade."

"These two look like prairie dogs cleanin' out their burrow," Carson suggested.

"More like gophers," Bridger countered.

"Ye'll look like *gophers* when ye're runnin' around with little red hats on," Joe said, snorting.

"Think we've done about all we can, Joe," Bridger said. "It's up to the *Pieds Noirs* now."

Meek thrust his shovel into the loose earth and scratched at a mosquito bite on his forehead.

"Tell ye what," he said. "Them Blackfeet are havin' second thoughts. Either they didn't know we was here, or else they were countin' on most of us bein' away from home. If Old Man

Coyote's in the right mood, he'll give 'em some excuse to head on so's they can find a herd of Absarokee horses to steal."

"Unless us coons has had the bad judgment to set up camp on some of their sacred ground. In that case, they've got no choice but to try an' drive us off."

Meek glanced at Bridger.

"Ye figger that's what we done, Gabe? Ain't no evidence of anything of the sort around here."

"Don't know, Joseph. Any case, I don't see any way for 'em to whup us. They got the numbers, but we got the guns. An' like most Injuns, they never quite figgered it out that the purpose of fightin' is to kill the enemy an' not just to count coup. Win a battle an' lose braves, an ye've got to go do 'er all over again until ye get 'er right. We're dug in, an' it's goin' to cost 'em some men to roust us out. But the damned drums is startin' to get to the boys. Me too, for that matter."

"Wagh!" Carson grunted.

"*Wagh!* is right," Meek agreed. "I'm with ye on that. The sound is just plain ghostlike."

The afternoon hours dragged on, tedious and seemingly endless. And even after sundown the pounding of parfleches and wild songs continued, increasing in fervor.

War dance.

Firelight and shadows drifted out across the swift-running Yellowstone, now high with spring melt, and owls called and coyotes screamed, the total result being a terrible, almost supernatural chorus of dissonant and yet peculiarly harmonious sounds.

Godin and Muckaluck proposed sending men across under the cover of darkness, by means of bullboats, and attempting to pitch a powder keg or two into the big fire on the island, but Bridger overruled the idea.

"As long as they're whoopin' an' yellin' an' singin'," he argued, "they ain't nothing but an annoyance. The Blackfeet is gettin' up a fine head of steam, but they won't be comin' at us until sunup. Whatever they do, we're ready for 'em. When they start across the river, it's goin' to be like target practice at Rendezvous. As long as we don't rile 'em any more than they already are, mebbe they'll dance themselves silly an' come to their senses. If we don't have to fight, we don't lose none of our boys."

Meek watched the goings-on across the water for some time,

Umentucken sleeping fitfully in her robes beside him, next to the small fire he had kindled to produce at least a minimal source of heat against the freezing cold of the early March night. It was past midnight, as Joe calculated the time, and still the Blackfeet were at it.

Doc Newell joined Meek, bringing with him a pot of steaming coffee. He greeted Joe, set the pot next to the fire, and gazed down at the sleeping Mountain Lamb.

"You're a lucky nigger, Joe. She'd never be out of your sight if she had choice in the matter. Me, I'm goin' to be older than Le Blueux before the chief gives in. . . ."

"Don't suppose ye brought a tin cup with ye?" Joe asked.

"Thought you just drank 'er straight from the pot, Bear-Killer." Newll laughed and then produced a pair of government-issue tins. "Didn't realize Mountain Lamb was here. . . ."

Meek poured the coffee and handed a cup to Doc.

"So old Gray's still holdin' out on ye? What's Bent Feather's price these days?"

"Entire state of Missouri or some such," Doc answered. "Come summer Rendezvous, though, I'm thinkin' about headin' for Spanish California."

"Don't work worth sour peanuts," Joe said. "I tried 'er, an' I know."

"Difference is," Doc replied, "this child's goin' to take the gal with him. If it comes to that, I'll do 'er, too."

Joe sipped the hot coffee, noted a strange light in the northern sky, and stared up at it.

"What the hell?" he mused.

"North lights, I guess," Doc said.

A pale red glow, increasing in intensity even as they watched—and within moments streamers and filaments began to appear, hanging curtains and dartlings of light pulsating in the heavens like some vast, living thing, expanding out from its center into a long, fiery band across the north and composed of nodules, luminous and darkening to crimson streaked with white and blue-green. Lights that danced and shifted, streamers and bundles of filaments.

"The Blackfeet see it too," Joe said, his voice tight. "Listen—the damned drumming's stopped."

He roused Mountain Lamb and pointed at the sky.

"What is it, Joe Meek? Has the attack begun?"

"Somethin' else is goin' on, Isabel. The whole damned sky's on fire. . . ."

"North lights," Newell insisted. "But this child's never seen anything like these before."

Sky-shapes, moving, shifting about, cloudlike forms appearing and glowing and vanishing.

"It is beautiful," Mountain Lamb said, clinging to Joe's arm. "When this happens, my people say that the Great Creator is dreaming again. If Old Man Coyote is not asleep, he will see it and know what it means. Then he will have to change things here on the earth."

A shudder went through Joe's body, and he burst out laughing in spite of himself.

"Do you think that is true, what I have just said?" Mountain Lamb asked.

"Sounds good to this coon," Joe answered. "Wagh! I never seen nothin' like 'er."

"I know what Godin will say." Newell chuckled. "He'll tell us the Great Manitou wishes us to go back to Europe, wherever the hell that is."

"Iggerant Iroquois," Joe said, nodding. "But the real question is what the Blackfeet are goin' to make of it. It'll either be that the Dreamer's tellin' 'em to attack at dawn or to go take their spite out on the Crows. Mebbe even to go home an' make love to their women."

"That sounds best," Mountain Lamb said softly, pressing against Joe's side. "It is much better for the men to do that than to go to war. I think so."

"Isabel's right, dammit," Joe said, laughing. "When the sun comes up, we'll know which it is."

The lights persisted, sometimes growing in intensity, sometimes fading, finally shifting to a long arch across the northern sky just before dawn, and then vanishing as the gray-white stillness spilled in over the low eastward ridges.

And as the sun rimmed the horizon, the trappers watched and thanked whatever gods they secretly exalted as the Blackfoot force, forming into a long line of men on horseback, withdrew without offering either battle or even a volley of shouted insults.

The spring hunt progressed, and Bridger's Irregulars moved south, working the mountain streams as they went, up Boulder Creek and toward Granite Peak and the Beartooth Range, then down country to the upper reaches of the Yellowstone and the land of geysers and hot springs, past the big lake and on toward Jackson's Hole. Joe Meek labored like a man possessed, bringing in enough plew to satisfy three trappers.

Bridger let it be known that Joe had sold his soul to one of the Yellowstone devils, and Carson wondered if he had not somehow come across another extensive American Fur cache.

"Costs money to *woman*," Joe explained. "Me an' Isabel are gettin' hitched proper. A coon marries the beautifulest woman in the entire Rocky Mountains, he's got to buy her one or two leetle things."

"Thought ye was already hitched," Carson said, laughing. "Sure looks that way to me an' the boys."

"Wal," Joe responded, "we is, I guess. But we got to have the ceremonies. Ain't ye got no respect for tradition?"

"Tradition is just what happens an' nobody questions it, is all," Carson said.

"What if old Milt shows up?" Bridger asked.

"Isabel's made her choice, whether Milt likes it or not," Joe said. "I love the man, but I love her more. Milt'll understand. Likely he's found him some high-stocking Saint Louis woman anyhow."

"What if he wants Mountain Lamb back?" Bridger persisted.

"Then he's got to fight me for 'er. This child ain't givin' up Umentucken, no matter what. Gawd hisself couldn't pry me loose from that gal. Don't ye know nothin' about love, ye dumb-ass greenhorn?"

Summer Rendezvous, '35, on Seedskeedee. Green River, as the newcomers called it. At the mouth of New Fork, between North Piney and Cottonwood, an area of extensive meadows, good forage, and plentiful game.

Five of Bridger's Irregulars had gone under that spring, these to marauding Blackfeet. And, as other bands found their way to the Rendezvous site, further tales of conflict with the Indians were told. Blackfeet, Utes, Cheyennes, some of the Shoshone groups, Crows, Arapahos—everyone was eating at everyone else, and the trappers were getting caught in the middle of it.

North of the Yellowstone, apparently, no one was safe—and out into the Bighorn Basin no horse was safe due to the predations of the Crows and the Cheyennes as well.

"With them boys," Meek laughed at a greenhorn, "ye might keep your ha'r, but ye won't have no pony."

Bonneville and Joe Walker and their men came in, and the captain let it be known that they'd had a *fair* hunt but had parted with many of their furs to Nathaniel Wyeth at Fort Hall on the Snake. Even so, the trappers were obsessed with the idea of attending the Rendezvous. Some had furs, and some had money. But all wanted to come.

Old Bill Williams and his boys drifted up from Taos and the Sangre de Cristos, and Bill the Preacher reported a good spring hunt.

Bands of Indians and free trappers showed up until the meadows along the Seedskeedee resembled a small city of elk-hide lodges. And Drips was there with his brigade as well.

The Blackfeet showed up too, stole eighteen horses, and made tracks for the mountains. Carson, Meek, and Mark Head chased the *thievin' Red divvels* for a good distance and finally gave up, returning to Rendezvous empty-handed. Bridger howled and moaned about *incompetence*, gathered together a party of fifty, and set off after the long-vanished *Pieds Noirs*, but after a day or so decided the horses were a lost cause. When he came riding back in, Carson, Meek, and Mark Head led the jeering, and for a time Gabe refused to speak to his old friends.

But then he got interested in a serious way with a Flathead girl he referred to as *Cora*, and his disposition seemed to change for the better.

Captain Bonneville approached Meek about the possibility of the Bear-Killer's working for him.

"You did a good job for me on the California expedition, Joe. Everyone respects you, and I need someone else to keep my men's noses to the grindstone, so to speak. Perhaps we could enter into some sort of arrangement?"

"Don't know," Joe replied. "Guess I'd ruther work for my own company, to tell the truth. A coon's better off in not having to account to nobody unless he wants to. Me, I sort of string along with Bridger, just like old Kit does. But both of us works our own cricks, just like Gabe an' his boys works theirs. We get along better because we ain't takin' a salary."

"Your own company?" Bonneville asked. "Well, Joe, how much does your company pay you?"

"Wal," Joe answered, scratching at his beard, "this child's

had a purty good year. Even at low dollar, I'll take in fifteen hundred dollars or more."

Bonneville shook his head.

"I need your help, Joe," said. "I'll pay you fifteen hundred to work for me next year."

Joe dug at the ground with the toe of his moccasin and thought about the offer before he answered.

"Wouldn't be wise, Cap'. Might be I'll never pull in this many plew again. Ye see, this year I had an object—somethin' particular that was pushin' me on. Ye'd lose money on me."

"It's not just beaver I need you for," Bonneville protested. "Think it over, Joe."

"Done thought it over," Joe answered. "Ye're a good man, Cap'. But once a coon gets used to workin' for himself, he just cain't go back to bein' hired help."

The Fourth of July arrived and passed, and the Rendezvous settlement was growing uneasy. Tempers were beginning to flare, and good-natured contests of skill among the mountain men sometimes turned into bloody brawls and knife fights.

"Whar the hell's Lucien Fontenelle?" Bridger demanded.

"A long history of bein' late," Meek said. "Now old Billy Sublette, he'd be here by now."

"Particularly if he was tryin' to outrun Fontenelle," Carson added, flinging his Green River knife through the firelight and sticking it into the trunk of a dead cottonwood. "Ye goin' to get hitched to leetle Cora, Gabe? Mitchell says ye been grumblin' about it."

"Fontenelle's probably dead drunk on the Wind River somewheres," Meek suggested. "Mebbe we ought to go look for 'im."

"An' whar's Fitz this time?" Bridger complained.

"He didn't run fast enough, an' the Big Bellies got him," Carson said. "Ye goin' to answer my question like a Whiteman, or not?"

"What question, Kit?"

"Ye know damned well what question, ye big stumblebum."

"Ye mean about Cora? Why, I might at that. She's a fine little gal, I'll tell ye."

"Humps like a prairie dog," Carson said, grinning. "That's what Drips' brigade tell me."

Bridger glared at the smaller man and slowly pulled out his own skinning knife.

"Ain't knife fightin'," Carson said, yawning. "My blade's stuck in the tree yonder."

"Go get it, you half-growed runt."

"Just joshin', Gabe. Just joshin'. Thought ye could take a joke."

Meek lit his pipe and propped his feet up on a stone.

"I heared somethin' else," he said. "Newell tells me old Kit here's been eyein' one of them Arapaho gals that come in with Crooked Nose an' his boys. Grass-Singing-in-Wind—that's the name I heard mentioned. Only Chounard, that big Frenchy in Bill Williams' bunch, he's been lookin' 'er over, too."

"He needs killin', that one," Carson replied, his expression suddenly serious.

"Goddamned bully is what he is," Bridger agreed. "It's just a matter of time until one of our boys gets his back up an' puts galena between his eyes."

"True or not, Kit?" Joe asked.

Carson grinned, the firelight glinting from his teeth.

"Everybody else is fixin' to woman," he said. "I might as well join in—if she'll have me. Hell yes, we been talkin' down by the river. I admit it. We'll see, coons, we'll see."

"Might be three of us, then," Bridger said, laughing.

"Four," Meek said.

"Who's four? Godin, mebbe?"

"Doc."

"Ye really figger Gray's goin' to let go of that daughter of his? Looks to me like the old rascal's plannin' to bed 'er himself. Any case, he sure ain't encouragin' Doc much."

"Doc's figgerin' to kidnap her an' take off for California. He told me that the night the Blackfeet got worried about the lights in the sky, up on the *Roche Jaune*," Meek replied.

"Doc just might do 'er, too," Carson said, rising and walking over to retrieve his knife.

Another two weeks passed, and no Fontenelle. Some of the free trappers had already deserted Rendezvous, heading for the Snake River and Fort Hall to take in supplies for the autumn hunt.

And Joe Meek couldn't stand it any longer—not knowing if Milt was coming or not—wanting to sell his big stash of furs—

wanting to put on a grand wedding for the benefit of Umentucken, Tukutsey Undenwatsy.

Muckaluck and Godin agreed to go with him in the attempt to find out what had happened to the supply train, and the three were loading their packhorses when word came in—an advance rider for the supply caravan.

"Two days south," Black Harris said. "I left 'em at La Barge Creek."

"Any word of whar Fitz is at?" Bridger demanded.

"Sure enough," Harris said, laughing. "He's with the caravan."

"With Fontenelle?"

"Nope," Harris said, pausing overly long to take a drink of water. "Not with Fontenelle. White Hair's the one bringin' your groceries. Him an' the boys ain't been trappin' this spring at all. They been down to Saint Louis. He's done sold ye to American Fur, Gabe. Coon, ye're workin' for the company now. We all are. How's them for apples?"

"He's done what?" Bridger roared.

Meek pushed forward, pounded Harris on the back, and asked, "Is Milt with 'im? Tell me that, Mose, an' I'll leave ye be."

"Joe," Harris responded, "this old man's got bad news for ye. Milt's still in the settlements. Had to have his leg cut off, but he's okay now. Gettin' around on a crutch an' none too happy about 'er, but fat an' sassy an' figgerin' he'll live to be a hundred or so. Got a letter for ye."

Harris fished into his buckskins and withdrew a worn, soiled, wadded-up envelope, which he handed to Joe.

The missive had been sealed with wax originally, but that had been broken—and clearly not a matter of accident.

"You done read it?" Meek asked.

"Ye know this nigger cain't read," Harris protested. "Besides, mail's private like."

But Harris was grinning.

Meek opened the letter and stared at it. Milt's handwriting, no question.

One sentence stood out. The words had been underscored:

Joseph, I hereby renounce all rights to Isabel—and if you don't marry her and take care of that child of yours, I promise I'll come west again and personally whip on you until you've done right by her.

Meek let out a whoop that startled everyone, fired his pistol into the air, and set out running for his lodge.

The caravan came in, escorted by nearly two hundred trappers and Indians who had ridden out to meet it. Fitzpatrick, after a brief and not altogether unpleasant talk with Bridger, set up shop and began buying furs. Prices were low again, just as everyone figured they would be.

Joe Meek netted $1,621—and demanded cash money.

"Ye gone crazy, Joe?" Tom Fitzpatrick asked.

"Got that much in coin? I'll bring 'er right back, honest. Be back in an hour or less. Then this child's goin' to do some fancy spendin'!"

Fitz glanced at Bridger, and Gabe said, "Give it to 'im if ye can, Tom. Coon catches as many beavers as Joe here, he deserves to act loco for a leetle while."

Meek took the bag of gold coins to his lodge and spread them out before Mountain Lamb and Little Salmon.

"We ain't rich, but we're damned near rich!" he gloated. "Just think of all the foofuraw we can buy with these. Tell me what ye want, an' I'll buy it. We're goin' to have us *some* wedding, Pretty Face!"

Little Salmon picked up a handful of the gold coins and stared at them—wondered if they contained some sort of magic that he did not understand.

"You gave away all our furs for these?" Mountain Lamb demanded. "Joe Meek, take them back and get us what we need. I do not understand you. No one could ever wear this many medallions!"

Joe roared with laughter, kissed Mountain Lamb on the mouth, and scooped the coins back into the bag.

Little Salmon looked keenly disappointed and started to turn away.

"Here, son," he said, handing the child one of the fifty-dollar golds. "You put that in your pocket now, ye hear?"

And with that the Bear-Killer was gone.

When he returned he had with him a string of ten beautiful spotted Nez Percé horses, one of which was an exceptionally marked dappled gray with a fine Spanish saddle and an elaborately decorated *maishoo-moe-goots,* a specially designed saddlebag for the gathering of roots and berries. The bridle was set with Mexican silver dollars.

"She's yours, Pretty Face Isabel," Joe said. "Three hundred dollars an' more she cost, an' worth every penny. The Nez Percés say her name is *All Fours*. Ain't she a beauty? That's a pony as will *shine* when ye ride 'er!"

Rendezvous was on, a virtual explosion of devilment, merry-making, and drunkenness. The first night a Flathead and a Crow played the hand game, and at length the Flathead lost everything. Still he wished to continue and, lacking anything else to wager, he bet his scalp. When he lost, the Crow pulled out his skinning knife and took what he had won. On the second night, the Flathead, having sold his squaw several times to various trappers, managed to secure a second grubstake. His head bandaged, he sought out his Crow gambling mate, and once more the hand game began.

But now luck was working the other way, and by midnight, with both Indians roaring drunk, the Crow was reduced to wagering his own scalp. He lost, and the debt was paid. But still the Crow wished to continue and made the ultimate wager—his life.

When, after some time and much gyration and taunting, the Flathead correctly guessed which hand held the stick, the Crow stood up, crossed his arms, and closed his eyes. The Flathead plunged his knife into his opponent's throat, watched him struggle for breath as he bled to death, and walked away.

Meek was of the opinion that things were getting out of hand.

Bridger got drunk that second night also and sent Carson to fetch the doctors—men who had come in with the Scot nobleman, Sir William Drummond Stewart—an old preacher named Sam Parker and a young man of the cloth, this one also a bona fide medical doctor named Marcus Whitman.

"Gents," Bridger said, grinning, and at the same time blinking and wondering if he was going to have to vomit, "I done thunk 'er over. Got this arrowhead in my back—been there for a spell now. I was wonderin' if ye could tickle 'er out for me."

With that Bridger pulled off his buckskin shirt, took another long drink of the arwerdenty, and lay down on a hewn-plank camp table.

Whitman was hesitant, but Bridger was insistent. The young doctor had no choice finally but to get his scalpel out and begin to probe the sizable lump on the mountain man's back.

Bridger swore once or twice while the operation was in progress but was otherwise quiet. Whitman cut away at the network of scar tissue and cartilage that had formed around the obsidian point during the years it had been embedded, and, with sweat standing out on his forehead and with Gabe clinging to the table and grunting like a grizzly, he managed to tease out the two-inch-long flake of sharpened stone.

Rivulets of blood were running all over Bridger's muscular back, and more blood was pooling along his spine.

Only when Whitman applied the solution of astringent alum and water did Bridger howl out—startling the doctor to such an extent that he dropped his flask.

"Wagh!" Bridger growled as he sat up. "What'd ye put on me, Doc, some divvel's juice?"

"To tell the truth, Mr. Bridger, I'm astounded that point didn't take infection and kill you."

Gabe started to pull his buckskin shirt back on.

"I've got to bandage that, Jim. . . ."

"If the arrer didn't kill me, a leetle scrapin' ain't goin' to. Kit, whar'd ye put my jug?"

In the morning Stewart's favorite horse was missing, and his new Kentucky long rifle as well.

"Know who might have done 'er?" Mark Head asked.

Stewart shrugged.

"Ain't seen that Iowa of yours this mornin'," Head suggested. "What's the coon's name?"

"Marshall," Stewart replied, "but he wouldn't . . ."

"Can't trust Iowas," Head declared. "Bridger run him off a year ago for takin' up two of my traps. We caught him red-handed, as you would say."

Sir William Stewart broke into a string of profanities and offered five hundred dollars for Marshall's scalp, if he was indeed the thief.

"Put it this way," Head suggested. "Five hundred, an' I'll bring ye back the scalp of whoever it was took 'em."

"It's a deal, sir," the Scot agreed.

Head walked off whistling. He asked a few questions, saddled his pony, checked his possibles sack, and rode out of camp.

A day later he returned, Marshall's scalp, quite fresh, dangling from the barrel of his Hawken.

"Kept my word," Mark Head drawled, wagging the scalp back and forth. "An' here's your horse an' rifle into the bargain. You still up for that reward?"

Stewart, whose temper had cooled in the intervening twenty-four hours, stared at the scalp and nodded.

"The return of the horse and the rifle would have been sufficient, Mr. Head. You didn't need to butcher the man."

"Just followin' directions, Yer Honor. Do I get my money?"

Stewart paid the reward in the amount previously agreed upon.

With the Reverend Samuel Parker presiding, Joe Meek was married to Umentucken, Tukutsey Undenwatsy-Isabel. The two sat their ponies as Parker spoke the English words of ritual, and the mountain men cheered continually during the ceremony.

Joe was wearing a handsome new set of buckskins that Mountain Lamb had sewn for him, having temporarily laid aside his bearskin capote at his woman's insistence. And Mountain Lamb wore a skirt she had made from the bolt of blue broadcloth Joe had bought for her, while both her bodice and her leggings were of scarlet silk, the finest fabric Fitz had brought up country. In addition, she wore a scarlet hood over her long, braided hair, and her new moccasins of white leather were decorated with blue and red glass beads.

Joe held his Hawken across his lap as Parker spoke the binding words, while Mountain Lamb had fastened to one side of her saddle a tomahawk, symbolic of war, and on the other a tobbaco pipe, emblematic of peace.

When Parker uttered the final words, "I now pronounce you man and wife," and the two lovers leaned toward each other to kiss, a mighty roar went up from the assembled throng.

The two paraded their horses about, and Joe shook hands with half the encampment. Mountain Lamb smiled, basking in the genuine outpouring of affection from this motley tribe of Long Knives and Indians to which she had become attached and to which she most certainly belonged. A strange tribe they were, but they were her tribe.

That night the newlyweds watched as the Arapaho contingent held its ceremonial soup dance, a communal ritual of courtship among their own people, but a *doin's* that soon became a great favorite at Rendezvous.

A big kettle of soup hung steaming over a bed of coals at the center of the dancing area, and the mountain men, most of them actually sober, wore their best and cleanest clothing and stood about in a circle, talking, laughing, and hoping.

Around the kettle danced the unmarried women, of whom, this year, there were some twenty or thirty who had chosen to participate. The men vied for the attentions of the dancers, who, in turn, were at liberty to make acknowledgment or not, as they chose. Should one decide to bestow special favor, she would dance across the circle carrying a ladle of soup and present it to the man of her choice. Thereupon, the man was entitled to robe-in with the young woman, provided only that the two stayed within plain sight of all, thus relieving the girls' fathers of undue concern. Beyond that, nothing might happen—as the young woman chose. Or, on the other hand, it was possible that a courtship might begin—something leading to the paying of a bride-price and hence to marriage.

The ritual was Arapaho, but women from all the groups present had joined in. Swallow-darting, the young Flathead woman who had taken Bridger's fancy and whom he called Cora, was among the dancers this night. So was Bent Feather, the Delaware. And so was Grass-Singing-in-Wind, the Arapaho girl with whom Kit Carson was infatuated.

The dance began, and the young women commenced the stylized gyrations peculiar to their own tribal customs. Many of the dancers were quite attractive, but Kit Carson's eyes were upon just one—and such was the case as well with Jim Bridger and Doc Newell.

Grass-Singing-in-Wind, as became evident, was the most skilled of the dancers, and a number of men, White and Indian alike, attempted to gain her attention. Among these was the big Frenchman, Jean-Pierre Chounard, one who had several times during the previous days asserted that he was more than a match for any man at the Rendezvous—and who had goaded several into fights, in each case rendering his opponent unconscious with a few well-aimed blows of his huge fists.

"The bull of the mountains is after your woman, Kit," Jim Bridger whispered. "I think one of us is goin' to have to put 'im under before she's over."

Carson nodded, but his attention remained with Grass-Singing-in-Wind.

The Arapaho girl approached the kettle, withdrew a ladle of soup, and danced toward Kit—whose heart began to soar. But then she reversed direction and danced up to the whooping Chounard, who had spent the afternoon, between fights, in following her about and suggesting, bluntly, that the two of them ought to go off to the willow brake together.

Now Chounard grinned, muttered a few phrases in French, and opened his arms, licking his lips at the same time.

Grass-Singing-in-Wind smiled and flung the hot soup into his face.

Chounard cursed and started after her, but those around him managed to restrain him.

Then the girl danced again to the kettle, withdrew more soup, and went directly to Kit Carson. She offered him the ladle, and he sipped.

Bridger whooped, and Joe and Mountain Lamb applauded.

Within moments Kit and Grass-Singing-in-Wind had withdrawn to the edge of the firelight and had wrapped a buffalo robe about themselves.

Chounard had disappeared—no one seemed to know where he had gone.

The dance continued, and Bent Feather approached Doc Newell and offered him the soup ladle. The mountain men cheered as Doc and Bent Feather withdrew from the circle—and most agreed that another marriage was soon to follow. Had Chief Gray not apparently changed his mind about the tenacious Newell, surely he would not have consented to his daughter's participating in the soup dance. Doc's patient devotion to the Delaware girl was going to pay off.

Other young women chose favorites, but Cora, though coming toward Bridger again and again, had not chosen to dip any soup from the kettle.

Gabe smiled, gestured with his hands at each approach, but every time the girl danced away—laughing, smiling, gyrating back and forth in a kind of subdued frenzy.

Gabe was looking gloomy.

"That's downright pathetic," Joe Meek said to Mountain Lamb. "She's just teasin' old Gabe."

"Yes," Mountain Lamb agreed. "That is what she's doing. But she will choose him yet. You will see. . . ."

At last, with only four dancers still within the circle, Swallow-darting ladled out a quantity of the broth, danced the full circuit of men, and finally presented the soup to Bridger, who grinned, sipped, and led his Cora toward the edge of the firelight.

"You see, Joe Meek? You must not ever doubt my intuition in these matters. I know what is in the minds of other women."

"Wal," Joe replied, "this child's glad it turned out right. Do ye also know what Whitefolks do on the night of their weddin'?"

"Of course," Mountain Lamb replied. "They go home to their lodges and go to sleep."

"Some don't sleep at all," Joe said, laughing.

"Well, we must convince Little Salmon to sleep first anyway. Then we will see what happens, Joe Meek."

And she made the hand gesture for wishing to lie down with him.

A to-do in camp the next morning.

Jean-Pierre Chounard had followed Grass-Singing-in-Wind after she left Kit and had wrestled her down and attempted to rape her. When he realized she was wearing the horse-hair chastity belt as was traditional among her people, he had attempted to cut it from her. But the Arapaho girl had managed to draw her own knife and tried to stab him, slashing his forearm before he could get the knife away from her. Then he had backhanded her into unconsciousness and stridden away, cursing and looking for more whiskey.

Carson learned this when he approached the girl's father's lodge and was greeted coldly by both the brother and the father.

Grass-Singing-in-Wind's face was badly bruised, and one eye was swollen shut.

"When I return, I will bring many gifts," Carson said and exited the lodge immediately.

Meek's tepee was pitched a hundred yards away, and it was to this lodge that Carson now turned.

"Don't mean to disturb the new-weds," Carson said, a note of apology genuine in his voice. "But I got a leetle problem to take care of, an' I was wonderin', old compañero, if I might borrow your new Norris fifty-four. Maybeso I'm goin' to need more than one shot, an' it's a long piece back to my own lodge, if ye see what I mean?"

"What's wrong, Kit?" Joe demanded. "Damned if this child won't come with ye."

"Can if ye like," Carson responded, "but stay out of my way, Joseph. It's summat I got to tend to myself."

"Kit," Mountain Lamb exclaimed, "your face is white as the clouds. Why do you need Joe's pistol?"

Carson explained, and Meek reached for his Hawken.

"Remember now," Kit said, "she's my show, Bear-Killer. . . ."

They had no trouble finding Jean-Pierre Chounard. The big Frenchman was holding court, and as Kit and Joe approached, he made it clear that there wasn't an American at the Rendezvous whom he couldn't handle—no two of them together, for that matter.

"Talk's cheap, nigger," Carson said, his voice low and steel-hard. "This here's one American as wants to take ye up on it."

Chounard bellowed with laughter.

"The leetle man?" he said. *"Le petit garçon? Non,* I wish to fight this one who claims to be Bear-Killer. *Enfant de Dieu,* he is the one I will have for breakfast!"

Carson held up his own pistol and Meek's new Norris in one hand.

"On horseback," he said. "Whatever guns ye want. Ye done laid hands on the Arapaho girl, an' I'm goin' to kill ye, Frenchman."

Chounard laughed again, but now it sounded just a bit forced.

"You wish to die for *la slut?"* he asked.

"If Kit don't kill ye, I'm goin' to," Meek said. "But I'll be usin' my fists."

"Stay out of 'er, Joe," Carson said, shaking his head. "Somebody give me the loan of a horse!"

The Frenchman slapped one leg.

"I kill Kit Carson and Bear-Killer Meek," he said, laughing. "I become very famous in the mountains, *c'est a dire!* Ouf! First one, then the other!"

Word spread that something was up, and the mountain men came running, delighted at the prospect of an honest-to-God duel on horseback.

Kit mounted, thrust Joe's pistol under his belt, and charged immediately toward Chounard.

The Frenchman drew his pony about, waited, and fired. The ball clipped Carson's shoulder, but Kit kept coming. Chounard grabbed for his rifle just as Carson leaped from horseback, and the two men, locked in each other's arm's, fell sprawling to the earth.

A momentary struggle for the pistol, but Kit wrenched the weapon free and brought the barrel across Chounard's head. The

Frenchman cursed, put his hands to his face. At that instant Carson stood up, drew down with his pistol, and fired.

The ball entered through the mouth and exploded out through the rear of Chounard's skull. The body twitched and lay still.

Carson stared at the dead man, reloaded, and fired once more into the recumbent form. Then he pulled out his knife and took ha'r.

"Kit, ye all right?" Joe asked.

"Fit as a fiddle," Carson answered, returning the Norris pistol. "Guess I didn't need this after all."

With that he turned and, scalp in hand, walked back toward the lodge of Grass-Singing-in-Wind's father.

CHAPTER FOURTEEN

Shiam Shaspusia

Andy Jackson was president.

Eighteen-thirty-five was a time of turmoil for the Union, a nation just fifty-eight years on the road and intent at the same time on expanding greatly and on splitting apart. Rights for the common man as well as the rights of some common men to hold others as slaves. Agrarian interests and industrial interests. Religious freedom and religious persecution.

The year was heralded in by an attempt on the president's life, and later the new constitution for Michigan prohibited slavery within that state. The Democrats selected Van Buren as candidate for president, and Texas colonists under Travis seized Fort Anahuac on the Trinity River. Chief Justice Marshall died, and subsequent tolling of the Liberty Bell caused a crack to form. In South Carolina, abolitionist materials were removed from the mails and burned.

Texas settlers defeated a troop of Mexican cavalry. The Texas Revolution had begun.

Tammany Hall Democrats shouted down an Equal Rights faction and turned off the gaslights—but the radicals produced candles and lit them with new self-igniting matches called locofocos.

Seminole Indians in Florida did not wish to move west of the Mississippi and rallied behind Chief Osceola. Many runaway slaves were with Osceola also.

Jackson backed the prohibition of antislavery materials from the mails.

At year's end there was a great fire in New York City, while in Florida, General Thompson and his soldiers were massacred by the Seminoles—Dade and his men were also massacred on the same day.

But the Cherokees had surrendered and had signed the New Echota Treaty. Jackson, the great egalitarian, had rejected Cherokee appeals for protection of property and rights. Justice Marshall's court had ruled in behalf of the Indians, but federal

*authorities ignored the decision. When leading Cherokees agreed
to the New Echota document, their action was repudiated by nine-
tenths of the tribe. In fact, a number of the signatories were put to
death as traitors.*

*It was a time of abundant real-estate speculation, though
some predicted economic disaster.*

*In the High Shinin', where the law was that of survival and
the ethics those of bravery, cunning, and endurance, the Rocky
Mountain Fur Company, born of the efforts of Ashley and Henry in
the early 1820s and sustained as a changing partnership until
1835, had vanished as an entity. Bridger, Fitzpatrick, Sublette,
Campbell, and all who had been loyal to them were now in effect
owned by American Fur under the leadership of Chouteau and
Pratt, victors at the end of a long struggle for dominance in the
hinterlands. But by this time the beaver trade was also nearly
finished.*

Silk hats—those would do it in.

Three more mountain weddings just before the breakup of
Rendezvous, and Kit Carson and Grass-Singing-in-Wind, Doc
Newell and Bent Feather, and Jim Bridger and Cora were united
under the eyes of God and man by the Reverend Sam Parker, who,
when the whooping and cheering had quieted down, proceeded to
preach a genuine hellfire-and-damnation sermon to one and to all.

The Indians present paid particularly close attention, even
though many of them understood not a word of this strange
English that sounded more like a protracted war chant. The
reverend's voice rose and fell in an admirable series of cadences,
and his face turned noticeably red as beads of perspiration dripped
from his heavy eyebrows. Perhaps this, then, the Indians
surmised, was at the root of Long Knife medicine.

Sam Parker had been holding forth for nearly an hour, and by
now the mountain men and even the Indians, standing about in the
hot sunlight and attempting to be respectful, were beginning to
grumble and doze.

At this point, a dozen buffalo came wandering right into the
encampment, and the Whitemen and Indians shouted with glee
and took off for their rifles.

Over the cookfires that evening were roasts of hump-rib,
sizzled boudins, various other choice cuts, and a simmering pot of
tongues.

Godin and Muckaluck got into a boudin-eating contest, each
man beginning on one end of a half-cooked six-foot length of

buffalo intestine and eating his way toward the center mark, indicated by a wrapping of red ribbon.

Muckaluck was clearly winning, gobbling his way toward the ribbon, when Godin reached forward, pulled a foot or so of intestine back up Muckaluck's throat, and redoubled his efforts to reach the red band. Muckaluck attempted to cry foul, but managed only to gag.

And Godin, biting off the boudin just beyond the ribbon, spat out the red wrapping and raised his arms in victory.

The men cheered and called for more whiskey.

Sam Parker was in his lodge, brooding over the apparent failure of his sermon and outlining a second attempt for the following day. But among the lodges of the Flatheads, the Nez Percés, the Utes, the Shoshones, and the Arapahos, there was much discussion of the great power of the White medicine man.

Had he not called the buffalo directly into the encampment so that they could be easily killed? It would indeed be good to know the secret of such strong medicine.

But Joe Meek and Mountain Lamb were not present at these doings.

This, they had decided, was as good a time as any to enforce the weaning of Little Salmon from his mother's breasts—though some Indian women continued to nurse their children until the age of four or even beyond. And besides, Joe and Mountain Lamb could see easily enough that this final week before the disbanding of the big summer encampment might provide their only real opportunity to be alone, just the two of them together with nothing else to do but to enjoy each other's company and to make love as often as they wished.

Little Salmon, not altogether happy about it, was left with Washakie's wives, and Joe and Isabel rode toward Table Mountain in the Wind Rivers, to the lakes where the Seedskeedee arose.

August sunlight with the sky blue and utterly cloudless, unflawed, as in the beginning of things. And the great column of stone, the mountain, half-dissolved in silver brilliance, sheer cliffs rising to a nearly level crown where remnants of winter's snowpack still lingered. A second mountain, inverted, a nearly perfect duplicate so that it was difficult for the man and the woman to know which was the dream and which was real.

The man and the woman. She was tall, full-breasted, narrow-waisted, her hair unbound and long and black, her eyes

*the color of mud in alluvial fans except clearer and gleaming with
sunlight, her mouth full and sensual, her hands delicate, her
laughter like the music of mockingbirds. And the man, powerful
and deep-chested, his skin lighter than hers and dark with hair
across his breast and belly and legs, his eyes also brown, like hers
but wide-set, the beard and head hair black, the arms long and
heavily muscled, legs long and hips narrow, the Bear-Killer and
himself a bear of a man.*

*These two unclothed and swimming together, side by side,
through the warm waters of the shallow lake, ripples moving out
from their bodies.*

*A man and a woman, in love with each other so completely
that the word itself had lost all meaning for them. Their long time
of waiting behind them, the time of uncertainty, of fear, even of
hope that what they felt might somehow miraculously be realized
in the dark embrace, in the clinging of flesh to flesh, male to
female and female to male.*

*They splashed about in the water and turned upon their backs
and gazed up at the yellow smear of sun that blazed down over
forests of whitebark pine and fir and hemlock and spruce and
willow and bitterbrush, that engulfed the flat-topped monolith
where snowfields appeared almost as if they were patches of
space, sections of the mountain that Old Man had not quite
completed.*

*The sun drifted across the water, and the man and the woman
continued to swim, sometimes resting upon the shore or clinging
to a floating log, sometimes lying in the shallows, and sometimes
speaking and sometimes being utterly silent.*

*The water was warm, and they made love among the
wavering shadows of pines, the fluid about them only a few inches
deep and the bottom sandy. And afterward they lay embraced
together on the bank, on the sandy earth where the chapparal
grew, drifting in and out of an orange-red drowsiness and not even
opening their eyes to slap at an occasional mosquito.*

*Venison steaks sizzling over an open fire. Horned owls
calling to one another from opposite shores of the lake in the pale
crimson of alpenglow.*

*A full moon rising eastward, the air sharp now, chill, and
drenched in silver illumination, long shadows, the lake water dark
and wavelets sipping at the shore, a faint rustle of pebbles stirred
by the water.*

A dim but frenzied yapping and howling of coyotes from the broad, forested flat above the lake. Mourning doves. Cracklings of dry brush as deer, taking their scent, bounded away toward cover.

More lovemaking, the joining of male and female animals who appeared to be human but who had long since forgotten who they were and knew that it did not matter, that nothing else mattered now but the two of them and the hunger that increased even as they attempted to sate it. A man and a woman, both of them exiles from their own people and exiled by choice, two who had come together in a society of exiles, all of them criminals, and all of them saints and all of them bound by a code so fierce and yet so simple and pure that none dared to question at all and in a land that stretched out endlessly diverse and alluring and dangerous and violent and benign and unconcerned with all of them and hence pure in a way that none but they themselves could understand and that they themselves could never explain to anyone who had not been one with them and who, for that reason, would have no need of explanation.

Sleep, and wind singing down from the mountains and hissing through stands of pine and fir—no, breathing, singing without words and no words were sufficient or needful.

A pair of timber wolves came close, sensed human presence, avoided it.

Loons cried at dawn, and a grizzly, ravenous with his own massive hunger, slashed with long claws at a rotted log and licked up the white capsules of carpenter-ant eggs, shredded the punky wood until nothing remained, and then lumbered down to the lake's edge and entered the water and swam about, drinking as he did so.

From the high cliffs a pair of mountain goats stared out and saw nothing unusual, then nibbled at ground-hugging foliage and blossoms in the land above timberline where spring comes with the late melting of snow and is followed by winter.

Four days, five days had passed by. But the number did not seem to matter. Only the rhythms of day and night, of morning and of evening, and the rhythms of their own bodies as well.

How many times had they lain together since coming to the lake? They neither remembered nor thought it important to remember. All that was important was that they could not seem to have their fill of each other.

They swam and loved and walked together, even climbed up through a chute between fractured cliffs and across snowfields *and found their way to the plateau summit of the mountain and stood wordlessly gazing at the raw granite expanse of peaks and canyons that rolled away from their feet in all directions—the Wyomings, the Snake Rivers, the Gros Ventres, the Wind Rivers, the dimly visible crowns of the far Tetons. . . .*

It do shine. . . .

What god created all this?

The earth itself must have heaved and shuddered, like birth throes, like forest fire, like earthquake and storm. . . .

Hawks drifting below them, a sky island of jagged rock and scant vegetation, a place where marmots whistled and Picas skittered into burrows beneath boulders, their mouths pouched out with lichen and thick-bladed grasses.

Near-darkness when they stumbled, arm in arm, as if drunkenly, exhausted, back to their camp, each vaguely regretful that they had not also made love on the granite crown of Table Mountain—almost too tired to fix a campfire and roast the last of their venison.

But now the forest was hushed, almost expectant. Thunderheads had been building over the high peaks all afternoon, and the man and the woman could hear the distant rattlings of thunder.

They did build a fire, and they did eat—almost ravenously, and wiped the grease from their mouths with the backs of their hands.

It would rain soon. Both knew it. And they undressed each other and slipped naked away from the little firelight and waded out into the lake, were waist-deep when lightning split the sky above them, an almost-blinding burst of white light, and the terrible roar of thunder moments later, like huge boulders crashing together, and the first drops of rain began to sting at the surface of the lake.

The man and the woman laughed and splashed water at each other as the lightning came again and again and the thunder pressed down upon them.

They emerged from the water and ran together through the ozone-filled air and the beating rain, wrestled each other down close by the campfire's hissing remains and the odors of smoke and steam, and made love one more time as the rain lashed across their flesh and the forest bloomed white and went black and the weight of thunder pressed down upon them.

At last they arose, profoundly shaken, and heard the screams and stampings of their frightened horses.

Come, lightning!

Here we are!

You tried to strike us, but you could not do it! We lay open to you, and you blazed all about us and did not harm us! Our medicine is powerful. Our medicine makes us invulnerable. Nothing will ever be able to separate us!

A final flash of lightning, a blinding brilliance, and waves of noise a moment after. Everything flared into astounding, blue-silver relief, held for an instant, was gone.

A big pine, wrapped in white fire. Odors of pinesap, odors of broken wood, bark pulverized, branches crashing down, falling, bouncing. The tree burning even under the continued cloudburst, the drenching rain.

"Watch out, ye damned fool!" Joe Meek shouted into the darkness, his eyes useless with the aftervision of immense light, his ears ringing with a noise like the ocean. "That war too gawddamned close!"

The taste of her sex was in his mouth and the taste of the milk from her breasts as well. Those sensations would linger for the rest of his life, and years later they would come back to him, and he would remember. . . .

The summer encampment on Seedskeedee was over, the various bands of trappers, mules and packhorses loaded down with winter supplies, drifted invisibly away, back into the fastnesses from which they had come or on to new country, new streams—to wherever the siren cry of Brother Beaver led them. North, south, east, and west they rode, into the lands of the Blackfeet, the Comanches, the Crows, and the Shoshones.

Nor did they say goodbye to one another, for that was thought to bring on bad luck. In a world filled with all manner of dangers, *goodbye* was simply too final a word. Only if Old Coyote Man smiled would all the coons be together at Rendezvous the following year. Invariably some did not make it, but that was the way of things. That was simply how the stick floated.

RMF was no more, and the beaver trade was dying. The men knew it, but they saw little point in worrying the matter. If the mountains called to a man and showed him visions of quick riches, why, that was sufficient to get him there. And if he survived his first year in the High Shinin', that was usually sufficient to keep him there.

"Wagh!" Jim Bridger complained. "Coons like us, what

other sort of world would have us? Starve or feast, I figger to end my days hyar. . . ."

And so Bridger's brigade headed for the forks of the Missouri, dangerous country, Blackfoot lands, and for that reason the streams had been less often trapped than other places. If Bug's Boys wanted a scrap, this was the bunch to give it to them. More often than not, even the *Pieds Noirs* weren't damned fools enough to take on a tight-knit band of mountain men—not one composed of the likes of Blanket Chief, Kit, Bear-Killer, Mose Harris, Doc Newell, Antoine Godin, and their kind.

Even with Saint Louis prices as low as they were and the trade completely controlled by American Fur, a heavy take of plew might make enough of a difference for the boys to avoid disaster—to keep them going for another year.

Everyone agreed that prices would come back up—everyone agreed, but in truth, not too many believed their own words.

Jim Bridger would be his own company, then. And Meek would be his. And Carson his. The men who rode with them were loyal, and all of them were seasoned trappers. If success was possible, they would succeed.

Bill Sublette and Tom Fitzpatrick could sit on their haunches back in the settlements, if that was what they wanted.

"Clever as old Billy is," Kit Carson mused, "he'll be runnin' the show for Pratt an' Chouteau before the season's out. Him an' Fitz, they was our kind—even if they done sold us out. When the time comes, they'll do right by us. . . ."

Meek was scouting ahead, across to the east slope of the Absaroka Range. He was working his way down the Rosebud, beyond Blackfoot territory now, into the lands of the Crows.

With numerous beaver dams along the big creek, Joe was in no hurry to turn back toward his reunion with Bridger's bunch at the mouth of Boulder Creek. He took time to do a bit of trapping as he moved northeast toward the Yellowstone, and by the time he reached the mouth of the Stillwater, he had accumulated some thirty pelts, including half a dozen otters.

Had he been a single man, he concluded, he'd have been tempted to spend the entire autumn along the Rosebud. The trapping was that fine.

No sign of Indians, and that was *good* sign.

He had just broken camp that morning and was urging his mule northward, away from the little river, figuring to cut across the rolling hills and to strike for the Yellowstone at a point just about thirty miles below the mouth of Boulder Creek.

But he smelled something and drew the animal to a halt. The three pack mules pulled alongside him, and they, too, came to a stand, their big ears forward, their nostrils nibbling at the air.

"Whiteman!" a voice called out from a thick stand of firs on the rise above him. "Throw down your weapon! We do not wish to kill you."

Meek leaped from his mule, set the triggers of Old Sally, his Hawken, and scrambled for the cover of some bitterbrush.

"You cannot get away!" the voice called out. "This is Apsaroka Betsetsa, the leader of the Crows. I am known to you as Long Hair."

"Ye be Crows?" Meek called out in response, his rifle leveled toward the firs.

Death-time, unless Gawd himself steps in an' saves this nigger's apples. . . .

A big, spotted horse, the animal wearing a war bonnet of hawk and eagle feathers. An old Indian astride the animal, a large man, still obviously powerful and perhaps sixty years of age, impossible to tell. A man who sat his horse with an air of total authority. His hair down over his back, jet-colored but touched with silver in places and bound up into a series of loops so that the total length was also impossible to determine.

Gawd save my hide, it's him. . . .

Long Hair rode slowly forward, alone, but Meek knew well enough that a considerable troop of Indians was concealed beyond the fir grove—there and perhaps all about him. The legendary head chief of the River Crows was not known to wander about unattended.

Mebbe Jim Beckwourth's with 'im. Beckwourth's with the Mountain Crows, but mebbe. . . . An' when I tell him I'm friends with Bridger . . . Le Blueux's with 'em too. Say your prayers, coon. It's goin' to take more than b'ar medicine.

"What is your name, Whiteman?" Long Hair asked, drawing his war pony around sideways and making no show of his own weapons. "Stand up so that I can look at you. We will spare your life if you tell us what we wish to know."

Meek rose, held his Hawken loosely, triggers still set but the barrel down.

"Name's Joe Meek," he said. "I'm with the Blanket Chief's

party, Jim Bridger," he said. "I'm old friends with Pierre Le Blueux—that's livin' with your people."

"Who is this Bridger that you speak of?" Long Hair asked.

"Casapy," Meek answered. "It's a name he got from the Crows."

Long Hair nodded.

"Bi-kas-o-pia," the Crow chief said, nodding. "Yes, Joe Meek. I am the one who gave him that name—the man in charge of blankets. That was ten winters ago, perhaps more. When we get older, we do not pay much attention to the passing of seasons. You are the one they call Bear-Killer, is that not so?"

Joe relaxed a bit now, breathed out. If the Indians intended to kill him, at least Long Hair wished to talk for a time first.

Spare your life if you tell us. . . .

"Are Le Blueux an' Beckwourth with ye?" Joe asked. "Pierre's my friend."

"You know the Medicine Calf, then—*Nan-kup-bah-bah?"*

"Never met 'im," Meek admitted. "But I'm friends with Le Blueux."

"The Frenchman, he has changed his name. Now he is Grayhair-on-His-Face. No, Medicine Calf and Le Blueux are not with me. They are with their own people. My warriors have grown lonely for their Siksika friends, so I am leading them to where we will have company. How many men does Blanket Chief have with him, Joe Meek? Perhaps we will wish to visit him also."

Two hundred and forty.

"Forty, countin' me," Meek replied.

The hint of a smile came across the old chief's weathered face, and he raised one arm above his head.

Within moments perhaps as many as three hundred Crow warriors had emerged, as if by magic, drawing out from all about the encircled Joe Meek. A number of squaws as well, several of them with children.

Damn near a whole gawd-awful village. . . .

"Just forty? Is that what you say, Bear-Killer?" Long Hair asked again. "If you have told me the truth, then I will give you your life."

Joe swallowed hard.

"Forty," he repeated, "if the Blackfeet ain't got none of 'em."

* * *

Long Hair and the Crows were apparently in no particular hurry and camped well before sundown. Joe's hands had been bound, but now they were untied so that he could eat—and for this purpose he was brought once again to Long Hair's side—a welcome relief after having been taunted by the women for half a day—occasionally prodded with sticks and called *masta-sheela*, a term of derision meaning *yellow-eyes* or *Whiteman*.

Long Hair said little as they ate jerked buffalo meat and dried plums. But when they had finished, the chief unwrapped his pipe, filled the bowl with tobacco, the wild kind, and lit it. He signed to the four sacred directions and to the earth and the heavens, and then sipped at the smoke and blew it back out his nostrils. Long Hair handed the pipe to Meek, who imitated the ritual and puffed likewise, returned the pipe.

"Forty men with Bridger?" Long Hair said, looking Meek straight in the eyes.

"Enough coons so they can protect themselves," Meek said, nodding.

"I am glad you have told the truth," Long Hair said reflectively. "Some of my warriors wished to open your belly so they could see how long your intestines are. We do that to Blackfoot captives sometimes."

Don't show no emotion. He's testin' ye. When we get close to Gabe's camp, mebbe ye've got a chance. If him an' the boys is there yet. . . .

Long Hair puffed again and once more handed the pipe to Joe.

"Blanket Chief and his men are at the stream you call Boulder Creek?" the old Crow asked. "That is where he was last winter."

"I'm supposed to meet 'im thar," Joe answered.

"And only forty men with him now. That is very strange, Joe Meek. I was certain there would be many more."

"Nope," Meek insisted, returning the pipe to the chief.

"Forty including the Bear-Killer?"

"Yup. I'm number forty."

"And you have only killed one bear?"

"Nope. Killed a bunch of 'em."

"Yes," Long Hair replied. "That is what I was told."

When it was time to sleep, the Indians did not bother to tie Joe's hands again. He was allowed his own robes, and his mules and his weapons were returned to him.

*It's a trick. They want me to light out so they'll have reason
to put me under. . . .*

Meek lay awake for a long while, considering the matter. But
at length he decided to play along, to wait until the band had
drawn close to Bridger's camp before making a move.

As it turned out, he slept quite soundly.

The following day brought them close to the mouth of
Boulder Creek. Long Hair signaled for Meek to accompany him
and three of his warriors, and together they rode to the crest of a
hill that overlooked the encampment of the mountain men.

The gathering was even larger than Meek had supposed it
would be—apparently a number of Flatheads had joined in with
Gabe and Kit and the boys. Perhaps as many as three hundred
now, with numerous women and children and a sizable herd of
horses and mules.

Long Hair feigned amazement and glared at Meek—but the
chief's eyes were glinting with what appeared to be amusement.

"I promised you that you would live if you told me the
truth," Long Hair said. "But now I think you have told me a great
lie. Once I gave Bridger a name, and now I will give you one also.
I call you *Shiam-shaspusia*, the man who can outlie even the
Crows. I think the Bear-Killer is actually a Cheyenne, for they are
great liars also. Now I want you to do something before I allow
my men to kill you. I want you to ride forward with my friend
Little Gun. When you get halfway to the village, call out to your
friend Casapy. If he is truly your friend, then perhaps he will wish
to give us some presents in exchange for your life. You must call
out to him and tell him that Long Hair and his warriors have come
to visit."

Meek, with Little Gun beside him, rode out—and Joe
shouted for Bridger.

"Gabe!" Meek yelled. "Long Hair an' his Crows has got
me. Parley with 'em an' get me out! They say they want to come
visit ye!"

Within a few moments Bridger and Carson appeared, drew
their horses to a halt within a few yards of Meek and Little Gun.

"Wal, tell the old renegade to come on in, then!" Bridger
laughed. "We been waitin' supper for the lot of ye!"

The Crows discharged their weapons and came riding down.
Several fire pits had been constructed, and fresh-killed deer were
roasting whole. Bridger and Long Hair embraced, and the Crow

warriors, on their best behavior, entered the trappers' encampment.

Bear-Killer was feeling just a bit put-upon, but even he had to appreciate the subtlety and grand extent of the jest.

Mountain Lamb came running out, Little Salmon struggling along in her wake, and Joe Meek's wife threw herself headlong into her husband's arms. When the food was ready, she sat beside him and smiled as Long Hair, employing his best English, related Joe's tale of only forty men in the encampment and once again explained the name-giving—*Shiam-shaspusia*, the one who, like a Cheyenne, is able to outlie the Crows themselves.

"If Long Hair here had just half as many warriors with 'im," Meek explained in turn, "why, I'd of skulped the lot of 'em. But the chief just had too many for me to handle all by myself. So I figgered, hell, might as well let Gabe an' Kit an' the boys have some of the fun too."

Long Hair nodded and thought the matter over.

"We were all afraid he would turn upon us," the chief agreed—to the great delight of mountain men and Crow warriors as well.

Early autumn had arrived, and most mornings a light frost glistened in the early sun. Beaver proved plentiful along the streams in the area, and the furs were improving in quality all the time.

Muckaluck had reported finding a fine grove of wild plum trees a few miles upstream on the creek where he was putting out his traps.

Mountain Lamb's face lit up, and she insisted upon accompanying Joe and Muckaluck and Godin the following day.

"Sounds good to me," Joe said, laughing. "Might as well bring the Whale along with ye. Boy's got to learn how to trap some time—cain't be my kid otherwise."

Mountain Lamb raised one eyebrow.

"I think he is still too young for that, Joe Meek," she replied.

"Mebbe, but bring 'im along anyways."

"Perhaps we will even find some Crow warriors to scalp," Muckaluck said, his face deadpan.

Meek scowled and put his hand on his knife.

But morning found them up among the grass- and sage-covered ridges above the Yellowstone, and by noon the little group had reached the plum grove Muckaluck had described. Much of the fruit had already fallen to the ground, but what remained was tight-skinned and very sweet, little red-purple globes of succulent, sugary flesh.

Joe, Antoine, and Muckaluck continued up the stream, and Mountain Lamb began gathering the ripe fruit into the elaborately ornamented *maishoo-moe-goots* that had been one of her wedding presents.

A group of wandering Bannocks, observing the beautiful woman alone, sneaked up upon her and surrounded her.

"What is this?" one of the Indians called out.

"A lost Shoshone," another cried. "Perhaps she wishes to lie down with all of us. That is the way Snake women are."

Mountain Lamb turned to her gathering pouch and withdrew the Norris pistol Joe had given her.

"I am Bear-Killer's woman," she said, her voice calm and steady. "He and his friends are close by. If you come any closer, I will have to kill one of you. Then Bear-Killer and the other trappers will kill the rest of you. Go away now and leave me alone."

"She has a little one with her," a Bannock said. "We will take that one with us and turn him into a Pun-nak warrior."

"Which one of you wishes to die?" Mountain Lamb demanded. "You can do what you wish with me, but I will kill one of you first."

The Bannocks laughed and taunted but did not approach any closer.

"Joe Meek!" Mountain Lamb shouted at the top of her lungs. "Help me! The Pun-naks are here!"

The Indians talked matters over among themselves. Was this indeed Meek's wife? And were any of the mountain men close at hand?

One of the warriors had spent a few days at the Rendezvous, and he informed the others that the woman had been there—but whether she was Meek's wife or not, he did not know.

"If you will lie down with us," one of the warriors suggested, "we will let you go. No one will be hurt that way, and you can take your child and return to the camp of the mountain men. Your husband, whoever he is, will never know the difference. Otherwise we will cut your throat, Shoshone. After you are dead, then all of us will fuck you anyway. Maybe we will fuck your little boy also."

"One of you," Mountain Lamb repeated, pushing Little Salmon behind her and moving back toward her horse, "will be dead. He will not wish to lie with anyone."

The Bannocks edged closer, the men grinning and laughing.

Mountain Lamb levered back the hammer of the Norris.

"Do not come any closer," she warned.

At that moment a Bannock lunged for her, and the pistol exploded. The Indian, his face a mask of disbelief, clutched at his abdomen, staggered another step forward, and fell face downward at Mountain Lamb's feet.

The Bannocks shouted with rage, and Little Salmon clung to the fringe of his mother's dress.

She held her skinning knife out in front of her, waving the keen blade back and forth.

"Now we are going to cut your head off, Snake," one of the warriors said.

Umentucken watched, her vision strangely detached, as the Bannock warrior started toward her. She turned her own blade slightly in anticipation and was aware of the low whimpering sounds Little Salmon was making. But no sense of reality about what was happening—as though she were watching indeed through her own eyes but from some point far removed, distant, safe. It was like being with Joe Meek high atop Table Mountain and looking down upon some insignificant human drama being enacted below—a dance being performed by people the size of ants.

She gritted her teeth, hissed, knew just where to strike with the knife in her hand.

But the Bannock's head came apart, a spray of blood and brains going up as if a rock had been thrown into still water.

A haze of gunsmoke on the rim of the grassy rise above the plum grove. The other Bannocks shouting and diving for cover.

Then the sounds of the three rifle shots—and Joe Meek's big voice, bellowing curses. Muckaluck yelling the war cry of his people, Antoine Godin yelling out in a language that was neither French nor Iroquois.

The Norris pistol. She reloaded instantly, sighted down on one of the fleeing Bannocks, and fired—the man stumbling, falling, rising to one knee as Muckaluck bore down on him, trampling him beneath the mule's hooves.

Within a matter of moments some eight men lay dead, their

bodies scattered irregularly. The remaining four Bannocks had vanished.

Mountain Lamb stood there, dazed. But it was all right now. Joe Meek was holding her, was kissing her face and hair.

"Father," Little Salmon said. "I wasn't afraid, Father. I could have fought them. See?"

The small hand was clutched on an egg-sized pebble.

CHAPTER FIFTEEN

Umentucken Leaves
Her Mark

Brother Beaver, where are you? We have depended upon you, and now you are passing away. Where are the herds of buffalo? Once they were plentiful to the west of the Shining Mountains and roamed through the basins where Snake and Seedskeedee begin—but now they are few.

No, it is not just the Whitemen who have caused this to happen, for we have also trapped the beaver and slain the buffalo for their robes so we could sell the furs for weapons and ammunition and for trinkets and bright cloth because our women desired them. We have needed the weapons, but we are all to blame.

Human things must end, and only the mountains live forever. That is what the old people say, and we have always seen that it is so.

A long time ago the waters stood in great waves, as high as the Rockies, and afterward Old Man made everything as we see it now. We must always be grateful to Old Man. For this reason we leave part of what we have killed for Little Brother, the gray-brown coyote. And we say prayers that help the spirits of the Animal People to find their way into the Spirit World. After that Old Man sends them back to live in the bodies of other animals.

Some say that in the old times the Animal People would go home to their lodges at night, just like the Humans, and then they would take off their animal costumes and act just as we do. It is not that way now, but perhaps someday it will be again.

But it will not happen for a long while, and soon it will be time for all of us to go to the place where the animals have gone. I do not think it will be very long from now.

I hear voices out in the forest.

An Irish free trapper named O'Fallon joined the encampment on the Yellowstone, and he had with him two Umatilla slaves whom he had bought from the Blackfeet.

Meek knew there would be trouble eventually, but he

shrugged and went about his business. A good trapper tended to his lines and didn't make a point of concerning himself with another man's business. Still, the Nez Percés and the Flatheads didn't like O'Fallon having Umatilla slaves—since the Umatillas were traditionally their allies. And, for that matter, they didn't like O'Fallon himself. No question—trouble of some sort was inevitable.

Jim Bridger declined to interfere, and so Muckaluck and the Flatheads and the Nez Percés came to Meek's lodge, even though Joe was out trapping, and explained to Mountain Lamb that something would have to be done. When Meek returned, Muckaluck was certain the Bear-Killer could be persuaded to lend assistance.

"Perhaps we should help the Umatillas to get away," Mountain Lamb suggested. "But why do they stay with this man? Is it possible that they wish to be his slaves?"

"Why would they wish that?" Muckaluck demanded.

"Maybe he saved their lives by rescuing them from the Blackfeet."

Muckaluck shook his head.

"I have seen this man tie the Umatillas and beat them. It is not right, Mountain Lamb."

The others, their eyes serious and intent, nodded.

"We will help the Umatillas to escape, then," Mountain Lamb said. "It should not be too difficult. This O'Fallon is only one man, and there are nearly twenty of you. Why don't we give the Umatillas horses and weapons? Then they can simply ride off. The freckle-faced man will never be able to catch them."

"Yes," Muckaluck agreed. "I think they would go if they had ponies to ride. They could easily cross the mountains and ride on down the Snake River to the place where their villages are."

"I have too many horses," Mountain Lamb said, nodding. "Some of you also have animals that you do not need. And an extra pistol or a rifle? Then, if O'Fallon follows them, they can shoot him. The Umatillas are not helpless—they will know what to do when the time comes."

Plans were laid, and supplies were gathered together. The following morning, while O'Fallon was away from the encampment, Muckaluck and Mountain Lamb brought two saddle ponies and a pack mule, fully loaded, along with an old horse pistol and well-worn Kain-tuck rifle, to O'Fallon's lodge.

The Umatillas promised to return both the animals and the

weapons as soon as they were able to do so and proceeded to ride away from the camp, heading upstream along the Yellowstone.

Muckaluck and Mountain Lamb watched the men ride off and then returned to Meek's lodge.

"I think we have done the right thing," Mountain Lamb said, smiling. "It is not good to be the slave of another."

Muckaluck agreed, but now he was beginning to worry about the Irishman's response to what had happened. He and Mountain Lamb had not been particularly covert in what they had done.

"Perhaps I should go find Joe," he said. "If there is going to be trouble, it is best for him to know."

Mountain Lamb nodded, smiled again, and turned to caution Little Salmon about the dangers of getting into his father's big can of black powder.

By noon O'Fallon had returned to his lodge, found his slaves missing, and began to ask questions. The answers to his queries led him first to the lodge shared by Antoine Godin and Muckaluck, the latter absent. Godin listened to O'Fallon's ragings for a moment or two and then reached calmly for his Hawken, set the triggers, tapped the pan, and pointed it at the Irishman.

"Dumb-ass Iroquois not like men with spotted faces," Godin said and grinned widely.

O'Fallon backed out of the lodge, walked a few paces, stopped, and then proceeded directly toward Meek's tepee. Halfway there he stopped again, went to his own dwelling, picked up his horsewhip, and turned his steps once again in their previous direction.

His actions, however, had been observed. Doc Newell's woman had seen the entire thing, and she had run straight to Mountain Lamb.

"The Irishman has gone to get his gun, Umentucken. You must come with me. I think he is going to kill you."

Mountain Lamb listened to her agitated friend, picked up the Norris pistol, and ushered Bent Feather out of the lodge.

"Go tell Carson or Bridger. Hurry. I am not afraid of this O'Fallon, but I do not wish to have to kill him either. Hurry now, Bent Feather."

The Delaware girl ran off, and Mountain Lamb and Little Salmon went around to the rear of the tepee.

"You must stay right here, no matter what happens," Mountain Lamb cautioned the child. "Do you understand me?"

"Yes, Mother," the child answered. "If you shoot anyone, will you take his scalp? I would like that."

"You are worse than Joe Meek," Mountain Lamb said. "Be very quiet now. . . ."

O'Fallon arrived at the lodge entry and shouted for Mountain Lamb to come out.

"Ye've set my damned Umatillas free," he roared, "an' this nigger wants payment! You come out or I'll pull the stinkin' tepee down on top of ye!"

No answer from within.

"I'm goin' to give ye a whippin', ye slut! You come out, or I'm comin' in after ye by the backside of Jesus!"

O'Fallon was about to enter when he heard a trigger being set. He spun about to find himself looking directly at the business end of a pistol.

"Were you going to use that on me?" Mountain Lamb asked, a smile on her face and lights glinting in her eyes. "Did you use it on your prisoners also? Now I have sent for Bridger, and he will have you whipped, perhaps."

"Goddammit, ye give my boys horses an' set 'em off ridin'. Careful with that there gun. Ye don't want it goin' off by mistake, now. Look—I lost me temper, that's all. Let's forget this whole thing, little lady. I'll talk with Meek when he gets back— somebody's got to pay me for my Umatillas. That's only right, by golly."

Mountain Lamb raised the pistol slightly, as if preparing to fire.

"If Joe Meek was here, he would kill you, O'Fallon. But he is hunting, so I will have to kill you myself."

"Careful with that thing—I lost me temper—I'm sorry about 'er. . . ."

O'Fallon started to back away.

"Get down on your knees, Man-Who-Owned-Slaves. That is how I want you when I kill you. Get down!"

O'Fallon did as he was told.

Bridger and Carson and about twenty others had come running as soon as Bent Feather had told them what was happening. Gabe arrived with pistol in hand, and Carson had out his Green River knife. But as soon as they saw that the situation was under control and that Mountain Lamb was controlling it, they formed a circle about the man and the woman and began to laugh and jeer.

"Gabe—ye ain't goin' to let 'er kill this lad, are ye?" O'Fallon called out.

"This coon figgerin' to use that horsewhip on ye, Mountain Lamb? Tell ye what. Me an' the boys'll tie him up, and ye can whup on 'im until your arm's tired out. Just don't shoot 'im, Isabel. How's that sound?"

The trappers clapped their hands and hooted.

"I do not wish to whip this man," Mountain Lamb replied. "I would rather shoot him. But if he asks me to spare his life, that is what I will do."

O'Fallon looked up at the pistol and then stared back at the earth once more.

"I beg ye for my life," he whispered. "I beg ye *please*. . . ."

"It is yours, then," Mountain Lamb replied. "Go away now and do not bother me again. I will not even tell Bear-Killer what has happened."

The men roared with laughter—more of them running up with each passing moment. O'Fallon rose to his feet, glanced about at the circle of malicious eyes surrounding him, searched for an opening, and walked toward it. The circle gave way to allow his passage, and the trappers whooped and whistled and yelled.

"Hurrah for the Mountain Lamb!" they cried out.

By nightfall O'Fallon was gone from the encampment, and when Muckaluck returned an hour after dark, Meek with him, Mountain Lamb was sitting on the sleeping pallet with Little Salmon, telling the child a coyote story.

When Muckaluck and Joe entered the lodge, she looked up as if surprised. But her eyes were gleaming.

"Take it my lady's pleased with herself about somethin'." Meek grinned, hanging his beaver cap on a peg.

The streams froze late that winter of '36, and the trappers continued their hunt, moving over into Crow territory, well down the Yellowstone to the area beyond the mouth of the Rosebud. And the high peaks of the Beartooth Range formed a nearly solid wall of white against the southern horizon. Along the Yellowstone, long days of freezing rain alternated with periods of cloudless blue sky, and the hunt for beaver continued.

Near the end of January, Long Hair and his Crows paid a second visit to the Bridger encampment, and, with spirits running high, a great feast was held—the mountain men having completed a successful buffalo hunt just two days earlier.

Long Hair and his men had been, as they said, visiting their *friends* the Blackfeet—and as a consequence had among them an extremely impressive collection of scalplocks formerly belonging to Piegans, Bloods, and Siksikas.

"But now," Long Hair reported, "the Blackfeet have found an enemy far more fierce than my warriors. We have encountered three death villages during our march. Many people dead, many more dying. Sores on their faces and bodies. Ough! The smell was terrible. This is the same sickness that came to our people many years ago. And that is why I have suggested to the leaders of my Foxes and Lumpwoods and Dog Soldiers that we should return to our own lands. Your people sometimes die of this disease also, Blanket Chief. It has come to our lands from up the Big River— other Whitemen have brought it to us. I had heard of some sickness among our cousins the Hidatsas last fall. Now we cannot go to visit them anymore either."

"Smallpox!" Meek whispered.

Bridger and Carson and the others nodded. The dreaded scourge was loose in the mountains again. The men glanced at one another and surmised what the warm weather of summer might bring. Rendezvous itself, with Indian bands coming in from all over the Rocky Mountain region, could well prove to be a powderkeg with an extremely short fuse.

"Any of your boys sick?" Bridger asked, holding his breath and dreading the answer.

"No," Long Hair said. "Old Man Coyote has been good to us. We have been very fortunate. But that is why I have not returned to the great village near Fort Union. If the sickness had touched us, it would have been better for us to die far from our people rather than to take it home with us. Kipp and Tulleck and others have told me that it spreads in the air that we breathe. Is this what you believe, Blanket Chief?"

"Guess so," Bridger replied. "Seems like it hits the Injuns worse than the Whites."

"We are safe for a time, then," Long Hair said, lighting his pipe and gesturing to the sacred directions. "Let us speak of happier things now. Is the Bear-Killer still happy with the beautiful woman who is his wife? Or does he already think of taking additional women into his lodge? I do not understand why Whitemen prefer to have only one wife. When you have seen as many winters as I have, then perhaps you will wish to have a younger wife to take care of you. When a woman gets older, she cannot work as she once could. Then it is better for the man and the woman also to acquire a younger wife."

"Ain't interested in no other squaws," Meek said. "Ain't never goin' to be, nuther. Me an' Mountain Lamb, we don't need nobody else."

Long Hair passed the pipe to Bridger and said, "This one, the *Shiam-shaspusia,* he is still young. He will learn. Medicine Calf, the man you called Beckwourth, he has ten wives—and that is too many. So he has sent three of them to live among the River People. Even your friend Le Blueux has taken a wife—did you know that, Joe Meek? Perhaps she will bear him a new little one soon, I do not know. My people and the Mountain Crows will meet for the spring buffalo hunt unless . . ."

"The smallpox breaks out," Meek said, finishing the old chief's sentence.

Spirits were still high the following morning when tragedy struck.

A vain young Crow warrior, having gussied himself up in the most outlandish fashion, with his hair bound in clumps and elaborate painting covering his stomach, arms, and face, had been strutting back and forth for some time near Meek's lodge, hoping to attract the attentions of Umentucken, Tukutsey Undenwatsy. Indeed, the beauty of the Shoshone girl was a matter of discussion among the Crow warriors, but only the one man, Two-Bulls, had resolved to initiate the first stages of a kind of courtship. The Shoshone's husband, he reasoned, had been captured by the Crows and had given no signs of wishing to fight. He had allowed himself to be taken prisoner and had in fact cooperated fully with Long Hair's wishes.

Such a man was without pride and not worthy of having so fine a woman.

Two-Bulls paraded back and forth, bragging of his prowess in battle and of the number of scalps he had taken from his enemies—and with each pass he drew closer to where Mountain Lamb and Joe were pressing beaver hides into a pack.

Meek half-understood what the Crow was saying but was resolved to ignore him. Long Hair would be gone soon, and there was no point in precipitating any trouble. As long as the trappers were in the good graces of the old patriarch of the Absarokas, they could ply their trade unhindered.

For Mountain Lamb's part, if she understood what Two-Bulls was saying, she also chose to ignore him.

Finally, when Joe went inside the lodge for a moment, Two-Bulls stepped to Mountain Lamb's side and placed one hand to her breast. She was astounded: the dandy stood there grinning from ear to ear and made no sign of withdrawing his hand.

She pulled back and spat into his face.

Two-Bulls glared at her, pulled the riding quirt from under his belt, and lashed her with it across the shoulder, barely missing her face as she turned away from the blow.

The report of a pistol cracked the morning air, and all who were close by turned to see what had happened.

Two-Bulls lay dead, a pistol ball through the forehead, and Joe Meek stood over him.

All hell broke loose within a matter of moments, with trappers and Crow warriors at one another's throats. Bridger, Carson, and Long Hair came bursting out of Gabe's lodge, the three of them shouting all at once and attempting to get things calmed down. But it was not to be. A pitched battle was on, with Indian and trapper alike rushing for his weapons.

Within minutes one trapper and another three Crows lay dead.

Bridger and Carson were still shouting, and Long Hair and Little Gun, the leader of the Dog Soldiers, were bellowing in Absaroka tongue.

The shooting subsided, and a terrible silence lay over the encampment. The trappers dragged their dead man back to his lodge, and the Indians took up their four and sullenly lashed the bodies onto the backs of horses.

Bridger and Long Hair gave each other a short, formal embrace, and Long Hair and his men departed immediately.

Bridger was furious.

"Goddammit, Meek, what in hell'd ye have to do that for? So a crazy-ass Injun took a shine to your woman. That any reason to put 'im under? Hell no it weren't."

Joe put his arm about Mountain Lamb's waist and stared steadily across at Bridger.

"He hit her with his riding crop, Gabe."

"But were it worth gettin' one of our own coons killed?" Bridger said, exasperation showing in his face. "An' now we're goin' to have to make tracks. Them dead Injuns' relatives will demand revenge—an' there's goin' to be hell to pay, no matter what old Long Hair tells 'em. He cain't control his young bucks any more than Washakie or any other chief can, an' that's a flat fact."

"I'm sorry about the dead man. Very sorry, this child is, but couldn't help 'er. No divvel of an Injun shall strike Joe Meek's wife."

"Ye damn hothead. No matter what happened, it wasn't worth gettin' anyone kilt."

"Sorry for the man," Joe replied, shaking his head. "Couldn't help it, though, Bridger."

Bridger's brigade pulled out of Crow territory, heading upstream along the Yellowstone and then across to the Madison Fork of the Missouri and then over the divide to the Henry's Fork of the Snake, into Shoshone county, and finally they set up a new winter camp on Blackfoot Creek, a tributary of the Snake River. Along the way they had passed near to two different death villages, avoiding these and moving quickly past them. In addition they had run directly into a sizable Blackfoot war party far up on the Madison, a group of two hundred warriors led by Little Robe, the Piegan war chief.

The leaders from both sides, not eager for battle, met under truce. But Little Robe asserted that the trappers and their friends were responsible for bringing the great sickness to his people. Indeed, he made a long speech and had listed numerous grievances before he came to the issue of the smallpox.

Bridger studied the Blackfoot's stern eyes and realized he had to say something, *something right,* in order to avoid having the chance meeting turn into a major battle.

"It weren't the Whites at all," Bridger explained. "Who's your greatest enemy, Little Robe? Who is it your people hate worse than anyone else?"

Little Robe's eyes narrowed.

"Medicine Calf of the Crows. Do you now tell me that he is the one . . . ?"

"That's it," Bridger said, his voice full and earnest. "Him that half-kilt one of As-as-to's daughters years ago an' has been killin' Blackfeet ever since. Beckwourth. He war a trapper then, but he ain't White. No sir. He's a Nigra, that's what. He left ye some infected blankets—that's the way I heard 'er. An' that started the sickness up."

Little Robe considered what Bridger had told him. Finally he said, "I like your words. I will not fight you, then. If you will give us some presents first, we will trade with you."

Bridger took in a few worthless robes and twenty beaver pelts, exchanged these for powder, lead, and a couple of old rifles, and was relieved to be on his way without a scrap.

"Quick thinkin', coon," Kit Carson said. "Don't know as Jimmy Beckwourth's goin' to take it all that kindly, though, in case he ever finds out."

"Hell, Kit," Bridger replied, "the Blackfeet hates old Medicine Calf worse than pizzen anyhow. One more reason for hatin' 'im ain't goin' to make no difference. . . ."

Once the new winter camp was set up, things quieted down; and the mountain men were able to get back about the business of trapping beaver. The interval did not last long, however, for the great cold of winter soon pushed down into the Snake River Basin, freezing the beaver streams solid and driving the big rodents into the semihibernation that would last until spring rains and gaining sunlight set the waters to flowing once again.

Now, during the quiet time, Joe and Mountain Lamb found themselves relaxed and happy together—with nothing to do but watch Little Salmon grow, go off hunting for meat together, and spend the nights in each other's embrace.

"We're married for sure," Joe said one day. "Gal, Pretty Face, we don't even talk to anybody else very much anymore. We just waste all our time playin' kissy-face."

Mountain Lamb looked up from the deerskin dress she was ornamenting with beadwork and porcupine quills.

"Don't you like that anymore, Joe Meek?" she asked.

"Wal, now," Joe answered, taking the dress out of her lap and pulling her down onto the sleeping pallet, "of course this child does. I ain't a complete gawddamned fool."

But by the first of March the streams had begun flowing once more, and so Meek shouldered his string of traps and, with Mountain Lamb riding beside him, set out for the promising beaver country around Gray's Lake. The days drifted by, sometimes catching them in a brief snow squall, sometimes the sun blazing down with the strange half-warmth of early spring.

After a week Joe said, "Let's head on back, Isabel. I keep

thinkin' I hear Little Salmon callin' to us. Ye don't suppose they's anything wrong, do ye?''

Mountain Lamb raised one eyebrow and pursed her lips.

"I think only that my Bear-Killer is a very foolish man," she answered. "Why should anything be wrong? Now he has two mothers to take care of him—Bent Feather and Grass-Singing-in-Wind. He will probably not even be glad to see us when we return."

"Kid has got no loyalty," Meek complained.

But he was grinning as he said it.

When Joe and Umentucken returned to the camp on Blackfoot Creek, the place was buzzing. A group of Bannock warriors had come in the previous evening and had left during the night, taking with them a dozen horses belonging to the Nez Percés. As soon as the theft was realized, the Nez Percés and the Flatheads and Godin and Marshall had ridden out in pursuit.

By mid-afternoon the mountain men were back, the borrowed ponies trailing behind them. Godin and Muckaluck drew up before Meek's lodge, and they and their companions began to yip-yip like a band of coyotes in celebration of pure moonlight.

"We caught 'em napping and just danced away with the whole bunch of ponies, ain't that right, Muckaluck?''

"This Iroquois has very strong horse medicine," Muckaluck agreed.

"Those Pun-naks, they are very angry now," Antoine Godin continued. "They do not like to have their stolen ponies stolen back from them."

"We have done well," Muckaluck added. "Perhaps the Fair One will give me a kiss? I have worked very hard."

Mountain Lamb laughed and placed her hands over her mouth.

"Kiss—my Virginy be-hind!" Meek growled. "Get the livestock out of our frontyard, an' mebbe I'll brew up a big pot of coffee for them as wants it."

The minions of mountain justice began to yip-yip again as they led the ponies away.

"Nothin' but damn kids, that's what they be," Meek said with a growl as he poured water into the king-sized speckled blue pot whose bottom was completely black with the stains of charred resin.

"I am very happy, Joe Meek," Mountain Lamb said, placing

one hand on Little Salmon's shoulder. "It is a good day to die. Now I have something to tell you."

"An' what might that be, Pretty Face Isabel?"

"Joe, I think I am with child once again. My woman's blood has not come for two moons now, and I have been feeling different for the past few days—just like before."

Joe scooped the crushed coffee beans and powdered licorice root into the pot before he spoke.

"Lordy, are ye sure, gal?"

"I think so," she answered.

Joe set the pot in against the embers and stood up, took his wife into his arms.

"By the dog-faced gawd," he whispered into her ear, "we'll get us a whole new tribe of half-breed heathens an' take over the mountains. King Joe an' Queen Isabel, that's what we'll be. About October, ye think?"

"Yes," Mountain Lamb answered, pressing her face against his shoulder, "in the moon of leaves-falling."

Godin, Muckaluck, and a few of their Nez Percé friends had just returned for coffee when Jim Bridger came swaggering up to Meek's lodge.

"Joseph, old compañero," he grinned, "this nigger's got news for ye. Goin' to have me a kid, for sure."

Meek's eyes twinkled.

"Ye told Cora yet?" he asked.

"Dumb-ass coon, it's Cora what's goin' to have the kid!" Mountain Lamb burst out laughing.

"Oh," Meek replied. "Didn't understand ye there at first."

"What's so durned funny, Umentucken? Is that good news or ain't it?"

"Very good," Mountain Lamb replied. "I am also with child. Perhaps Cora and I will give birth about the same time. Then Muckaluck can name both of the new little ones."

"Wagh!" Bridger cried out. "Ye think I'd let this hyar Red savage name Jim Bridger's kid? He ain't even civilized."

Muckaluck yipped like a coyote again, apparently not having yet tired of his new word game. But then he turned to Bridger and drew on a serious expression.

"Muckaluck is more civilized than the Blanket Chief," he asserted.

"What do ye mean by that?" Gabe demanded.

Muckaluck yipped again and grinned.

"I know how to write my name with a pen and ink," he said. "Antoine showed me how to do it. I do not think that even Bridger knows how to do that."

At first Bridger was impressed, but almost immediately he became suspicious.

"Prove ye can do 'er," he insisted.

Muckaluck threw up his hands.

"I have no pen. I have no paper. I have no ink. First I would need those things, and they are back in the lodge, in Antoine's little wooden chest."

"Do 'er with a stick—right hyar in the dirt," Bridger said. "Then mebbe I'll believe ye."

Muckaluck looked doubtful, but then he took a twig, sharpened the point, and carefully inscribed some letters upon the damp ground.

Meek squinted, looked twice at the writing.

Red Devil.

Bridger scratched his nose and looked into Muckaluck's eyes.

"Be damned," he said. "I thought ye was bluffin' cards. Mebbe I'll get old Antoine to show me too. Milt or Fitz could of, but I always figgered my mark was good enough. But hell, if a damned Flathead knows how to do 'er. . . ."

Meek was biting at the back of his hand, but he could restrain himself no longer. He roared with laughter. Then he pounded Bridger and Muckaluck on the back and turned to pour coffee.

Rifle fire from the far end of the encampment, and Joe turned, accidentally upsetting the pot as he did so.

"Somethin' up," Bridger said, growling. "Grab your Hawkens, gents. . . ."

More rifle fire, and now the distinctive snappings of pistols as well.

Indians on horseback, charging through the camp, whooping and firing at random.

"The Pun-naks!" Godin shouted. "They have brought their friends with them!"

"Isabel!" Joe cried out. "Quick! Get the rifles out of the tepee. . . ."

Men were diving for cover. Powdersmoke was rising, the air suddenly filled with the blue-gray haze. One of the Flatheads shot through the throat and thrashing about, bleeding to death. A

Bannock spun from his saddle, and Godin was upon him, slashing with his knife.

Mountain Lamb emerged from the lodge, two rifles in hand, and gave one to Joe.

"Load an' I'll shoot," Joe said, pulling off a round at a charging Bannock. But the pony swerved, and Joe's ball had struck the animal in the neck. The horse crumpled forward, its front legs splayed out.

The rider landed on hands and knees, leaped for the pistol he had dropped, grasped the weapon, and turned and fired. Meek, his own weapon empty, drew his knife and hurtled atop the Bannock and drove the blade into the warrior's chest, clear to Green River. He started to take the scalp—knew something was wrong—turned back to Mountain Lamb.

She was lying on the ground, attempting to push the remaining rifle toward him.

Bridger leaped to her side, but Meek shoved his friend away, took the stricken Mountain Lamb into his arms.

"Joe Meek," she managed, "I am bleeding all over you. Listen to the coyotes calling. I see a path—it was never there before. . . ."

There were no coyotes.

Umentucken, Tukutsey Undenwatsy was dead—dead in her husband's arms.

Joe's vision blurred. He was crying, sobbing. Flames burst through his skull, a great wave of heat and terrible light, and then subsided.

He lifted her, turned from the battle at hand, and carried her into the lodge, placed her down upon the sleeping pallet.

Little Salmon stared up at his father. The child's eyes were wide, his mouth was open.

It's a good day to die. She said that. When did she say it?

EPILOGUE

What the Grizzly Told Joe

Word of Mountain Lamb's death spread like wildfire through the encampment on Blackfoot Creek, and the mountain men, utterly enraged, poured rifle fire at the retreating Bannocks.

Joe Meek's shock turned to absolute numbness and then to a terrible need for revenge—against the Bannocks, against fate, and perhaps even against God himself. He shouted out to his fellow trappers, his voice breaking as he did so, and they followed him in a wild pursuit of the renegade Indians and within an hour had driven them into cover in some old earth-forts on a seasonal island in the flooding Snake River—a rocky point covered with willow and bitterbrush during much of the year, but now separated from the shore by a fifty-foot-wide stream of gray-green water.

All through the afternoon and into the night the mountain men continued to pour a rain of gunfire. A half-moon drifted through bandings of thin cloud, and trailing mists moved along the river.

By midnight, Joe had used up nearly all his ammunition, and the hex barrel of his Hawken was hot to the touch. He lay the weapon aside and slumped forward, his hands and his entire body trembling.

"Joe," Kit said softly, "why don't ye try an' get some shuteye? Don't worry—these murderin' bastards ain't goin' to get away from us, not a one of 'em. Ain't many left now, I'm sure of 'er. When dawn comes, we'll cross an' wipe out the last of 'em."

"I cain't get it through my head what's happened," Meek said. "Ain't nothin' seems real anymore. She's all like a gawddamned bad dream, ye know? Kit, what's this child goin' to do?"

Carson placed his hand on the big man's slumped shoulder, patted him softly.

"Remember the mule fort, Joe? You an' me, we've been through some tough times together, but we been through some good ones too. Sometimes a coon's got to be stronger than he's got any right to be. Not much of an answer, compañero, but they ain't no other. Get some sleep. I'll keep an eye peeled for ye. Sure we ain't goin' to cross over to the island without ye, Joe."

Meek sprawled out against a shelf of rock and fell down through a profound darkness, a welcome and complete darkness.

It was nearly light when he stirred, reaching out for Mountain Lamb. And the touch of cold stone brought him instantly and fully awake.

"Joe?" Carson said. "Ain't nothin' stirrin' about down there at all. Guess mebbe it's time to go take a look-see."

When the sun finally rimmed the eastward horizon, the mountain men were ready to swim their horses across while half the boys kept up a cover of rifle fire from behind.

At that point a lone figure appeared—an old Bannock woman, the peace pipe on her arm.

"You have killed all our men!" she called out in half-discernible English. "Now only women and children are left. We wish to make peace with you. We are helpless, and that is why I do not think you will wish to kill us."

The mountain men glanced at one another, and then all eyes turned to Joe Meek.

Joe stared across at the old woman, raised his palms in the sign of peace, and turned back toward where his pony was tethered. Bridger and Carson and the other mountain men hesitated only a moment, and then they, too, turned and walked away.

Meek did not—could not—return to camp as yet. He was dimly aware that he was going to construct a tree-hung grave for Mountain Lamb, but he could not find the strength within himself to do it as yet. The neutering numbness had fallen over him once more, and he rode eastward, across the low hills toward Gray's Lake—the last place he and Mountain Lamb had been together.

What had it been? How long since he and Mountain Lamb, riding together with their pack mule behind them, had returned to the encampment along this same route?

A single day—twenty-four hours. And now it's all changed, it's all spoiled, it's never going to be the same again. The mountains ain't never goin' to shine no more. . . .

By nightfall he had reached the place where they had camped together, just downstream from where the big creek spilled from the shallow lake. Joe had intended to spend the night there, at one with his pain and his memories of the woman he loved—still loved—always would love. But the campsite seemed cold, deserted, void of her presence.

And so he continued to ride, aimless now, circling to the east of the lake and finally directing his pony upstream along a ravine that fed down from the sentinel peak of Caribou Mountain.

The horse was struggling over loose rock and against heavy brush, but Joe urged the animal onward. At last he came to a clearing where snowbanks, thin white in the moonlight, lay in against a stand of firs.

Meek dismounted, turned his horse to graze as it could, and approached the snowbank, stood staring at it for a time, and then threw himself down upon it. He was crying again, couldn't help it, dug his fingers into the coldness.

After a time he rose and kindled a fire, held his aching hands above the flames, and stared out at the moon as it dropped westward toward the invisible darkness of the horizon.

The horse was making a ruckus, stamping about, then crying out. Meek reached for his Hawken, set the triggers, and rose to his feet.

Something was close by—something or someone.

Then he recognized the smell.

Ephraim the grizzly.

Joe lifted his rifle, aimed toward the sound of the bear as it pushed its way through chaparral. He waited.

The bear emerged at the edges of the firelight, moved its big head back and forth, perceived the human being. Then, quite uncharacteristically, it sat down on its haunches and began to make snuffing sounds.

Joe started to pull the trigger, stopped.

"Gawddammit, leave me be! Get out of hyar! I ain't goin' to shoot ye unless ye make me do 'er. Now git!"

You have suffered pain, Joe Meek, but you have suffered pleasure also. You have known a love such as few men ever know, but now the time of that love has passed. Do you know who I am, Bear-Killer? You may shoot me if you like, but I will not die. No, I have come here to tell you that you must return—you must bury her properly so that she may enter into the Spirit World in honor. You must do what is fitting, just as she would have done for you. Do you understand what I am telling you? You must listen to my thoughts, you must hear them. She was the child of the bighorn sheep of the mountains, and now you must assist her to wander the long pathway to the Other World. Joe Meek . . .

The huge bear rose, turned, and ambled away downstream. Its fur burned silver in the failing moonlight. And then it was gone.

Meek waited for daybreak, and then he mounted his pony and followed in the direction the bear had led. He knew what he had to do. He had to give Umentucken, Tukutsey Undenwatsy a proper sendoff to the Spirit World that she and her people believed in—and, yes, that he also believed in. Perhaps, in some impossible way, they might yet be together again. The Mountain Lamb. She was Joe Meek's wife, the beautifulest animal that Old Man ever created, and by gawd she had a right to go in style.

Author's Note

Mountain Lamb is based upon the true story of a portion of the life of Joe Meek, one of the great figures of the fur trade. Umentucken, Tukutsey Undenwatsy is, likewise, a historical figure—as are many of the characters in *Mountain Lamb*.

Those who wish to avail themselves of nonfictionalized accounts of the same material should turn first to three books by Stanley Vestal (Walter Stanley Campbell): *Joe Meek, Jim Bridger,* and *Kit Carson.* Other fascinating sources, among a host of related volumes, are Frances F. Victor's *The River of the West;* Washington Irving's *The Adventures of Captain Bonneville;* John E. Sunder's *Bill Sublette: Mountain Man;* Bernard DeVoto's *Across the Wide Missouri;* and Don Berry's *A Majority of Scoundrels.* Beyond these few references, I will merely remark that the literature is extensive and that excellent bibliographies are available. I should, however, suggest at least five other volumes: Tom McHugh's *The Time of the Buffalo;* George Hyde's *Indians of the High Plains;* Virginia Trenholm and Maurine Carley's *The Shoshonis;* Harold Driver's *Indians of North America;* and Winfred Blevins's wonderful volume, *Give Your Heart to the Hawks.*

Joe Meek was born in Virginia in 1810 and grew to be a big, tall man with shining black hair. He found his way to the Rocky Mountains in the spring of 1829, in the employ of Bill Sublette and in company with Doc Newell (another greenhorn). Riding out from Rendezvous on the Popo Agie during the summer of 1829, Milt Sublette and Joe Meek found Jed Smith on his way back from his disastrous second venture to California. In the late fall of '29 Joe became separated from his party and wandered for days in heavy snows, through the geyser country of Yellowstone, finally rejoining his party on the Wind River. By this time Meek had become "Old Joe," an accepted mountain man, even though he was only nineteen years of age. The following year he accompained Jed Smith and Jim Bridger into Blackfoot country, had some scrapes, was walked on by a grizzly, killed the bear, was buried alive in a collapsed fur cache, and dug his way out.

That summer's Rendezvous was held at the headwaters of the Wind River, near South Pass. Bill Sublette brought two hundred new men to the mountains, and Smith, Jackson, and Sublette sold out their interests in RMF to Tom Fitzpatrick, Milt Sublette, Henry Fraeb, Jean Gervais, and Jim Bridger. Joe Meek, just twenty years old, became Milt Sublette's right-hand man. That winter Joe and Legarde went overland to reach the settlements with messages. Legarde was captured by Pawnees, but Joe made it and returned to the mountains. He met his party at Powder River, and the trappers lost their horses to the Crows. Meek, Godin, Newell, and a few others pursued the thieves and regained a few of their ponies.

Rendezvous 1831 was held on Green River (Seedskeedee), and the trappers set off to their winter camps. Legarde showed up alive and well. The rival concern of Drips and Vanderburgh (working for the American Fur Company) was now operating in the interior of the mountains.

Mountain Lamb begins at this point.

Joe Meek lived until 1875. When the beaver trade was finished, Joe and Doc Newell headed wagon trains to Oregon. Once there, Joe served in the provisional government's legislature, and was sent to Washington, D.C., as a special envoy to President Polk, making himself at home in the White House and addressing the House of Representatives.

The year 1849 found him back in Oregon as a commissioned U.S. marshal. He lived the remainder of his life in Oregon. In the mountains he was the Bear-Killer, owing to his numerous scrapes with grizzlies. But in Oregon he was a leading citizen, respected, honored, and widely known as "Uncle Joe."

Throughout his life he was a man with a keen sense of humor, a love of the absurd. He feared nothing, but he understood well that discretion is indeed the better part of valor. And he was given the name of *Shiam-shaspusia*, the one who could outlie the Crows, one who could lie like a Cheyenne. It may indeed have been the great Crow chief Long Hair who so named him, just as I have it in the novel. But in battle, men like Bridger and Carson knew that Joe Meek was worth a dozen normal men—and that was by mountain standards.

—BILL HOTCHKISS

Woodpecker Ravine
Nevada County, California

ABOUT THE AUTHOR

BILL HOTCHKISS is a poet, critic, and novelist whose most recent books include *Spirit Mountain, Ammahabas, Soldier Wolf, Crow Warriors,* and *The Medicine Calf.* Born in New London, Connecticut, in 1936, Hotchkiss grew up in California's Mother Lode country and was educated at the University of California, San Francisco State University, and the University of Oregon. He's the holder of several graduate degrees, including a Ph.D. The author and his wife, Judith Shears, live in Woodpecker Ravine, near Grass Valley, California. He is at work on two more historical novels to be published by Bantam Books in the near future.